The air around me ch... a moment, catches me up and carries me along with it. Silken wings pulse against my throat—faster than a racing heart, more dangerous than an exploding locomotive—and then they're gone. The fairy swarm from beneath the cypress surges past in a rush of glittering flesh and sharp teeth, snarling high-pitched, baby-voice snarls that would be hysterical if this wasn't a matter of life and death.

Cane's life. Cane's death.

I run, slower than the fairies had flown, but faster than I've run in years, closing the distance between me and Cane in seconds. The Fey are already on him, swarming around the hole near his palm as he bats and swings, but they haven't started gnawing on the suit yet.

There's still time. Not much, but enough. It *has* to be enough.

Praise for Stacey Jay

"Jay's writing is light and engaging, and the characters are lively and likable."

—*Publishers Weekly* on *Undead Much*

"Peppered with gross-out humor, the camp flows freely. . . ."

—*Kirkus Reviews* on *My So-Called Death*

"Super entert... —*R*...ad to Me

Dead on t... Book

STACEY JAY

DEAD ON THE DELTA

POCKET BOOKS

New York   London   Toronto   Sydney

Pocket Books
A Division of Simon & Schuster, Inc.
1230 Avenue of the Americas
New York, NY 10020

This book is a work of fiction. Names, characters, places, and incidents either are products of the author's imagination or are used fictitiously. Any resemblance to actual events or locales or persons, living or dead, is entirely coincidental.

First Pocket Books paperback edition June 2011

POCKET and colophon are registered trademarks of Simon & Schuster, Inc.

For information about special discounts for bulk purchases, please contact Simon & Schuster Special Sales at 1-866-506-1949 or business@simonandschuster.com

The Simon & Schuster Speakers Bureau can bring authors to your live event. For more information or to book an event contact the Simon & Schuster Speakers Bureau at 1-866-248-3049 or visit our website at www.simonspeakers.com.

Designed by Jacquelynne Hudson
Cover design by Lisa Litwack; illustration by Elena Dudina.

Manufactured in the United States of America

10 9 8 7 6 5 4 3 2 1

ISBN 978-1-4391-8986-3
ISBN 978-1-4391-8988-7 (ebook)

To my father, Bill, for the title and so much more.

Acknowledgments

Thanks so much to the people of Donaldsonville, Louisiana, who charmed me utterly. Your hospitality was incredible. You are gems. Don't give up on your town or rest until every chemical plant is adhering to clean air standards that protect your health and the health of the next generation. (Please feel free to threaten the nearby factories with killer fairies if you think it will help.) And please forgive me for any fictional modifications to your lovely town. Sometimes I needed things to be a bit different.

Thanks also to my critique partners, Stacia Kane and Julie Linker, both of whom are just plain kick-ass. Thanks to my adorable and hilarious editor, Jen Heddle, for the straight shooting. Thanks to Jennifer Estep and Jeri Smith-Ready for their time, and to the Debutantes of 2009 for a feast of such awesomeness that I'm still feeling stuffed two years later. Thanks to the entire staff at Pocket and to every reader who takes a chance on this book.

And, as always, a special thanks to Grandma Stumpy, my husband, and my two little boys, who inspire me daily to hope for the future. And a super special thanks this time around to my dad. In the mid-1990s Bill Branscum started a gritty contemporary mystery titled *Dead on the Delta*. He died before he could finish the book. I was nineteen years old and I promised I would finish it for him. It took me over ten years and this story now in *no way* resembles what you started, Dad, but this one is definitely for you. Hope you're well and stirring up fun and trouble on the other side.

DEAD
ON THE
DELTA

One

Losing your lunch sucks. It sucks even more when you're not hungover.

My view on upchucking is that you should've earned your punishment. But I haven't earned it, and neither had she. I don't need those last three years of med school to know the body at my feet was a child not too long ago. Before the animals got to her face, before the bugs crawled inside to investigate the holes the animals made, before—

I barely make the one-eighty turn in time.

The guilty contents of my stomach—cherry Pop-Tarts, coffee, and a touch of last night's burger and fries—spill out onto the damp earth, adding another layer to the stench of the bayou. I can barely smell the body over the stink. A few of the fairies have laid their eggs early this year. They don't usually drop their sacs until September, but there's no mistaking the smell of fairy babies baking in the noonday sun. Smells like a homeless man's crotch.

Not that I've ever been up close and personal with a homeless man's crotch, but . . .

"Annabelle? You okay?" It isn't the first time Cane's asked. His voice is pinched, strained, not the sexy rumble that made my ribs vibrate less than an hour ago. We could still be tangled up in each other, bitching about the heat in my poorly air-conditioned bedroom if I'd only said "yes" instead of "no" to his offer to play hooky.

As my stomach voids itself and I continue to gag, I wish I'd kept Cane in bed. I wish I'd let him call in sick and stay with me, his big hands warm on my skin. But he's been scary lately. He wants to stick a pin in our relationship and label the specimen.

I fear labels. I fear dead bodies more.

In the three years I've worked for Fairy Containment and Control I've seen my share of dead things, but nothing like this. I force myself to turn around, take another look. She isn't much more than a baby and her face is . . . gone, eaten away by the scavengers our toxic patch of the Mississippi River Delta hasn't killed yet.

The chemical spills along the river did their part to make the marshland from southern Tennessee down to Mobile unfriendly to living things. The mutated fairies have done the rest. Fairies can live on animal blood, but the Louisiana Fey hunt humans with a terrifying single-mindedness. Still, most people have the sense to keep safe. Almost no one ventures outside the iron grid that runs throughout Donaldsonville.

As soon as it was confirmed that iron repels fairies, the D'Ville city council cut any program not necessary to keeping people alive, declared downtown refugee central, and sank a million dollars into nailing iron cables to every roof. A sturdy fifteen-foot iron fence completed the protective measures, enclosing the original Donaldsonville of the early 1800s in a metal cocoon, taking the town back to its roots.

As a result, Donaldsonville is one of the few southern Louisiana towns that still welcomes the Adventurous Tourist to its historic buildings, Cajun restaurants, Delta Fairy Museum, and refurbished town square. Despite the modern-day highwaymen that terrorize the roads, tourism is our top source of revenue, and everyone in town acts accordingly. We're friendly, welcoming, and pride ourselves on being one of the safest places in the South. If you score a ticket on an armored shuttle and actually *make it* to Donaldsonville, you can breathe easy.

This girl shouldn't have died.

"Annabelle? Annabelle, do you need me to come over there and—"

"No." My voice doesn't sound like me. I sound . . . small.

"Crawl on back, girl, I can get a suit and—"

"No."

"Come on, Lee-lee," he says, using a pet name in public, a capital offense in the Annabelle Lee dating handbook. In a different context, I might have flipped him off. If he wasn't thinking about risking his life to come hold my hand and there wasn't a little girl behind me. A *dead* girl, but still . . .

Still.

"Get the suit."

"No! Stay there." Even with an iron suit, Cane won't be totally safe. The August heat makes the fairies crazy. They've been known to bite through metal in their hurry to find a meal. Ingesting iron kills them, but the bite still does its dirty work on the person inside the suit.

For seventy-five percent of the human population, Fey venom leads to insanity, with a slow build to batshit crazy that makes syphilis look gentle by comparison. Another ten percent develop ulcers on the spine that twist healthy bodies into torturous shapes before causing death. And yet another ten percent die instantaneously, hearts stilled within seconds of infection. The convulsions of the severely allergic snap the spinal cord and break teeth, making sure the dying suffer on the way out.

I've seen that firsthand. It's as horrible as it sounds.

"Just . . . give me a second." I motion toward the clutch of anxious policemen a few hundred feet away. They're waiting for me to tell them what I've seen, to come back and pick up the dummy kit and collect the evidence they need for their investigation—dirt samples, tissue scrapings, bug larvae, etc.

Bile rises in my throat again.

I've only had to do this to a human once before. It was an adult male, dumped in the bayou outside the grid. Come to find out, a gunshot wound did him in long before he hit the Ascension Parish county line. The coroner in Baton Rouge discovered the truth easily enough. Amazing what they can do with forensics these days, even with hacks like me occasionally collecting the evidence.

Shit. I hate the thought of touching that girl. There are times—more than the non-immune would imagine—when I wish I wasn't part of the lucky five percent. But I know I'm in the minority on that, as well. Most immune people think they've been blessed, that collecting fairy shit and egg sacs is a holy calling. They feel *lucky* when they're called in to do non-immune people's work for them.

Especially cop work. Everyone wants to be a crime fighter. I blame *CSI.* I've never watched it, but I've heard it's like Breeze. Breeze—dried fairy crap mixed with bleach—is the new crack. Brown is also the new black and forty is the new thirty and up is the new down.

God, I'm dizzy. I take a deep breath and immediately wish I hadn't. I can smell her now, a sickly sweetness beneath the rest of it.

There's some murmuring from the assembled company. The parish sheriff wants me to hurry it up. He has places to go, people to see, graft to collect from businesses vying for liquor licenses. His brother's the head of the Alcohol Beverage Commission and the pair of them make a tidy sum extorting the thirsty.

I wonder if he knows it's a kid out here, probably

the Beauchamp girl who's been missing. I'm guessing not. If he did, there'd be less impatience. The Beauchamps are Important. Their classic (and gigantic) Greek Revival home lures visitors from all over the world. Camellia Grove Plantation is one of Donaldsonville's biggest tourist draws, and we need it. Badly.

Most of the other rich folks moved north after the mutations, fleeing their Victorian houses, abandoning their restaurants, antique stores, and art galleries, leaving the rest of us to clean up their mess and reorganize the town. Only a few stubborn, hard-core wealthy stick around by choice. The rest of our citizens are here because they don't have the resources to move somewhere else. The ratio of black and Hispanic to white in Donaldsonville has settled in at around ninety-eight percent to two, confirming that a pasty redhead like me is the true minority.

It's statistics that I would be dating a black man; it's good fortune that I'm dating a gorgeous black man who cares about me and makes the best jambalaya I've ever had. Cane developed a special recipe without the shellfish so I won't puff up like a marshmallow the second shrimp protein touches my lips. He also brings me herbal insomnia remedies, fixes my leaky toilet, and calls to remind me to put out my trash on Friday morning. He takes good care of me.

I know his family thinks he's too good for a girl who gets around on a bicycle, has no discernible urge to better herself, and isn't grandchild-birthing material. No matter how sweet they are at Sunday dinner, I'm pretty sure they want Cane to dump me. I honestly don't know what I want him to do.

"Lee-lee?" Right. I want him to quit calling me that in public. Immediately. "We've got to—"

"One second." My finger shakes, and the sweat dripping down my forearm makes me shiver. It's nearly a hundred degrees and humid enough that my hair still hasn't dried from my shower. I shouldn't be cold, but I am. "I'm going to take another look. Then I'll come back for the evidence bags."

I turn back around, trying to take in the body with as much detachment as possible. Blond hair in braids—one tied with a heart-shaped elastic, one starting to unravel. No eyes left to judge eye color, not much of her nose either, and the soft curve of her upper lip ends in a jagged tear.

I drop my gaze.

No shoes, bare legs, and a white nightgown with red bows sewn on by hand. A few of them are missing. So is her right index finger. There isn't any dirt under the remaining nails or on her feet. She looks pretty clean considering she's been out in the bayou for . . .

I crouch down and inch a finger under the curve of her back. The dirt beneath her is drier than the surrounding ground. She's been here half the night, at least. Her body blocked the light rain that fell sometime between midnight and two.

I'd heard it on the roof when I got up to chug

one final beer before finally falling asleep. I ran out of my sleeping pills a few days ago and have been forced to rely on booze to knock me unconscious until I make it to the field office in Baton Rouge to pick up another bottle of Restalin . . . or two or three. Getting to sleep and staying asleep has been a battle since I was sixteen, since the night I saw my first dead body and toted it home in the backseat of my car.

No. Not going to think about that. Now isn't a good time. *Never* is a good time.

I take one last look, searching for anything else that might help Cane identify the body as Grace. Her fingernails are painted a pale pink with sparkles, but there's no jewelry, no defining marks that I can—

Scratch that, there's something peeking out from under her sleeve. I lean over, snagging the elastic with two fingers.

It's a tattoo, one of the temporary variety. Even the douchebags down at The Rusty Pin—who'd been all too happy to ink me when I was sixteen and so drunk I'd passed out on the table—won't work on babies. I pull her sleeve higher, revealing a unicorn with glitter flowing down the tail. It looks like it's shitting pink sparkles. Who knows? Maybe unicorns are real, too, and they crap cotton candy. After the fairies, we're all a lot more willing to believe in imaginary things.

Hmm . . . *fairies.*

They *will* feed on a human corpse, as long as it hasn't been dead for too long. If the girl was killed somewhere else and carried here, there should still be bites on her skin. But aside from whatever critter's been at her face—weasel maybe, or possum—there isn't a mark on her. Not even a mosquito bite.

Of course, mosquitoes have been hunted to the brink of extinction. Fairies don't mind getting their human blood secondhand. I watched a couple of Fey feed on a mosquito swarm in a containment unit during my first year of FCC training. Intense doesn't begin to describe it. With their precious faces and delicate wings, it's easy to forget that fairy mouths are full of fangs coated with deadly venom. For millions of years, those mouths were too small to close around human flesh. But after the mutations, that isn't a problem.

I can see a clutch of the little sharks circling in the shade of the cypress trees down near the water. The pink and gold glow of their skin gives them away, an insect-luring adaptation that serves as an early warning to humans.

If you see the glow, it's time to go. Marcy teaches the rhyme to her kids right along with *Stop, drop, and roll*.

There isn't much need for concern at the moment, however, even if I weren't immune. Fairies aren't fans of direct sunlight. They won't come out of the shade unless there's a tempting meal—two or three food-friendly humans, maybe more. It would probably be safe for Cane to come down and collect the evidence himself.

Probably. And if not, you've got more blood on your hands.

Blood. Another one of my least favorite things.

I stand and climb up the rise to claim the dummy kit. Cane holds it out as I slip inside the gate, but doesn't look me in the eye. He knows better than to make eye contact when I'm upset. He's smart. And prepared. And probably going to make captain after his brother retires if I don't mess up his life first. I don't want to mess up his life. He's a good man and he's already been through hell with his first wife. I should leave him.

Instead, I let him put an arm around my shoulders, and pull me close.

"Is it her?" he whispers, voice pained.

I nod. "I'm pretty sure. White nightgown with red bows, pink nail polish, and a temporary tattoo of a unicorn on her right arm."

"Shit." He runs a hand up his forehead and back over his shaved head.

There's a shushing sound as the rough skin on his palms brushes the hint of stubble, the same sound my fingers made a few hours ago. It makes me want to get even closer, to wrap my arms around his neck and pull his scratchy head down for a kiss.

But I don't. I can't. Now that the kit is in hand, real panic is beginning to set in. The world spins again, and my brain screams in protest. I take a breath and turn it off, promising it a nice, strong toddy when we've finished the dirty work. I pull away from Cane and turn back toward the thing in the field, to the thing I will poke and prod and eventually drag within the iron gate for the coroner to collect.

I can't think of Grace as Grace or I won't be able to finish this. At least not while I'm sober.

Two

The Beauchamps are standing on the veranda of their massive, be-columned home as I bicycle by. Thanks to a fresh coat of paint each spring, Camellia Grove always looks bright and new, a virgin awaiting a bridegroom who never came back from the Civil War.

A creepy virgin, with vacant eyes and clutching hands.

I've never liked the house. Camellia Grove is one of the only plantation homes that wasn't wrecked in the riots following the mutations and a true treasure of Louisiana heritage, but it's also . . . haunting.

Today, the lingering creepiness is worse than usual. I can't help but imagine a new spirit drifting through the live oak trees lining the drive, mocking the sentries' aura of safety and permanence. Nothing is safe; nothing is forever. So I don't slow to watch the lacy moss that hangs from the trees sway in the breeze. I just pump my legs a little harder.

Cane is still cataloguing the evidence, the coroner's loading up the body, and Percy hasn't mustered the courage to haul her ass back to the house and tell her employers what's happened. I know she hasn't. The Beauchamps are looking at me expectantly. Even from a hundred feet away I can see the tension in their faces. Barbara and her two adult children—James and Libby—shuffle to the porch railing, a trio of well-dressed zombies searching for something that will make them human again.

Barbara adopted Grace late in life, when her own kids were nearly grown. I remember the head-line—local Christian saint adopts baby with heart condition from New Orleans. They'd showed the baby's picture, a beautiful one-year-old girl with white-blond hair. Heart condition or not, I wasn't impressed.

What about all the kids around *here* who need someone? Kids whose parents have been infected and are no longer fit to care for them? At the moment, there are over two hundred orphans at Sweet Haven, the halfway house where Marcy worked when I was sixteen. There are kids right here in Donaldsonville who need homes. But a lot of them are older, or fucked in the head, or black, or in some other way undesirable to a woman like Barbara.

I know her kind. I was raised by someone just like her.

But my hovering mama doesn't speak to me anymore, not since the night I left our own well-appointed home in New Orleans. Accident or not, my sister, Caroline, was dead and I was alive. I was never going to be forgiven. It was better to leave. I'd thought distance, time, accomplishment . . . *something* might make it easier to go back. But it didn't, and I eventually gave up on med school and my mother.

It's for the best, really. She wouldn't approve of her daughter dating a black man and I don't want to hide Cane the way I hid Hitch all those years ago. Hitch was poor, not "colored"—as my mother drawls when in the company of her fellow bigots—but, to her, that's nearly as bad.

Barbara reminds me way too much of Mama Lee, making me grit my teeth as I get closer to the house.

The trio on the porch shuffle closer. Libby hunches and rubs at her arms, but Barbara is by far the most tragic figure. Her usually perfectly arranged blond hair is loose and wild, her face makeup-free despite the fact that it's nearing two o'clock, and her clothes look like they've been slept in. She leans against her son, fingers tangled in his blue button-up shirt. James, at least, seems to be holding it together. He's twenty-something, doing his residency at the heart hospital in Baton Rouge, and the head of the household. Mr. Beauchamp died before I moved to Donaldsonville, long enough ago that James is comfortable with the role of family pillar.

Good for him. It can't be easy. Barbara's a handful.

From the corner of my eye I see her waving at me, an impatient gesture that makes it clear she assumes

I'll scurry to do her bidding. Unfortunately for her, I don't scurry. Ever. For anyone.

I pretend I can't hear her cry out for me to stop. There's a reason I put in my earbuds and slipped on my official orange FCC vest before I left the crime scene. I want everyone to see that I am *busy*. And also can't hear jack shit. I'm not going to be the one to tell Barbara her daughter is dead. I'm. Just. Not. Going. To. Do it.

I pump harder, breathing easier when I reach the bend in the road and put the Beauchamp mansion and all the pain hovering around it behind me. I would have taken the long way around the swamp behind the house and avoided the scene entirely if I weren't late for my real job. But I *am* late, and I have to snag samples, whip up a report, and get to the FCC field office in Baton Rouge before five o'clock or—rare, premed-qualified, immune field agent or not—I'll have my ass handed to me on a platter, cut up hors d'oeuvres–style with a sweet-and-sour dipping sauce. My deadline for turning in my new samples passed days ago and Jin-Sang is already going to give me shit.

Wretched Jin-Sang.

I thought supervisors couldn't get any worse than his sister, Min-Hee, with her OCD fixation with filling out forms in triplicate. By hand. With "black ink, not blue, damn you, Lee!" But after four weeks, I'm counting the days until her maternity leave is up. Unfortunately, the FCC gives immune operatives six *months* of paid leave. Something about hoping the immunity to fairy bite can be transmitted through breast milk and blah blah blah. They also give you a hefty bonus if your child is immune. Shady government spending if you ask me, but it's a powerful incentive for some women to squeeze out a few puppies.

Not me. No kids, no puppies, no kitties . . . well, no kids or puppies.

Somewhere between the crime scene and the Beauchamp house, I've acquired a tail, a fat black and white cat with a limp. It has no collar or tags, but it looks cared for and seems to have taken a "shine" to me, as Marcy would say. Too bad I'm not in the market for a pet.

I'm not good at keeping things alive. Not pets, not plants, probably not even intestinal bacteria. I forget to feed myself half the time until I start to get dizzy. Definitely not mommy material.

I assumed the cat would get the hint when I tossed it out of the trailer behind my bike a half a mile back, but so far, not so good. It still rambles along behind me, yowling, cursing me for making it walk. It's so damned loud I can hear it over my punk rock cover of "Islands in the Stream" by Fairies Will Die—surprisingly good stuff for a band out of Detroit, but then I'm a sucker for a good cover.

"You're asking for an alligator bite, cat." I glance over my shoulder to see how it takes the news.

It yowls again and plays up the limp, as if it knows I'm looking.

"Go cry for someone who cares." I turn back around and snag my drink—Coke bottle emptied halfway, with that medicinal rum I promised myself poured in to fill it back up to the top—and take a long, deep swig.

The numbness is a soft blanket pulled across my soul, shutting out the horror of the afternoon. The alcohol makes the unbearable heat even hotter and I'm dizzy by the time I reach the edge of the swamp, but that's okay. Better dizzy than sober.

"Reeow." The cat lets out a sound of triumph as I pull to a stop and climb off my bike, giving it the opportunity to leap into my trailer and snuggle up next to my blue cooler.

"Get out." I toss it to the ground, but it's back in seconds, growling as it once again claims the coldest seat in the house, shooting me an affronted look that reminds me of . . . myself. Probably similar to the look I gave Cane when he said he wanted to call in sick and make love to me again. *Gag.* We don't *make love.* We screw each other's brains out . . . or so I thought.

But when a man tells a sure-thing kind of girl he wants to make love, he means it. At least, I'm pretty sure he meant it. Sure enough to be scared.

After Hitch, I opted out on love. I'm too independent, too distant, too obnoxious to be lovable. Even taking into account that I have a decent sense of humor, shoot a mean game of pool, am generous with blow jobs, and know how to spiff up in my Sunday best and play sweet with his mama at lunch once a week, there's no way Cane could love me.

But what if he does? What will I do?

The FCC pays *very* well, but I live in a three-room shack without central air and ride a bicycle, for Christ's sake. I can't even muster the gumption to commit to a large purchase, let alone a relationship. *Any* kind of relationship.

I reach for the cat. It narrows its eyes and presses closer to its new best friend. He—I can see now that he's *definitely* a he—seems ready to make a romantic connection with my blue cooler. His bad leg hitches up over the edge, claws catching on the handle, as intertwined as Cane and I were a few hours ago.

Damn. Just . . . blechk. I give up and grab my waders. The cat will either be gone before I get back or he won't. I can't waste any more time.

I struggle into my dark-green boots and pull the rubber pants of the waders up around my waist, hooking my arms into the suspenders. The khaki straps cut into my skin as I bend to snag my kit, but I'm still glad I went with the light green tank top. It's better to wear a T-shirt for field work, but it's just so damned hot. Better blisters than any more sweat. Even with perspiration that doubles as a natural fairy deterrent, there's such a thing as too much of a good thing.

My sweat scares away the fairies. Something in the iron content keys them in to the fact that my blood will kill them. On a hot summer day, the

Fey won't come within two feet of me. I'm that . . . potent.

"Just in case." The cat narrows his eyes as I run the sweaty back of my hand over his fur. Fairy bites don't affect animals the way they do humans, and the fairies probably won't bother with something so furry when there are plenty of insects around, but no need to take chances. I don't want the little bastard bleeding on my cooler.

He growls as I reach around him, fetching my gloves and a few tubes that have fallen out of my kit. Jin-Sang would shit himself if he saw the disorganization. He'd probably try to get me fired, if he hasn't already.

"Later, cat." I toss my iPod onto my seat—I can't afford to drop another one in the water—and take one last swig of my drink, tipping it back until the lukewarm mix of sugary rum and Coke flowing down my throat makes my nose tingle.

I can't bring it with me, either. Not enough hands and fairies like red—being the color of blood, that isn't surprising. They'd swarm around the bottle and get in the way. That can be useful when I need a live specimen, but I'm only after water, egg, and shit samples today, though I will take a body or two if I find any floaters.

Ugh. I don't want to think about dead things. Even fairies.

My drink churns in my stomach as I wade into the shallows, sticking to the shady areas, gathering

my samples, keeping an eye out for logs with eyes.
I trudge farther and farther, deep into a part of the
bayou where nothing human dares to walk anymore.
Under a cluster of fungi sucking the life from a live
oak, I find a few early eggs and scoop a sample into
my blue test tube, ignoring the tiny, pissed-off faces
of the fairies that flit close enough to smell that it isn't
a good idea to bite me and buzz angrily away. A few
more vials of water and I'll be done. All I need is poo.

As I search the patches of dry land for a mound of
fairy dung, my mind drifts into melancholy territory.
I think about white nightgowns and pink fingernail
polish and a time when Caroline and I both loved
unicorns. We'd been best friends when we were
babies, but by the night of the camping trip, she'd
barely been speaking to me.

She only agreed to go to piss off Dad. She thought
if he and Mom came home from his conference in
Mobile and found out we'd been smoking pot and
drinking beer and being generally disreputable with
two boys in a camper all weekend that he'd let her
go to Smith for undergrad instead of making her
stay in New Orleans. Dad and Mom were resigned to
me being a failure, but they wanted better things for
Caroline. She assumed that if her proximity to me put
her at risk, they'd let her go.

She might have been right. If she'd made it home,
she might have gotten the green light to head north
and become a future Yankee of America. If the newly
mutated fairies hadn't attacked our campsite, if she

hadn't been bitten and died in my arms, going from perfect daughter to dead body so fast she was gone before I could say goodbye.

Bodies. Caroline's body, and now that tiny body they'd lifted into the ambulance. What had happened to Grace? How did she die? Was it over quickly or did she suffer? Was the murderer someone she trusted, or a stranger who—

"None of my business." I don't realize I've spoken aloud until someone answers

"Damn straight, bitch. This ain't none of your bidness." The high-pitched voice is accompanied by a bony fist. I duck in time for the punch to connect with my head instead of my jaw and hear the woman behind me cry out. I have a hard head . . . or so my mama always told me.

I drop everything and twist around, landing my own punch in the middle of the scrawny woman's face before I've quite regained my footing. Bright red explodes from her nose—a crimson target in the center of skin as black as my cream-free morning coffee. The fairies are on her in seconds.

I might have felt bad—even though she hit me and called me a bitch—if she weren't already covered in bite marks. This chick has been out here awhile. Her fate's already sealed. A camp is in her future. The bitten aren't allowed to live among the average population. Back in the early days of the mutations, a few of the infected transmitted the disease to friends and family. Fey venom can't survive in human saliva and doesn't contaminate the blood—humans can't spread it by biting each other or having sex or sharing needles—and there's no airborne virus, so I have no idea *how* it spread. But the government said *it did*, and the soldiers in charge in the days of martial law came to take the infected away.

Even now that we're back to a more standard "rule by the people" method of government, that's still the way of things. Bite victims who don't die right off the bat are sent to a containment camp. Keesler Air Force base over in Gulfport, Mississippi, is the biggest in our area. I visited it when I was in training. Nice facility, especially considering most of the people living there are raving lunatics.

But the immune officers keep the peace. Of course, they do have four hundred officers on active duty. The abundance of immune operatives at the camps is a big reason we're so understaffed in the field. Sometimes, that's just an irritation. Sometimes, it's a matter of life and death.

Like now, perhaps. If I had a partner, I wouldn't be alone out here with no backup, getting my ass kicked by someone half my size.

"Bitch!" Skanky chick swings at me again, her diamond chandelier earrings swinging wildly around her ears. The jewelry's ridiculous paired with her stained T-shirt and sodden jeans, but there isn't time for a fashion intervention even if I were that kind of girl.

I duck, and back away. She comes after me,

seemingly oblivious to the creatures grunting and screeching as they tear into her flesh. She fights her way through a tangle of tree roots, while the fairies suck and slurp and fall off of her in a drunken stupor, hitting the water with the *plunk* of pennies dropping into a wishing well.

Crap. She's a Breeze head. I should have known.

Her blood wouldn't make the Fey drunk unless she'd been eating or snorting Fairy Wind. She isn't just venom-crazy, she's flying the wind, pumped up on a toxic high that will make her impossible to overpower. I'm only five eight and a hundred and forty pounds on a good week—when I've remembered to eat and not earned my morning vomit once or twice—and even six-two, two-hundred-and-ten-pound Cane would have had a hard time with this one. Unless he resorted to something more serious than fisticuffs.

Cane bought me a gun last year, when he thought New Orleans gangs were setting up a secret drug-running operation in the bayou. But I refused to get my concealed-weapons permit. I'm too lazy to take the eight-hour "super-secret carrying-heat class" he teaches on weekends. And I've always assumed I couldn't kill a person, even if that person was trying to kill me.

I'm beginning to think I've been wrong about that.

"Ahhh!" Skanky screams as she lunges for me. I try to step back, but slam my head into something hard. The next thing I know, I'm under water with the woman's hands around my neck.

Swamp surges into my nose, but I have the sense to hold my breath after the initial invasion. I don't try to swallow it or spit it out. I just drive my hands up, grabbing the woman's wrists, digging my fingers into her tendons until her grip fails. As soon as her fingers spasm, I throw her off and surge to the surface, spitting out swamp and sucking in a deep breath.

"Don't do it!" I scream, loud enough that even a Breeze head with a death wish and ears full of water has to have heard me. But she doesn't listen. She comes for me again, and I do what I have to do.

She's off-balance when I push her under. It isn't hard to take her all the way to the bottom or stomp rubber-booted feet firmly into her back. She bucks and thrashes at first, but stops moving faster than I expect. Still, I don't get off of her until I count to sixty. I don't want to take a chance that she's faking it.

Harsh, yes. But she tried to kill me, and I'm not Saint Mother Mary Margaret of the Immaculate Church of Forgiveness. By the time I pull her up, she isn't breathing. I have a feeling I should be panicked about that, but I'm not. (Thank you, rum and Coke.)

I drag her limp body to the closest patch of land, struggling with my waterlogged boots and pants, and haul her up and onto her back. Lucky for me, a few chest compressions are all it takes to have her coughing up bayou and blood, and there's no need to get into a mouth-to-mouth situation, because I have a good idea where that mouth has been.

"You've been eating shit, you know that, right? You know what Breeze is?" I roll her onto her stomach and pull her hands behind her.

She's still too stunned to fight back, and I figure I'd better get her secure while I have the chance. But what to use? I can see my kit floating not too far from shore, but there's nothing but specimen bottles and chemical solutions in there. I could use my tank top, but that would involve letting her go. Maybe she has something that—

"Nice belt." I reach underneath her, pry open her buckle, and pull it, hissing, through the loops.

I tie her up and am feeling pretty proud of myself until I stand and see it. There, floating in the shallows, is an ancient camper . . . houseboat . . . thing. I scoped out this location a couple months ago and didn't notice it, but it had to have been here. It's hemmed in on all sides by gnarled tree roots bursting from the water like knobby-kneed girls sitting on the wall at a debutante ball. It must have floated in during the rainy spring and gotten trapped. Which is probably exactly what the owners had planned.

This part of the bayou is a perfect place to make Breeze. When this many fairies occupy the same hunting ground, they designate areas for shitting and pissing, usually patches of dry land in the middle of the swamp, high enough out of the water that they won't be subsumed after a heavy rain and contaminate the area.

Fairies have the sense not to eat their own poo, or

sniff it up their noses, or liquefy it and shoot it into their arms. Many *people*, however, do not. What this says about the chance of humanity outliving the Fey I don't want to think about.

I also don't want to think about what Jin-Sang will do to me when he finds out I missed something like this during my initial scout. He's going to send a report to the regional head at Keesler and I'm going to get reamed. They won't be happy to hear I screwed the annual report by letting a Breeze house sit for months on land that was cordoned off for research seven years ago.

I'm suddenly possessed with a powerful longing for my iPod. A little "Islands in the Stream" would really cheer me up. Or maybe a stiff drink would be better.

"Or maybe a drink and some music." I pat the woman on the back before grabbing her under the armpits—ugh, as gross as I feared—and pulling her into a seated position under a nearby tree. She's still groggy from her time under the water, but if she's too high or crazy to stay upright and un-drowned until I get back, that's her problem. At least the fairies seem to be keeping their distance, so she shouldn't lose any more blood.

Just to be safe, I catch a bit of sweat from my forehead and brush it across her pulse points. That'll keep the bloodsuckers away and considering the way she smells, a recently bathed person's sweat is probably a hygiene improvement.

"Don't touch me . . . bitch," she mumbles. "Stupid . . . bitch."

"*I'm* rubber and you're glue," I whisper.

There's probably no one in the camper—surely they would have come outside while Skanky and I were thrashing in the water—but I prefer not to take chances. I already have a goose egg on my head, and have reached my scuffle limit for the day. I learned how to fight during my time at Sweet Haven, but only when it's unavoidable. In an ideal world, I prefer to fight with a smartass comment. Or a thumb war. Thumb wars are a great way to settle conflict.

Of course, I've got big thumbs.

I back away from the boat, grab my kit, and hustle to my bike as fast as my waterlogged britches will allow. I'm not doing anything else out here without backup. They can call in the immune chief of police from New Orleans. It's an hour trip up from the Big Easy, but she'll hightail it to the next shuttle for a Breeze house. Gathering evidence for a murder is something they'll pass on to a local immune field agent with a dummy kit and an enforcement order until they find out if the victim is someone worth caring about. But this . . .

Shutting down the Breeze operations is Governor Schmidt's pet project. He's pinning his hopes of reelection on his fairy-drug-fighting image and everyone in New Orleans knows it. Captain Munoz won't risk letting Schmidt find out she's passed a Breeze investigation on to a sample-collecting field agent without a lick of crime-fighting training.

I make a solemn vow to continue avoiding the criminal justice seminars Cane tries to drag me to. Untrained = Not responsible. Exactly the way I like it.

"Reeeoow. Owww." Gimpy the Cat yowls as I toss my kit into the trailer behind my bike, and hisses when my soaking waders follow after.

"Don't," I warn, but I don't try to throw him out.

And—I realize as I climb on my bike and book it back to the gate—I've named him. So much for avoiding responsibility.

But really, in the scheme of things, how much trouble can a cat be?

Three

That's a nasty beast." Dicker backs away from my bike and sticks his finger in his mouth, sucking at the place where Gimpy scratched him.

"That's real sanitary, Dicker." Dom, Dicker's partner, a lanky Italian boy who grew up in Donaldsonville, tosses an antibacterial wipe at Dicker's feet before heading back around the house. He's a compulsive hand washer, but usually an upbeat guy.

Today his springy step is decidedly unsprung. I've never seen him so down. Dom's the guy who's always smiling, even when he's hauling drunks into the tank. But today his duties are a lot more intense than wrestling Shane and Nell away from each other after the newlyweds have a few too many at Swallows. He's making a third pass of the Camellia Grove grounds, looking for clues to help find the man who killed a little girl.

Meanwhile, Cane's questioning the Beauchamps inside the house and Dicker is . . . using his mad detective skills to think of where the investigation should proceed next? Watching the car? Slouching in the shade doing jack shit?

I'm betting on the last option.

Dicker leaves the wipe on the ground and continues to suck at his wound.

"Dom's right," I say. "You shouldn't stick your finger in your mouth. It's a good way to get an infection."

"Spit's cleaner than cat claws."

"Really?" Doubtful. The human mouth's a pretty gross place, but I don't want to get into it with Dicker. He'd argue with a stump.

I cast another look toward the front door of the Beauchamp home. Still shut tight. I didn't think questioning the family would take this long. Hmm . . . could Cane be thinking that the Beauchamps . . . In cases like this it's often someone close to the child who—

Nope. Once again, none of my business.

I snag the wipe from the ground and swipe my face. What I really need is a long, hot shower to wash off the swamp nasty, but that's not going to happen anytime soon. I have to get my ass to Baton Rouge before the FCC office closes for the weekend.

"Hell, yes, cats are filthy." Dicker says. "Where you think cat scratch fever comes from? Damn *cat scratches*, that's where." He has the lack of foresight to point at Gimpy a second time, earning himself another swipe—which he narrowly avoids—and a hiss.

In the cat's defense, I wouldn't want Dicker's pudgy sausage fingers anywhere near me, either. He's a round, cheery-looking guy, but skeevy. Like a perverted, cranky black Santa, complete with chubby cheeks and a graying beard Cane lets him keep against county regulation and common sense. What kind of nut job wants fur on his face during a southern Louisiana summer?

Dicker, apparently.

"Nasty. Little. Bastard." Dicker shakes his head. "You should get that thing put down."

"Can't. He's not mine. I just can't get rid of him," I say. "And I'm not up on cats, but cat scratch fever is caused by bacteria."

"Oh, yeah?"

"*Bartonella* bacteria, two different strains." I learned a few things in med school, though I don't like to admit it. "*Bartonella henselae* and *Bartonella*—"

"Yeah, yeah. You're a smart-ass."

I grunt in agreement and steal another look at the house. Doesn't seem like Cane's coming out anytime soon. *Dammit*. I'll have to give Dicker my request. Suckity suck. Cane would have kept my mistake quiet, or as quiet as possible considering Captain Munoz is going to be called in. But with Dicker doing the paperwork, Theresa's visit is ensured to be A Deal. And maybe even A Big Deal.

Unless . . .

Dom would probably take care of the request for me without a fuss. I could wait for him to come back from the other side of the house where Grace's window—the window she was allegedly pulled through the night of her disappearance—is located. Or I could sneak under the crime scene tape and go find him. Cane won't be happy to know I contaminated the scene with another set of footprints, but I figure I've earned the right to contaminate with what I had to do this morning.

"Watch my cat, Dicker." I head out of the shade and across the wide side lawn.

"I thought it wasn't— Hey, you can't go back there," Dicker calls after me as I duck under the bright yellow tape. "You're going to piss everyone off."

I ignore him, but keep to the stone path as I walk around to the back. He doesn't come after me. A glance over my shoulder reveals he hasn't even left the shade of the live oak where my bike and the squad car are parked. Real dedicated to the job there, Dicker. I would tattle on him, but who am I to throw stones? I'm the girl who's over a week late with her field samples and somehow missed a Breeze lab sitting right in the middle of her location, that's who. Poster girl for Dedication and Excellence I am not.

I spot Dom's stabby brown hair near the steps leading to the back porch, and hurry over. "Hey, Dom. Can I ask a quick favor?"

"You're not supposed to be back here," he says, but he doesn't sound upset.

Or surprised. He doesn't even stand up, just stays in a squat, staring at some mud near the side of the house. It looks like there was a hose leaking there not too long ago. It's damper than the light rain last night could have managed on its own.

"Yeah, I know, but I didn't want to ask Dicker. You know how he is."

"What do you need?"

"I need you to call in Munoz from New Orleans," I say, relieved now that I've confessed. It always feels good to pass the buck. "I found a Breeze house while I was collecting samples today."

"You're kidding." He still doesn't look at me. Must be something really interesting there in the mud. I inch closer, peering over his shoulder. Are those footprints? They're enormous.

I look up. Grace's window is on the first story, about four feet off the ground. If I stand on tiptoe I can peek through the pink curtains, see the unicorn mural on the wall. There's a blond girl riding one of the unicorns, a big smile on her face. I wonder if the guy who took Grace saw the mural, or if it was too dark. I wonder—

"Nope." Focus. I have to focus. I don't want to think about Grace or who killed her. I did my part. I can put it behind me now. "Found a Breeze house and a Breeze head who tried to drown me."

"What?" Dom finally turns, brown eyes wide. He actually looks concerned. I always thought he was more Cane's friend than mine, but maybe he really cares. "Are you okay?"

"Yeah." I shrug, glad the goose egg on the back

of my head is hidden by my hair. I don't want any pressure to get checked out. Hospitals remind me of other things I'd rather put behind me. "I tied her up with her belt, and propped her up against a tree."

"You didn't."

"Um . . . I did," I say, the shock in his voice making me wonder if maybe this is a bigger deal than I'd thought.

"You didn't."

"I did. For real."

"Annabelle." He blinks four or five times in rapid succession. "You can't just tie someone up and leave them in the swamp, what the—"

"What else was I supposed to do?" I ask. "She tried to *kill* me, Dom. And she's already been bitten, so . . ."

"Crud. Crud, crud, crud." Dom doesn't cuss. He says his mama raised him right. "Crud" is probably the nastiest word I've ever heard come out of his mouth. "There's alligators out there. And crazy people." He stands with a sigh, hands on his narrow hips. He looks skinnier than usual. With a metabolism like his, even twenty-four hours of increased stress and poor appetite can make a difference. This isn't a man who should be forced to think about murdered kids.

But then, what sort of man should?

"And snakes and all kinds of . . ." He runs a frustrated hand through his spikes, making them prickle. "We could have another dead body on our hands, Annabelle! Crud! Fudgin' crud."

Hmmm . . . fudgin' crud indeed.

Maybe I should have asked Dicker, after all. At least he wouldn't have cared that I left a Breeze head to chill out in the bayou for a few hours. Really, she'll be okay. I didn't tie her feet, so she'll be able to run if she sobers up. Not that she should need to run from anything. The fairies have already had their piece of her and most of the other predators don't come out until after dark. *She's* probably the most dangerous thing in the swamp at the moment.

Still . . . Dom's crudding makes me feel guilty.

"You're right." I take a big breath and let it out. "I'll just . . . go get her."

"No, you can't go get her." He shakes his head. "You don't have the training to handle a violent suspect."

Whew. Thank God. What would I have done if he'd taken me up on my offer? Screamed "prank call" and made a run for it on my bike?

I need to stop saying things I'm not sure I mean.

I wince as a memory flashes through my mind. Me, Cane, and two Big Gulps full of Jack Daniel's and Vanilla Coke. It was his night off. We'd walked to the town square to see the summer movie in the park and then back to my house. We were drunk by then, and laughing, and he'd felt so good. Too good. The words had been out of my mouth before I realized what I was saying. Those three little words that I didn't really mean, that I hadn't meant since I was nineteen and Hitch was . . . everything. And then Cane said them back.

It still makes me queasy. I wonder if he remembers?

He hasn't said it again, or mentioned the incident, but today, the way he held me afterward felt . . . different. Safer and more dangerous at the same time.

"So you'll call Munoz?" I ask.

"Yeah, I'll call her." Dom takes another long look at the ground beneath the window. Definitely some footprints in the mud. Huge footprints. If they belong to the guy who took Grace, he wears a size thirteen or fourteen. Maybe even bigger. "Come on, let's go get the paperwork out of the cruiser. I'll call while you scribble."

He heads off across the lawn and I hurry after, forcing my brain not to start running through every man in town with clown feet. Cane will do that. He's good at investigative work. "Actually, Dom, I was hoping you could do the paperwork for me. I'm already late to turn in my samples and—"

"Sure, no problem. You did your share for us today." He slows and turns back to me with a pained look on his face. I know what he's going to say before he opens his mouth. "I'm so sorry you had to do that. I know some things have to be done before we move the body but—"

"I really have to run, Dom." I edge around him, uncomfortable with his apology. Cane hadn't bothered. He knows I don't know how to handle apologies. He knows me better than I realize sometimes. Maybe he even knows that I didn't mean what I said the other night.

The thought makes me sad, which means it's

probably time to put an end to things. I should have done it before now. A year and a half is too long for a casual relationship, and those are the only kind I want.

"Sure, go ahead. I'll fill out the forms after I call New Orleans. I'll give them straight to Cane, no one else."

"Thanks, you're the best." I hurry toward my bike, oddly pleased to see Gimpy still wrapped around my cooler. Maiming Dicker has edged him onto my good side. For now.

He yowls as I pull onto the road, pedaling toward town. It's a low, pained sound, different from his usual complaining. He's probably hungry. Who knows the last time he was fed? Maybe I'll swing in and buy him a can of food at the Quik Mart on the way to the bus stop. I have twenty minutes until the shuttle to Baton Rouge leaves the square. If I hurry I can—

A rustling sound ruffles the air above me. My head snaps up. Spindly brown legs hang from a fat tree limb, and child-sized feet wave listlessly in the breeze. I almost scream, but swallow the sound. It's just a girl. An *alive* girl. There's no need to freak out, even if the small toes are painted the same pink as Grace Beauchamp's.

It must be Deedee, Percy's daughter. She and Grace are the only two kids on this side of town. Most of the families with little ones live close to the square, in renovated apartments near the town center. It makes people feel safer to be farther from the bayou.

I'd thought that silly even a few days ago, but now . . .

I wonder how much Deedee knows. Has she been told that her friend is dead?

"Hey." I wave at the feet. Deedee stares down at me, dark eyes glittering like stones under water. Then her legs and feet are gone. The branch shakes as she disappears into the dense leaves close to the trunk.

Odd. Deedee's usually friendly. Too friendly. She likes to show up when Marcy and I are having Saturday coffee on the square and spend thirty minutes talking Marcy's leg off. She prefers Marcy to me, but I would have said we're friends, and it's not like I'm a scary person.

At least not until you get to know me better.

"Deedee? You okay?" Silence, but I can see a patch of skin near the top of the tree. "Deedee?"

Nothing from the girl, but Gimpy hisses, protesting our lack of motion or his empty stomach or some other cat thing. Who the hell knows? Stupid cat. I should have left it in the swamp with the Breeze head.

"Do you need anything?" I ask the tree, feeling obligated to try one more time. If Deedee's heard about Grace she's probably devastated. Not that I'm prepared to deal with a seven-year-old girl traumatized by death, but there isn't anyone else here. "Want me to call your mom?"

"No. I'm good, Miss Annabelle," the girl hurries to say, making it clear she wants to talk to her mom even less than she wants to talk to me. "I'm just . . . playing."

Ah, the evasive "playing." How many times did I tell my mom the same thing, usually when I was setting Caroline's dolls on fire?

"Oh. Okay. So you don't need anything?"

"No. I'm good." Gimpy hisses again and Deedee sticks one hand through the branches to point at my trailer. "That's a mean cat."

"Yeah."

"Can I hold it?"

Kids, so dumb and . . . kidlike. "Probably not a good idea."

She sighs and pulls her hand back in. "Yeah. Probably not."

"But I'll see you, okay? You come see me and Marcy for coffee on Saturday?"

Silence and another sigh, then finally, "Maybe."

"I'll buy you a brownie."

"Okay . . . maybe."

Wow. A "maybe" on a brownie. It's all the confirmation I need. She knows about Grace. *Shit.* At least I was sixteen before someone I loved died on me. I feel bad for the kid, but what can I do? What can anyone do?

I mumble my goodbyes and Deedee mumbles something back and my nasty cat and I head toward town. A quick glance at my watch reveals just enough time to zip into the Quik Mart for cat food and a little something. My rum and Coke wore off between my sample taking and near-drowning, and sobriety isn't any more appealing than it was earlier in the day.

I have a feeling it won't be one of my favorite states of being until Cane and Dom catch the man who killed Grace. Until then, I'm prescribing myself a late-afternoon buzz followed by an evening of more intense therapy.

After Jin-Sang rips me a new asshole, there's no doubt I'll need something to ease the pain.

Four

The trip to Baton Rouge seems endless.

An hour in an armored vehicle with no windows and iron sides too thick to allow a cell signal is rarely fun, but today it feels like the wheels will never stop rolling. It makes me long for the early days of the mutations, before a few blood-hungry fairies smashed their way through the supposedly impenetrable glass windows of the shuttles and ruined the view for everyone.

Admittedly, there isn't much to see on the road from Donaldsonville to Baton Rouge aside from the toothy ruins of petrochemical plants, miles of abandoned strip malls, posh residential ghost towns, a theme park, and a trio of giant crosses angry citizens pulled to the ground after the existence of killer fairies was confirmed.

All in all, it makes for depressing scenery, but at least there would be *something* to look at. Something to keep my mind from flipping through the Beauchamp murder investigation, worrying the pages, doodling notes in the margins of mental pictures of a dead girl.

Why did someone kill Grace? Was it just some sick fuck who got off on brutalizing children? A kidnapping gone wrong? Or something else entirely?

I slouch lower in my seat, hiding from the driver's mirror as I tip my can back for a drink and try to focus on other things. Like what I'm going to tell Jin-Sang when I arrive at the FCC office in Spanish Town. There has to be some way to spin the discovery of the Breeze house, to make it seem like I wasn't—

"You gonna share?" The vaguely familiar woman across the aisle casts a pointed look at my brown-bag-wrapped can.

I'd gone with a twenty-four-ounce import—higher alcohol content, superior taste—since I'd lost my storage for a six-pack. Gimpy wasn't keen on letting me actually touch my cooler. He was even less keen on being shoved into one of the animal compartments under the shuttle for the trip, but I was afraid animal control would snag him if I left him roaming the square without a collar and tags. Still, I'm probably going to lose an eye when it comes time to pull him out.

The thought makes me take another swig.

"You better have brought enough for everyone, or I'm going to have to tell the driver you're breaking the rules," my new friend threatens, holding out a thin, bony hand.

"What is this, third grade?"

"Don't mess with me, girl," she warns. The smell of old cigarettes drifts from her fingers, making my nose wrinkle. Why do some people's bad habits have to stink so much more than mine?

"Aren't you on your way to work?" I hug my can tighter. Her Happy Helper maid uniform looks clean and her frizzy hair is tucked up beneath a white bandana.

She smiles. "That's why I need a drink."

"I feel your pain, but this is my only can. Sorry."

"You don't have to be sorry, sugar, just hand it over." Her voice rises, making the two boys three seats up twist to stare at the back of the bus. Despite my wild hair and bayou stink, they'd eye-fondled the front of my tank top when I boarded the shuttle.

"I would," I say, a little too loudly, "but I have oral herpes, open sores all over the inside of my mouth." The boys turn back around. Take that, raging hormones. "You don't want to drink after me. It's really contagious."

She rolls her eyes like she isn't buying my excuse, but turns back to digging through her purse without hitting the call button to alert the driver to trouble in the cabin. I hadn't expected her to. Most normal people—no matter how cranky and alcohol-deprived—won't risk making the driver stop outside the iron gates of Baton Rouge. There's the very real danger of the shuttle being attacked by venom-crazy highwaymen, as well as some scary urban legends about fairies sneaking in through the exhaust systems of parked cars.

In truth, the buggers push their way in through the outdoor vents. If they want in badly enough, fairies can get in, whether the car's running or not. That's why people without a death wish take the shuttle. It isn't safe to drive a normal car between iron-protected towns. Of course *I* could have driven without any worries, if I'd been so inclined. But I'm not. Guess I didn't want to see the view as badly as I thought.

I take another drink and close my eyes, feigning sleep between sips.

Ten minutes later, the shuttle pulls to its first stop outside the state capital. It's still the tallest in the nation, the better to view the wreckage surrounding the impressive white building. I chuck my empty into my purse along with the few samples I salvaged after my scuffle, ignore Skinny Cigarette Chick's condemning snort as I ease into the aisle, and amble down the steps and around to the animal compartments, giving the driver a chance to fetch Gimpy from his cage.

Outside, the air's even more stifling than it was an hour ago, a steamy, oppressive dog-lick to the face with a side of yuck. My lungs struggle to find oxygen hidden somewhere in the humidity. Hopefully, if I dawdle, the driver will accidentally set the Gimp free to roam the streets of Baton Rouge, looking for another owner with a bigger, better cooler.

But Gimpy's still there when I turn the corner,

entwined with his true love and only moderately cranky. He even tolerates being lifted and set into my red shopping cart, though now I have no place to put the weird groceries I'm supposed to fetch from Capitol Gourmet. That's fine by me. I'm not in the mood to hunt down the ingredients for Cranberry Nougat–Stuffed Pork Chop Lamb Shank or whatever Cane's planning for dinner. It's doubtful he'll be in the mood to cook it, either.

Even if he isn't mad at me for leaving the Breeze head out in the bayou, he'll be wrapped up in the murder investigation. He's only had a few murder cases in the time I've known him, but they always tie him in knots. Knots that make him so much more attractive. There has to be something wrong with me that I find the tense, brooding, noncommunicative version of my fuck buddy sexier than the sweet, laid-back, tolerant version who cooks me gourmet meals.

Probably many things wrong, which I'm sure Jin-Sang will underline, highlight, and footnote for me in a few minutes.

The slight Korean man is prowling the front porch of the FCC bungalow when I rattle up the street, his knobby knees poking annoyed jabs at his pants legs. In contrast to my clearly piqued supervisor, the office itself is cheery and welcoming, a crazy grandma you love to visit after school. The aging wood has a fresh coat of purple paint with orange detail in keeping with the hippie vibe of Spanish Town. Yellow rockers on the front porch complete the "come on over, y'all" look, inviting the curious to come sit a spell and read the Fairy Containment literature proffered in plastic holders nailed along the railing.

There are no curious tourists about today, however. Jin-Sang probably scared them away with his frown brow and prune face. The man's mouth spirals into a cat's anus when he's pissed—which is most of the time as far as I can tell. He's obviously in a mood this afternoon. Playing nice would be a waste of time. Better to come out swinging and hope the "a strong offense is the best defense" theory works in my favor.

"Sucking on lemons again, Jin?" I ask from the bottom of the steps, smiling when he turns to glare. He hates it when I shorten his name. His brow-crease grows deeper, a canyon where his uni-brow goes to die. "That'll destroy your tooth enamel."

"The office will close in two minutes." Jin-Sang checks his watch with the requisite amount of drama. "Now . . . one and a half."

"Then why are you out here? Shouldn't you be inside making sure all the coffee mugs have been washed and put away?" I nearly lost a hand for leaving a lipstick-stained mug by the kitchen sink a couple of weeks ago. Another reason not to bother with makeup: you're less likely to leave trace evidence at the scene of the crime.

"I will tolerate you today, but just mostly. Don't press it, Annabelle." Jin-Sang was raised in Dallas with his sister, but you can't tell it by his creative use of the English language.

"So . . . I guess you heard about the murder?" I can't imagine any other reason he'd be willing to "mostly tolerate" me.

"I did. I also heard you very closely vomited on the evidence," Jin-Sang says, descending the steps with sharp jabs of his threatening knees.

"Yeah." My beer roils in my stomach and I wish I'd popped a piece of gum. Jin-Sang isn't afraid to get up close and personal when he's in a snit, and I don't want him smelling beer on my breath. I don't make a habit of drinking on the job. It's just been . . . a day. To put it mildly.

Still, I should've waited until after this meeting before declaring it five o'clock somewhere. But the metal walls of the bus had been pressing in more than usual. Almost everyone living in the Delta struggles with anxiety—there's a reason the medic trucks hand out Xanax like candy when they sweep through a town—but most people have real reasons for it. They aren't immune, any of the lucky people to get a free pass.

Too bad having no excuse for the apprehension pricking at your insides doesn't make it stop. When I was younger, right after the emergence, anxiety had made me a prisoner in the halfway house, a shy freak of a kid who considered ending my own torment . . . until my new roommate introduced me to vodka. I was a pot girl in my old life, but after Caroline's death the smoke that had once made me giggly and relaxed only made me more paranoid. But alcohol . . . Just a shot or two and the fear went to sleep—a baby with whiskey slipped into its milk—and I was free to say and do and be the things that anxiety and regret had stolen away.

"Yeah," I repeat, tucking my chin to my chest. Jin-Sang stops inches away, hands propped on his hips, carefully manicured nails pressing into his belt so hard the tips turn white. "It wasn't easy. It was a kid. I knew her. Not well, but . . ."

I keep my eyes on Jin-Sang's hands, relieved when his white nails flood pink and his breath rushes out with a sympathetic sigh. "Those things are always difficult. But part of the road we've been chosen to travel."

Jin-Sang is one of the immune who consider themselves blessed by God. He's a loyal attendee at one of the churches that have popped up like mushrooms on cow shit in Baton Rouge in the past decade, one of the people who shun free tranquilizers and sleeping pills, preferring to shoot up every Sunday and Wednesday with the opiate of the people.

I haven't been to church since I left New Orleans. I don't see the point. Churches are run by people, the same people whose filth and stupidity and violence and hatred helped bring about the fairy mutations in the first place. All in all, people could color me unimpressed and God . . . well, I doubt he's that impressed either.

"Yeah." I shove my hands in the damp pockets of my cotton pants. "So I was already late getting to the site and then—"

"Then you did something stupid. I've been contacted."

Thanks, Dom. It would have been nice if he'd waited a couple of hours so I could break the news myself before making the required call to my supervisor. What happened to "I'll give the paperwork straight to Cane"?

"I wouldn't call getting attacked by a Breeze head stupid." I shrug and shift my weight to my back foot, putting more distance between us. "Maybe unlucky or—"

"Don't shit on me, Annabelle."

I laugh. I can't help myself. The snort's out before I can suck it back in. Jin-Sang scowls so blackly that his eyebrow furrow turns into an ominous "V" that stretches to his hairline.

"This is not funny. This is serious business time. That drug house could have compromised all of your samples. You should have scouted that sector and made sure it was clear."

"I did. I tracked through the entire area twice a couple of months ago." And I had. The fact that I was hungover and sleep-deprived at the time is a matter better kept to myself. "They must have had the Breeze house covered or camouflaged or something or I'm sure I would have seen it."

"You should have seen it anyway," Jin-Sang says,

obviously not impressed with my excuse. "And you definitely shouldn't have left a bite victim alone in the bayou. That was a big mistake for you, Annabelle, a very big mistake."

"She isn't just a victim." My voice rises, summoning a growl from Gimpy. "She's a junkie who was trying to *kill* me. She's crazy; how was I supposed to—"

"Make a review of your handbook. The protocol is clear." His brow smooths, his irritation decreasing in direct proportion to my own. The smug note in his tone makes me want to growl along with my cat. "You should have restrained the woman and then called for help if you were unable to bring her into the proper authorities alone. You should have waited with her until—"

"And what if she had friends out there? With guns? I'm supposed to sit around with my thumb up my ass and wait for some Breeze head to shoot me?"

"Rules are rules, and you knew this work could be dangerous when—"

"I'm a shit and egg collector!" I yell. "Why would I assume that would be a dangerous line of work?"

It *hadn't been* when I first signed up to train with the FCC, before some freak figured out that fairy droppings can get people high. You have to wonder about things like that. Who was the first person who decided it was a good idea to eat fairy poo? Or, better yet, mix fairy poo with bleach and snort it up his nose? I'd like to meet that freak. And punch him in the face a few dozen times for making my job suck more than it had in the first place.

"I'm sorry you see your work with those eyes." Jin-Sang looks as if he genuinely pities me for not believing that wading around in the swamp putting water in tubes and scooping dead fairies into jars is the most noble work on the planet. "Perhaps we should discuss a transfer to a different department."

"Jin, come on, I don't want to transfer. I just—"

"*After* you deal with the FBI."

Five

W hat?" The FBI? He must be confused. Captain Munoz is New Orleans police, not federal government. "The DPD are calling in immune law enforcement to get the woman who attacked me, but it's not—"

"The FBI liaison called twenty minutes ago. They're sending a team from New Orleans on the eight o'clock shuttle to Donaldsonville." Jin-Sang turns his attention to the cat in my basket and absentmindedly reaches down to scratch Gimpy behind the ears.

Amazingly, the Gimp's glittery green eyes narrow in pleasure and a garbled, mucus-y rumble that might be a purr fills the air. It figures the bastard would bond with someone equally evil. Or maybe it's just Jin-Sang's cat-anus mouth that's fooled Gimpy into thinking the man is one of his kind.

I cross my arms and curl my lip at the spectacle Gimpy's making of himself as he rolls over and offers Jin-Sang his belly. "There was a murder. I'm sure the FBI is—"

"It is the Fairy Investigation division, not normal FBI."

His words give me pause, just as he knew they would. Surely the feds haven't been called in because of one lousy Breeze house. The government does its share of cracking down on fairy drugs, but only the big-time operations. If they're coming to Donaldsonville, it means one of two things: either my find isn't the first in the area, or they're coming to town in more of a "policing their own" sort of capacity.

I've only known two FCC workers who were arrested. One was taken into custody by military personal at Keesler, the other hauled off by the Fairy Investigation division of the FBI.

"Immune agents or non-immune?" I struggle to think of anything I've done that might warrant arrest. I haven't been the busiest worker bee, but I get the job done. A little late, a little sloppy, maybe, but I wasn't worried about getting fired, let alone arrested.

But maybe Dom and Jin-Sang are right. Maybe leaving that woman tied up out in the bayou is a more serious offense than I'd thought . . .

"They didn't say," Jin-Sang says, the hint of a smile twitching at his lips. Either he's really in love with my cat or really enjoying my misery. "They only advised me to make sure my local field agent was available to them."

Only. Whether he knows it or not, Jin-Sang's given me an angst-reprieve.

Doesn't sound like the feds are coming to haul me off to the hoosegow. Sounds like there's an excellent chance that the FI unit is coming to Donaldsonville for reasons that have nothing to do with me. Or mostly nothing. If they aren't immune, the FBI will need the local FCC field agent to wade out into the swamp and take pictures of the Breeze house and collect evidence and yada yada yada.

But with Captain Munoz on her way to town, I'll get a break from that sort of thing. At least for a few days.

"Well then, I guess I'd better get back to town and see if they're going to need any help." I pull my cart away from Jin-Sang, interrupting the love fest. Ten minutes ago, I would have given Gimpy to the first interested party, but now I'm feeling strangely territorial. I don't really want my new pet, but neither do I want my new pet that I don't want to want a chode like Jin-Sang more than he wants me. I reach into my purse and grab the box of test tubes I fished out of the water. "Do you want these? I know the area's contaminated as far as habitat research is concerned, but—"

"Of course. I enjoy evidence that you've actually tried to do your job."

"Ha ha," I say, though I know he's not joking.

Jin-Sang takes the box, being careful not to make bodily contact, reminding me how filthy I am. Mud lingers beneath my nails, emphasizing the square end of each finger. It would probably be a good idea to run home and snag a shower before I head to Swallows for a beer and something fried. But even as the thought passes through my mind, I know I won't bother.

Who cares if I'm frizzy and stinky and have obviously skipped my last seven or eight manicures? The only person I bother getting pretty for is going to be busy locking up the Breeze head Munoz brings in and filling out the paperwork to get a collection team from Keesler to come pick her up. Then he'll have to stay at the police station to welcome the feds arriving on the eight o'clock shuttle.

Cane and his big brother, Abe, are the senior officers at the DPD and will be in charge of making the introductions between the FBI and Captain Munoz. They'll also have to arrange housing for the feds, get Munoz settled in the visiting police guest quarters, and so on and so forth until God knows when. As long as I turn off my phone, I'll be able to eat and drink in scruffy peace.

After the day I've had, I know I should be upset that the person I'm closest to isn't going to be around to offer comfort and support. Instead, I'm relieved. I don't want comfort and support. I just want a beer or four, some buffalo wings with blue cheese dressing, and a few sleeping pills.

Which reminds me . . .

"I'll come into the office with you," I say, stopping Jin-Sang halfway up the stairs. "I need to pick up a bottle of Restalin."

Jin-Sang sighs and his angry face returns. "Didn't you pick up two bottles the last time you were here?"

"Um . . . yeah." I shrug, making it clear I don't care if he thinks I take too many sleeping pills. Who doesn't? Once you've been taking them a few years, one Restalin stops working. After that, you either up your dose or spend half the night tripping out with the sweats and shakes and weird half-waking dreams that accompany withdrawal.

According to the FDA, the pills are supposed to be non-addictive, but just about everyone knows better by now. The detox from Restalin is supposed to be miserable. Not that I'd know. I've never gone more than a few nights without my pills. Why bother? It's not like I'm some hippie who wants to cleanse my body of toxins. I like toxins. I figure they're human preservatives. I'll probably live to see Cane and the other organic-eating, healthy-living people dead and buried. I'll be like a cockroach, obnoxious and toxic and indestructible.

"That's a sixty-day supply." Jin-Sang frowns. Again.

"Not if you take more than one at a time." I smile, refusing to let him get a rise out of me.

"You should still have at least thirty pills left, Annabelle. It's dangerous to chew so many pills."

"That's why I don't chew them. I swallow them."

"Don't use words with me," he says, just begging for me to ask if he prefers elaborate hand gestures. I resist the urge, but just barely. "Come back in two weeks. You can have more then."

I shake my head, refusing to believe I've heard him correctly. "But you can't do that. Meds are a part of my employment package." They have been since the early days, when the immune were in charge of cleaning up the dead. It was the only perk to dealing with the horror, one the government hasn't gotten around to taking away yet. And I want my perk. Now. "Those pills are free for field ops."

"I'm not asking you to pay me for them. In two weeks, I will give them—"

"I can't wait two weeks. I need to sleep now. And last time I checked, you weren't my doctor. Dr. Doughtry told me to take two if I couldn't sleep."

"This was during your last physical?"

"Yes. She also told me to take iron supplements and eat more red meat." I've been doing the latter religiously. Nothing like an excuse to have steak twice a week.

"And your last physical was what? Two . . . nearly three years ago?"

My mouth opens and closes. Surely it hasn't been that long. Min-Hee's been after me to get in to see the doctor at one of the monthly well calls, but I kept brushing her off. I have better things to do on Saturdays then get poked and prodded and told I'm not dead yet.

"Dr. Herget is the new physician for Baton Rouge," Jin-Sang says, all smug and full of his rightness. "He'll be in tomorrow from noon to six. If you aren't too busy with the FBI, perhaps you can come talk to him about your drug problem."

"I don't have a drug problem, I have a people

problem," I say, angrier than my casual tone suggests. Min-Hee has never questioned me like this. She just lets me into the med room and gives me a paper bag like any reasonable adult who knows to keep her nose out of other people's habits.

"I apologize, but I'm your supervisor." He cradles my samples in his hands, as if they're some kind of treasure instead of a bunch of stinking egg sacs and vials of polluted swamp. "As such, I am entitled to supervise your work and your access to FCC equipment and benefits. You will not be allowed inside the medical cabinet until your file is up to date with a current physical."

It's all I can do not to scream. "What happened to two weeks from now? What the fuck is—"

"You will use nice words or this conversation is over."

"Jin-Sang, please . . ." I soften my voice, open my green eyes wide, and think precious, baby-kitten thoughts. "The work's been hell today. I could really use a little—"

"I understand. But I truly think your work would improve if you were to chew fewer sleeping pills." Then the bastard has the nerve to smile, like this is some sort of friendly chat, not a power-play smackdown with my sanity on the line. Two more weeks with the kind of non-sleep I've had the past few nights will make me crazier than I am already. "Maybe then your eyes will work better when you're awake."

Or maybe I'll come back here and strangle him with his own shoelaces.

"Great idea. I'm sure that will work." I bare my teeth in an expression more snarl than smile. "Tell Min-Hee I miss her."

"I will." He bows slightly, pretending he doesn't get the message that I can't wait for him to take his pointy knees and prune face and go back where he came from. "And please give my greetings to the FBI. I'm sure they would appreciate it if you were waiting at the shuttle station when they arrive."

"Right. Another great idea. Thanks. See you, Jin." I turn and clatter off down the street. My cart rattles over humps in the pavement, making Gimpy's face jiggle and his gurgly purr morph into the more familiar yee-owl. I ignore him and hustle toward the shuttle stop. The wretch is on my shit list for kissing up to Jin-Sang and deserves shaken-cat syndrome.

Meet them at the station, my ass. The *last* thing I'm going to do is seek out the FBI. I'll lay low with the usual crowd at Swallows, let Captain Munoz take immune-personnel point, and hope this all blows over in a few days. It *is* Friday and after five o'clock. Well-paying job or not, the FCC is still just a job, not my life's calling.

So what is *your life's calling? Professional slacker? Pill-popping loser and future cat lady of America?*

My phone screams in my purse, the horror movie shriek I chose for Cane's ringtone startling me from my unusually self-critical thoughts. I wouldn't say that I particularly love myself, but I've come to a place where I'm content with my choices. I slack at my job, I need help getting to sleep. So what?

At least I took a job with the FCC like a good, community-minded immune member of society. There are other people with my good fortune who use their privileged status in more selfish ways. One man took over hundreds of acres of farmland just south of D'Ville—not to mention a few *very* expensive historical homes—and declared himself the cotton baron of southern Louisiana.

He, along with the other immune he's convinced to work for him, makes millions every year, profiting on the fact that there's no one else left to farm the rich Delta soil. Most immune folks are busy at the camps or collecting samples for scientists or running the river ports, helping keep the trade routes functioning despite the fact that it often seems the rest of the country has declared Mississippi, Louisiana, and parts of Alabama a dead zone.

It's like the "normal" states are afraid to interact with the infested areas, as if eating Louisiana crawfish or wearing delta cotton will infect them with fairy venom. What they really fear, of course, is that the mutations will find a way to live in other climates and expand their territory.

"Your phone is screaming." A narrow woman with hot pink hair gelled into a star shape points to my purse as she eases by me on the sidewalk. The sparkles on her cheeks send images of Grace's glittery pink nails surging to the front of my mind.

There are definitely reasons to feel lousy about myself today.

A girl's life was stolen, her chance to grow up and be whatever she'd dreamed of being obliterated by a monster who deserves to die in one of Louisiana's many electric chairs. Professional slacker or not, I should do everything in my power to help catch and destroy that person.

I fish out my phone, but freeze before I hit the green square to accept the call.

This call isn't about the Beauchamp murder—Cane wouldn't tell me anything about an ongoing investigation. Once my evidence collections duties are over, I'm as excluded from official police business as the next citizen, at least until they need me for other "immune only" duties. This call is probably about the Breeze house or the Breeze head. Or maybe he's calling to yell at me for touching Grace's sleeve or tromping through the Camellia Grove grounds. Or maybe this is personal, a call to ask how I'm holding up, or gently criticize me for making poor choices . . . *again*.

Cane cares about me. Eighty percent of the time, he makes me feel like a better person. The other twenty, his sad brown eyes and quiet disapproval make me more miserable than I've been in years. Letting Cane down reminds me of all the other people I've let down—Mom and Dad and Marcy and my professors and all the others who once believed I could be something wonderful. And Hitch, who loved me for the mess I was. Who was nearly as big a mess, and yet still found a reason to hate me.

No, not *found* a reason. I gave him a reason. Like I gave everyone a reason. No matter how hard I tried—and I *did* try—the whole *trying* thing never worked out. In the long run it's better for everyone if I don't try. If I clock in, toe my line, and go home alone. As soon as the investigation's over, I'll make sure I go home alone again. I have to end things with Cane, before I hurt him and add another name to the list of people who think I suck donkey balls.

Gimpy yowls and rolls his eyes, flexing a claw at my phone as if he'll answer the call himself.

"Oh, shut up." I tap the red rectangle, sending the call to voice mail.

According to my display screen, it's five after five. Cane knows I turn my phone off at the end of the day. He actually approves of it—though I'm sure he wouldn't want me telling his big brother, Abe, that he thinks it's a good idea for the only immune person in Donaldsonville to make herself unavailable after quittin' time.

But Cane believes it's good to disconnect, to spend time playing cards and taking walks on the levee instead of watching the mutation update boards on the Internet. He's an unusual man, and a general class act. How he got mixed up with me, I haven't a clue, but it's a mistake I'll remedy for him soon enough.

The thought threatens to make me sad, but Gimpy banishes my angst with a hiss and a swipe at my face as I pick him up and shove him back into the animal containment unit under the shuttle. There's no time to comfort him, even if I were in the mood. The shuttle driver fidgets impatiently near the door, as ready for the end of the workday as I am.

I hurry to fold up my grocery cart. "Two seconds," I say, scanning the tightly packed luggage compartment. Looks like Donaldsonville is going to be tourist-filled this weekend.

Wonder if our visitors know there's been a murder in town? Probably not. The only news program covering Louisiana comes out of New Orleans and they have bigger, scarier things to report. New Orleans never really recovered after Hurricane Katrina, when the iron gates were ripped from the ground and the fairies turned my hometown into a death zone. The mayor, police, and National Guard barely pulled the Big Easy back from the edge of complete annihilation. It still isn't safe to go out at night, even in the Bourbon Street area, no matter what the tourism board tells the Mardis Gras revelers every year.

"Here, let me get that." Nelson, the driver, has worked the route between Donaldsonville and Baton Rouge for as long as I can remember. He knows I fail at spatial relationships. There's a reason my purse is big enough to fit a lawn gnome and still have space left over.

"Thanks." I hug my giant purse—the better to

conceal the empty can I've forgotten to throw in a recycling bin—and head for the door, casting a final glance at the Capitol building before I climb inside.

I don't know why I turn to look. I've seen it a million times before and find it more depressing than inspirational. The upper levels are posh apartments for rich people who moved downtown when the suburbs turned deadly, and most of the bottom level has been bought out by a bank. Only about an eighth of the structure has anything to do with democracy. There's a tiny courthouse, a tinier meeting room for the shrunken number of state representatives, and a couple dozen cramped offices. The FCC was in one until Min-Hee threw a fit, demanded more room to safely store our samples, and got the office moved into a house down the street.

So why the hell is Barbara Beauchamp hurrying up the white stone steps like a woman on a mission? On any other day, I might assume she has business at the land office or the DMV—she drives a specially designed iron minivan—but today . . .

What could be so important that she left her family only hours after learning that her youngest daughter is dead?

I step around the corner of the shuttle, watching her newly curled blond hair bounce as she climbs. She clutches her thousand-dollar purse to her side, but I'm sure she isn't hiding empty cans or bottles. It looks like she's hiding *something*, however. The tense line of her spine, her rushed steps, the nervous glances she casts at the men in suits streaming out the front doors, all reek of secrets. Bad secrets.

Whatever Barbara Beauchamp is doing in Baton Rouge today, I have a nasty feeling it has something to do with her daughter's murder. It's hard to believe she'd hurt Grace—she obviously loved the girl—but my gut screams that I should follow her and see what she's up to. Just in case . . .

Instead, I turn and board the shuttle, heeding Nelson's warning that he's ready to head out. This is none of my business. I'm not a detective; I'm a shit scooper.

And I'm officially off-duty.

Six

Less than an hour later, I ease through the battered red door of the tavern and take a deep, healing breath of central air. Yet another reason—aside from draft beer and food that doesn't come from a box—that coming to Swallows is so much better than going home. My ancient window unit never cools down the kitchen; it barely makes it comfortable enough to sleep in my bed.

Some nights I still end up dragging my mattress onto the floor in front of the screen door where a hot summer breeze blows from the front porch to the back, proving shotgun houses are both cheap *and* practical. Sure, someone could theoretically shoot a bullet straight through my living room, bedroom, kitchen, and out into my backyard if all three doors were open, but what are the chances of that happening?

People in this town need me too much to shoot bullets through my house, even if I weren't a decent neighbor and friend. Which I am. I love this town, these people.

Especially *these* people. Swallows is filled with several of my favorites. Shane and Nell, sixty-plus each and newly married, snuggle near the end of the gleaming bar nursing a pitcher of Blue Moon. Bryce, Alvin, and Patrick, old friends who make arguing look like more fun than most marriages, dominate a table for six in the dining room, while Fernando and Theresa huddle in the curve of the bar near the entrance, dark heads bent together, in the midst of some serious gossip. As usual.

Fernando turns as the door slams closed behind me, his amber eyes sparkling above his freshly shaped goatee. "Annabelle! You little slut, we were just talking about you."

"Don't call her a slut." Theresa pinches Fernando's well-muscled arm. He's wearing one of his many skintight black tank tops, the ones that cling to each sculpted pec and washboard ab, showcasing the perfection of his body. The better to taunt we straight women with the majesty of the Latino god we'll never have, I suppose.

He certainly isn't hoping to hook up with someone at Swallows. Most of Theresa's clientele is over the hill and all of them are straighter than the broom shoved up Jin-Sang's ass. Fernando's own bed-and-breakfast/antique shop/wine bar is the best (and only) place to meet and mingle with other men in Donaldsonville. It's at the end of Railroad Street, and aptly named The First and Last Chance Wine Bar and Flophouse.

"It's okay, she knows she's a slut." Fernando grins, dimple popping. "Right, honey?"

"That's right, Fern." I lean down, letting Fernando kiss my cheek just for the joy of seeing his nose wrinkle.

"Shut the front door! You smell like ass."

"You would know." I grin and plunk my purse down on the floor before sliding onto the stool next to Fernando's.

"Oh, bitchy *and* slutty today. So, tell me, is it true you were shacking up in the middle of the day with both your doors wide open and—"

"Buffalo wings or cheeseburger?" Theresa interrupts, rattling her armful of bracelets at Fernando like he's a cat to be scared away. Speaking of cats . . .

I turn to peer at where my bike and trailer are parked in front of the bar, feeling oddly pleased to see Gimpy still asleep in the back. I'm starting to get attached to the bastard, and would have brought him in if I didn't know for a fact that Theresa would cut me if I toted something hairy into her place of business. She's only five feet tall and small enough to wear her twelve-year-old daughter's clothes, but she's tough and not a fan of four-legged things.

She grew up in White Castle, the next town over, in a trailer full of six brothers and sisters and triple the number of cats. Rumor has it she drowned them all— the cats, not the brothers and sisters—the day her mother died of a fairy bite, just shoved the rheumy-eyed mongrels in a sack and pitched them into the Mississippi on her way into Donaldsonville.

I'm not sure the story is true, but I've seen Theresa draw a gun on a dog that lingered too long near her Dumpster. She didn't kill it—just fired in its general direction—but still . . .

"Which one?" she pushes when I hesitate a second too long. "Or are you going to appease my motherly side and order some grilled chicken or something healthy?"

"You have a motherly side?" I ask, grabbing a handful of peanuts from the bowl in front of me.

"My kids think so, but the brats don't know any better." She doesn't bother smiling. We both know she's kidding. She'd give her life for Dina or Diego. "So, wings, I'm guessing?"

I nod. "With extra blue cheese and an Abita Amber."

Theresa clicks her tongue and turns away, but not before reaching out to pat my arm. Just once, a swift pat-squeeze that's over before it begins. Still, the gesture throws me. Theresa isn't touchy-feely. She must have heard about the body . . . about what I had to do to the body.

Looking around the room, I spot the sympathetic glances from Shane and Nell and even Patrick—who I haven't seen look anything but red and angry since the Saints were sold to some frigid state up north where they can't even pronounce "who dat"—presses his lips together and nods. Ugh . . . it's almost enough to make me get up and go home. If I hadn't already ordered, and Fernando wasn't acting as catty and gossip-hungry as ever, I might have seriously considered it.

"So you were Afternoon Delighting with police boy, weren't you?"

"I was. And if Bernadette doesn't want to hear, then she can close her door or turn up her soaps or something." I make a mental note to steal my eighty-two-year-old neighbor's newspaper on Sunday morning. Nothing makes her madder than someone taking her coupons. A petty gesture, perhaps, but I'm sick of her spreading the sordid tales of my love life all over town. Honestly, what does the woman expect? Our houses are less than three feet apart. Even if I closed the doors—which I won't because it's too hot to have sex in the summer without ventilation—she'd probably still be able to hear every sigh and moan.

Theresa returns with my beer in record time, proving she's going soft and feeling my pain. I grab the chilled mug and take a long, cold swig, hoping I'll be beyond feeling anyone's pain before the sun sets on this miserable day.

"I don't see how you drink real beer and don't get fat." Fernando shakes his head as he surveys my admittedly flat midsection. "Not to mention all that chicken skin and lard."

"I'm a skinny fat person, what can I say?"

"So you're covered in cellulite under those dykey clothes you wear?"

"Totally covered. It's disgusting, but Cane loves to count my ass dimples, so . . ." I shrug, keeping a straight face, doing my best to destroy Fernando's fantasy life. He's one of my best friends, but I know he has a crush on Cane and rather enjoys Bernadette's blow-by-blow descriptions of his sexual prowess. "And my clothes aren't dykey, they're functional. Not all of us dust shiny things for a living."

"I don't *just* dust shiny things." He takes a sip of his Chardonnay. "I also order wine and occasionally pour it myself when Tanner has a day off. And I have been known to wash sheets and make beds occasionally."

"Very occasionally."

"Very, very. Why bother when those Mexican girls are so great at getting their maid on for me?"

"Shut the hell up, Fernando." Theresa plunks down my wings. Wow. Wings and a beer in less than ten minutes. At this rate she's going to give McDonald's, the only fast-food restaurant still trucking frozen patties down into the Delta, a run for their money.

"Those Mexican girls will *rule* this town in ten years," Theresa says, pointing a tiny finger at Fern's perfectly sloped nose. He's had work done, but you wouldn't be able to tell if you didn't know him before and after. "My sisters are saving their money. They're going to lease those two big houses next to the courthouse and open a spa and bed-and-breakfast in a few years and take *all* of your business."

"Just what D'Ville needs. A spa," Fernando says

dryly. "I think they'd be better off opening a strip club. At least then Amity's crowd would have some place to go when she closes at two."

I kick Fern under the bar, and shoot him a "shut up" look.

Amity Cooper's new bar—a renovated warehouse filled with big-screen TVs and a stereo system that makes the entire street throb from 9:00 p.m. to 2:00 a.m. every Thursday, Friday, and Saturday—is the bane of Theresa's existence. Coop's is three blocks away, but loud enough to disrupt business at Swallows. Theresa doesn't get many families eating late dinner Thursday through Saturday anymore. People with young kids aren't comfortable near the noise and the roaring SUVs and the general "gangsta" feel Amity has deliberately cultivated at her new place.

And it isn't like Theresa or any of the other restaurant owners can complain. Amity clearly slipped a wad of cash in the mayor's pocket to score the building. The church was after the warehouse for years to build a skating rink—Father Reginald offered a decent price and threatened the mayor with eternal damnation and was *still* refused—so there would be no help coming from that direction. The only other route for complaint was to appeal to the city council, who are in the mayor's pocket, or the police force, and Amity's brothers make up a third of that.

It's kind of hard to believe Cane and Abe don't realize their sister's new enterprise is screwing the laidback, homey vibe of Railroad Street, but I suppose they have bigger things to worry about than noise control. Like policing the iron fence, or processing bite victims needing to be deported, or writing tickets for people who keep throwing perishable trash in the town's non-perishable dump and putting our town at risk for some kind of medieval, fleas-on-rats, plague situation.

Or trying to catch a murderer.

Jesus. There's a murderer in our town. It *has* to be someone from inside. The average tourist wouldn't know their way around the Beauchamp mansion so well. They wouldn't know about the hidden path that cuts through the garden to the family quarters, to the place where Grace slept.

I drown my thoughts in another deep drink of Abita Amber.

"I'm just saying I think your sisters would be hot naked," Fernando says, his playful tone indicating he's trying to make nice in his own obnoxious way. Maybe that's why I like Fern so much. He's even more offensive than I am. "Not to me, personally, but most straight men think you Swallows girls have the hottest—"

Theresa curses in Spanish, calling Fern a filthy homo who can suck her mother's eggs—or something like that, *my* mother made me take French—and sticks her pierced tongue out before going to refill Nell and Shane's pitcher. Looks like they're steering clear of the whiskey tonight. Hopefully that will mean a peaceful evening for Dom and a drunk-free drunk tank down at the station. The last thing any of the town law enforcement needs is more crap to deal with.

"But for real, Miss Lee." Fern lowers his voice as he leans closer. "We need to have a *tête-à-tête*."

"Okay. Can I eat while we head-to-head?"

"What?"

"*Tête-à-tête*. It means head-to-head." I take a bite of spicy, blue-cheesy goodness and sigh. So good. Buffalo wings are all the proof I need that God loves us and wants us to be happy. Benjamin Franklin once said the same about beer. Because he was a wise, wise man . . . and buffalo wings hadn't been invented yet.

"I'm not getting anywhere near your head." Fernando curls his upper lip. "It looks like you have bugs living in that straw. A deep conditioning treatment should be in your immediate future."

"Okay," I say, skipping the usual smart-ass banter. Fern's heart isn't in it. I can tell. There's something in his eyes, something . . . spooked that I didn't notice before. "So what's up your skirt?"

"You shouldn't talk with your mouth full. It's gross."

"You shouldn't look at my mouth if you don't like seeing what I'm eating."

"And hearing it. Could you smack louder?" He turns to twirl the stem of his wineglass. "I can't believe you're dating the hottest piece of ass in town. You must be as filthy in bed as you are out of it."

"Really?" I throw my naked wing bone back to my plate. "Is this what you wanted to talk about?

My disgusting eating and living habits?" There's hurt in my tone. He's getting to me. I usually have rhino skin when it comes to Fern—I know he doesn't mean ninety percent of the crap that comes out of his mouth—but tonight I'm feeling fragile. A strange wetness lingers at the edge of my lashes when I turn to grab my beer.

The wing sauce must be spicier than usual.

I slam my empty beer down and swipe the back of my hand across my nose. Runny. "Could you hand me a napkin?"

"Of course. Yeah. Here, take the whole thing." Fernando stammers, fumbling one of the tightly packed napkins from the metal dispenser between us. "Nards, girl. I'm sorry." Fernando wraps his arm around me and hugs me to his side, not even flinching when a bit of hot wing sauce transfers itself from my fingers to his forearm.

"It's okay. It's just been a rough day."

"I know. I heard. We all heard. We promised not to talk to you about it."

"Good idea. Let's stick to that plan."

"Okay, then let's talk about something else upsetting."

"Do we have to?" I reach for another wing.

"Well, Theresa didn't want me to tell you." Fernando pauses, making sure that Theresa is still in the back rustling up food.

"So maybe you shouldn't tell me." I'm not really in the mood for more bad news.

"I think you need to know this particular bit of nasty." He drops his voice further, playing up the drama. "Amity Cooper was in here about twenty minutes ago looking for the 'redheaded slut.'"

"How do you know she was talking about me? Patrick's a redhead and I hear he's a real whore when he's loaded."

I know Amity doesn't care for me. The hateful glares across the supper table on Sundays tipped me off even before she cornered me at the grocery and threatened me with the wrong end of a loaf of garlic bread. She'd actually poked me in the chest and warned me not to "fuck with Cane." I assumed she meant metaphorically, but maybe she was being literal and the rumor of my afternoon tryst with her brother has pushed her to the edge.

But whatever. She could tumble over that edge and lose her crappy weave on the way down for all I care. "Meh. Sticks and stones."

"No, seriously," Fernando says. "I think she's out for white-girl blood. I've never seen her so pissed. She was out of her mind."

Hunh. Odd. Amity isn't usually the type to make a public scene. Even the garlic bread incident was conducted in a quiet, otherwise abandoned corner of the Piggly Wiggly in appropriately hushed tones. "Did she say why she was so angry?"

"No, and none of us were about to ask." Fernando shakes his head, real fear in his eyes. "Her claws were all the way out and jewel-tipped."

"Weird." It *is* weird. I wonder what I did?

"I was just glad you weren't here. She could totally take you in a bitch fight." Fernando steals a piece of my celery, carefully wiping off a lingering bit of sauce with a napkin. "You should talk to Cane about her, asap. She needs to realize she can't mess you up just because she's related to half the policemen in town."

"She won't 'mess me up.' Her mother would kill her for being that tacky." I wave at Theresa as she exits the kitchen with a tray full of cheeseburgers and cheesier, gravier fries, giving her the universal sign for "bring more beer." "She's not nearly as tough as she likes people to think."

"No, she's not, but she's crazy. She really is, Lee, you need to listen to me." Fernando grabs my wrist, squeezing hard enough to make me wince before letting go. "Some guy got knifed last night at Coop's," he says, casting a nervous glance over his shoulder, as if the knife-wielder might be lurking in wait behind the poker machine. "They kept it quiet and off the police scanner, but there's gang shit going down at that club. You can talk 'town reclamation' all you want, but this place is starting to get skankier than a—"

"Ease up." I refuse to let him finish his no-doubt colorful simile. "I moved here right after the mutations, and I heard people talk about what it was like before. Donaldsonville was post-apocalyptic before a single terrorist set off a bomb in a chemical plant."

Fern sighs, and does another spooked scan of the bar. "Maybe so, but—"

"We came together and made this town something better," I say, genuinely irritated with him for the second time in one day. "It's Mayberry around here compared to those last few years before the mutations. So give it a break."

He stares at me for a beat before smiling and snatching me up in another hug. I stiffen at the unexpected display. "We love you too, slut."

I shrug him off with an eye roll. "I just like it here. I like the people. Even Amity. We were cool before Cane."

"Well, she's certainly not cool with you now," he says. "Stay away from her, Lee. I'm serious. She wants to rip your face off."

"Maybe she'll like me more in a few days." Or weeks, or however long it takes for me to get up the ovaries to break up with her brother.

Fern gasps. "You're not! Are you? Right now? You can't, not when he's so in love with you that it sickens people walking down the street to see you together."

I squirm. "I don't know. I don't want to talk about it." The bell above the door tinkles again, and I turn to look over my shoulder. I intend to make certain it isn't Amity coming to gut me, then maybe do a quick check on Gimpy to ensure he's still asleep. But when I see who's stepped into Swallows I forget I have a woman out for my blood, or a cat, or a huge smear of wing sauce on my chin.

The smell of him hits first, a smell so achingly

familiar I would know who it belonged to if I were blind. It's sage and soap and a hint of clove cigarette, topped with the spice of that gross green shampoo he loves, the one we'd called Martian Spooge and squirted all over the shower making alien-orgasm sounds one of many nights we had a few too many. It's mint gum and the hint of the garlic-laden something he ate for lunch. It's cotton and sunscreen and cherry Chapstick, because he's allergic to synthetics, sunburns easily, and prides himself on having girly-soft lips that he knows exactly what to do with.

It's just . . . Hitch. It's him. It *really* is.

Something horrible I've forgotten I know how to feel fists around my chest, crushing my ribs. I forget how to breathe, how to think, how to move my napkin to my open mouth to wipe the mess away. All I can do is stare, and watch his cool blue eyes register a slight surprise as he recognizes the girl at the bar and then . . . nothing.

Nothing. Seeing me doesn't affect him. He doesn't feel the weight of everything that was once between us pressing down on his face, smothering the life out of him. He doesn't feel regret and loss and misery slamming into his gut, followed closely by a flash flood of memories of the way it feels to hold my hand, to run down the street giggling and gasping for breath after we let the neighbor's annoying yapping dogs out of their kennel, to slip all the knots free on my bikini and coax me, naked, into the dark water of the pond behind his house.

He doesn't remember that he loved me. That he should *still* love me.

Because he *should*. If it was ever real, it should still be real. Love doesn't stop just because you start hating someone. I still love my mother so much it makes me hate her even more every time I think about her. Seeing, remembering—it should hurt Hitch like that. It should hurt him the way it hurts me.

Seven

It feels like my skin's been turned inside out and every secret, pathetic part of me is grotesquely exposed, a hot sloppy mess of organs and shame. What a lame-ass I am. What a dumped-so-long-ago-it-shouldn't-matter-but-for-some-stupid-reason-it-does lame-ass.

I recover fairly quickly—jaw closing, fingers spasming around the napkin Fern places in my hand—but I know Hitch has seen it. My weakness. He's seen that I still love and hurt and regret. He knows that I'm the big loser in the game of love.

Some game. Some dumb, shitty game. It makes me remember why I don't want to play anymore.

I silently resolve to end things with Cane immediately, before we have the power to do this to each other one hot, sunny afternoon down the road. I have to live in this town; I can't deal with having a *real* ex tromping about, flashing his sex eyes and smelling his perfect smell where I could get a glance or a whiff at any time. It'll kill me. I'll have to move, and I can't imagine that. Donaldsonville is the only home I have left, the only place that's somewhere I want to be.

"Hello. Annabelle? I'm Stephanie Thomas." The voice is tight and perky, but with a husky undertone, hinting at a sensuality her conservative black suit and casually upswept brown hair are doing their best to conceal.

Still, it's obvious this woman is pretty. Very pretty. And standing very close to Hitch, who is also working the business look. I scan him up and down, taking in the dark blue summer suit with the light blue shirt underneath, pulled together with a conservative white-and-blue-striped tie. His wavy brown hair is so short it barely teases his ears and he's evidently tried to tame it with some sort of "product." There's a crisp, damp look to the curls despite the fact that they're dry, and not a hint of the usual scruff on his chin.

He looks so amazingly tidy, professional.

I've never seen Hitch in anything but scrubs or cut-up jeans and T-shirts so threadbare you could see his skin through the fabric. Occasionally he'd whip out an ancient flannel or sweater he saved from high school, for warmth during the brief Louisiana winter, but I hadn't realized he could look so damned fancy. Even when we'd gone out, we'd gone in jeans and T-shirts. My mind doesn't know what to do with the dressed-up, business-ified Hitch standing next to this dressed-up, business-ified woman.

What the hell is he doing here? Why does this

chick know my name? How long will I sit here staring at her outstretched hand before I shake it?

Hmm . . . I don't know. How long? It's already been too long. Way too long. Probably best to avoid it altogether. I'm not much of a mind to touch "Stephanie," anyway. I rather hate "Stephanie" at first sight.

"Yeah, I'm Annabelle." I glance at her hand and then at mine and shrug. "Sorry. Wing sauce." I waggle my fingers in the air and smile, watching irritation flicker behind her soft brown eyes with the green flecks. My smile widens. It pleases me to annoy Stephanie, gives me something to work at besides pretending that seeing Hitch doesn't make me want to puke for the second time today.

Speaking of Hitch, I have to acknowledge him sometime. With words instead of gaping.

I turn, keeping my grin in place, but the second our eyes connect I flinch. Even that still feels so intimate. "Hey, Hitch. How are you?"

"Not so good," he says with an answering grin. "Someone was supposed to meet us at the shuttle station, but apparently everyone in Donaldsonville is too busy for the FBI."

"The FBI?" I parrot, my mind refusing to believe what my gut has already realized. "You're kidding." Surely he's . . . surely that wouldn't . . . and he couldn't . . . and . . . and . . . and—

"I'm Special Agent Stephanie Thomas, fairy investigation division." Stephanie flashes her badge with more aggression than necessary, punishing me for my refusal to touch her evil FBI flesh. "And you know Special Agent Dr. Herbert Rideau, fairy forensics."

"Herbert?" Fern—who up to this point has remained mercifully silent—can't resist commentary. "Did you punch your mama on the way out?"

"It's a family name, Herbert Mitchell. My friends call me Hitch," he says, his unsinkable grin still in place. The man could smile while fishing maggots out of the garbage. Nothing dents his damned cheeriness. Almost nothing, anyway. "But y'all can call me Dr. Rideau while I'm in town."

Oh, no. He didn't. He didn't just said *"y'all."* If he expects me to call him "Dr. Rideau," he can take his fancy new badge and shove it up his—

"Right. Absolutely, doctor, Ms. Thomas. Glad to have y'all in town." Fernando nods respectfully, picking up on the angry vibe beneath Hitch's superficial pleasantry. He's off his stool a second later. "Well, Miss Lee, I think I should head back to the ranch, make sure all the boys are settled for the night."

A pathetic part of me wants to latch onto his arm and beg him not to leave, not to abandon me to the scary people in suits, but I can't. Fern has every right to flee this uncomfortable situation. I, however, have nowhere to run. They're right. I should have met them at the station. Or at least *someone* should have.

I wave goodbye to Fernando and take a moment to wipe my face and hands, hoping to win back a few having-my-shit together points by not being covered in sauce. "Listen, I'll be glad to help y'all out with whatever you're here to do." *Please, God, don't let them be here to arrest me. Not Hitch. And "Stephanie."* "But getting visiting law enforcement settled really isn't my responsibility. The Donaldsonville Police have a couple of—"

"The Donaldsonville Police are pretty busy tonight." Stephanie slips her badge back in her pocket and crosses her arms, doing her "tough" impression. She looks like she's chastising a five-year-old for eating too much ice cream, and I'm not scared. I can imagine hating Stephanie—am actually well on my way to hating all people named Stephanie in her honor, in fact—but not fearing her.

It's hard to tell who's supposed to be the good cop and who the bad cop. They're both pretty pleasant. Of course, I know the unpleasant potential hidden beneath Hitch's sweet, Southern exterior. I've seen him screaming angry, veins standing out against his forehead, hands curled into fists I suspected he wanted to punch me with.

But he hadn't. He'd just screamed, cried a little, and walked away, leaving me alone in the house we'd shared. I'd packed my things that night, signed the official paperwork to withdraw from school the next morning, and left New Orleans without bothering to say goodbye. I was enrolled in the FCC training program at Keesler before supper, and shacked up in my new dorm by nightfall.

Six years have passed since then, six years without a hint of what Hitch Rideau might be up to. He'd sold his house, changed his phone number, and left to finish up his residency at another hospital without telling anyone where he was going. Every drunken phone call to old friends and late-night Google hunt came up empty. Hitch didn't social-network, he didn't blog, he didn't post on the fairy message boards. He wasn't listed in any public database or phonebook. It was like he'd vanished off the face of the earth.

Or joined the FBI.

"The man we spoke to on the phone . . ." Stephanie pauses to consult a small notebook she's pulled from one of her many magic pockets. "Captain Abe Cooper. He said half his force just got off a double overtime shift, he's got one officer on fence patrol, and the other is working an iron suit job in the bayou at the edge of town. His dispatcher is out sick, so he wasn't able to leave the station to—"

"Wait. What suit job?" Concern for Cane sizzles along my skin, banishing some of my Hitch-induced angst. Cane's always the first to volunteer for suit jobs, no matter how many times I beg him to call me before he sets foot in the fairy-infested areas.

Call me. *Shit.* He *can't* call me.

I fumble in my purse, searching for my phone. I have to check my messages, find out where Cane is. Surely he's called, probably more than once. "What kind of job, why are—"

"He's retrieving an assault suspect." Hitch watches me paw through the mess in my purse with raised brows, as if he's vaguely repulsed by my disorganization. Or maybe it's the giant empty beer can rolling around at the bottom of my bag.

Shit again. Why didn't I throw that away?

"Captain Munoz couldn't make it up from New Orleans. She's two weeks from her due date and her doctor said it wasn't safe for her to travel," Stephanie provides, her expression making it clear she isn't any more impressed with the contents of my purse than her partner. "There wasn't anyone else available to pick up the woman you left tied up in your research area and law enforcement couldn't get in touch with you. Captain Cooper recommended we look for you here." She pauses, brown-and-green eyes lingering on my empty beer glass. "At the bar."

Oh, shit. Oh, shit. *Ohhhhhhh. Shit.*

My hand finally closes around my phone. I jam the on button and jump off my stool without waiting for it to complete the series of swishing sounds. I head for the door, but Stephanie blocks me with one thin leg and a sensible black pump.

"We're going to need you to answer some questions, Annabelle."

Crap! I can't deal with this right now. I really can't.

Stephanie continues in her soft, sensible voice. "Restraining an allegedly infected person—"

"There was nothing 'alleged' about it. She was covered in bite marks."

"As I said, restraining someone you believe to be infected and leaving them—"

"Can we argue about this on the way to the site?" I interrupt, wincing when I see the red dot on my phone announcing seven missed calls. "I need to get out there and help."

"I think the police station would be a better place for you to give your official statement," Stephanie says. "I'm sure Lieutenant Cooper is qualified to retrieve a suspect."

So it *is* Cane. *Dammit.* "Sure, he's fucking qualified," I yell, making the young mother seated a few feet away "hmm-mmm" in annoyance and tell her two boys to close their ears. I lower my voice, blushing. "But he's not immune to fairy bite. It'll be dark soon and fairies are more likely to swarm when—"

"I'm a special agent with fairy investigations." Stephanie's smile turns patronizing. "I'm aware of the typical behavior of the—"

"Good for you. Someone should give you a cookie." The smart-ass is so thick, the people in the next room can probably taste it settling on their French fries. "I'll make you one myself, but right now you need to get out of my way."

"Come on, Steph." The familiarity in Hitch's voice and the ease with which he shortens his partner's name add to my suspicions that they're more than colleagues. "We need to check out the site, anyway. Might as well give this guy some help. I'm sure he's using one of the old suits that weigh a damned ton."

"He's definitely using one of the old suits," I confirm. The new, lightweight iron cling overwear is ridiculously expensive. Not even the New Orleans police department has more than a few.

In Donaldsonville, where people refuse to vote in a half-cent sales tax despite the fact that we can barely pay our city workers and are half a million dollars in debt to the federal government, it's doubtful we'll be getting those new suits anytime soon. Or ever.

"We can put off the questioning, don't you think? I mean, you're the boss, but I'd hate to see someone infected if Ms. Lee here can help prevent it." Hitch's honeyed drawl, the one that once made me melt, seems to have a similar effect on "Steph." I shift my gaze in time to see the hint of a secret happiness smear the edges of her lips into a smile.

"You're right." She nods and shifts out of my way. "Where's your car?"

"I don't have a car."

"You don't have a car?" she asks, as if I've just confessed that I like to skin kittens for fun on Sunday afternoons.

"I ride a bicycle. It's environmentally friendly."

Hitch grunts under his breath before pushing through the door and out onto the sidewalk. The grunt could mean that he knows damn well I don't drive a car because I'm rarely sober after five o'clock. Or maybe he's just pissed that we're going to have to walk. Maybe he's forgotten that I like my hooch, or that he once enjoyed it as much as I do.

Right. And maybe Stephanie is going to take me

up on that cookie offer and we'll become best friends and spend hours braiding each other's hair.

"I'd like to remind you of your right to have an attorney present before you discuss the events of this afternoon." Stephanie reaches for the door and holds it open, letting the sticky evening ooze inside Swallows. "Everything you say in front of myself or Agent Rideau will be considered on the record and could be—"

"Close the door! I'm not paying to air-condition the street!" Theresa calls out, hustling to the front of the restaurant with a pitcher in each hand, either oblivious to the fact that she's yelling at the FBI or not giving a good goddamn. Stephanie releases the door and opens her mouth, but I beat her to it.

"Hey, Theresa, can I borrow your car?" I ask, the thought of the long walk to the bayou with Hitch and Stephanie enough to inspire a panic attack even if I didn't know every minute we waste could be bad news for Cane. The sun isn't down yet, but it will be soon. I don't want him out there in the shallows when the air starts to cool. "I can have it back in an hour or two."

"Are you drunk yet?" she asks bluntly, staring me straight in the eye, ignoring Stephanie now that she's allowed the door to swing back into place.

I feel my cheeks heat and for the first time in a long while I wish I wasn't a beloved "regular" at my local bar. "You served me one beer, how could I—"

"That's not what I asked. I asked—"

"No." I cross my arms and clutch my phone as it vibrates. A glance down reveals a text from Cane's older brother and boss, Abe, warning me that the FBI is looking for my ass. He's actually used the words "my ass," confirming he's as pissed with me as I assumed. I wonder how many of the missed calls are from him, reaming me for putting his brother in danger on the same day he found the body of a murdered girl.

"Good." Theresa nails me with another of her piercing looks. "Don't get that way until you get my car back. Keys are by the cash register."

Then she turns and walks away without asking why I want the car or waiting to be introduced to my new acquaintance. But then, Theresa isn't a nosy person and doesn't particularly care for people who upset her friends. I guess it's obvious Stephanie and I aren't long-lost sorority sisters.

I grab the keys and hurry out the door, not bothering to see if Stephanie's following. I do, however, stop to check on my cat. Gimpy's still asleep. Hopefully he'll stay that way until I come back to get my bike. If not, he's a big boy and can take care of himself. He might have to someday soon, since I'm pretty sure they don't allow cats in federal prison.

Hitch is waiting for us outside the door, smoking a clove cigarette. The murky sweet scent curls through the air, teasing at my nose. I want to stick my tongue out and taste it, let it sneak inside me and burn. As powerfully as I hate the stink of tobacco smoke, I just as intensely love the tang of a clove. I would smoke them myself . . . if they didn't remind me so entirely of Hitch.

"We've got a car. Are you smoking?" Stephanie asks. "I thought you'd already had one today." She sounds like his mother, or his girlfriend, or a terrifying mix of both. I watch a hint of irritation flit across Hitch's face before his lips stretch into his usual, easy smile. He winks at Stephanie, then takes one long, last drag.

"Well, shit." The smoke spirals from his lips with a sensuality that compels me to watch. "I guess I decided to have two." He crushes the cigarette out on the brick wall of Swallows and tosses it into the trashcan nearby. "I may even have three."

Stephanie sighs, but it isn't an easy sound. "Fine. I don't think—"

"We should get going," I say, plowing between them, reaching for the door of Theresa's Taurus. Cane's waiting and I can't take another minute of the Hitch and Stephanie show. They're tripping me out. It's too weird to stand next to a man I screwed in ways too filthy and wonderful to be spoken of in broad daylight while he stares into the eyes of another woman and pretends I was never a part of him.

But maybe I wasn't, maybe—

"I'll drive." Hitch plucks the keys from my hand. The place where his skin brushes mine screams in protest, revolting against the sudden sense memory of what it feels like to touch this man. "I'd feel safer, wouldn't you?"

"I'm an excellent driver." I stare him down, daring him to contradict me. The intimacy is there again, and for a second I would swear he feels it too, a secret thing that swims between us, electrifying the air.

"You've also got an empty container in your purse."

Without breaking eye contact, I reach into my purse, grab the can, and hurl it toward the trashcan where his cigarette disappeared a moment before. The clatter of the can knocking against the rest of the trash as it lands inside is one of the more satisfying sounds I've heard all day. The second Hitch turns over his shoulder to ascertain that I really am *that* awesome, I snatch the keys and slide into the driver's seat.

Where I intend to stay.

Eight

Turns out driving is just like riding a bike. Except you get where you're going faster and there's less sweating involved. We're off Railroad Street, through the historical district, and heading down the half-mile stretch of road toward the southwestern edge of the gate in minutes.

"The Beauchamp house is going to be on the left," Stephanie says over her shoulder to Hitch, who's thankfully taken the backseat.

I don't want to sit next to him. Being trapped in a vehicle with his smell—that damned smell that keeps making my body remember things I don't want to remember—is bad enough.

"We should stop by tomorrow morning," Hitch says, "and show the parents the pictures."

They're stopping by the Beauchamps'? With pictures? Then this visit isn't solely about the mess I made.

"There aren't parents. Just a mother, no father," I

say in my most helpful voice. *See how helpful I can be, FBI? See how easy it would be to just let my mistake slither under the rug and stay there? Forever?* "Barbara Beauchamp adopted Grace when she was a baby. Barbara's also got two grown children, James and Libby."

"That's in the file." Stephanie doesn't approve of helpful Annabelle anymore than unhelpful Annabelle. I can practically hear her frown deepen. "Hitch just didn't have time to look over the Beauchamp case. He was too busy reading up on the protocol for your particular code violation."

"And collecting all our data on the Breeze houses in the area," Hitch says, throwing me a bone. Repulsive ex-girlfriend or no, he doesn't seem as determined to play head games as his partner. "Y'all have quite an epidemic on your hands."

It's exactly what I was hoping to hear, but the news that there are other Breeze houses is far from comforting. Sure, it means the FBI has bigger fish to fry than yours truly, but it could take months to dismantle a Breeze network. A series of Fairy Wind–producing houses, all offering each other materials and sanctuary, acts like a toxic underground railroad, ferrying a mind-melting product north to freedom. Freedom to steal the lives of countless people with Breeze's instantly addictive high.

A part of me protests that I'm the last person who should be preaching against addiction, but alcohol doesn't make my brain bleed or my teeth fall out.

Alcohol doesn't make me dangerously violent or supernaturally strong; it doesn't drive me to steal and kill in the name of my next fix.

And besides, I'm not an addict. I am a *habitual consumer*. There's a difference.

"So you're here to dismantle a Breeze network, and slap me on the wrist," I say, hurrying on before they can confirm or deny that all I'll be getting is a slap on the wrist. "But what about the murder? You think that's related to the Breeze houses in some way? Is that why your unit's involved?"

"Not that we know of," Hitch says. "We're looking into the Beauchamp case as a favor for the—"

"Should we share details at this juncture?" Stephanie interrupts, leaning forward to peer at Camellia Grove as we pass by. Darkness has fallen early at the plantation, hastened along by the live oak trees arched protectively over the house, mourners at a funeral that can't take place until the autopsy is performed.

For the zillionth time today, sadness settles along my skin. No matter how much I believe in Cane and Abe or how much I hate having "Hitchanie" on the case, it's good to know the FBI is going to be involved. I want Grace's killer found. Soon.

"Unless you want me to suit up and do all the work myself, then she'll have to be told what we're looking for sooner or later. It's up to you." Hitch casually defers to his partner's seniority once again, as if he doesn't care if she decides to send him into a potentially life-threatening situation just because she doesn't want to share information with a slacker FCC agent.

I'm getting ready to tell Stephanie exactly what she can do with her condescending, dangerous attitude—ex or not, there's no way I'll allow Hitch to put himself in danger—when she speaks. "No. You're right. We don't want to put you at unnecessary risk." She turns back to me as I pull onto the dirt road leading to the iron fence. "We're aiding the New Orleans criminal division of the FBI. They couldn't spare a team, but they think Grace's murder might be the latest in a string of serial killings. There are four other girls dead. All found in Louisiana, all between the ages of seven and ten with blond hair and blue eyes. They have a few suspects, men with a history of abuse who were in the right place at the right time. We're hoping the family might remember seeing one of them on the property in the past few weeks."

"God." I don't know what else to say.

"The killer usually leaves a clue at the murder scene as to where he'll strike next," Stephanie continues, hand moving to her seat belt buckle even before I pull to a stop next to Cane's empty police cruiser. "We're hoping we can find the clue in time to make this murder the last one."

"There was a snow globe with a plantation inside buried near the body of the last victim," Hitch says, his voice gentler than it has been.

He knows about my sister. He knows about the

camping trip that ended with me lugging Caroline's dead body into the backseat of my car while the two boys we'd brought with us ran screaming as the newly mutated fairies tore into them. We'd all thought the highway signs warning us to watch out for killer fairies were a joke. A lot of people had. A lot of people who were now dead.

I swallow and cut the ignition. "So I'll get to go on a treasure hunt tomorrow. Sounds great."

Hitch makes an angry sound. "Your sarcasm isn't appreciated, but your help would be. A girl is dead, and—"

"I wasn't being sarcastic." I turn to him, meeting his judgment-filled blue eyes, hurt that he thinks I'd be flippant about something so awful. Seems he has an even lower opinion of me than I assumed. Hitch must have forgotten that there's a good person buried beneath my bullshit.

Or maybe he never believed I was a good person, maybe he stayed with me for three years for the sex, drugs, and rock 'n' roll. Not that there was much drug use—aside from beer and the occasional upper to get us through a long night at the hospital—or rock 'n' roll. Hitch liked to play bluegrass, sing old country songs in a voice that oozed like molasses through the night, filling me with such simple happiness I wasn't sure my body could contain it. And sometimes it hadn't: sometimes the joy spilled over in tears, or laughter, or into Hitch's mouth as I kissed him and kissed him, certain I'd never have to come up for air, that I could survive on the taste and feel of the man I loved.

I was never happier than when I was with Hitch. I can remember that happiness, even though I cut away a long time ago the part of me that grieved for it. I can understand amputating a poisoned limb, but you shouldn't forget it had once served you well. It had once held your morning coffee, scratched the places that itched, smoothed softly over where you hurt and left pleasure behind.

But Hitch has forgotten, the disgust on his face proves it.

I drop my eyes to the floor at his feet. "I had to collect the initial samples on Grace this morning and carry her body back to the fence. She didn't weigh much more than my cat." I turn and hit the buckle on my seat belt. "Anything that will help you catch the person who killed her *does* sound great. Sincerely."

Hitch sighs, and for a second I think he might apologize. But he doesn't. Instead, he pops the top of his briefcase and begins rustling through a pile of neatly organized folders. From what I can see in the rearview, he's now a color-coding and tab-using kind of guy. This from the man who was officially reprimanded twice during his residency for misplacing paperwork and only believed in folding clothes if there wasn't a clear piece of furniture left to throw them on.

Maybe this isn't Hitch at all. Maybe he's been body-snatched by aliens, and this anal, dressed-up, cold-eyed version of him is a virus from another planet masquerading as my ex-boyfriend. The thought, though unlikely, makes me feel better.

Leaving alien Hitch in the backseat, I slam out of the car and follow Stephanie to the edge of the fence, scanning the dirt road beyond. The air blushes with sunset glow, and the pink and gold lights of the fairies flash brighter than they did earlier in the day. They're moving faster, shaking off the sluggishness inspired by the August heat. Watching them dive and dance, pausing to pop a mosquito or tear into a wasp here and there, makes my heart beat faster. Cane is out there, walking among those beautiful predators, risking his life because I couldn't be bothered to keep my damn phone turned on.

"I'm going over the fence. I'll walk down to the . . ." My words fade when I hear the distant, rhythmic rattle.

"What is it? Do you—"

"Sh! Listen." The rattle grows louder. I watch the road beyond the fence, gravity easing its death grip on my shoulders when a tall, iron-clad figure trudges around the corner. The suit is ridiculous-looking—the tin man from Oz crossed with a robot from a '50s horror flick—but I've never been so happy to see it whole and intact.

"That's him!" I'm through the gate without another thought, running down the stretch of road that separates me from Cane. I'll feel better so much better when I'm by his side, protecting him with my unappetizing-to-fairies stink.

I don't slow until I'm a few feet away, close enough to see the suit is indeed hole-free . . . and the anger in Cane's dark eyes. Oh. Dear. Even through the plexiglass shield covering his face, I can see that he's pissed. *Really* pissed. In a way I haven't seen him since Amity forgot his mother's birthday last year.

Yes, my six-foot-two, buff, gun-toting lover is a big ol' mama's boy, and not the least bit ashamed of it. His mama raised three children on her own and put herself through nursing school while working two jobs to keep her kids in clothes and shoes. She's a hero to Cane, his first true love . . . but he stood up to her. For me.

I'd barely poured my sweet tea at my first Cooper supper before Mae was grilling me about my past, my future, my goals, my faith, my family, and dwelling at length on my feelings about children. Did I want them? How many? How soon? Blah, blah, blah, until I was a stuttering mess.

I can understand her eagerness to grow a crop of grandkids—Abe is forty-two and married to his job, Cane's nearing forty and his ex wasn't able to have children, and Amity is thirty-five and still busy partying until three in the morning. I can feel Mae's pain, but I am *so* not the girl she wants me to be. I care about Cane, but I don't even want to *think* about babies. Ever. I'm with him for the laughs, the companionship, and the damned fine, totally protected, non-procreative sex.

But try explaining *that* to your man's mama. It was easier to fake a stomach virus and run for home. Literally *run*, even though I'd been wearing high-heeled sandals. Cane, however, stayed behind and gave Mae a talking to. I know he did. He never told me what went down, but the change in Mae's behavior made it clear that her son had asked her to back off. He'd done that—gotten tough with his beloved mama—on my behalf. It's just one of the things that proves he's a better man than I deserve.

"I'm sorry." I wrap my hands around his iron-covered arm and fall into step beside him. "I'll never turn off my phone again. I suck. I know I suck. I'm so sorry. I'd never want you to get hurt," I say, all my noble, ending-our-relationship intentions vanquished by the relief rushing through my veins. I'm just so glad he's okay.

More than glad. I'm giddy, dizzy with gratitude. I can't wait to feel his skin against mine, to have his hands everywhere, to kiss him from the top of his scratchy head to the tip of his moon-shaped toes and show him how truly sorry I am. It might already be too late for a merciful breakup. If his safety is this vital to my existence, I'm probably already in too deep.

"You are in a mess of trouble, girl," Cane says, his voice tinny, echoing inside his suit.

"I know. The FBI is here."

"Already? I thought they weren't getting in until eight."

"Guess they got here early. That's them waiting at the fence," I say, glancing back to where Hitch and Stephanie stand just inside the gate. "I think I'm going to be officially reprimanded for . . ." I freeze. The fact that Cane and I are alone finally penetrates my thick skull and injects my brain with a healthy dose of panic. "Oh . . . *fuck.*" I was so happy to see Cane safe that I forgot the reason he was out here in the first place.

"Oh fuck and a sack of shit," Cane agrees. "I couldn't find that woman anywhere. I walked every inch of your research area, even went beyond the borders just in case you'd wandered too far." He sucks in an only slightly labored breath, despite the fact that his suit weighs close to one hundred pounds. "Didn't see a damned trace of that Breeze head or the Breeze house, either."

"What?" I shake my head. How can that be? The woman could have freed herself—or been freed by someone else—but she couldn't have taken the houseboat with her. "That boat was locked in by tree roots. There's no way it's going anywhere until the water rises."

We're only fifty or so feet from the fence now. Cane slows almost imperceptibly. Next to him, the giant cypress that hovers over the split in the road sways in the breeze. The fairies lurking in its shade churn and hiss, angered by my existence. I shiver, glad I'm standing close to Cane. That patch of deep shade is the perfect place for a suit-penetrating swarm to get started.

"I don't know," he says, beneath his breath, "but I know we need to find that woman. Abe got a call from Keesler about ten minutes after Dom faxed your report to New Orleans, telling him you were going to be investigated by the FBI. Leaving an infected person tied up out there was a big mistake, Annabelle."

Oh, no. He's calling me Annabelle, not Lee-lee. I'm definitely in big trouble, but how big? "Is this official-write-up kind of big, or pay-cut kind of big, or lock-me-up-and-throw-away-the-key kind of—"

"Didn't have a lot of time to look over the FCC regs," he says, "but I'm thinking it's going to depend on whether or not that woman is found and what state she's in at the time. If she's good, I think you'll be good. But if she hasn't made it through the afternoon . . ."

My mouth goes dry and my tongue suddenly feels thick and stupid. For the first time, the immensity of my mistake hits me squarely between the eyes. That woman could be *dead*. Because of me. Sure, she's a Breeze head and a bite victim and marked for an early grave, but she could have lived a year or two in one of the camps. Maybe more.

But what if tying her up led to her getting drowned or sucked dry by fairies or eaten by gators? Her blood will be on my hands. I'll be a murderer, or at least a manslaughter-er. I didn't intend to kill her—I was only trying to keep her from killing me or getting away—but in the end, will that really matter? To a judge and jury? A *military* judge and jury, no less?

Oh God. This is bad. Why didn't I realize just how bad before?

My knees buckle and the ground swims before my eyes, but Cane catches me with an iron arm around my waist.

"Just hold up. This is going to be okay. This woman assaulted you, you weren't thinking clearly," Cane says, making me feel a tiny bit better. I *do* have a nasty bump on my head. "We all know you didn't mean to hurt anyone."

"I don't think *they* know that," I whisper, fighting a full-fledged panic attack. "I think that Stephanie woman wants to send me up the river."

"It doesn't matter what she wants. She's got nothing on you. We're going to find that Breeze house and if the woman who attacked you isn't there . . . Well, we'll make sure this thing is buried. They can't force you to testify against yourself and no one else saw anything with their own eyes." Something in Cane's choice of words makes my stomach clench. He's the most honest, life-valuing person I know, but a part of me wonders how far he'll go to make sure a certain body is never found.

A *body*. I might have caused a person to become a *body*, just like Grace, like Caroline, like all those corpses littering the highways after the first mutations. Like the bloated bodies I helped pull from the wreckage after Hurricane Katrina, when immune teams took the brunt of the cleanup, hoping to spare anyone else from infection. We worked twenty-four-hour shifts until we could barely stand, and still there were more dead left to find.

That's when the drinking during the day started. Just here and there, a little something to block out the horror and the smell of death. Just a little, a little, and the little became a hand to hold, a habit that stayed even when the death was gone.

Or mostly gone. Once you've seen certain things, when they've crawled inside you and made themselves at home, you can't ever really be free of them. Not ever. I would imagine seeing the body of a person I caused to die would be like that, a thing I will never escape.

My breath comes in shallow gasps and my forward motion slows to a crawl.

"You've got to calm down, baby," Cane says, the affection in his tone making it even harder to breathe. How can he love me? How? "This is what we're going to do. I'm going to tell these folks I wasn't sure where I was supposed to look. You see if you can remember where you left her, I'll get a drink of water, and we'll head out again in a few minutes."

"No, *I'll* head out again in a few minutes," I say, forcing myself to focus on tangible details, anything to distract my mind from the disaster at hand.

I catalogue the color of the stones beneath our

feet, tick off the number of trees between us and the fence, then start in on the number of branches on the giant cypress. Even as my heart slows and I begin to pull myself together, a vague feeling of misgiving nags at the back of my brain. Something about the cypress is bothering me, something more than the fact that hungry fairies spin beneath it. But what? What . . .

"You're not going out there alone, especially not now."

"I'm fine," I say, trying to sound it. "You don't need to be out here after dark. It could take hours. If she wasn't in my research area, then I have no idea where to start looking. I'm positive I left her . . ."

Left. I usually make a *left* at the tree to go to my research area.

I turn in a slow circle, staring down the path to the right. Tire tracks. Bicycle tire tracks. Three of them. One for the wheels of the bike, and two for the wheels of the trailer pulled behind. They have to be mine. No one else would ride their bike beyond the iron gate. A car, maybe, but not a bike.

I bet if I get closer, I'll see cat prints trailing beside, prints that would disappear when Gimpy leapt into my trailer and reappear when I stopped to toss him out, and then got back on my bike and went the wrong way. The. Wrong. Way. Damn that blasted cat.

"What's wrong?" Cane's iron-covered finger trails down my arm.

"I went the wrong way," I whisper. I'd spent the entire morning tromping around the *wrong* part of the bayou.

This screwup is getting bigger with every passing second. I hadn't missed that Breeze house in my earlier scouting. There *is no* Breeze house on my research land. Cane spent an hour in a tin suit and risked his life for *nothing*. That damned woman is still out there, sitting in the wrong part of the swamp, where I'll have to go fetch her after I explain how I managed to perform my job as crappily as I did this morning.

The panic tries to surge back in, but I push it away with a promise to indulge it fully at a later date.

"You went the wrong way?" Cane asks. "You mean—"

"I wasn't in my research area." I meet his eyes through the thick glass of his visor, knowing it's pointless to lie though a part of me is tempted. "I was somewhere else. You were looking for the suspect in the wrong place."

"Shit, Lee-lee." Cane turns, following the tire tracks. "Come on. I don't need that drink of water."

"No." I stand my ground. "Go back to the gate. I'll get her by myself. You've been out long enough."

Cane keeps walking, trundling with a clank and an occasional screech through the gathering dusk. "I told you, I'm not going to let you fetch some crazy Breeze head by yourself."

"Cane, come back." I cross my hands at my chest,

suddenly acutely aware of the audience observing our every move.

Hitch and Stephanie probably can't hear us, but they can see that something stupid is going down. I have to convince Cane to come back to the gate and show them he has no part in the stupid. He's a professional who was looking in exactly the place I told him to look. It isn't his fault there was nothing there to find.

"I mean it," I say, raising my voice a hair. "I'm not going to—"

"Lee-lee, don't you tell me what—" Cane's right foot shuffles forward, catching on a gnarled root that's elbowed its way up from the packed earth.

The heavy suit throws him off balance; he stumbles, and would have fallen if he hadn't reached out with one big hand. A hand that lands on a rock hard enough to rip a hole in the iron suit keeping all his yummy, salty, human skin safe from the hungry things buzzing through the night.

The air around me churns, a mini-twister that, for a moment, catches me up and carries me along with it. Silken wings pulse against my throat—faster than a racing heart, more dangerous than an exploding locomotive—and then they're gone. The fairy swarm from beneath the cypress surges past in a rush of glittering flesh and sharp teeth, snarling high-pitched, baby-voice snarls that would be hysterical if this wasn't a matter of life and death.

Cane's life. Cane's *death.*

I run, slower than the fairies had flown, but faster than I've run in years, closing the distance between me and Cane in seconds. The Fey are already on him, swarming around the hole near his palm as he bats and swings, but they haven't started gnawing on the suit yet.

There's still time. Not much, but enough. It *has* to be enough. I launch myself into the air, grab Cane's swinging hand, and take a punch to the stomach that knocks the wind out of me, but I refuse to let go. I cling to his arm, covering the hole with my body, pinning his hand to my ribs.

As soon I make contact, Cane freezes, proving he's an even cooler customer than I thought. He doesn't panic, doesn't lash out or run. He simply presses his palm closer and pulls me into his arms, until my back is glued to the front of his suit and my fairy-repelling scent lingers in the air all around us. The fairies hiss and snap. A few of them get so close to my face that I catch a whiff of their metal-flavored breath. For a second I'm sure my plan will fail, and Cane and I will both be savaged by the swarm.

But then, slowly, one by one, they give up and flutter away, back to the shade of the cypress where they fall to fighting over a few unfortunate horseflies. My heart races as the insects disappear into their mouths and the fairies' detachable jaws ooze back to their closed positions. Rows of teeth transform into pretty, pouted lips, and their faces once again resemble something humanoid with flat, feral eyes.

I shiver and clutch Cane's arm. It's by far the closest I've come to being bitten. I'm almost completely immune to fairy venom and, were a fairy to choose suicide via Annabelle, I'd suffer nothing more than a headache and a barfing spell. But I've seen immune people at Keesler with fairy bite scars. The Fey die when our blood hits their stomachs, but in those few seconds between nibble and death, they can do some hefty damage. It's only luck that I haven't been bitten before.

Luck, and the fact that I don't make a habit of diving into fairy swarms or prowling outside the gates at night. I play it safe—only going out during the day, steering clear of large concentrations of fairies—but tonight I'll gladly put myself at risk. I'll walk the bayou until the sun comes up, anything to make sure Cane stays on the other side of that iron fence.

Nine

"Are you okay?" My heart is still slamming so hard against my ribs that I suspect Cane can feel it against his hand. "Did any of them bite through, did they—"

"I'm fine. We're good. You did good." He hugs me, a gesture of comfort and affection, not desperation. "Now, let's start walking back toward the fence, nice and slow, right foot first. You ready?"

"Ready. Sounds good." I move my right foot with his and then my left, the rhythmic amble taking me back in time to the nights I danced on my father's shoes.

We'd gone to the Daddy-Daughter Valentine's Ball in New Orleans every year when Caroline and I were little. It had felt so special to spend an entire night as even one-half of my father's sole focus. He was usually too busy with work and other men to waste time with his family. It made me angry when I was a teenager—inspiring bad behavior I hoped would get me the attention my good grades and soccer trophies hadn't—but in the end, his apathy made losing him so much easier than losing my mom.

And now I'd almost lost Cane.

"Are you sure you're good?" I ask again. "No stinging anywhere, no—"

"I'm fine. And you're doing great. Just a little farther." The low, easy rumble of Cane's "calm down" voice makes me realize how hysterical I sound. I try to talk myself back to my happy place as we close the last few feet to where Hitch and Stephanie wait at the fence. We dance through the narrow opening with a final one-two step and Stephanie pulls the gate closed behind us, slamming the handle down, locking the horror out for the time being.

I jump off Cane's ironclad feet and spin, reaching for his headpiece, but Hitch is already there beside me, hands at Cane's neck, lifting the iron away.

"I'm Dr. Rideau. Is it okay if I check you out?" he asks Cane.

"No problem," Cane breathes, meeting my eyes with a comforting smile.

Hitch sets the hood on the ground and probes gentle fingers along Cane's sweat-slick skin, checking for the telltale swelling of the lymph nodes that begins within seconds of venom infection. "And . . . you feel good, no enlargement."

Ugh. This is weird. Call me crazy, but it seems wrong for two men who've both had their you-know-whats in me to have their hands on each other. There should be some law against it, in fact. A serious one.

"Open up and say 'ah,'" Hitch says. Cane obeys, the pink tongue that teased between my legs earlier today slipping from between his lips.

I squirm and shuffle back a few inches while Hitch stands on tiptoe to see inside Cane's mouth. Hitch is tall, five eleven in bare feet, but Cane's pushing six foot four with the addition of the iron under the soles of his shoes. Seeing Hitch look so small after years of having him loom so large in my mind is . . . strange.

This entire afternoon has been strange. In a someone-slipped-acid-into-my-juice-then-knocked-me-over-the-head-repeatedly-with-a-sledgehammer-until-I'm-nearly-unconscious kind of way.

"Tongue looks good. No swelling inside the mouth." Hitch sighs, a sound of relief that makes me like him more than I have all evening. "Now let's get you out of this suit and do a quick check for any surface abrasions."

"I'm good. I just need to get this hole patched and get back out there," Cane says. "The suspect wasn't where I expected her to be. I—"

"I screwed up," I say, spilling my guts before Cane can cover for me. "I was collecting samples in the wrong place this morning when I was attacked and found the Breeze house. I . . . wasn't thinking straight. The body and everything . . . it kind of screwed me up."

Hitch doesn't say a word, just nods and drops his gaze to the ground. Guess he suspects foul play or slacker play or drunk play or some sort of play, but who gives a crap what he suspects? There's no way to prove anything, and I know the rum and Coke isn't to blame. I was shaken by what I had to do to Grace. I've seen the bodies of dead children before, but I've never had to stick cotton swabs up what was left of their nose.

I shudder, blinking the memory away. "I'm sorry. I really am, and—"

"Wait a second." Stephanie steps forward, disbelief crinkling her perfectly arched brows. "So that woman's still out there somewhere?"

"Not 'somewhere.' I know exactly where she is," I bluff, not certain I know exactly where anything is anymore.

"It's getting dark." Stephanie's calm exterior begins to crack, making me wonder what kind of work she's done for fairy investigations before now. I'm guessing desk jockey stuff. Fieldwork seems to be getting to her.

"I'll borrow a flashlight. I'm sure Lieutenant Cooper has one in his car." I catch Cane's eye. "But I'm going alone. Patching that hole will take time if you do it right. It'll be better if I get out there and get back before it gets dark."

Cane shakes his head. "That woman is violent. The report said she tried to drown you."

"She didn't try to drown me." I wave an impatient hand through the air.

"So you were lying to Dom?"

"No, I wasn't lying to Dom, I just—"

"Then don't lie to me. I know that Breeze head got rough with you." Cane's arms cross with a clang. "After a year and a half together I can tell when you're telling stories, Lee-lee."

My mouth opens and closes and my cheeks burn. The confirmation that Cane and I are more than good friends settles like dust around the assembled company, making me, for one, feel vaguely dirty. Why did he have to talk about us being *together*? Why? When it would be so much better for the both of us if the feds assumed we *aren't* doing it?

Cane's full lips press together and I see the awareness that he's made a mistake flit behind his eyes. Maybe he's more shaken by his near-death experience than I'd thought. "I can't let you go out there alone. You're FCC, but you're still a civilian. If I believe your safety is at risk, I'm obligated to suit up and offer you an armed escort."

"You could just give me your gun," I say, frustration and panic warring within me. I love Cane for being the good, law-abiding man that he is, but can't he just give it a rest? I can't worry about him any more today. My heart can't take it.

"I can't give you my gun," he says. "Law prohibits me from—"

"Who cares!? You almost died! Don't you get that?" I bang my fists on his iron-covered arms, figuring it's pointless to act like we don't touch each other at this juncture. "I'm not going out there with you."

"Then I'll have to go by myself."

"I won't tell you where she is."

"I'll comb the area until I find her."

"Will you stop this? Please?" I beg. "That was so close. I can't believe you—"

"Let Hitch go." Stephanie pipes up from a few inches away, making Cane and me jump. "His suit is back at the police station with our luggage. It's lighter and more durable and you'll be able to get to the woman faster. And he's pretty good with a gun."

Pretty good with a gun? This woman must be the sharpshooter of the century if she dubs Hitch only "pretty good" in comparison. I've seen him shoot a line of beer cans off a fence from two hundred feet mere minutes after he finished emptying several of them himself.

He grew up hunting to help feed his mother, brother, three younger sisters, and eventually a couple of nieces and nephews whose daddies couldn't be bothered. His entire family depended on Hitch. He was the bright, shining star, the one who was finally going to pull them out of poverty.

But salvation hadn't come quickly enough. His entire family—save his asshole brother who was trapped at a local bar and couldn't get home—died in the first weeks of the mutations. Hitch's mom refused to camp out at the Superdome. She was too afraid of the looting and violence that threatened to destroy New Orleans. She was born on the bayou and knew a thing or two about fairies and folk tales, and had thought she and the younger girls and grandbabies would be safe as long as they lined the windows and doors with iron and stayed inside. She'd thought wrong.

I wonder if Hitch told Stephanie about the day he finally fetched his family's bodies, over a week after their deaths? I wonder if he'd cried into her lap the way he'd cried into mine?

Our eyes meet in the hazy orange dusk, and for a split second I see the old Hitch lurking beneath the surface of this new, professional man. There's a hint of that wild, sad boy inside him still, enough to make me guess he hasn't told Stephanie, just like I've never told Cane about my sister. There are things people like us only do once.

"That would give Lieutenant Cooper and me the chance to chat about the Beauchamp case," Stephanie continues, turning to Cane. "I'd love to hear about your initial questioning of the family."

So the FBI isn't here to take the case away from the DPD. In the old days, they surely would have, but every law enforcement agency in the Delta is overburdened and understaffed. Now the feds and the state often work with the local departments.

Which means Cane and Hitch will be working together for the next few months, maybe longer. Which means it's probably a good idea for Hitch and me to grab a few minutes alone and get our story straight. Do we tell all or keep our past buried beneath a big mound of fairy poop? I'm not a fan of meeting problems head-on, but, like it or not, Hitch and I have to decide how we're going to deal with being thrown back into each other's lives.

"Sure, sounds good," I say, at the same time that Hitch announces a trip into the bayou is "fine with him."

For once, it seems we're on the same page.

Ten minutes later, Cane pulls his cruiser into his spot at the station. I pull in alongside, stealing Dicker's spot. He won't be in until tomorrow morning, and I have to get Theresa's car back to her before then.

Luckily, I'm going to have help with that and a few other things that need accomplishing while I tromp out into the marsh looking for the woman who nearly killed me. I made a call on the way in, and Marcy is on her way.

No, scratch that, Marcy's already here.

I spot her as I step from the car. She's wearing her comfy jeans and a green, Blessed Hands T-shirt with the day care's logo on the front. Despite the lingering heat, she leans against the faded beige brick at the corner of the station. Her eyes are closed and her head tilted back as she soaks in the last of the dying light. The way the sun hits her face makes her look younger, softer than usual.

Twenty-eight years as a social worker—five of those spent as den mother to a bunch of angry, teenage orphan girls with enough angst between them to sink a dozen battleships—and another five years in the toddler trenches at the helm of her day care have deepened the lines near Marcy's brow and the frown

parenthesis around her mouth. She'd look perpetually angry if it wasn't for her eyes, those bright hazel
lights that shine from her midnight skin.

Marcy's eyes are the most beautiful things I've
ever seen. They are love, pure and simple, the tough,
fierce kind that never lets you go and never lets you
down. Without Marcy, I wouldn't have lived to see my
eighteenth birthday, let alone applied to college or
scored a half-dozen scholarships to pay my way.

She is my rock, my surrogate mother, my best
friend and—

"What do you want, Mess?" she asks, sensing my
approach but not bothering to open her eyes. She
has some kind of sixth sense where I'm concerned.
She can feel me coming from a mile away, she says,
a storm ready to blow through her ordered existence.

"Thank you so much for meeting me, Marcy, you
don't—"

"Don't you thank me. I was two feet from my
house when you called, and I don't want to be here."
Her eyes open, but stay squinted, taking my measure
and finding me lacking. Her "harrumph" comes from
that place deep inside her that hates dirt stains with
a passion verging on obsession. Marcy's clothes are
always clean, soft, pressed, and stain-free, even at the
end of a workday.

"But how do you really feel? Don't hold back."

"I didn't plan on it." A grin teases her lips as she
crosses her arms over her generous chest. Despite the
grin, she looks tired.

But it *is* Friday. The end of a long week of chasing kids and wiping noses and butts and all the other things that leak in the under-four set. Marcy is pushing sixty. She's getting too old to handle eight kids at once all on her own. I've tried to convince her to hire another full-time girl at Blessed Hands, but she won't. She says the babies keep her young and out of jail.

She swears she'll kill her husband, Traynell, if she's home with him all day. He retired three years ago and does cabinetwork in their backyard, but evidently wants sex constantly whenever Marcy's home. You'd think men would get over that after their fifth or sixth decade. Apparently not.

Speaking of men . . . Cane's already on his way into the station with Stephanie and Hitch, and will be back with his suit in a few minutes. I have to hurry. Cane's letting us take his patrol car with its superior fairy protection, Hitch's suit is the best of the best, and there's a good chance he won't need to get out of the car, anyway, but I'll still feel better if I have all non-immune people back within the fence before it gets too late.

The later the hour, the darker and cooler the air, the more vicious the Fey.

"So, the cat is in the back of my trailer over in front of—"

"Annabelle, honey, I sure as heck don't need another cat." Marcy shakes her head and gives her patented "just how stupid are you?" look, the one that really makes you look to yourself and wonder. "Do *you* think I need another cat?"

"I'm not trying to give you another cat," I say. "I'm going to keep this one."

"You're going to keep a cat? Alive?"

I ignore the insinuation that I kill things, not finding it amusing tonight. "I just need someone to pick him up from Swallows and keep him safe for a few hours, give him a can of food and some water."

"That's it?" Her face stretches outward in all directions, as if she's shocked by how little has been asked of her.

The look makes me feel bad. I try not to bug Marcy that often, but there are times when I have to ask favors. I don't have anyone else and I'm not ready to ask Cane to check my mail or take out my trash when I'm forced out of town for my quarterly training at Keesler.

"What about supper? Did you eat?" she asks. "Or do you need me to put a plate in your fridge?" And I certainly don't ask her to bring me food, though I do enjoy eating it. Marcy's chicken and grits with extra butter will be my last meal if I'm ever facing the chair.

The thought makes my semi-normal pulse speed anew. I need to take care of business and get that woman in police custody asap.

"No, I ate." I hold out Theresa's keys. "I just need you to drive Theresa's car over to Swallows, grab that cat, and drop the keys behind the counter at the bar. That's it."

She snatches the keys from my hand. "Done. But you come get that cat as soon as you're finished tonight. I'll be up late, you know I don't sleep anymore."

"I will."

"And be careful," she says, looking over my shoulder toward the entrance of the station. When she speaks again, her voice is strangely soft, nearly a whisper. "I know you don't have to worry about the bites, but I think there might be a killer out there."

"I know . . . I was there when they found Grace's body."

"I know." Marcy takes my hand, squeezing softly. I can feel her strength and empathy flowing into me even though her expression doesn't change. Marcy doesn't worry about "making faces for people," but she feels as deeply as anyone I know. "But she might not be the only one. Some woman called today asking about Kennedy."

"Kelly's daughter?"

She nods. "They think they might have found her body over in Lafayette. They won't know until they finish the autopsy, but this Agent Thomas woman who called still wants to ask me some questions tomorrow."

"What?" My mind rejects the information, even though I know Stephanie and Hitch are looking for evidence that Grace's murder is one in a string of serial killings. "But I thought you said Kennedy's dad took her? That she went with a white guy she seemed to know?"

"That's what Naomi said, but she never met Kennedy's daddy." Marcy sighs and releases my hand. "And you know Naomi. She might have just been covering her skinny butt."

Naomi was the woman on playground duty at Blessed Hands the day four-year-old Kennedy Grayson disappeared about a year ago, the woman who was promptly fired when Kennedy's mother tried to sue the day care for negligence. Naomi let the girl leave with a man claiming to be her father without bothering to make him go inside and type in the code required to pick up any of the kids.

A few hours later, the mother, Kelly, also came to pick up her daughter. She lost her mind when she learned Kennedy was gone. She and Kennedy's father were getting a divorce. Kelly had just given birth to Kennedy's little brother, a baby boy with dark mocha skin he certainly hadn't inherited from either of his pale-as-they-come parents. The Graysons were both Caucasian with light hair. Kennedy's was so blond it was nearly white.

A pale, blond girl who liked sparkles and unicorns, just like Grace.

"So they think a serial killer pretending to be her dad might have taken her?" I ask. "And then come back for Grace?"

"The agent didn't say anything about a serial killer, but that's good to know. I was under the impression she thought I might know more about Kennedy going missing than I'd let on. I'm from Lafayette. She seemed to think that was interesting." The furrow between Marcy's eyes deepens. She's worried, though she certainly has no reason to be. Marcy could never hurt a soul. She can't even kill spiders. She collects them in jars and sets them free near the levee.

Anger burns along my skin. Stephanie can act like I'm enemy number one all she wants—I've actually done things to deserve her attitude—but Marcy is one of the best people I know. Playing head games with her is just harassment, plain and simple.

"I'm going to tell that witch to back off."

Marcy shakes her head, and one finger snaps up to point at my chest. "You'll do no such thing, Annabelle Lee. You'll watch your mouth and be respectful to the FBI and kiss tail until you're out of trouble for this Breeze business."

Crap. I was hoping Marcy wouldn't find out about that. "Cane called you?"

Her skin smooths. She loves Cane. She'd never push the way his mother does, but I get a feeling she has her own fantasies about a big wedding and a surrogate grandbaby or two. Marcy doesn't have any biological kids. Traynell, for all his legendary virility, is shooting blanks. "He did. That boy's worried about you."

"He shouldn't be. I'll be fine." And I will be. Hopefully. "I've gotta go, the other FBI agent will be out any second and I should be in the car and ready to scoot."

For a second I feel icky inside for neglecting to tell Marcy that the other agent is Hitch, *my* old Hitch, the one she's heard so much about, but never met. I ignore the feeling and head toward the car. There isn't time for a thorough debriefing, and if Hitch and I decide to keep our past a secret I may be able to avoid spilling my guts altogether.

Even Marcy doesn't know what wrecked me and Hitch, only bits and pieces of information she pulled from me in the months after. I prefer to keep it that way. I'm honestly not sure what happened that August night.

Was it what little I remembered? What I'd told myself later? Or what Hitch heard floating around the halls of the hospital?

I don't know. I don't want to know. It's better if it all stays buried.

Hopefully Hitch will agree.

"Okay. Be good, be safe," Marcy says, following me toward the cars. "And come over straight after. You've got clothes at our place. You can shower and have something real to eat before you go home."

"Do I smell that bad?"

"Not a bit. You never do." Marcy is baffled that my sweat repels fairies. She swears I "don't smell like a real person."

It's true I don't usually get really foul, but I don't usually go around with swamp dried in my hair either. It's nice to get confirmation that I'm not completely repulsive. I couldn't care less what my ex thinks of me, but we *are* going to be in a cramped car together. I don't want to disgust or offend.

"But you look like hell," Marcy continues, snatching away her scrap of encouragement. "Like you were hung up wet, and you've got a sunburn on your nose. Again. It's red as fire."

My fingers drift to my nose, where telltale heat throbs beneath the skin. "I forgot my sunscreen."

"You're going to get skin cancer, and when you do," she says, grunting as she lowers herself into Theresa's car, "I don't want to hear any complaining about having a hole cut in your face. You were warned. From the time you were—"

"Yeah, yeah. You told me so. 'Bye. Go. Thanks." I peck her cheek, close her door, and give a wave, breathing easier when she starts the car with a final wag of her finger and pulls out of Dicker's spot.

Hitch is on his way out of the station, but doesn't seem to notice who's driving Theresa's car. There's a chance he would recognize Marcy. He saw pictures of her when we lived together and was hurt that I wouldn't take him home to meet "mama."

I just . . . hadn't wanted to share him with anyone. I never thought about marriage or "forever" or any of those things I probably should have thought about; I just wanted us to be on the same team. In a way, now we are.

Irony. It's less tasty than usual.

"You ready to get this over with?" he asks, not bothering to look me in the eye as he pulls Cane's keys from his pocket. His iron suit is folded in a clear plastic tackle box in his other hand.

"Aren't you going to suit up first?"

"Nope." He circles around to the driver's side and places the box in the backseat before sliding into the front.

I open the passenger door, but don't get in. "We're going a good way past the fence and it'll be getting dark soon. Don't you think—"

"No, I don't." His blue eyes meet mine, as cool and unimpressed as they were in the bar. He's still distant, a stranger. The part of me that hoped this would get easier when it was just the two of us withers and dies. "Get in the car."

If had been anyone else, at any other time, I would have told him to go fuck himself.

Instead, I force a smile and get in the car.

Ten

I sit in the strained silence for ten long minutes, determined not to be the first one to break it. We're nearly to the gate when Hitch speaks. "I read your file today. The entire thing. It took twenty minutes."

"Glad it didn't suck up too much time."

"You haven't been promoted once in five years. Isn't that unusual in your line of work?"

He knows damned well my job is reserved for the newest FCC recruits, a way to pay their dues for a year or so before they're advanced to cushier jobs at the ports or the camps or the occasional research facility. If the person in question has a college degree and any kind of medical training, it's a no-brainer they'll be on the fast track to ruling a research facility.

The U.S. government isn't the only employer for the immune. There are other countries running investigative operations in the Delta, each wanting to be the first to unlock the secrets of the creatures who've hidden among us for thousands of years. I've been approached by representatives from France and Brazil, but I told them both no thanks. I don't want to rule the world or even a research facility. I just want to scoop shit in peace and go home to a cold beer or four.

But Hitch will never understand. He works even harder than he plays. He's driven, in the way that makes people captains of industry or Peace Prize winners or eventually eats them alive and leaves them drooling in a corner.

"It *would* be unusual," I say. "If I'd applied for a promotion."

"And you've been passed over for two pay increases. Because of habitual lateness? If I was reading between the lines correctly?"

"You probably were." I shrug. "I make enough money."

I make more than twenty average D'Ville residents combined, but you'd never know it from the way I live. I don't need the excess. I grew up with an entire floor of a house to myself and unlimited charging privileges. I know firsthand that money doesn't buy happiness. Or safety.

Speaking of safety . . .

"Do you want to put your suit on before we go through?" I ask, as Hitch brakes in front of the gate.

"Nope." He hits the button on the dash, the automobile portion of the boundary tilts upwards, and we drive through the iron mesh at the mandated five miles per hour. The mesh slithers across the hood and over our heads, scratching like a hundred tiny fingernails. "I'm assuming we're going right."

"Right for about a mile. I'll tell you when to stop."

He nods. "So what happened to all the ambition?"

"It became more environmentally friendly."

"Like your bike?"

There's the smart-ass. I'd known it was coming. It's almost a relief to hear the derision in his tone. The pleasant neutrality was hurtfully impersonal.

"Let's talk about you," I say, shifting in my seat, giving him my full attention. "Do you have a death wish? Or has the FBI developed some kind of vaccine I don't know about because—"

"No death wish, no vaccine. I don't plan on getting out of the car."

"You don't plan on getting out of the car?" I'd considered that he wouldn't have to, but assumed he'd at least want to be prepared.

"Nope." It's his turn to shrug. "This is your mess, you should clean it up. It'll be dark by the time we get there and I'd rather check out the Breeze house during the day when I can see something. I'll come back suited up tomorrow."

"So why'd we waste time going back for your suit?"

"I didn't want an innocent man risking his life," he says, giving no sign that he realizes the "innocent man" is *my* man or that he cares one way or the other. "And I needed my guns."

"How are you going to shoot someone from inside the car?"

He sighs. "I think we both know there's not going to be anyone there to shoot."

"We do?"

"If this woman had friends they either untied her and got the hell out of town, or left her there and got the hell out of town. They're going to know they've been discovered and react accordingly."

"Right. Because Breeze heads *always* react the way they should." My eye roll is so intense my head gets involved. "Are you the same man who spent a year in the ER? Because I know you've seen your share of—"

"No, I'm not," he says, his words shutting me down as thoroughly as he knew they would. "I'm a different person, and I'd appreciate it if you'd respect that."

"The way you've respected my differences?"

"I wouldn't call being a drunk and lousy at your job respect-worthy differences."

My jaw clenches, but I manage a soft laugh. "You don't know anything about me."

"I know what I read, what I see." He casts a look exquisite in its disdain toward my side of the car.

It's all I can do not to run my hand through my hair, straighten my stained tank top, do something to make myself less repugnant. Instead, I search the road ahead, breathing in and out through my nose, fighting not to say things I'll regret.

"Pull over. Park at the end of the gravel." I point to a stretch of dry land that reaches further into the water than most. I should be able to see the Breeze house from . . .

Yep. There it is, floating among the gnarled branches, gray clapboard sides nearly black in the fading light, tiny windows as flat and empty as fairy eyes.

"That's it?" he asks. I nod. "I don't see—"

"We won't be able to see her from here. I pulled her around to a dry patch on the other side." I'm pretty sure that's where I put her. I pray so, anyway.

As I grab my flashlight from my bag, I honestly *do* pray for the first time in a long time, sending out a promise to suck less at everything if God will help me find this woman and let her be okay. Or as okay as when I found her.

"Guess you'd better get going," Hitch says. "Unless you've got something you'd like to share with the class."

I take a deep breath. "No, nothing to share. I just guess I'd rather be a drunk than a condescending asshole."

Hitch smiles, a stiff curve of his lips I can barely make out in the near dark. "I'd rather be a condescending asshole."

"Clearly." I hit my seat belt and reach for the door, but pause to check for fairies.

None have dared get close to the iron-plated car, but the rest of the dusky bayou is aglow with orbs swooping through the air, their reflections dancing in the still water beneath. It's beautiful, like a house fire or a tornado writhing in the sky. There are times when you can't help appreciating something, no matter how deadly it is.

I pause a second too long, and Hitch lets out a frustrated sigh.

"If you really think you're in danger, you can have one of my guns. I have two."

I turn, surprised to see the handle of his semi-automatic hovering near my face. "Am I supposed to be carrying an FBI weapon?"

"I don't care."

"I thought you were a big rule follower these days."

"Sometimes. Sometimes not." The gun inches closer. "If it will make you feel safer to have a gun, take it. I know you know how to use it."

It's not much of an opening, but I could try to make this lead into a chat about how much of what we know about each other we're going to admit to in our new, shared workplace. But I can't muster the gumption. Hitch is sending me out into the bayou alone. He isn't even going to suit up so he'll be ready in the unlikely event I need backup. He doesn't care if I live or die. He volunteered to come out here solely to spare the life of a stranger.

If that isn't confirmation that he'd just as soon forget he ever knew my name, I don't know what is.

"Thanks." I take the gun, but keep my eyes lowered. I don't want him to see that he's hurt me. Again. "If the fairies get too close, turn on the lights up top." I gesture toward the control on the dashboard. "They don't like the white and blue." Police lights are no longer red. Red attracts fairies.

"Got it. Good luck."

I don't bother to respond. For all the sincerity in that "good luck," he might as well have told me to go fuck myself. I slam out the door and head toward the bayou, realizing I neglected to fetch my waders from my trailer only seconds before I reach the water's edge.

Christ on a cracker. How could I have forgotten? People are creatures of habit and today's been anything but routine, but I spent most of my early twenties thriving in a stressful, rapidly shifting reality. When I want to excel, I do. And I *honestly* want to excel right now. I want to find this woman and help dismantle the chain of Breeze houses around Donaldsonville. I want to assist Cane and the FBI in finding Grace's murderer, and make my town a safe place again.

But despite my good intentions, I'm failing. And Hitch is watching. The knowledge makes me tuck my borrowed gun into the back of my waistband, flick on my flashlight, and keep going.

I step into the water, wincing as the gritty, oily bayou soaks through my thin cotton pants. I've barely made it five feet when something slithers against my leg, churning through the water with a muscular thrust of its long, thick body. I freeze, heart racing, tongue pressing against the roof of my mouth as I fight the urge to scream. Even when the snake is gone, gliding away, tracing elegant S-shapes in the water, the need to turn and race back to the shore is almost more than I can handle.

"Crap," I hiss, shaking one hand at my side in a vain attempt to release some of the adrenaline coursing through my system.

I'm immune to fairy bite, not snakebite. There's a reason I wear thick, rubber waders and search the ground very fucking carefully before I reach my hand near a place that could hide a snake. This is insane. I should go back to the car, see if Cane has a pair of waders in his trunk. I could even ask Hitch to loan me his suit. If he isn't going to wear it, I might as well. It'd be pretty damned hard for a snake to bite through iron.

Now a gator, on the other hand . . .

Panic dumps into my bloodstream. The black water with its dancing fairy lights isn't pretty anymore. It's deadly, filled with things I have good reason to fear. This isn't groundless anxiety; it's my body's attempt at self-preservation.

I turn, but stop before I take a step toward the shore. It's still light enough for me to see that Hitch's head is tilted down, as if he's reading something in his lap. He isn't even watching. If I go back to the car I might get the comfort of his suit, but I'll also get more of the "Annabelle is a loser" show.

I don't like that show. I don't like Hitch much, either. Unfortunately, growing to loathe him isn't making it any easier to be in his company. The only remedy for the nasty way he makes me feel is to get rid of him, to make sure he has no reason to be here.

Hand strangling my flashlight, I wade forward, one foot after another, until the water reaches my waist and begins to recede, inch by merciful inch. By the time I reach the low limb where I busted my head earlier in the day, the bayou barely tickles the tops of my thighs. A few more feet and I slog—dripping, pants clinging to my skin—onto dry land.

Several fairies prowl the air beneath the trees, but they give me a wide berth, flitting on to other hunting grounds as I draw near. At this point I've been sweating onto my clothes for nearly eight hours. No matter how non-stinky Marcy insists I am, the Fey are obviously catching my scent. They're so averse to contact that I'm alone in the glow-free shadows by the time I reach the place where I tied up my Breeze-head friend.

Or where I *thought* I tied her up.

Shit. The ground where I left her is empty. I stalk forward, tennis shoes squishing, sweeping my flashlight back and forth, eyes straining as I search for some sign of where she's gone. But there's nothing. *Nothing*.

Shit, shit, shit.

I follow the gentle slope of the land downhill, thinking maybe she's rolled somewhere nearby. Like into the water . . . where she's *drowned* or been eaten by gators or sucked dry by fairies or something equally horrible. My head spins with all the possibilities, my gut certain I'm going to find a body floating in the shallows. A body I'll have to drag back to the police car, a gruesome trophy to my shame. I'll have to live with her blood on my hands for the rest of my life, I'll probably do jail time, I'll—

"Ohthankgod." My breath rushes out, half sigh of relief, half hysterical laugh, as I pluck the twisted scrap of leather from the ground. The belt! She untied herself and got away!

Not usually something I'd celebrate, but I know Cane's right: far better for her to escape than be found dead. I stuff the cheap accessory down the front of my pants, and draw Hitch's gun from the back. Juggling my flashlight, I remove the safety, and load the chamber with a quick snap of the slide back and forth, glad Hitch gave me the semi-automatic. He has a revolver, as well, but I prefer the added heft of the semi. It makes me feel . . . safer.

My finger hovers over the trigger, not touching, but ready to squeeze—light and steady—if the need arises. Unlike *some* people, I'm not certain my former captive has the sense to get out of town. She could still be close by, sniffing Breeze, picking at her scabs, lying in wait for round two of our own personal WWE smackdown. It pays to be prepared. I don't want to shoot her, but I will if I have to.

No sooner has the thought pinged through my mind when something much harder—a meaty fist backed by some major muscle—crashes against the side of my head.

My entire body clenches as I fall, including the finger lingering above the trigger. A shot goes wild into the trees. My flashlight falls to the ground and my gun nearly joins it, but at the last minute I curl my finger, hanging on to the trigger guard as my hip and shoulder hit the ground. I make the most of my small good fortune, spinning the gun back into position as I roll onto my back, aiming at where I guess my attacker will be standing. I twitch my arm back and forth, but find . . . nothing. Nothing at all. The air is quiet but for the rasping of my desperate breath.

Here I am, the heavy breather. Come and get me.

I swallow, blink, fight for a clear thought. Tree limbs dance a creepy mambo against the dark-blue sky and my head pounds out an accompanying rhythm. I scramble into a crouched position, low to the ground. I can't stand up; I can barely sit. The world spins and tilts like every carnival ride that ever made me puke when I was a kid.

I turn, searching the shadows, trying not to tip over. Halfway around my circle, my right wrist cramps and the gun wavers, but I prop it up with my left, squinting for a flash of skin, the shine of an open eye, the slightest sign of the man who hit me. It has to be a man. I don't know many women who can pack a punch like that. My head feels like it's about to explode; my eyes pulse with their own unhealthy heartbeats. Everything is blurry, but I can see well enough to know that there's no one, not even—

Sudden warmth at my neck, and rough fingertips tease over my racing pulse.

I throw an elbow into a mass of flesh and dive back to the ground. I hit the earth and roll as a howling sound fills the air, making me flinch and scream. The gun fires again—though I can't remember squeezing the trigger—and a bullet bolts into the sky. Blue and white lights pulse through the night, helping my brain make sense of the howling. It's the siren on the police car. Hitch must have heard the gunshot.

Now, if only he can get suited up in time. Even the gun in my hand doesn't make me feel safe. That gut I jabbed was ridiculously immense, a brick wall of an abdomen belonging to someone large enough to wring my neck with a single hand. Someone who also has the agility to move scary fast. He's gone again, the space where he stood is empty and . . .

No. Not empty. The light sweeps through the trees, casting racing, writhing shadows everywhere. Everywhere, but for a patch of pitch black at forty-five degrees. A shadow. A man's shadow . . . with no man attached.

What the . . .

The flashlight a few feet away snaps off of its own accord. A second later, the gun flies from my hand, and a man's voice growls in the darkness. "Where is it? We know you have it." He's close, close enough to touch, more than close enough to see. My eyes flick up and down, back and forth, desperate to find what my brain assures them they should. "Where is it!"

"Wha-wha-wha—"

"Where did you hide it?"

"Annabelle! Annabelle, answer me!" Hitch's yell booms through the night, louder for the sudden absence of the sirens, sounding closer than the door of the police car. I hear a splash and then another. He's in the water; he's coming for me.

"I'm over here! In the trees!" Now it will be two against one.

My attacker must have had the same realization and decided he doesn't care for the odds. The leaves crunch and whisper as he hurries away. He has a soft tread for a big person and is distancing himself quickly, fleeing the scene of the crime.

Crime. Has there been a crime? Assault is certainly against the law, but how do you press charges against someone you *can't see*? I don't know. I don't want to think about the impossibility of what just happened. I just want out of here.

I snatch Hitch's gun from the ground, decide I can buy another flashlight, and make a run for it. My eyes search the darkness as I crash into the bayou, aiming my body toward Hitch's splashes, wondering how I'm going to explain to him—or anyone else—that I was attacked by an invisible man.

Eleven

▼

When I see Hitch fighting his way through the water, my first thought is that he's as handsome as I remember. The old Hitch was a smooth, Southern sex god of epic proportions. Despite the slightly crooked teeth and too-thin lips, his sleepy blue eyes and lean boyishness made women crazy.

All kinds of women. Old, young, married, single, straight, gay—heads turned when he walked down the street. But I was never jealous of the attention Hitch received when we were together. I understood it was impossible *not* to look. I was just grateful that I was the one who woke up beside him, who watched his lips move while he sang and his eyes light up when my clothes came off. The new Hitch, though physically the same, and admittedly better dressed, lacks that ineffable irresistibility.

Or he has until now.

Now, his eyes spark with that old . . . *something*, that quality that makes you certain there's a brilliant man with an amazing heart and a hell of a sense of humor lurking beneath the handsome exterior. A man enchanted by love and life, a man who will make you believe in magic when his skin is hot against yours. Making love to Hitch is a soul-deep experience, like stepping through a secret door into a world of pleasure, where powerful forces are at work healing the universe one orgasm at a time.

The memory of those orgasms might be to blame for how long it takes me to realize what's wrong with the picture before me. Or maybe it's the blow to the head or the white specks still flickering at the edge of my vision.

It doesn't matter. What matters is that Hitch is waist-deep in swamp water, wearing nothing but his dress suit and an *"oh shit"* expression. He has a gun, but that isn't going to help him now; he's too far from the flashing lights spinning atop Cane's car. He might be able to take down one or two—maybe even ten—of the itty-bitty targets flying his way, but not a swarm of a hundred or more.

There really are hundreds of them. *Hundreds.*

They surge from every corner of the bayou, drawn by the smell of unprotected flesh. The reflection of fairy glow turns the water into rivers of molten lava that stream through the night from the north, south, east, and west, racing each other for the first bite.

It's that afternoon with Cane all over again, but so much worse. There's nothing I can do, no way I can get through the water fast enough, no way to reach Hitch before—

"Look for my gun!" Hitch sucks in a breath and plunges under the water seconds before the swarms collide above his head in a mess of battered wings.

The screech of so many small voices raised in one combined wail of frustration brings home the threat humanity faces in a way I haven't felt in a long time. After a few years, you learn to live with the terror of knowing there's no safe place in your world. You push it aside and ignore it, blunt the sharp edge of reality with comforting lies. Or God. Or sleeping pills and alcohol—whatever it takes to get through the day and the long, fearsome nights.

Even as one of the immune, the Delta is terrifying. Sometimes it's *more* terrifying to know you might be left alone, to realize the people you love are perpetually on the verge of losing everything. Their freedom, their minds, their lives . . .

Hitch. I have to get to him. Now. Ten seconds ago.

I jolt into motion, churning through the water, using my hands to help me move faster, faster. Above my head, tiny bodies knock against each other, wings bending and bruising. Dozens of fairies fall into the water with the delicate plops of skipping stones. They break the surface and sink, but bob quickly back up. Fairies can't hold their breath for more than a second or two. They won't be able to dive down into the swamp to feed on Hitch.

He's bought himself a few precious moments.

Now it's up to me. How fast can I make it through the heavy swamp that sucks at my legs and feet? Will I be able to spot the tip of Hitch's gun poking up from the water in the maddening flash of white and blue light? Do I have the—

"Shit!" Pain, sharp and fierce, cuts away at my right ring finger, making every nerve ending from my hand to my shoulder scream.

I pull my fingers from the water and shake my wrist, trying to dislodge the fairy that clings to me, without dropping my gun. The thing is pink and green, a young female with tiny breasts and only the slightest hint of golden hair between her legs. From the glassy look in her eyes, she's already dying, but her damned teeth are sunk too deep for my frenzied shaking to do much good.

Finally, I reach over and squeeze the place where her detachable jaw connects to her face, shivering at the feel of her skin. It's unbearably soft and hot, like a newborn baby born in a rush of blood. Our contact is brief—her jaw pops wide and she falls into the dark water a second later—but it leaves me shaking. I've never touched a live one before. I didn't realize they felt so different, so . . . human.

When they're dead, fairy skin is scaly and hard like an insect's shell. Why didn't anyone tell me they felt any other way? Did they assume I knew? Did anyone? Surely other people who have been bitten had to—

The gun. I see it six or seven feet away, moving steadily through the water, back toward the police car. Hitch isn't waiting for me to come save him, he's doing his best to save himself. Unfortunately, he isn't going to be able to hold his breath long enough to reach the shore, and the cop lights aren't going to scare this mob away. There will be a few Fey who will brave the glaring light for fresh, human blood, just as there are a few who are stupid enough to feed on an immune woman.

Tiny, razor-sharp teeth dig into my shoulder and another set nip at my elbow. I dispose of them the same way I did the first, but by the time I reach Hitch, I have half a dozen throbbing bites, jangled nerves, and am well on my way to full-blown hysteria.

If my smell isn't keeping the Fey off of *me*, how am I going to protect Hitch? A little sweat behind his ears isn't going to work. The fairies are too hungry, angry, riled up and feeding off the fury and frustration of their comrades. The mob mentality has taken over. Hitch is as good as dead; there's nothing I can do.

Another fairy dives for my neck. I slap at it with a wild sound, sending a drop of blood flying from the wound on my hand. The dive-bombing fairy—and several others circling nearby—retreat with staccato howls different than their usual screeching. The sharp barks almost sound like language, like . . . a warning.

Blood. My poison blood.

Hitch surges from the water, gasping for air. The fairies dive, but I dive faster. My bloodied arms wrap around his neck, smearing red. I drive my fingers into his hair and around to his face, finger painting frantic trails down his cheeks before reaching for his hands. He tries to shove me away, but I hold on tight.

"I have to go back under," he gasps, nostrils flaring as his body seeks to pull every bit of oxygen from the air.

"No, you'll wash it off!"

A confused look. More pulling away. Not good! I tug him in tight. "They don't like my blood. I'm putting it on you," I yell, sounding as crazy as I feel. I swipe at the wound near my elbow and reach around to his back. I dab spots across his shoulders and down his arms and pray it will be enough. "If you go under, I don't know if I'll have enough left to get you to the car."

Thankfully, my words penetrate before Hitch takes another dive. He looks up, scanning the swarm. They're still close, but not nearly as close as they'd like to be. A few of the braver bastards buzz a foot or two above our heads, but none dare get closer than that. The feeding—and dying—on Annabelle frenzy seems to have come to an end.

The older Fey are angry with the ones who bit me. They bark threats into the darkness, spraying venomous spittle and rage. One ancient man with a wee face like a wrinkled white raisin shoves at the younger fairies, sending them spinning.

Back, back, you stupid fools, back!

Strange. So, *so* strange. To date, researchers have no evidence of a fairy language. The Fey exchange information, but their communication is primarily based in body language and scent cues used during the mating season. I've certainly never heard anything from a fairy's lips but earsplitting screams.

But now . . . I swear I can read the meaning of their "words," that a part of me—

"So this is your blood?" Hitch lifts a hand to his cheek, and his fingers come away red. There are streaks all up and down his face, painting him like some tribal warrior. *Jesus*. All thoughts of fairy chatter fade. He's *covered* in blood, dripping with it. I didn't realize I was gushing that much. Immune or not, I should probably seek medical attention. "Why are you bleeding? Did—"

"They bit me," I say, taking a slow step toward the shore that Hitch mirrors.

"They— Are you okay?" The concern in his eyes makes me acutely aware that our faces are only a few inches apart, that his hands have found their way around my waist beneath the water, pulling me close.

"I'm immune. I'll be fine. We just need to get you to the car." We take another two-step toward the shore, dancing just as Cane and I did, but nothing about our contact reminds me of my father.

Our hips bump together, our stomachs kiss as we pull in deep breaths, and when he hugs me tighter, my breasts flatten against his chest. Despite the danger, my body reboots a million memories I was certain I deleted.

"Are you sure?" he asks. "I heard the gun fire."

"Yeah . . . it did," I mumble, fighting through all the wretched *feeling*. I'm drowning in it.

How did I convince myself I was over this man? That I don't long for him every day, with everything in me? Time, distance, general assholishness on my part and his—none of that matters when his forehead drops to mine.

"Just talk to me. Are you okay?" He cups my face, pressing our skulls tight. He always did this when we hit a rough patch and I wasn't talking as much as he would like. It's as if he thinks he can tap into my brain via our connected skin and bone. There were times when I was sure he did.

I hope now isn't one of those times. I don't want him to know how much I miss him, or that I'm thinking about things like love and the way he used to kiss me. His life is still in danger. I should be focused on saving him, nothing else.

"Why did you fire the gun, why—"

"Why did you get out of the car without your suit?" I ask, suddenly angry. None of these feelings or worries would be relevant if he'd just stayed in the damned car. "What were you thinking?"

He swallows, licks his lips. "I heard the shot and called your name and when you didn't answer . . ." He shakes his head, evidently as shocked by his behavior as I am. "I thought you'd been shot. I thought . . . And I just . . ."

"I wasn't shot." My heart races faster. He cares. He still cares. The knowledge fills me up like helium, making me dizzy. "Neither was anyone else. But there was . . . something out there."

"Something?" he asks, hands at my neck, warm, soothing fingers kneading the knots there. I press even closer, fisting his shirt in my hands, hanging on to him for dear life. His dear life. We're getting closer. The water drops to our knees and then our shins.

Still, I'm almost afraid to believe we're going to make it to the car. The cloud that pulses and hums and hisses above us is bigger than anything I've ever seen. The fairies fill the sky, blocking out the moon, replacing its cool light with a toxic mix of pink and gold. Surely they're not going to let such a big, juicy food source escape just because he's donned a little war paint?

"Something big." I pause, swiping blood from one of the free-flowing bites on my arm and dabbing it on the wet fabric of Hitch's pants. A few more steps and we'll be out of the water.

"Something big like what? A person? An animal?"

"Let's talk about it in the car." My words are a whisper. What am I going to say? I can't tell him the truth, especially since there's a good chance it *isn't* the truth. It was dark; I have a head injury. I'm probably just . . . confused. There's no such thing as invisible men.

Just like there was no such thing as killer fairies a dozen years ago.

No. This is different. Fairies have always existed; we simply lacked the technology to observe them until after their mutation. An invisible man reeks of magic, or science so advanced it might as well be magic. Humans aren't capable of making a person invisible, and I don't believe in voodoo.

So what hit me out there? And how to explain that voice in the dark?

"Let's get in on the passenger's side," Hitch says, the tension in his grip increasing as we ease from the water and start the slow sideways shuffle back to the car. Six feet have never loomed so large. The Fey press closer, swooping down to investigate the ground at our feet, though they keep a safe distance from Hitch's blood-smeared pants legs. "Then you can crawl over to the driver's side."

"Too shook up to drive?" I ask.

He laughs, a short, breathy sound. "Yeah. A little shook up, a little high on life. I thought I was a dead man."

"You almost were." I don't say what we're both thinking, that he still *could* be a dead man if the fairies get up the guts to attack before we make it to the car.

I glance toward the cruiser, squinting into the bright blue and white. Three more feet. I turn back to Hitch, stare up into his eyes, breathe his breath, will a shield of safety to surround him. His fingers dig into the skin at my hips and his head tilts just the slightest bit closer to mine, making my breath come faster.

"We're almost there," he says.

"We are." The urge to hurry him to safety presses

in, but I force my feet to keep step with Hitch's slow, steady pace. Rushing the last few feet will only attract the fairies' attention, make them realize their chance at a big feed will soon be gone. Instead, I concentrate on keeping my body as close to Hitch's as possible, trying to ignore the way the feel of him pressing against me makes me shiver.

Finally, my ass bumps up against the cool iron and steel of the police car. I fumble behind me, finding the door handle and pulling it open the barest crack. I glance over Hitch's shoulder, scanning as much of the ground and air as I can see. "I think we're clear. Mostly. Probably."

"Good. Let's go back to front, you slide in sitting on my lap," Hitch says, spinning me carefully around, keeping his vulnerable non-bloodied front covered.

His arm comes tight around my waist and then, suddenly, I'm in the air, stomach lurching as he hauls us both into the car with a speed that makes my head spin. The door has barely slammed closed behind us when splashes of pink and gold thud against the window, fairies dashing in too late and ending up eating glass instead of human flesh.

"Holy shit," I gasp, flinching when another fairy hits and then another before they seem to realize they're not getting through police-grade glass.

"Sorry." Hitch's breath comes fast and shallow. "Adrenaline overload."

"It's okay." I search the car, making certain nothing has followed us inside before turning back to the door and hitting the power locks. Outside, the fairies are starting to disperse, flitting away in twos and threes and batches of fifteen or twenty.

They're leaving. We're safe. *Hitch* is safe.

For the first time in the past half hour, the tension level in my body cruises down to something near normal. Ready for a break from the flashing lights, I punch off the white and blues, the subtle movement reminding me that I'm sitting in my ex-boyfriend's lap. His arm still circles my waist, his strong thighs cradle mine, and my ass nestles close to where I swear I feel the beginnings of something . . .

Maybe I'm not the only one thinking of the way we used to be, the ways we used to move together.

"Thank you." His breath is hot against my neck, lips so close they kiss at my skin when he speaks. My pulse picks up, throbbing in my throat. "You saved my life."

"Thanks for trying to save mine." I turn to look at him, knowing I should hurry into the driver's seat, but enjoying this brief intimacy too much to end it. As I move, our noses almost touch and his hand slides lower, trailing into dangerous territory. Long fingers curl over my inner thigh with an air of possession, and something at the heart of me catches fire.

"I don't deserve thanks." His eyes watch my lips and I fight the urge to slip my tongue out to wet them. "I wasn't even thinking, I just . . . I had a moment of clarity."

"An unthinking moment of clarity?"

He smiles, a flash of teeth that's quickly absorbed by the darkness. It's harder to see without the strobes, but I prefer the shadows. They're safer, more inclined to keep my secrets. "If I'd thought about it, I would have taken the time to suit up. But when I heard those gunshots . . ." He shrugs, shifting me slightly on his lap, bringing me closer. When he speaks again, his voice is a whisper that feathers across my lips. "I didn't want to think of a world without you."

"Hating me is that much fun?"

His fingers squeeze my leg; I pull in a shaky breath. "It wouldn't be nearly as satisfying if you were dead."

"So you really do hate me?" I try to keep my voice light, but fail. It's impossible to sound carefree when asking him the question I've held inside all these years. A part of me wants to know if I have a chance to be forgiven, if maybe someday we might be friends. The other part of me doesn't want to hear the truth, doesn't want to know that I hurt a man so deeply that he hates me six years later.

Hitch's index finger traces a gentle path back and forth across my soaked pants, making me burn.

Who am I kidding? Hitch and I will never be friends.

"I don't hate you." He sounds so sad. Hating me is a commandment he's broken. *Thou shalt hate the girl who broke your heart:* it's right after *Thou shalt not sleep with your boyfriend's relatives.*

A sour taste rushes into my mouth. I try not to think about Hitch's brother, but I can still recall the smoke and salt smell of his skin the morning I awoke naked in his bed, whiskey scalding my stomach and pain all over.

I raced to the bathroom and was sick until it felt like my insides had been scooped out with a shovel, but purging did nothing to banish the self-loathing, to blunt the disgust when Anton shuffled into the bathroom wearing nothing but a smile and told me I was the best he'd ever had.

The wildest, the most shameless, the dirtiest little slut.

I didn't say a word, just clenched my legs to hide the dried blood on my thighs, gritted my teeth against the bruised feeling inside, grabbed my clothes, and rushed out the door. I couldn't remember the night before. Maybe he was telling the truth and I'd banged his brains out by my own free will. Maybe he was lying and I'd fought him the way my body told me I had. There was no way to know for sure. Just like there was no way to know if Hitch would have believed me if I'd told him what really happened, if I'd met his anger the night after he found out with truth instead of my own misplaced rage.

It's too late, and that memory is a rotted piece of the past that should stay dead and buried.

Too bad the past feels so present with Hitch's arms around me, Hitch's lips so perilously close to my own.

"No, I don't hate you," he says again. "I should, I guess, but I don't."

I swallow, willing my throat to loosen. "You don't sound like you're too happy about that."

"Happy." His voice fondles the word before chucking it toward the bayou with a soft grunt. "I haven't been really happy in awhile . . ."

Me either. Despite my beautiful, sweet lover, my charming hometown, and my well-paying job, nothing has felt truly *good* for so long. So, so long. I haven't allowed it to, I haven't dared. But maybe I could . . . if I could get up the guts to tell Hitch the truth, to tell him I don't remember, and that I'm sorry. So sorry.

"I know it was . . . a long time ago." My heart slams in my chest, fear and exhilaration rushing inside me. "But I'm sorry, and I want you to know I—"

"Shut up." And then he kisses me, soft and slow and so, so sweet.

Hitch's kiss is morning sunshine creeping through the window to warm the sheets, it's honey in smoky tea, it's a blues song that oozes through your mind and leaves more space for your soul behind. But tonight, it's also a bucket of tears, rain that will never quit falling, an ocean that gobbles up ships and sucks them down into the depths.

There's always been sadness hidden at the core of Hitch, but it's never been big enough to taste. Occasionally, I'd get a whiff of it, salty on the wind, but it never pressed in between us like it does now, threatening to drown us both. His tongue flicks against mine, his teeth nibble at my lip, his hands wander over my body with an easy familiarity, but beneath every wave of desire, every swift breath, there is the pain.

Pain and hurt and betrayal.

Our past and present are tainted, poisoned and wrong despite the fact that touching Hitch feels so right. His hand up my shirt, sliding to cup my breast, is like coming home—and being kicked out onto the street—all at the same time. And then there's Cane. I never promised him anything, not even exclusive dating privileges, but he deserves better than this. I care about him, I care about Hitch, and a part of me even cares about myself. This isn't a good idea for any of us. No matter which way you turn it.

From this place, there is no future, no way out to anything better.

I was going to pull away and tell Hitch so, tell him we had to at least *try* to talk. I really was . . . even before he ripped his mouth from mine and vomited into the driver's seat.

Twelve

Oh, shit." Hitch groans and the curdled smell of sickness fills the car. My nose automatically closes itself off, but breathing through my mouth doesn't help much.

"What's wrong?" Is my breath really *that* bad? Sure, I had some wings and a beer, but I practice excellent oral hygiene. I'm a religious flosser. I love to floss. I *live* to floss.

"Something bit me while I was under the water. I thought it was just a nonvenomous water snake," he says, squeezing his eyes shut and clenching his teeth. Even in the dim light I can see the sweat breaking out on his forehead. "Thinking now . . . it might have been a cottonmouth."

My stomach turns to stone. It's peak water moccasin season and peak bite time. We're less than fifteen minutes from the hospital, but if the snake hit an artery or vein or near a primary lymph node, Hitch could be dead before we reach the iron gate.

"Where's the bite? Let me see." I shift over, sitting on the center console, my neck twisting as my head hits the roof of the car.

Hitch yanks up the right side of his pant leg, revealing two puncture wounds below his knee. They're already red and swollen, and leaking a light pink fluid. It's definitely a cottonmouth bite. *Shit*.

I reach for his leg, but he bats my hand away. "No, don't touch it, I just need to stay calm and keep my leg below my heart until we get to the—"

"You need to take your shoe off," I say. "If your extremities start to swell, you—"

"They can cut my shoe off, I don't care."

"What about necrosis?" I ask. "They might have to cut your *foot* off if—"

"There's going to be some tissue death associated with a moccasin bite. The sooner you get me to a place with a good store of antivenin, the less extensive the necrosis."

I sigh, giving up on his damned shoe. "Fine, whatever you say, doctor."

"That's right, dropout." He's trying to make a joke, but the sickly beads of sweat popping out on his lip ruin the punch line. Time for less talk, more driving.

"Just relax, the hospice is only a block from the police station. We'll be there before you know it." I slide into the driver's seat with a full-body cringe as warm vomit soaks into my already wet clothes.

I could have tried to open the door and scoop some of it out, but there are still a few fairies outside and

I can't waste any more time. I start the car and pull out with a spray of gravel, ignoring the oozing sensation around my legs and the way my tongue cramps at the back of my throat, begging me to indulge my gag reflex. It's just vomit. I've seen and *handled* worse on a daily basis. Usually with gloves on, but still . . . I can stomach this.

Despite the opinions of some, I am a professional.

The trip to the hospital is a blur. I vaguely remember slowing down at the gate—heart racing as we waited the seemingly interminable three seconds for it to swing open—and swerving to avoid a black SUV with its bass turned up loud enough to throb in my chest, but it's almost as if the narrow drive leading to the hospice's emergency room simply appears before me. Like magic.

I've never driven that fast, especially while chattering on a police radio and placing a few phone calls. Luckily, Cane and Stephanie were still at the station when I jumped on the radio. Now, they wait outside the emergency room doors, next to Jonathan, the burliest male nurse in D'Ville, and Connie, our one and only doctor.

It must be a slow night. I've never seen Connie curbside. She usually makes everyone wait at least an hour, even if they're nursing a stab wound. But I suppose the FBI gets preferential treatment, and a venomous snakebite is nothing to mess around with.

Jonathan pushes a wheelchair chair around to

Hitch's side of the car and Connie follows, throwing open the door and helping Hitch out. "We've got the antivenin prepped, Dr. Rideau," she says, a chubby brown hand patting Hitch's shoulder as she eases him down into the chair. "We'll have you up and fighting bad guys in no time."

She peeks into the car long enough to wrinkle her nose and shoot a disgusted look in my direction before she and Jonathan are gone, wheeling Hitch around the front of the cruiser. I can't tell if the nasty look was for me or for the vomit, but I decide to blame the puke. Connie's never been my biggest fan—she resents the fact that I refuse to come in for treatment until I'm practically dying of pneumonia and have to be admitted—but I don't think she has anything personal against me.

I reach for the handle of my door, but Cane gets there first. "How fast did you drive, girl? I can't believe— Hot damn." The hand he'd reached in to help me moves to cover his nose and mouth.

"The snake venom made him sick. I'm sorry. I'll clean it up," I say, easing my legs out of the car.

"You don't have to clean it up. That's what Dicker's for." Cane recovers with a tight smile. "Come on out of there. I'll call him back in, have him pick up the cruiser, and get it detailed tonight."

I stand. Chunks of whatever Hitch last ate fall from my pants to plop onto the concrete. Ew. Blechk. Gag. I peer down at myself, wondering if it would be appropriate to strip off my clothes and burn them where I stand. As I tip my head, the ground tilts and the world spins. I stumble and might have fallen if Cane hadn't grabbed me and held tight.

"Baby, what happened to your arm?" Cane's touch is gentle as he adjusts his grip, transferring the hand at my elbow to my waist.

"A few fairies bit me. It's okay, I just need a shower and some Band-Aids." I lean into him, grateful for his strength but feeling guilty for the taste of Hitch that lingers on my tongue. "Will you take me home?"

"You can't go home," Stephanie says from her spot near the entrance to the ER.

"She's right. You need to see the doctor." Cane guides me toward the automatic doors. I resist the urge to dig my heels in and fight him. I hate hospitals. They remind me of my many past failings and I've had enough of that for one night. "Or at least get one of the nurses to check you out."

"And I need to know what happened out there." The doors swish open and Stephanie follows us inside.

The harsh, fluorescent lights make me squint. They seem so much brighter than usual, glaring and awful, pointing out every black scuff on the cracked tile and piss stain on the faded paisley seats of the waiting room. The smell of melon disinfectant and hand sanitizer and a poopy diaper someone must have shoved in the trash a day or two ago swim inside my nasal passages, making me dizzy.

I stumble again, earning a concerned look from

Cane. He slows, giving Stephanie the opportunity to angle in front of us, blocking our path to the reception desk.

"Did you find the suspect?" Stephanie asks.

"This can wait. She's hurt," Cane says, his professional voice deeper, more threatening than it normally would be. He's losing patience with Stephanie. I can sympathize, but thankfully I have a "get her off my ass free" card in my front pocket.

"No, she got away," I say, "but I found the belt I used to tie her up on the ground. She's free. Probably running around in the swamp right now, eating fairy crap and attacking more innocent people."

Stephanie's upturned nose wrinkles—apparently she's not convinced of my "innocence"—but I read the relief in her eyes. She's glad I didn't bring a dead body back from the swamp. "Did you collect the belt? We can try to find some prints, see if we can get a positive ID on the woman and alert all the local agencies."

"Yeah, I—" One hand drifts to my waist, to where I tucked the belt into the front of my pants. It's gone. Shit. *Shit!* "I . . . I don't have it anymore."

"So you have no evidence that the woman you tied up is free?"

"No, I *do* have evidence." The room swims again. I blink and keep my lids lowered. It feels like the light is stabbing me in the eyeballs. "It must have fallen into the water while I was trying to get to Hitch."

"Right." Stephanie's arms cross and her business face returns. I can feel Cane's muscles bunch against my back. "Hitch, who was in the water without his suit on because. . . ?"

"He heard gunshots and jumped out of the car. He thought I'd been shot."

"Had you been?"

"No, Hitch's gun went off when somebody hit me from behind." Cane turns to stare at me, but I hurry on before he can say whatever's on his mind, probably something about guns and how I shouldn't have been carrying Hitch's. "It wasn't the woman from this morning. It was a big guy, *really* big. I didn't get a good look at him, but I elbowed him in the gut. He felt like he weighed three hundred pounds. Maybe more."

"But you didn't see him?"

No, I didn't, because he's invisible. An invisible man! Right here in Donaldsonville, can you imagine?

I wisely edit my reply to a simple: "No, I didn't."

"And he hit you on the head?"

"Yeah, you want to see?" I turn, parting my hair around a nasty lump and a bit of sticky I'm guessing is dried blood.

"Oh my God." Stephanie's words are soft, but I hear the shock in her tone. My head must look bad if it's disturbing her more than the bite marks peppering my bare arms. Maybe the head wound is responsible for my dizziness, not the blood loss I was planning to blame once I got around to blaming something. "You should go see the doctor. We'll talk more tomorrow, during your official interview. I'll expect you at the station at noon."

Crap. Official interview. Why didn't I thread the damn belt through my belt loops? Why couldn't this all go away?

"Right. If you'll excuse us." Cane pushes past her without waiting to be officially "excused."

I glance over my shoulder, displeased by the displeasure on Stephanie's face. I get the feeling she isn't buying my "lost belt" story and is plenty pissed that her partner's life was put in danger—whether or not that was really my fault. She isn't going to make my life easy, and she isn't going to let me off the hook for what I did this afternoon. I'm still in deep doodoo unless I can prove that Breeze head is okay.

If she's okay. What if the invisible man did something to her? He's clearly violent and confused. What was it he kept asking me? Where is it? Where I put *it*? He thought I'd taken something that belonged to him. His invisible treasure, perhaps? Or maybe something more sinister.

Could the man be connected to the deaths of Grace and the other murdered girls? I flash back to those big footprints in the mud outside Grace's window. The giant I elbowed had to have equally gigantic feet, and he was plenty heavy to push a print deep into damp earth. He could have crept onto the Camellia Grove grounds unobserved and had Grace a few hundred feet from the property before she recovered from the shock of being lifted from her bed by someone she couldn't see.

An invisible serial killer with a yen for children.

It's a terrifying thought. He might never be stopped. Even if someone realizes what's happening, they'll be too afraid to say anything. Afraid people will think they're out of their mind. I've been labeled a slacker, borderline alcoholic, pill-popping loser by too many people. There's no way I'll be able to convince them there's an invisible person wandering the swamps outside D'Ville. I barely believe it myself and I saw it. Or *didn't* see it.

I sigh again, a mournful sound that makes Cane hug me closer.

"You're going to be fine, Lee-lee. Don't worry, we'll get this sorted out."

"Thanks." But his words offer little comfort. Cane can't help me with this. No one can. I'm going to have to go back into the bayou tomorrow and search for something on the man who hit me.

If I can find footprints, I'll be able to prove there was someone else out there, someone who will divert the sole responsibility for the Breeze head's fate from my fairy-bite-covered shoulders. Surely, even an invisible man has to leave footprints. He certainly left other physical marks. I touch the lump on my head again, flinching at the size of it.

"Don't touch it." Cane stops at the front desk. A pretty, big-eyed, coffee-with-cream-skinned woman I haven't seen before holds out a clipboard and pencil.

"Just sign here to verify none of your information has changed, Miss Lee, and Benny will bring you right back." The girl—*Infinity*, if her name tag is to be believed—passes me the clipboard before darting a swift, admiring look up at Cane. Somebody must have told her my name, but not that I'm intimately attached to the cop who has me by the waist.

I wonder who she thinks I am? A victim of a crime? A suspect?

No, Cane's too gentle with me. She must think I'm a victim, and that Cane will be finished with me once he makes sure I'm in a nurse's capable hands. Maybe that's why she's so eager with the clipboard; she's ready to get the Lieutenant alone. A stab of jealousy I have no right to feel makes me glare at her as I sign the form. I just kissed my ex-boyfriend; I have no right to be possessive. But I am.

"Miss Annabelle?" Benny, a forty-something nurse with the most chapped hands I've ever seen, appears at the door leading into the exam stations. She comes into Swallows every now and then with her two teenage boys, mostly on nights when the boys are jonesing to watch a basketball game not being aired on network television. She's very nice, very tolerant, and doesn't judge people for having a beer or two to unwind at the end of the day.

Hope sparks within me. This emergency room visit might not be a total waste, after all. Benny can probably be convinced to slip me a few Restalin before she hands over my discharge papers. After the day I've had, I need to sleep tonight, and that won't be happening without serious chemical assistance.

I move toward the door, but Cane stops me with a

soft squeeze. "I'll wait for you, and drive you home. Tuck you in," he says, in true knight-in-shining-armor fashion.

On impulse, I stand on tiptoe and press a kiss to his cheek. "Thanks. I . . . I appreciate you."

He smiles, that smile that makes his eyes crinkle at the edges. "I appreciate you too." There's something in his tone, something that speaks of his assurance that I more than *appreciate* him that makes guilt gurgle in my stomach. But then Benny calls for me again, and I go.

I follow her down the narrow white hall, trying not to think about what happened with Hitch. It was a mistake, a weird reaction to stress and a near-death situation. For better or worse, it won't happen again.

Less than two hours later, I'm showered, bandaged, dressed in a loaner pair of Benny's scrubs, and checking my reflection in the full-length mirror nailed to the door of my room. The pants are short—Benny's closer to five four than five eight—but the pale peach color makes me look healthier than I have all day. My cheeks flush pink beneath my freckles, my burnt nose seems kind of cute, and my frizzy auburn curls are drying in relative ringlet fashion in the cool hospital air.

More importantly, I don't stink the stink of a thousand stinks. That's definitely a plus when going out to meet the man in your life.

The door handle twitches. I step away as Benny eases back into the room she commandeered for our use. It is indeed a quiet night in the ER, with only a handful of patients for an equal number of nurses.

"Here you go." She hands me a paper to-go sack full of yummy drugs. Yay. "I put in a two-week sample pack of Restalin, but don't take one tonight. You hear me? Wait until you're symptom-free for at least twenty-four hours."

"Yes, ma'am." Mentally, I cross my fingers behind my back.

"I put some six-hundred-milligram ibuprofen in there for the pain. Take that, avoid alcohol or anything else that will make you sleepy, and you should be good to go."

"Thanks, Ben. And thanks for the clothes and tennies."

She makes a pooh-pooh face that tells me what she thinks of my thanks. "Girl, it's nothing. I've got ten pair of shoes and double that of scrubs. No rush getting those back. I know you're busy."

"Thanks."

"So you really didn't see who hit you?"

"No, he snuck up behind me. It was already getting dark . . ." I let my words trail off. I feel bad for lying, but I can hardly tell the truth.

"Too bad. That's a nasty bump. I wouldn't be surprised if you've got a hairline fracture in there somewhere." Benny already consulted with Dr. Connie, who confirmed what I already knew: there's nothing to be done for a crack in the skull other than to avoid getting hit again. I can be sent home without an X-ray or an MRI as long as I only have symptoms of a mild concussion—minor dizziness, blurred vision, etc.

I have none of the above. My dizzy spell's passed, and I actually feel pretty good. The hot shower worked wonders for my worldview. I can barely feel my bites and bumps. Either that ibuprofen Benny gave me is magic or I'm made of tougher stuff than I thought.

"Seriously," she says, "the man who did this to you should be locked up."

"I'm going to work on that tomorrow," I say, figuring there's no harm in telling Benny my plan. "I'm thinking I'll head back to where I was attacked and see if I can find any footprints."

"Well, be careful. Make one of the tough guys out there suit up and go with you."

"Will do." I shift my weight toward the door, but Benny doesn't move. Instead, she crosses her arms and stares at the ground, lingering a few moments too long. I get a bad feeling in my stomach even before she speaks.

"So . . . do you know if they found out anything about that Beauchamp girl's murder? You were the one who found her, right?"

"No, I didn't find her. The perimeter patrol saw something this morning and called me in to have a look since the body was beyond the gate." I shrug, not really wanting to get into this, but feeling obligated: Benny *has* slipped me prescription drugs without a prescription. "I don't know much about the investigation. Just that the FBI is going to help out with it while they're here."

I leave out the part about the suspected serial killer. If that particular piece of gossip gets out, there won't be much doubt where it came from. I don't want to be blamed for having loose lips in addition to all my other flaws.

"Hmm. Well, I hope they find whoever did it soon."

"Yeah, me too." I would leave it at that, but there's something in the way she said "whoever" that makes me think she's got a person in mind. "Did you know Grace?"

"Not really. But I treated her about a year ago." Benny snags a bottle of lotion off the nearby sink and squeezes some onto her chapped hands. "She was brought in for an overdose."

"Of what?" I ask, figuring Benny's already violated nurse-patient confidentiality.

"Xanax. The family said she got hold of her mother's prescription and it was a big old accident, but I don't know . . ." Her narrow shoulders rise and fall. "Usually, you don't see children six or seven years old chewing a bunch of nasty-tasting pills. It's not like they taste like candy."

"Wow . . . so you think . . ." I don't even want to speak the words out loud. It's a big accusation, especially against the Beauchamps. Without their plantation, there's a good chance D'Ville would have gone the way of so many other small Louisiana towns and died a swift death after the mutations.

"I don't know what I think," Benny says. "But Cane should take a damn long look at everyone living in that house. That's all I'm saying."

Like Barbara Beauchamp, who was dressed up and running around Baton Rouge hours after her daughter's body was discovered. The thought makes me sick. I know as well as anyone that mothers aren't always what we'd have them be, but why would Barbara kill her adopted daughter? She seemed so dedicated to Grace, to all her kids.

"Not that I'm saying anything, you got me?" Benny's newly moisturized hands rise at her sides in the universal sign of "I had nothing to do with this."

"Got you." She wants me to pass on the information without letting anyone know where I got it. I fist my bag o'goodies and reach for the door, making a mental note to tell Cane what I saw in Baton Rouge and relay Benny's message on the drive back to my house. I'll wait until we leave the hospital so he'll be less tempted to come back and start nosing around himself.

"I mean, I know that girl wasn't right," Benny says as we emerge into the hall. "But she was just a little girl."

I slow, waiting until Benny walks beside me. "You mean her heart condition?"

"Well, yes." Benny shoots me a sideways glance. "And . . . other stuff."

"Like what?"

She lowers her voice to a whisper. "For a while, the

Beauchamps had some big-shot child psychologist from New Orleans up here every week. He worked with Grace in the behavioral therapy room. Rumor was she'd scream the entire time, and even bit him once."

"Really?" That's . . . hard to believe. "But she came to Marcy's when she was a toddler for the drop-in program. Marcy never said anything about her being hard to handle." But then Marcy is amazing with kids. Even the most messed-up kids get their act together under her care. I'm living proof of that.

Benny shrugs again. "Yeah, well, she seemed like a sweet girl to me, but . . . whether she was sweet or not . . ."

"Right." Whether she was sweet or not, she didn't deserve to be murdered.

We walk the rest of the way to the discharge desk in silence. Benny leans over, hollering at Infinity's back. "You need anything else from Miss Annabelle?"

"No, she's good. We'll file with her insurance." Infinity waves over her shoulder.

Benny motions me back to the door leading into the waiting room.

"Hey," I say, hoping to get one last piece of info. "Do you know how the FBI agent with the snakebite is doing? Is he going to be okay?"

"He was doing good last I checked. Stable and comfortable, but Connie's going to keep him overnight for observation. Did you want to stop by his room?"

"No, that's okay. I'll check in with him tomorrow." I smile, relieved that Hitch is going to be locked up for the night and there'll be no risk of seeing him again until I have some much-needed sleep. "I'll get the scrubs back soon."

"No worries." Benny opens the waiting room door, dismissing me with a smile before plucking a chart from the wall and calling the next name.

There are a few people occupying the ugly paisley chairs—a woman with a red-cheeked baby who stands at Benny's call, a man with a black eye, and an older couple with an oxygen machine shooting judgment-filled looks at the man with the black eye—but it still isn't crowded. I should be able to spot Cane right away.

But I can't find him. Not in the chairs, not by the water fountain, not trolling the hall near the snack machines. I spin in a slow circle. He isn't inside. Maybe he's gone to supervise the cleanup of the squad car. I walk through the automatic doors, out into the muggy night. Even at nearly eleven, the air is hot and heavy. My ringlets begin to puff and frizz. Not that it matters. There isn't going to be anyone to admire my pretty hair.

The squad car has disappeared from the front drive, and the parking lot across the street is police vehicle-free. Cane is gone.

Thirteen

I check my cell for missed calls. Nothing. Odd.

Cane wouldn't usually leave without telling me. And even if he's on an emergency call, he'd find the time to send a text. I try his cell and then his work line at the station. Both calls are sent to voice mail. Weird, and . . . unsettling.

My house isn't far, but now that I know I won't have a ride, those seven blocks seem daunting. I'm tired. Very, very tired, and past ready to pop a couple of Restalin and hit the sack. For a second, I contemplate heading over to fetch my bike, but it doesn't make sense to walk half a mile in one direction only to turn around and bike a mile back.

With a sigh, I start down Magnolia, sticking to the cracked sidewalk. My borrowed shoes start to pinch almost immediately. Benny's feet are a couple sizes smaller. Not many women her height wear a size ten, or have long, bony toes that jab at the end of a shoe like they're trying to start a fight. Ow. I consider taking the sneakers off, but the street is lined with thick trees that block the glow of the streetlights. With my luck, I'd step in an unseen pile of dog poo in my sock feet. Better pain than poo.

I walk faster, ignoring my squished toes.

The faint throb of the music from Coop's pulses through the air, audible even from three streets over, an annoying *dum-dum-dum* that overpowers the peaceful chirping of the frogs and crickets. But other than that, the night is oddly quiet. No barking dogs, no beeping horns, not even the soft chatter of neighbors out on the front porch with a glass of sweet tea. Even this late, there are usually people up and about, especially on a Friday night. But maybe news of the murder sent everyone to bed early, even people who normally have trouble—

"Crap." Marcy. She's always up late. I was supposed to stop by her place, but in all the excitement of the head-bashing and snake-biting, I'd forgotten.

I pull my cell back out of my purse and mash Marcy's name. She picks up on the second ring. "You done? Are you hungry?"

"Yeah, I'm done. I guess. And no, I'm not hungry. I'm actually not going to make it over tonight." Before she can yell at me for "failing to honor my social obligations," I fill her in on the events of the evening. Most of the events, anyway, minus the invisible man, kissing Hitch, and getting ditched by Cane.

"Are you all right? Do you need anything?" Marcy

asks, gearing up into full mother-hen mode. "Do you need me to come bring you some food, or medicine, or—"

"No, I'm fine. I'm just beat. I'm going straight to bed."

"Are you supposed to sleep when you have a concussion? Won't you need someone to wake you up every few hours?"

"No, that's just on soap operas."

"I don't watch soap operas, I watch telenovelas," she says, the familiar huffiness in her tone as she realizes I'm messing with her and therefore, probably going to live. "And that's only so I can work on my Spanish."

Right. Marcy is addicted to telenovelas on the Spanish language channel. At the moment it's the melodramatic tale of twin sisters separated at birth who have been reunited only to be torn apart by an evil drug lord who wants to marry the twin who worked as his secretary before she knew he was a drug lord and not an innocent baron of industry. Or something. I do my best not to pay attention when Marcy starts summing up the latest episode of *Teresa's Secret Sin*.

"Well, you be safe and call me in the morning."

"I will." I smile. I'm lucky to have Marcy, to have someone who loves me despite what a messed-up kid I was when I first met her. Which reminds me . . . "Hey, Marcy, you remember when Grace Beauchamp used to come to Blessed Hands, right?"

"Sure. Been a few years, but she came most every Friday there for awhile, when her mama went to her Junior League meetings in Baton Rouge."

"What was she like? Was she a good kid? Hard to handle? Or—"

"No, she was a good girl. Very good. She was a weird eater, only ate peanut butter sandwiches and bananas, wouldn't touch nothing else you put in front of her, but real sweet." Her voice holds a note of sadness. It isn't right to be talking about Grace in the past tense. She should have grown up to discover the joys of eating more exotic foods than peanut butter. "She was shy, but I figured that was because she wasn't in the class all the time with the rest of the kids. She played real good, though, went down for her nap, toileted without any—"

"Okay, okay. I don't need the potty rundown."

"Fine. But it was fine. Why do you ask?"

"I was just . . . wondering. I heard something about her seeing a therapist last year."

Marcy grunts softly. "Well . . . it might have been for the food issues. I've had a couple of kids who needed therapy for that sort of thing," Marcy says. "But then, I haven't seen the child since she was four years old, so I can't say for sure."

"Yeah. That was kind of weird, right? She just stopped coming all of a sudden?"

Marcy sighs. "Mrs. Beauchamp said she pulled Grace because Libby decided to stay home to do her college work on the Internets."

Marcy refuses to recognize the fact that "Internet" is singular. I quit trying to correct her years ago.

"But I'm guessing she had other reasons. A lot of people stopped doing the drop-in program after Kennedy disappeared with her daddy . . . or whoever took her."

"Listen, I haven't had the chance yet, but I'm going to talk to the FBI before they question you," I say. "I'll make sure they know you had nothing to do with that."

"No, I'll be fine. You just take care of yourself. Don't worry about me."

"I *do* worry about you. I love you, you know that."

I can hear her surprised smile. Marcy and I love each other, but we don't talk about it much. Okay, *I* don't talk about it much. I grew up in a family that considered displays of affection—even verbal displays—uncomfortable and rather gauche. Those three words still feel funny in my mouth, even when they lack romantic connotations.

"You *should* love me," Marcy says. "I'm keeping this pain in the ass cat of yours overnight."

"Oh, shit." Gimpy! "I'm so sorry. I totally—"

"You're hurt, and had to rush a dying man to the hospital. This time, I'm going to say you deserve to cut yourself some slack."

Maybe she's right, but still, I need to get my act together. And I will. Come tomorrow morning. I'm not up to getting anything together tonight except the energy to change into pajamas before I fall into bed. "Thanks, Marcy. I'll come get him first thing."

"Take your time. He's not so bad . . . as long as you don't touch him or talk to him or feed him. Or look at him too close."

I laugh under my breath as I hurry off the corner and move onto the street. The junkyard comes into view, great piles of trash silhouetted against the night sky. There's no sidewalk surrounding the oversized block that serves as the dumping ground for the large, non-perishable items D'Ville residents are finished with. The trash sprawls all the way to the edge of the hard-packed dirt, occasionally trickling into the street if we go too many months without a visit from the Baton Rouge solid-waste division. Broken television sets, old mattresses, and the rusted remains of cars create a mini-mountain range at the northeast side of town, a kingdom a few homeless men have claimed as their own.

I walk faster, not wanting a run-in with the Junkyard Kings tonight. I haven't brought any alcoholic treats, and I'm not in the mood to deal with the heckling I receive on treat-free nights.

"He's cranky, isn't he?" I ask Marcy, keeping my voice low.

"He is. You two should be a match made in heaven."

"I'm not cranky."

"No, you're prickly. Like a sticker bush."

"Thanks." I've proudly cultivated my sticker bush

personality, but for the first time in a long while, I wonder if maybe I should try to soften up a bit, tell people I care more often, make sure Cane knows how much he matters to me whether or not what we have is true love.

"Good thing I like sticker bushes," Marcy says.

A rattling tickles through the air, closer than I would like. Maybe it's just trash settling, maybe not.

"I figured you might," I whisper, trotting the last ten feet to where the sidewalk picks up again. I smell cigarette smoke, the cheap kind the Kings buy in bulk at the Piggly Wiggly when they've saved up enough loose change. They aren't too close yet, but they will be if I don't hustle. Eli and Nigel, the youngest Kings—two scruffy black men in their late forties—have excellent hearing.

"Why are you whispering?" Marcy whispers.

"No reason." I jump the curb and move back onto the sidewalk, toes protesting inside my borrowed shoes. A quick glance over my shoulder reveals the street behind me is still empty. Eli has trailed me to my front door once or twice, but apparently tonight I've slipped by unnoticed.

Or maybe the Kings deliberately left me alone. As I draw closer to my house—the last shotgun shack on the right—I see the shadow of a police cruiser parked under the willow at the end of the road. Cane. I must have misheard him. He must have said he'd *meet* me at home, not give me a ride home.

"I gotta go, Marcy. See you in the morning."

"Okay. Be safe and sleep well."

"You too." I hit the power button, ending the phone call and shutting down for the night. The only person I want to talk to is already sitting on my front step.

Maybe Cane will want to stay and watch some mindless television before he heads home. Despite the lingering heat, being curled up in bed with Cane, watching the flat screen flicker, drooling on his bare chest as I'm sucked into sleep by a couple of pills, sounds like the most wonderful thing in the world.

I smile as I cross my front lawn. "Hey, you," I say, still in something close to a whisper. My spying next-door neighbor, Bernadette, is probably asleep, but it pays to be careful. "I tried to call, but your phone was off."

"I turned it off." Four words. Only four words, and I already know something bad has happened. Cane's voice is so deep I can feel the reverb dancing along my ribs from five feet away.

I freeze, eyes straining in the dim light. I don't make a habit of eating my carrots, or any other vegetable for that matter, but tonight I'm seeing better in the darkness than I normally would. I can make out the tense outline of Cane's shoulders against the blue wood behind him and the way his head hangs down, the curve of his neck expressing an eloquent mix of anger and defeat.

"What's wrong? What happened?" I close the distance between us, and run light fingers over the bunched muscles at the back of his neck. Instead of relaxing into my touch, he turns away and the knotted muscles grow knottier.

"I wasn't going to come over. I know you need your rest." His voice is so low I can barely make out his words. "But I couldn't stay away."

"You can come here anytime."

"Really?"

"Yes. Really." I continue kneading softly at his neck until he stands and paces across the yard, hands on his hips, head still hung low. My stomach clenches. "Listen, I know I haven't said that enough, but I mean it. You're always there for me, and I want to be there for you. If you need me, all you have to do is ask."

It isn't a profession of love, but it's sincere. I hope it will be enough to let him know he doesn't have to keep whatever's bothering him locked away.

"There are two cameras in the police car," he says, stating the facts in his smooth, steady voice. "One on the hood, one in the ceiling." *Oh . . . no.* Cameras. In the police car. Where I'd kissed Hitch, the FBI agent I had pretended not to know.

I'm suddenly reminded that no matter how bad things are, they can always get worse.

Cane turns. I can feel him watching me, but I can't see him. His features are cast in shadow, the street light behind him offering only enough illumination to emphasize the amazing breadth of his shoulders.

"The cameras turn on automatically when the blue and whites are activated," he continues, "but they don't turn off until the officer on duty shuts them off.

After he finished cleaning the car, Dicker turned the camera off, then skipped back through the recording to see if he could find anything that might help us identify the man who attacked you."

Which meant Dicker saw me kissing Hitch, too. Cane won't even been able to keep his cheating girlfriend a secret. If I know Dicker and his big mouth, the entire police force will know by tomorrow morning. Not that anyone else knowing matters to me. Cane's the one I care about.

I do care. I really do. I've never wanted to hurt him.

But you did. Big surprise.

I take a breath, gathering my courage, determined to at least try to make this better. "Cane, I don't know what to say, but I—"

"You were driving ninety miles an hour on the way back to town. The camera recorded your speed. You were up to a hundred in some places. It's amazing you didn't kill yourself and that agent." Cane ambles a step closer. His tone is easy, but his muscles are strung so tight it makes my body ache just looking at him. "You've got some damn fast reflexes. Better than I gave you credit for."

"Not really." I'm shocked to hear I was driving that fast. I'm not particularly skilled behind the wheel, and usually feel anxious at speeds above seventy-five. "I guess it was the adrenaline, thinking someone was going to die and . . . all that."

"Someone." A loaded word if I've ever heard one.

"Yeah . . ."

Cane stops a few inches away. The tension spikes between us, making it hard to swallow. I take another breath and inhale Cane's cop smell—soap and polyester and a hint of bug spray. Inexplicably, it makes me want to cry. It isn't a particularly nice smell, but it's Cane's. Cane. My friend, my lover, a person I don't want to lose.

Especially not today. Not like this. I thought I was done with moments like this, spared the risk of betraying someone I care about by refusing to commit in the first place. But bonds can be forged without words and they can be broken without them, too, despite the fact that no one has "technically" done anything wrong. Cane and I aren't exclusive, at least not in words, but in our unspoken hearts . . .

Well, we both know we're more than friends with benefits. He deserved my honesty about how well I knew Agent Rideau. I hadn't given it to him. And then I'd upped the ante by sticking my tongue in another man's mouth. On camera. So Cane could watch.

God. I have to think of something to say.

"Were you going to tell me?" His hurt and anger make me flinch.

"No." Why lie? It's too late for lying to do any good. "I wasn't going to tell anyone. I didn't think . . . I didn't mean for that to happen."

"Obviously. Seemed like you two weren't getting along so well up to that point. Must have been a tough breakup." The sarcasm is a slap in the face. Cane doesn't do smart-ass, especially not nasty smart-ass. The contempt in his voice is shocking.

"Please, don't—"

"Don't what? Don't call you on your bullshit?" His enraged face is suddenly inches from mine. My breath rushes in and my paper bag falls to the dry grass with a heavy *thwick*. "Answer me!" he yells, loud enough to make me jump.

"I—I don't know. What do you want me to say?"

"Say something so I don't feel so stupid." His hands fist by his face and shake the air, but I know he'd rather be rattling my teeth.

I hate that he's angry and hurt, but at the same time, on some level, this is a gratifying exchange. This is what I've been waiting for, confirmation that Cane knows he's too good for me. Now it can be over; now I can wash my hands of the terrifying business of trying to love again.

"I'm not that man, Annabelle," Cane says, soft and low, under control once more. "I'm not going to become that man for you."

I swipe at my nose and sniff, only realizing I'm crying when I feel the wet mess on my cheeks. I bite my lip, willing the tears to stop. "I don't understand."

"I think you do," he says. "I'll paint your toenails, I'll play hooky from work with you, I'll stay up late and read books to you when you can't sleep."

So much for stopping the tears. "Cane, I—"

"I'll take care of you when you're sick," he interrupts, continuing in that safe, sane voice that scares me more than his anger. "I'll take out your trash, I'll cook you meals, and I'll tell my mama to leave you be so you can eat your dinner in peace when we go over to her place. But I won't let you lie to me or treat me like a fool. I'm a simple man in a lot of ways, but I've got too much pride for that."

"I . . . I know."

He catches my gaze and holds it until I squirm and drop my eyes to the ground. He sighs, and I can hear that he's not happy with whatever he saw in me. "I erased the recording. There wasn't any sign of the man who attacked you, and I couldn't see the sense in keeping it. I told Dicker to keep his mouth shut, too, at least until we find who murdered the Beauchamp girl. We don't need personal shit getting in the way of what's important."

"Okay," I say, eyebrows drawing together as I sniff again. What's going on? Is everything okay now? Or are we breaking up? Why can't I ever tell the difference?

"I'll see you tomorrow. Good luck with the questioning. Just stick to the truth, and Agent Thomas shouldn't have any reason to give you more than a warning." He turns, striding back toward his squad car.

"Cane, wait!" My voice breaks, and my hands claw at the thin fabric of my borrowed scrubs, but I can't seem to get my feet to move. Thankfully, Cane comes back, crossing the yard in four steps.

He reaches for me, cupping my face in his big,

rough hand. "I love you. I want it to be you and me. If you decide that's what you want too . . . you call me." He leans down, presses a kiss to my forehead, whispering his next words against my skin. "But be sure you mean it."

"I'm sorry." I want to grab him around the neck and pull him down for a kiss, to pull him inside the house and show him—skin to skin—how sorry I am, but I sense he won't allow it. He's drawn a line in the sand, way up ahead of me, maybe too far down the trail for me to follow.

"Don't worry about it," he says, pulling away. "I forgive you."

My eyes open wide, then squint again. "You do? Just like that?"

"Just like that." Wow. That's . . . unexpected. And he really doesn't seem mad anymore. The electricity popping in the air between us has died away, absorbed by the sticky heat of the night. "I don't care that you kissed some man you used to know. I just need to be sure that you and I want the same things before we do this anymore."

"What do you want?" I ask, afraid of the question, let alone the answer.

"I want love, and trust, and a commitment." He shrugs, like he hasn't just delivered a laundry list of Big Emotional Stuff. "And maybe a kid or two."

"A kid?" What the hell? We've gone from breaking up to having children in less than two minutes? Even considering we've been dating for over a year, it's shocking. To me, at least. I hadn't seen this coming. *At all*. Had I?

"I'm thirty-eight years old, Annabelle. I want to have a family."

"With me? But . . . but . . . I . . ." My mouth opens and closes before my shell-shocked brain gives my lips the information they need. "But I'm not good with kids. I'd be a horrible mother, and probably a horrible wife, too. And your sister hates me, and I kill plants, and I forgot I even had a new cat, and—"

"I know who you are, Annabelle." The conviction and unflinching affection in his words shock my tongue into immobility once more. "And I love you."

Oh God. He does. He really does. And maybe I do too? Do I?

"But . . . I . . ." Panic and elation and the strange, trapped feeling I've always associated with airplane bathrooms flood through me. I don't know what to say. I don't know what I feel, what I want. I don't know whether to punch Cane in the chest or throw my arms around him and never let him go.

"Take your time. Like I said, if you get to a place where you're sure, just give me a call." He walks back to the car, and pauses with the door in hand, the *ding-ding-ding*ing sound escaping from the interior indicating he's left the keys in the car, probably to facilitate a fast getaway. "And just in case you hear anything tonight, nothing's going to happen until tomorrow morning. So don't get fired up. Get some rest. You need it."

"What?" Is he talking nonsense or is my brain just too fried after the baby talk to think clearly?

"See you tomorrow." He eases into the car and starts it up. I watch the red tail lights move down the darkened street and turn right at the junkyard, disappearing into the night, leaving me confused and snotty and feeling like gremlins have been set loose in my rib cage to rough up my internal organs.

Emotions. Jesus. They *suck*.

Fourteen

I snatch my paper bag off the ground with a huff, suddenly angry. My chat with Cane has managed to do what repeated head trauma had not. I feel lousy. Completely, *physically* lousy. Achy and horrible and damaged. And worse, wide awake.

There's no way my brain is going to shut down and let me "get some rest," no matter how exhausted I am. I'll be up all night, tossing around everything Cane said, the voices in my head arguing for and against the chances of Happy Ever After and then doing their best to convince me to pack my bags and leave town.

But I can't leave. I have friends here, a review tomorrow, a Breeze operation to shut down, and a killer to help find.

Yep, good job with that so far. You forgot to tell him about Barbara and what Benny told you and—

"Whatever." It's not like Cane gave me the chance to tell him anything.

I fumble in the bag, stab two Restalin from their

punch card, and shove them into my mouth. I dry-swallow as I stomp up the stairs and into the house, not bothering to kick my heel back to keep the screen door from slamming. Bernadette's awake. I would swear I heard her blinds snick shut as Cane pulled away. By tomorrow afternoon the entire town will have heard the story of our lover's spat and Cane's sort-of proposal.

It *was* a proposal . . . I think. Or at least a strong hint that a proposal is around the bend. Despite his penchant for eating organic and avoiding technology, Cane isn't hippie-rific enough to shack up and squeeze out a few puppies outside of wedlock. He'll want a ring on my finger, the Cooper last name on my Social Security card, and a jointly filed tax return every April . . . which could be tricky.

Cane doesn't know how much money I actually make. I mean, he knows FCC agents are paid well, but I don't think he knows *how* well. I've always secretly wondered if he'd be bothered by the fact that I make more money than he does. Probably not. He'd probably take a look at my tax records—and the hundred-thousand-dollar per year donation to Sweet Haven—and think I'm a goddamned saint. Which I'm certainly not, which is why I make the donations anonymously. I don't want anyone to think well of me for giving to those kids. I *was* one of those kids. Giving to Sweet Haven is like giving to myself. It's a selfish act, because I'm largely a selfish person.

Why can't Cane see that? Why does he have to love

me and look at me with those sweet brown eyes and make me wonder if I'm something better than I've assumed?

I lock the door behind me, making a mental note to find my house key so I can start dead-bolting my doors when I leave the house until Donaldsonville feels safe again, and flick on the light. Inside, life seems shabbier than usual. The overstuffed yellow love seat and tiny, antique coffee table I filched from the junkyard sit smugly in the front room, confident they'll never be traded in for furniture more conducive to a family of two or more. The pictures on the walls—surreal sketches of dead fairies pinned like butterflies that an old med-school friend drew for me before we lost touch—are macabre and inappropriate for children.

But that's fine. I've never wanted children. I don't want them now. But Cane . . . I want Cane. I *do* want him . . . don't I?

Sure you do. That's why you kissed Hitch like the world was on fire.

Ugh. No. I'm not going to do this right now. I'm too worn down to spend the night thinking about the past and Big Mistakes or the future and Big Decisions. I don't like to think about those things even on the best of days.

I stalk through the living-room door, passing through the bedroom without sparing a glance for the rumpled sheets. Once inside the kitchen, I plunk my paper bag down on the scarred wooden table and cross to the fridge.

The door is full of a vast collection of condiments—mayonnaise, two kinds of mustard, three hot sauces of various scorch levels, and an entire shelf devoted to all things pickled. The large compartment, however, houses only a half-empty case of beer, three Cokes, and a couple of Marcy's Tupperware containers. The Tupperware is empty, but I haven't gotten around to washing or returning it. The containers crouch on the top shelf, festering, the remnants of home-cooked goodness turning toxic within.

Like my life, or my potential, or some other such analogy I could draw if I was in the mood.

Ugh. Blah. Blergh.

I reach for a beer.

I know I shouldn't, a head injury and two Restalin are pushing things already, but I pop the top and chug while standing in front of the open fridge, letting the cool air soak through my scrubs and into my skin. By the time I finish the first and reach for the second, my core body temp feels normal for the first time all day.

It was a typical, late-August-in-Louisiana scorcher and it's likely to be worse tomorrow. I have to get up and around early if I hope to be out in the bayou before the worst of the heat sets in. I don't usually *do* early, but it seems like a good idea to start looking for those footprints as soon as possible. I can do a scope of the Breeze house while I'm out there, and take some pictures for the FBI's evidence file. Some kissing up before my review with Stephanie can't hurt

my chances of getting off the hook for my past trans-
gressions.

The last of my second beer sloshes into my tummy.
I put the empty back in the case with the rest and
think about looking for some pretzels in the pantry.
Instead, I reach for my third, and slide to the floor in
front of the fridge.

The third I drink more slowly, savoring the sharp
taste of hops, the slight tang of orange rind, and the
gradual dulling of the jagged edges of my mind. Alcohol is a sanding tool that leaves me shinier, glossier,
better than I was before.

At least I *feel* better. After a couple Restalin and a
few beers, nothing seems quite as scary. Hell, I could
probably do motherhood as long as I stay buzzed for
the first few years, until the kids learn not to eat electrical cords or toddle out into traffic. Too bad intoxi-
cation is frowned upon during pregnancy and the
raising of small children.

Children. *Babies.* God.

I tip my cool brown bottle back and pour the liquid straight down my throat.

By the time I stand and close the refrigerator door,
my knees are wobbling, making me think I may have
underestimated my head injury. Normally, a few
beers—even drunk in swift succession—and a couple
of sleeping pills are barely enough to calm me down,
let alone mess me up. But I bang my hip on the door-
frame on my way to the bedroom and trip on the rug
as I shuffle into the bath. Peeing is another adventure

in body control as I wrestle with pants and underpants and paper and hands and fingers and all those little things that suddenly feel very big. And annoying. And stupid.

Sleep. I need sleep. And less light. The row of giant bulbs above the sink are killing me. I lift my eyes to the mirror. And cringe. There I am, heavy-lidded and slack-faced and obviously in less than stellar shape. Dark circles smudge the pale skin beneath my eyes and my pupils are pools of black that flood out the green.

Dilated pupils, a possible late-onset sign of a serious head injury, the wanna-be doctor within me chirps. *You should call the ER.*

Right. I should call the ER and tell them I popped two Restalin and had a few beers. And they'll send an ambulance to drag me back to the hospital for observation, and probably a one-way ticket to some sort of twelve-step program.

So . . . you're going to put your life at risk because you don't want to look like you have a problem?

"I *don't* have a problem," I mumble to my reflection, then spit out my toothpaste, not sure whether to laugh or cry when the frothy glob lands on my hand.

Screw my reflection and the voice of reason. I'll be fine, as soon as I get some sleep. My wonky pupils are probably just a sign that the fairy venom's still working its way through my system. If I can just . . . sleep . . . oh, sweet elixir of sleep . . .

"Ahhh." I sigh as I fall into bed, not even caring that the faint, spicy scent of Cane lingers on the sheets. It's almost . . . comforting, like a part of him is still here with me. I'm not as alone as I feel right now. I have friends. I have . . . a cat.

I sniff, wishing I'd made the time to swing by and pick up Gimpy. It would be nice to hear his cranky yowl from the back porch. Or maybe I'd let him sleep at the end of the bed, with his blue cooler tucked in beside him.

God. I'm longing to sleep with a cat that hates my guts? What's wrong with me?

I grumble something to myself that I can't hear over the *thub-thub*ing in my ears. My pulse has picked up, another bad sign that my heart is working too hard to adjust my blood pressure, but I ignore it and reach for my clock. I have to set my alarm. I've forgotten why, but there's some reason I have to get up early and pretend I'm a fully functional human being.

I swipe at the clock, missing the glaring red numbers that announce it's one in the morning—once, twice, three times. Grunting with frustration, I swing my hand out again. I swear I miss a fourth time, but it flies across the room, hitting the wall before sliding to the floor.

Blargh. I stumble out of bed, grab the clock, and am crawling back when I notice the blinking green light peeping on my landline's base. A message. I didn't think to check. No one ever calls my landline.

I force myself to aim my finger at the button on the phone.

"Annabelle, are you there? If you're there, pick up. Please . . . pick up." In the seconds of static-filled silence that follow, my brain connects the low, anxious voice to a face. Fernando. "Okay, so I guess you're not there . . . Listen, I only get one phone call. I know you turn off your cell after five, but hopefully you'll get this message sometime tonight. I'm at the police station. They're acting like they're going to hold me overnight."

What? What what *what*? I fall on the bed and squeeze my eyes shut, willing my ears to suck less.

"They'll have a bail verdict tomorrow morning," he says, the utter seriousness in his tone leaving no doubt this isn't a prank. "I could really use your help . . . arranging that. I . . . I just don't know who else to call. I can't believe this is happening." He sucks in a deep breath and for a second I can see his face, see how close he is to losing his famous sense of humor. "Anyway, if you could come see about me in the morning, I'd appreciate it. I'm counting on you, slut."

The last word makes me feel better. If he's still calling names, he'll be okay until morning. And it isn't like the Donaldsonville jail is a hotbed of danger. Cane will—

Cane . . . *damn. This* was what he was talking about. That "thing" that could wait until morning if I "heard anything about it." That bastard.

"And . . . be careful for me, will you?" Fernando speaks again, his voice not much more than a whisper. "Make sure your doors are locked. There are some bad people out running loose while the police are locking up minor offenders. See you tomorrow."

Minor offenders? So he has done *something* illegal, but in typical Fern fashion he isn't going to share the gossip over the phone.

The message beeps off, and a shiver passes over me, making the hair on my arms prickle. He's right. There are bad people roaming around out there. I ran into two of them myself, and one might be a bad person that no one can see, no can stop . . .

I reach for the clock again, this time managing to slide the alarm button without knocking it to the floor. I roll onto my back with a sigh and close my eyes, blocking out the spin of the ceiling.

Surely that man isn't *really* invisible. It was probably my head-injured eyes playing tricks on me. Or maybe he's just really, really fast and stayed out of my line of sight.

Even the fairies, creatures that myths through the ages have imbued with a wide variety of magical powers, are animals like the rest of us. They glow and fly, but they aren't magical. They don't grant wishes or cast spells or put princesses to sleep for hundreds of years.

Sleep. Sigh . . . sleep . . .

Unconsciousness creeps upon me, sucking me down before I can worry any more about invisible predators or friends in trouble or the fact that I've ignored Fern's warning and left my back door wide open.

Fifteen

Morning comes—bright and beautiful—and I hate it. Fiercely.

I hate the wind blowing through my hair as I bike toward the gate, I hate the soft lowing of the cows grazing near the levee, I hate the sun that has yet to poke its slacker head over the horizon. I hate all the old people fussing in their gardens with big smiles on their faces like it's fun to dig in the dirt at the ass crack of dawn.

There should be a law against getting up before five-thirty. Or at least a law against *me* getting up before five-thirty.

To add insult to injury, I haven't even had any coffee. My creamer expired two weeks ago, and I didn't have the stomach to drink it black. I awoke dizzy and nauseous, like I'd spent the night shooting tequila instead of drinking a few beers. My guts are icky, my brain stem cramps at the base of my skull, and my eyes protest the invasion of even the soft morning light.

I'm wearing my biggest, darkest sunglasses, the ones that make me look like a giant insect, but the light still isn't pleasant. Neither is the chafed feeling around my armpits where my seldom-worn leather holster rubs against bare skin, taunting me for being stupid enough to wear a tank top—black this time— again this morning. I have a T-shirt and change of jeans in my bag, but I'm saving those for my pre-interview freshening up.

For now, I'll just have to ignore my progressively irritated skin. There's no way I'm going to risk losing track of my gun today. After fitful dreams of invisible men sneaking into my house and fairies rushing at my face with teeth bared, I'm not going anywhere without a gun. Even if the license is expired and there's a good chance Cane will know that. But whatever. He can arrest me for all I care.

Hell, he might. Who knows what Cane is up to?

I still can't believe he arrested Fern. Even when I called the station a little after six and was told the bail hearing is set for nine-thirty via virtual court, I couldn't believe it. But the woman at the front desk— a temp I didn't recognize—said Cane was the arresting officer, last night around ten-thirty. He must have dashed out of the ER a few minutes after I went back with Benny, which makes me worry Fernando is in more trouble than he let on.

If not, why the big rush? Fern has no record, isn't immune, doesn't have access to an iron vehicle, and a single phone call could have ensured he wasn't allowed a seat on any of the shuttles out of town. It must be a serious charge for Cane to pull him in and hold him overnight.

Or maybe Abe gave Cane the order and this has more to do with Fern's lifestyle than his infraction. Abe's the kind to cross the street to avoid saying hello when I'm hanging out with Fern and his more flamboyant guests. Unlike his sister, Abe's friendly when we run into each other one on one, but not if there's "a gay" around.

Ugh. Small towns. Small-town mentality and small-town hassles.

If Cane and I are really over, this town is going to be a far more uncomfortable place than I imagined it could be. It isn't just Cane I'll have to avoid, but his entire family. Why didn't I think of that before? Why didn't I end our relationship after those first hot, heady nights? Why did I have to go meet his blasted mama?

"Stupid." I slam on my brakes at the edge of town and jab my remote, opening the pedestrian gate. I found my long-lost gate remote while digging through my junk drawer for my house key. No more getting off the bike to open and close it by hand. At least not until I lose it again.

"Reeeooowr." Gimpy yowls from the trailer behind me, protesting our stop.

I snagged him from Marcy's front porch on my way out of town, determined to get as many of yesterday's fires put out as possible. He's mellower this morning and I can tell he's pleased I brought ice for his cooler, but he doesn't seem interested in food. It lies untouched next to his paw, where his claws flex in a vaguely threatening fashion.

Don't screw up any more today, Lee, those claws say.

I don't plan on it. I'm prepared to kick ass, take names, and snap pictures of the kicking and the taking. My uber-megapixel, waterproof camera hangs around my neck. Any pictures I take can be blown up nice and gigantic, perfect for hanging on the evidence-room push board. Hopefully, I'll come back with a few incriminating footprints and maybe even some Breeze house evidence to keep Stephanie busy and off my back.

Unless you don't come back at all.

The thought doesn't scare me. Stupid or not, I don't think I have anything to fear in the bayou this morning. Even when I steer my bike onto the inlet where skid marks in the mud speak of just how fast I hauled ass out of here last night, I don't feel the slightest apprehension. All the fairies are tucked away sleeping off their nightly feeding, white and blue herons stalk lazily through the shallows, and the air rings with frog song. The swamp is as peaceful and safe as it will ever be. I feel that truth in my gut.

No . . . not my gut. It's more a nervous-system thing. My skin feels different this morning, tingly and hyperaware, sensitive to the slightest vibrations.

Maybe the head injury has reactivated some part of my brain dulled by alcohol and the general blehness of being in my late twenties.

"Or maybe I'm just crazy," I whisper into Gimpy's fur as I snag my waders. He makes a sound half-purr, half-growl, but doesn't swipe at my face. I figure it's a step in the right direction.

After pulling my hair into a quick braid, I push the bike into the shade, ensuring the Gimp and his cooler won't get overheated, and head for the water. Amazingly, even the murky depths of the bayou hold no fear for me today. The fact that the sun has broken the horizon and turned the swamp a charming ruddy gold helps, and my waders certainly don't hurt. A thick layer of rubber between skin and reptile teeth is a good thing.

It makes me wonder how Hitch is doing. I thought about calling the hospital this morning and checking on him—for all of five seconds, before deciding that was just stupid. I don't want to talk to the FBI right now. Or my ex-boyfriend. Considering Hitch is both, I figured an inquiry about his health could wait.

The wade over to where I was attacked is relatively uneventful. I spot a couple of dead fairies drifting in the reeds near the shore, but nothing truly menacing. Still, I pull my gun from its holster before tromping onto solid ground. Today is about being safe, not sorry, about thinking ahead and cutting trouble off at the pass. Or at least not giving it a head start.

But the narrow clearing is deserted and the energy in the air calm. After a few moments, I feel dumb holding a gun on an innocent circle of trees, so I holster the weapon and turn on my camera.

A closer look at the ground reveals there was definitely someone with me last night. Giant footprints—the tread of the shoe makes me think my attacker was wearing work boots—form a circular pattern around a pair of smaller prints. The man's feet make my size tens look ridiculously precious. It's scary to imagine how big the rest of him must be, but also a little exciting.

Surely there can't be *that* many bad guys with feet this large. This is going to narrow down the police search, and maybe help confirm the identity of Grace's abductor. If the prints here match the prints Dom found outside Grace's window . . .

I snap a few dozen pictures, wider shots and close-ups of the tread marks, before wandering back to where I left my Breeze head tied up and taking a few more. The prints aren't as easy to find, but I get a decent shot of what looks like a size six sneaker heading off toward the water. It isn't the belt or a fingerprint, and I have no way of knowing if the woman made the print before or after I tied her up, but it's something, some small clue that might lead to a positive ID down the line.

Satisfied with my progress, I turn toward the Breeze camper/houseboat and pull my gun back out, making sure the safety is off. For the first time this morning, a shiver of apprehension does a shimmy down my spine. I still don't think I'm going to run into anyone, but who knows what I'll find inside that house? Something disgusting, no doubt. And awful. And filthy to the yarf degree. I don't imagine Breeze heads—especially Breeze heads who are also venom infected and hot on the trail of batshit crazy—are known for their housekeeping skills.

Visions of rotted food, mounds of fairy poo, and the bloated bodies of rodents dance in my head as I mount the three steps to the rickety screen door and pull it open. It squeals on its hinges, announcing my presence, but I feel obligated to knock. Just to prove that some people still have manners.

"Hello. This is Annabelle Lee, Fairy Containment and Control." I bang again, long and loud. "I need you to open the door."

I think about adding that I'm armed and dangerous and that anyone inside should "come out with their hands up," but decide it's lame to play cops and robbers at my age. After a few seconds of silence, I also feel too stupid to keep talking to people who aren't there. I reach for the cheap metal handle and am both pleased and pissed when the aluminum door swings inward.

So much for a good excuse *not* to check this place out. I flip my glasses on top of my head and squint into the darkness.

Hot air puffs from inside, carrying a pungent mix of bleach, the feared fairy shit, and fried-onion-scented sweat that's dried and re-dried so many times it's taken on a musky, animalistic odor. But still . . . the stench isn't as bad as I feared. There's nothing dead in here—I would know if bodies large or small had been baking inside this thing—and the cramped room is actually in fairly orderly condition. For a drug den.

Filmy black curtains hang on the windows above a sagging black pleather couch, and a black shag rug—now matted with grass and mud, but obviously once intended as a decorative statement—lies heavy on the floor. The tiny aluminum sink and cracked counter-top to my left are painted red, and the red folding table across the room is covered with Breeze-making equipment—glasses, burners, beakers, and piles of ash-gray shit left to dry on foil. A larger pile of fresh poo awaits treatment in the corner in a red trashcan.

Red and black. It's a theme. How gothic chic of her. Or them . . .

Next to the door, two jackets hang on bronze hooks. One of them is obviously intended for a small female, but the other is large. Not large enough to cover a giant, but a man's coat. I snap a few pictures, then, being careful to breathe through my mouth, step inside.

My gun leads the way, sweeping back and forth only once before I feel safe tucking it in its holster. There's no place for a bad guy to hide. Even the bath-room, a cramped affair with a toilet and a shower so small I doubt a grown man could fit inside, is visible from the main room.

I snap wide shots and then move in for close-ups of just about everything: the chipped coffee cups and glasses in the sink, the box of Nilla wafers and the wide variety of Cup O'Soup boxes on the counter, the red pillows on the couch, and all the drug paraphernalia from the smallest dish to the biggest bottle of bleach. I'm not sure what I'm looking for, but I suspect more is more where Stephanie and evidence are concerned. She seems like the anal-compulsive type.

I'm moving into the bathroom, intending to get a shot of the toilet for the sake of thoroughness, when I see it—the litter box.

A cat. This woman had a *cat,* one she cared for quite a bit, if the snazzy black ceramic litter box with the words "Satan's Helper" scrawled in red paint pen along one side are any indication. It's very craftsy, and makes me sad to think about Skanky being dead or on her way to a containment camp. Crazy, drug-peddling, head-bashing bitch or not, she went to the trouble to paint-pen her cat's litter box. It's sort of . . . sweet.

God, what's *wrong* with me? I'm becoming a cat lady. For real. Might as well paper my bedroom with kitten posters and buy a calendar. Or a mug with a kitten dangling from a tree with "Hang in there, it's almost Friday!" in pink bubble letters underneath. Or maybe a flask is a better idea . . .

For the first time since last night, a nip or three doesn't sound bad. Encouraging. Hopefully that means my head is healing and I'll soon be back to normal. Or close to normal, newfound soft spot for furry things aside.

Hmmm . . . furry things.

I turn back to the main room, crossing to the couch, eyeballing the red pillows. There, a medley of black and white hairs cover the fabric, just as they coated my tank top yesterday after I plucked Gimpy from the shuttle. There are no pictures or other hard evidence, but I'm willing to bet my next paycheck that *my* Gimpy is also the Breeze head's Satan's Helper.

As much as I hate to admit it, Skanky picked the better name.

"Well, he's Gimpy now," I mutter, feeling strangely territorial. Maybe it's the way Gimpy nuzzled my hand for a split second this morning after I refilled his cooler with fresh ice and a few cans of Coke. Or maybe it's just that I need something safe to love.

I swipe my hand across my forehead, determined to get out of here before the morning gets any hotter. Thankfully, my nose went numb after the initial stink-invasion, but the fairy shit in that trashcan isn't getting any fresher. I shove my hands into my waders and dig out a pair of plastic gloves and a few Ziploc bags from my jeans pockets.

Perfectly prepared. It feels good.

I pull on my gloves and head for the cabinets above the sink and the surrounding drawers. If there's a paper trail connecting this Breeze house to others in the area, I assume I'll find it in there somewhere.

There isn't any other place for it to hide. Aside from the couch, the Breeze-making setup, and a few laundry bins full of clothes stacked near the bathroom, the place is pretty spare.

I glance into the cabinets—empty but for cans of cat food and some cereal that rodents have already infested—then move on to the drawers. I tug open one after another, snapping pictures of their contents, but not bothering to shove anything into my baggies. Utensils, a collection of needles I'm not going to touch with a ten-foot pole, and a charger cord for a cell phone. There's nothing that gives me any clue who ran this house or whether they're connected to a larger operation. It's as if someone's been here before me to clear away the evidence.

But if that's true, why didn't that someone take the Breeze-making equipment or the fairy shit? Or at least the Breeze that's already prepped and ready to sell?

Wait a second . . .

Ready-to-go Breeze would probably be in cold storage. It doesn't have to be refrigerated, but it stays potent longer if it doesn't get too hot.

I slam the final drawer closed and step back, scanning the tiny kitchen. There it is, a brighter square on the once-cream linoleum. It isn't big enough for a full-sized fridge, more likely one of the mini numbers, but I still can't imagine my scrawny Breeze head carrying it away. Even pumped on a toxic high, she wouldn't get far with something so heavy. It must have been someone else. Her partner, maybe? Or . . . or . . . maybe . . .

Where is it? Tell me, where did you hide it? The invisible man's words drift through my head.

What would a man wandering around near a Breeze house be looking for that would get him het up enough to start bashing heads? A few hundred thousand dollars' worth of Breeze—roughly the amount that would fit in a fully stocked mini-fridge—would probably do it.

My gut, the one that assured me I'd be safe out here today, cramps in silent confirmation. Fabulous. My invisible man could be a Breeze head dealer as well as a kidnapper. I won't know the latter until Dom takes a look at my pictures and compares the footprints to the ones he found under Grace's window, but selling drugs and ransoming rich little girls don't seem like contradictory career paths. Maybe he didn't intend to kill Grace, maybe something had gone wrong, maybe—

The rumble of an approaching engine cuts through the stale air inside the camper, making me reach for my gun. I hurry to the door, sticking my head out into the increasingly muggy morning only to curse and pull back inside. The sunlight is still *killing me*. I flick my glasses over my eyes as I hustle down the steps and through the clearing, but the light still makes me squint, which means my pupils are probably still as big as saucers. I'll have to get Connie to run that MRI we skipped if things don't improve by this afternoon.

Or if I'm not killed by Breeze heads looking for their stash.

I can't see what's coming down the road just yet, but by the sound of the engine, it's big. Bigger than a police car or a pickup, but not as big as a shuttle bus. Which makes sense. The shuttles don't come this way. Nothing does. That's why the camper went undiscovered for so long. A body could go undiscovered just as easily, assuming you're careful where you pitch it.

So why was Grace's body laid out in plain sight, so close to the Beauchamp mansion? Where the patrol would be sure to see it from the fence?

Excellent question, brain. One I'll have to think on if I get out of here alive.

Sixteen

Death isn't in my future. At least not immediate death of the murdered-by-Breeze-heads-and-tossed-into-the-water-for-the-alligators-to-munch variety.

Even from my hiding place—crouched in the long grass across the water—I recognize the iron-sided van pulling into the inlet. It's the Beauchamp family van, the one Barbara Beauchamp probably used to drive into Baton Rouge yesterday for whatever urgent errand pressed her into the city on the day her daughter's body was discovered.

Today, however, there's someone else at the wheel, an obviously distraught Libby Beauchamp, Grace's much older sister. Even before she twists the key in the ignition, shutting down the roar of the van, I swear I can hear her sobbing.

If I didn't know better, I'd think she had the window down on the passenger's side, but there's no way she'd be that stupid. The fairies are drowsy and sluggish this time of day, but if they smell fresh blood they'll come swarming from whatever mud hole or hollow tree they've shacked up in. Rolling down the windows during a drive outside the iron gates is suicide.

But then . . . people have done crazier things after the death of someone they love.

There were times, after Caroline died, when I contemplated sneaking down to my parents' garage and turning on all four cars, crawling into the tarp-covered boat in the corner, and taking a very long, very permanent nap. There were times when I think my parents would have preferred that I sentence myself to the ultimate punishment for the crime of getting my beautiful big sister killed.

Libby and Grace were adopted sisters, but did that really make a difference? From the grief in Libby's sobs, I'm guessing it didn't. Losing a sister is still losing a sister, and losing a sister to murder when she's still so young and innocent and full of possibilities . . .

Well, I know how that feels. I also know there's nothing I can do for Libby.

I move into the water with a deliberate splash, and begin the journey back across the bayou to the inlet. Libby must not have noticed my bike parked in the shade, but I'll make sure she knows I'm coming.

In my peripheral vision, I see her pale blond head snap up, scanning the water. I can feel the second I'm spotted, prickles along my skin that make me want to cringe. Her last sob is swallowed by the sticky air. An uncomfortable silence, broken only by the water sloshing against my waders, follows me onto the shore. I wait until I step out of my rubber pants and shake off the water before lifting eyes to the van.

I intend to give a wave, dash to my bike, and be on my way. I don't anticipate that Libby will look so happy to see me. We've run into each other at Grapevine—the nicest restaurant in town, with the wine list Fernando adores—but we've never been officially introduced. Aside from a friendly smile or two, we've never exchanged pleasantries or names or *anything* that should make her feel obligated to wave me over.

But that clearly doesn't matter. Libby seems eager to make contact. Her slender fingers flutter a few seconds too long, and a shaky smile twitches at her lips before fading into a look of such longing even *I* can't ignore it.

I force a smile, cast a glance at where Gimpy lies curled around my cooler—obviously preferring me to his last owner as evidenced by the fact that he's stayed in my trailer rather than jumped out to roam his old stomping grounds, take *that*, Skanky—and trudge toward the van. No matter how much I want to run for it, I can't. The part of me that knows what it's like to lose a sister demands more human decency than that, and the amateur sleuth in me wonders . . .

Why did Libby drive out to the middle of nowhere to cry? Surely, that giant mansion has a place where she could grieve in private. But instead, she's driven out here, into fairy country, risking madness or death if one of the Fey gets ballsy enough to push through the ventilation system into her van. She must need to get away from her house pretty badly. Benny's warning that Cane should take a close look at everyone in the Beauchamp house swirls through my head, finishing the job of making me very curious.

Like that cat. The one that died.

I push aside the dramatic thought, do a quick check to make sure nothing winged and Fey is hovering nearby, and hurry into the van, slamming the heavy door closed behind me. Curiosity might kill me someday, but it won't come stabbing in the form of Libby Beauchamp. The girl is the definition of non-threatening.

I know she's in her early twenties, but with her white-blond hair swept into a ponytail and makeup-free face, she looks about fifteen. The steering wheel she clutches in her hands is bigger around than her wrist and I'm guessing the blue silk sundress she wears is a size zero.

Or maybe a double zero. Such things exist at the types of places her family shops.

"Hi." I can't think of anything better to say. I also can't bring myself to offer the usual apologies or ask the expected questions about how she's holding up. Obviously she isn't holding up, and me being sorry won't make her feel better.

"Hi." She holds out her hand, Southern manners kicking in. "I'm Libby . . . Grace's big sister."

I take her hand, but end our contact as quickly as

possible. Libby has the dead-fish non-grip of many Southern ladies, that gentle lying down of a cold, limp palm that makes my skin crawl. "Yeah, I know, I'm—"

"Annabelle. I know." There's a trace of playfulness in her tone that hints at the sense of humor she has under normal circumstances. "I . . . We heard that you were the one . . . I just wanted to say thank you." Her fingers worry at her ring finger, where a white circle marks skin usually covered by jewelry.

"You don't have to thank me. It's my job. I'm just . . ." Hell. I'm going to say it; I can't help myself. "I'm so sorry for your loss."

"Thank you." She sucks in a breath and her big, tear-filled blue eyes meet mine, punching me in the gut with her sadness, so eager to connect that I flip my sunglasses on top of my head. I can't let her eyes be naked alone, despite the fact that the sunlight flicks at my eyeballs like the fingers of mean little boys. "I just can't believe she's gone. I thought she was playing one of her games . . . I thought we'd find her hiding out in the barn or the attic or . . . or somewhere."

"She liked to play hide-and-seek?" I ask, partly because I'm curious, partly because I know it helps to talk about the person you've lost.

It's one of the things I regret most about losing contact with my family. Maybe some day they would have forgiven me, and we could have talked about Caroline together. It's no good remembering alone. It only makes Caroline feel more gone.

Libby shakes her head, a sad smile tugging at one side of her mouth. "No, she wasn't much for hide-and-seek. She preferred magical adventures. She had such an imagination. She'd start pretending and forget there was a real world."

There's a wistfulness in her tone that makes me think she envied Grace's ability to shut out the world.

"One time," Libby continues, "she told me she'd pretended so hard that she could hear the song the mermaids in her game were singing. She sang some of it for me. It was a beautiful, original composition. I'm sure she would have been an amazing musician." She breaks off with a breath that she holds as she fights another round of tears.

My chest aches with a combination of empathy and terror. Anxiety threads through my veins as I search for the right words and come up empty. I'm not equipped to counsel the grieving. Libby deserves better. I have to think of some way to get her in sturdy enough condition to drive out of here, and get myself out of this van.

"They're going to catch the person who did this, Libby."

"Is that why you're here? Did you find something that will help them figure out who killed her?" Her words are so filled with hope that a part of me itches to tell her everything, but I can't. I'm not supposed to be here without adult supervision myself, let alone spilling all to the victim's family member.

"I definitely found some interesting stuff," I say, "but . . . I can't really share . . . if you know what I mean?"

"Right. Of course." She twists her absent ring, and blushes, embarrassed. "I understand. I'm sorry, I—"

"No, it's okay. Just know that the FBI is here and Cane and Abe are good at what they do and I'm going to help any way I can. We're going to make sure this person is put away."

She nods, sniffing. "I know. My mother said they already have a suspect in custody."

"She did?" This is news. "Here in Donaldsonville?"

Libby nods again, and dread clutches at my throat. Fernando. He's in custody here in Donaldsonville. But she *has* to be talking about someone else. Fernando would never hurt anyone, especially a child, and there's no way Cane or Abe would have found evidence to the contrary. Still, I can't help but ask, "Did your mother say who—"

"She wouldn't tell me anything else. I'm too emotional to hear the ugly truth." Her voice holds a note of "my mother makes me want to slice open a vein or drink myself into a stupor" bitterness I completely understand. I was just thinking yesterday that Barbara reminds me of my mom.

But my mom stayed in bed for a month after Caroline died. She barely ate, nearly overdosed on Valium and vodka, and lost so much weight she had to get fat injected into her face to look semi-normal again. She certainly hadn't been running around the state

Capitol building hours after her daughter's body was found. It makes me wonder how much Barbara is really keeping from her "fragile" daughter.

"I bet I can find out who they're holding this afternoon and let you know," I say, throwing out the friendship rope before I think better of it. "I mean, since your mom already knows and everyone will know if charges are filed."

"Really?" Libby grabs the rope and holds on tight. "Would you do that?"

"Sure. I have to meet the FBI at the station anyway. I've got a few connections. I'm sure I can get someone to spill something."

"I would really appreciate it," Libby says. "I just . . . want to know. The waiting is killing me. My brother, James, too. He hasn't slept in three days."

"I'll do what I can. Do you want me to give you a call after?"

"Could you stop by the house? I used to have a cell phone, but my mother took it away," she says with an awkward shrug. "After I quit the symphony, no one really called me anymore."

Her words end in a sigh and an eye roll befitting a younger girl. But then, it seems her mother has done her best to keep Libby young and fragile and dependent. There's something a little off about the woman next to me, and I'm betting her controlling mother has something to do with it. I have no idea how that might factor into Grace's murder—I don't get a killer vibe from Libby, that's for sure—but there's no way

I'm passing up the chance to observe the Beauchamp family up close and personal.

"Sure, I can stop by. Maybe sometime this afternoon?"

"Afternoon would be fine. Or you could come for supper. We serve at six. Girls usually do dresses, but business casual would be fine," Libby says, sending a lightning bolt through my gut. I haven't dressed for dinner since I was fourteen and started eating all my meals in my room. "Percy's making shrimp and grits and she always makes way too much for just the five of us."

"Thanks, but I'm severely allergic to shellfish. I'd swell up and die," I say, grateful for the excuse. Sitting down to a formal dinner with a grieving family sounds about as fun as taking Stephanie for a beer after my official review.

Ugh. Review. I glance at the dashboard clock. Eight-fifteen. I have plenty of time before I have to meet Stephanie, but I should probably get busy with the whole bail issue before Fernando's hearing. Despite my delinquent youth, I have no idea how one goes about posting bail.

A part of me hopes the judge will be reasonable and release him on his own recognizance. With a potential child murderer also in custody, surely Fernando's been downgraded to threat level not-very-serious.

"Well, that's a shame." Libby wilts, narrow shoulders hunching. "You know, you don't have to come over at all if it's a bother."

"It's no bother."

"No, I know you must be really busy helping the police and the FBI and the whole town, really, so—"

"Libby, really, it's no big—"

The sound of a car horn blaring in the near distance makes us both jump. It's just so out of place. I've lived in Donaldsonville for years and never encountered this much action outside the iron gate. On instinct, I draw my gun and turn, catching sight of a long, metal storage container behind the driver's seat. It looks a lot like the one Cane uses to store his metal suit, but shinier, newer.

I know the Beauchamps are loaded, but seriously, an iron suit's a pricey item, one that's usually reserved for law enforcement and research facilities. Very few private citizens own them. Most people who are *that* rich and afraid of fairies either move north or invest in an iron-lined underground bunker.

So what's with the suit? Does someone in the Beauchamp clan like tromping about in nature? Hunting? Fishing? Enough to risk their lives outside the gates? No matter why they purchased it, the suit certainly would make it easier for one of them to dump Grace's body outside the iron gate. What if Benny is right? What if one of the Beauchamps . . .

Beside me, Libby presses herself against the driver's side door, obviously freaked out by my firearm. "Please, you can put down the gun down. It's probably just my brother. He hates it when I come out here."

Seconds later, an iron-plated BMW with a fairy-repelling floodlight mounted on the roof pulls up behind the van and slams to a stop with a crunch of gravel. As Libby predicted, behind the wheel is an angry James Beauchamp. His usually carefully feathered blond-brown hair sticks up on one side as if he's slept on it wrong, and his face is flushed and puffy. He tugs off a pair of sunglasses as big as my own and glares straight down the barrel of my gun, blue eyes so bloodshot I can see the red from seven feet away.

"Please, put the gun down!" Libby turns to wave frantically at her brother, almost as if she fears retaliation. Is her brother armed? A part of me wants to keep my own gun right where it is just to find out. "I'm fine! We're just talking!" Libby calls, her shriek shrill enough to make my ears ring. Her bony fingers are on my arm a second later, clawing into my skin with more strength than our handshake revealed. "Please, I don't want him to get out of the car. It isn't safe."

"It isn't safe for you, either. You shouldn't be out here if you don't have to be." I shove the gun back into its holster and give James a wave. He doesn't wave back. Or smile. Or stop glaring at me like he'd like to peel pieces of skin from my face with his surgical knife. But he doesn't get out of the car, either. After a few seconds, Libby's hand slides from my arm with a shaky sigh.

"I know," she says, still staring at her brother though her hands come back to worry her ring finger.

"Sometimes I just feel so trapped, especially since . . . since Grace went missing. It helps to go for a drive. You know what I mean?"

"I don't own a car, but yeah, I know what you mean." And I do. If I were a different kind of woman, I might even give her a hug. Instead I reach for the door. "I'll see you this afternoon, okay?"

"Yes. Thanks. Wonderful." Libby stops me with a hand on my shoulder. "Would you mind telling James I'll see him at home? Tell him I'll drive straight there."

Great. Silently, I curse Libby's mother for taking away her cell phone.

"Sure thing." I flip my glasses over my eyes, hop out of the van, and wave as Libby starts it up.

She won't be going anywhere until James backs away since he's blocked the path back to the road, but I'm glad she's taking the initiative. A part of me hopes James will get the message and head for home. I certainly won't be offended if he bolts without saying "hello." But he stays, BMW idling at a low purr, pinning me with a "what rock did you crawl out from under" look as I amble toward the car.

I've never been officially introduced to James, either, but we've exchanged words at the shuttle station a few times. He's always been friendly and pleasant, if a little bland. But there's nothing bland about him now. He looks like someone rammed a pole up his ass. A hot pole.

This is going to be fun.

I reach for the door, but the passenger's window

zips down a few inches before I can open it. Guess James isn't worried about fairies this early in the morning. Or maybe he's just *that* determined to keep me out of his fancy car.

"What were you doing with my sister?" he asks.

I force the smart-ass remark on the tip of my tongue back into my mouth. I have to remember this man has been through hell and has a good excuse for being a dickweed. "I was out here for work and saw she was upset. I thought she might want to talk."

He laughs, a short, ugly sound. "Libby doesn't talk. Not to strangers."

It hits me as a condemnation, not a warning.

"Okay . . ." Looks like brother is on the Libby-is-too-fragile-to-live bandwagon, too. Charming, the way families get together and decide what you are and aren't capable of, whether you'll be the golden child or the drunk, misfit loser.

Or maybe I'm projecting . . . the *tiniest* bit.

"Just leave my sister alone," he says, a protective note in his voice. "You have no idea what she's been through."

"Actually, I—"

"And please tell her to come straight home. The FBI is at the house."

The FBI? The Stephanie-flavored FBI or the Hitch-flavored FBI? Or both? Hmm . . . this doesn't bode well for me delivering my new evidence before the meeting and getting my bonus points for kissing up. Dammit.

"Would you mind? Please?" he asks, when I tarry too long before rushing to do his bidding. "She doesn't have a cell."

"I know. She told me." I smile, enjoying the irritation on his face. Take *that*, Mr. My Sister Doesn't Talk to Strangers. "She also said she's going straight home, so—"

"Good." James zips up the window with a suddenness that makes me start. Before I can close my mouth, he's shifted into reverse and backed away. Libby follows, raising her hand in one final, limp salute, and mouthing "thank you," before hurrying down the gravel road after her brother.

It isn't until I've wandered back to my bike and bent down to pull a fishing lure from Gimpy's mouth—because apparently plastic and fake hair taste better than the perfectly good food I've offered—that I realize neither of them offered me a ride.

"So much for Southern hospitality," I say, earning a growl when I toss the fly Gimpy was gnawing into my tackle box. I push the untouched can of cat food closer to his paw, and the growl becomes a full-fledged, teeth-baring hiss.

Satan's Helper. Hmph. Indeed.

Seventeen

These are amazing. Thank you so much," Dom says, fondling my camera in his long fingers, hazel eyes shining suspiciously. For a second, I'm afraid he might cry, or try to hug me, or something equally scary. Instead, he punches my arm and gives my braid a tug for good measure. "You done good, Lee."

"Thanks. I try." At least I've *started* trying. Harder, anyway.

"Hey . . ." Dom's hand moves to my shoulder as he peers into my face. "Are you all right? Are you feeling okay?"

"I'm fine."

"Okay . . . it's just, your eyes." He leans closer, until his nose almost touches mine. "Your pupils are *huge*."

"Yeah, I know." I laugh as I pull away, and flip my sunglasses back down with a self-conscious twitch. Rocking the sunglasses-indoors look is awkward, but better than being stared at like some sort of specimen. "It's a head injury thing, totally normal. I feel fine."

Mostly fine. Except for the light sensitivity, the slight, lingering headache, and the occasional auditory hallucination. All the way back to town, I swear I heard *whispering* in the trees, soft voices saying things I could almost understand. Things about "going away" and "staying away" or . . . something. But every time I stopped, straining to hear, the sound faded. By the time I reached the gate, the voices had vanished completely.

I'm probably just suffering from brain damage. Or finally losing my mind. Both are comforting thoughts.

I make a mental note to get to the doctor after my afternoon social call if things don't improve. I still plan on visiting Libby to fill her in on whatever I learn, despite the fact that her brother's about as friendly as my cat—who's outside chewing a patch of grass by the front door instead of eating the cat food in the trailer. I'm beginning to think the Gimp has an eating disorder.

"I'm going to go download these right now," Dom says. "Is that cool?"

"Very. That's why I stopped in early."

He cocks his head. "I thought you were here to give me your statement about what happened last night. Dicker's been up my ass about it all morning."

"Um . . . I don't remember anything about giving a statement." It makes sense, and is probably something I should do, but Cane didn't say anything about it when we talked. Had he? In all the excitement of the sort-of marriage proposal, that's the kind of thing that could have slipped my attention.

"Dicker's been calling your house for an hour."

"I haven't been at the house. I was out accomplishing great things." I point to the camera in Dom's hand. "Why didn't he call my cell?"

"I have no idea. Because he's Dicker? Because he can't imagine anyone being out of the house before six o'clock?" Dom rolls his eyes before glancing back at the camera's viewscreen, zooming in on one shot. For the first time, I notice how rough he looks, dark-circled and sallow-skinned, like he's been up half the night. Which he probably has if they brought in a murder suspect sometime this morning. "Honestly, I think it can keep. You'll be here at noon, anyway, right?"

"I'll be around all morning. Either here or over at Swallows grabbing some breakfast." And coffee. God, coffee. I need it in a major way. My stomach has finally settled and I'm feeling the caffeine withdrawal at a cellular level.

I need a strong cup, especially if I'm going to give an official statement about what happened to me and Hitch last night. I'm already planning to leave out the part about the invisible man—mostly because I've convinced myself my head injury is to blame for that particular bit of weirdness—but I should think hard on what else I might want to leave out.

Such as the fact that I was carrying Hitch's gun in a concealed-type fashion, which I'm not legally entitled to do.

"Good. I'll catch up with you later. I want to blow

these up on the big screen and get a closer look." He squeezes my arm with a tired, but excited, smile. "I didn't see you. You dropped this off and were out the door before I could stop you."

"Right," I say, catching a bit of his excitement. "So you think the pictures are going to help with the investigation?"

"Definitely. Especially the footprints. I think these are going to be key, no matter what Cane . . ." Dom shoots me a nervous glance through his long, baby-llama lashes. "Never mind. But, yeah, I think—"

"It's okay, Dom. It's not a huge deal." I shrug and try to smile, even as I casually sneak a glance across the open front office, back to where Cane and Abe usually camp out in the glass walled conference room with the Bunn coffee maker and the Little Debbie snack machine. This morning, the room is empty, making me wonder where they're holding the virtual bail hearing for Fernando. As far as I know, the conference room's the only place equipped for something like that. "Anyway, it's cool."

"It is?"

"Yeah. It is." More shrugging. See me shrug. See how little I care that a bunch of people who are friends with my boyfriend watched me make out with my ex-boyfriend. "Cane and I are in a fight. It's not a big deal."

"You are? Really?" Dom's shock makes me want to slap myself in the face. Fabulous. Cane actually made good on that promise to keep Dicker quiet and I've ruined it with my big mouth.

"Um . . . yeah. Sort of."

"But you two are so great," he says, lowering his voice. "Is it because of Fernando?"

"Yes. It is." I seize the easy out. Not only is it a great excuse, but I smell a chance to find out more about Fern's situation and I'm not about to let that pass me by. If the judge deems it necessary, I'll be trucking down to the bail bondsman's and plunking down fifteen percent of Fern's Get Out of Jail fee, and I'd like to know what breed of trouble I'm paying to get him out of. "I'm pissed about it."

"I can imagine. Well, I can't, really, but . . . yeah . . . it's pretty hard for me to believe. Even with the evidence."

My skin prickles. Oh no. No way. There's just *no way* they could be holding Fernando for Grace's murder. The thought is ludicrous. He's a snarky slut with a heart of gold. He'd do anything for a friend and a hell of a lot for a stranger. Fernando sincerely tries to make the world a happier, if slightly more gossip-filled, place. I can't imagine what he did to earn an overnight in jail, let alone a bail hearing, and there's no way he has anything to do with what happened to Grace.

But maybe the DPD isn't as enlightened as yours truly. Time to pump Dom for information. "It's hard to believe because it's not true," I bluff. "Fernando would never do something like that."

"I can't really say anything on the record." Dom's voice is hushed, complete with a glance over his shoulder to where the temp mans the phones a few feet away. "But I think you're right. And I think these pictures are going to help prove it."

"You think? How?" I ask, desperate for more information as the bad feeling inside me blossoms into a full-fledged stink-flower of worry. Why would my pictures of a killer's footprints help Fernando's case unless . . .

"This is crazy, Dom." I flip my glasses back onto my head, needing eye contact. "Fernando would never hurt *anyone*. You're not honestly telling me they think—"

"I'm not telling you anything."

"Dom, this is me! You know I—"

"Sorry, Annabelle. I can't discuss a case with a civilian. I hate to think of you like that since you help us so much and all, but I can't."

"Right, I get it." I've heard this before, every single time I've been out for beers with the boys after an interesting arrest and they ask me to leave the table so they can get their gossip on. Small-town cops or not, the DPD is fairly professional when it comes to keeping outsiders uninformed.

But right now, I *have* to have information. Fernando's future could depend on it. If he's been wrongly accused, I've got to do more than bail him out. I've got to find him a damned fine lawyer.

"Can you at least tell me whether you think I'm going to have to post bail?" I ask, hoping Dom can bend enough to give me a hint if my fears are grounded. "If

Fernando's not going to be released on his own recognizance, then I'm in charge of the bonding."

"You're going to need to post bail," he says. "There's no way he's getting out without bail. He's got Judge Wade."

Judge Wade. Evil Judge Wade, the only judge in Baton Rouge who still puts people away for pot possession. In the wake of the Breeze epidemic, and all the other crap we deal with, being the infested armpit of the United States, most judges in the Delta don't bother with weed convictions anymore. But Wade does.

It makes me feel better. Maybe Fernando is just getting the sharp end of the stick. Maybe he isn't in as much trouble as my gut's telling me.

Right. And maybe you should start hunting down lawyers. Asap.

I sigh, and check the clock. Nine thirty-five. They've only been live with the judge for five minutes, and that's if Wade showed up on time, which he probably didn't. Louisiana government types are never on time, especially on Saturdays. I have plenty of time to get to the bail bondsman down the street, figure out how to post bail, and get back before the verdict comes down. And I certainly have no urge to linger here. The last thing I want to do is spend the next half hour giving a leering Dicker my statement.

And he *will* leer when the time comes, of that I have no doubt. Catching a woman cheating on tape is the kind of thing Pervert Santa lives for.

Decision made, I slip back through the doors, into the increasingly sweltering morning. It's going to be brutal. Already, the sidewalk burns hot enough to feel it through my shoes.

"Reoowr." Gimpy welcomes me back with a groan.

He crouches near my bike in the shade, pressed up against a trailer wheel, evidently too spent from munching grass to jump inside. I lift him in, and watch him snuggle up next to my cooler with a slightly arthritic hitch of his back leg. It makes me wonder how old he is. Dr. Hollis, the town vet, will probably be able to tell me. Maybe I'll swing by and see if she's in on the way back from the Beauchamps'. Her office is on the way, a good ten blocks from the human hospital where I should be taking myself directly.

"Blah, blah, blah."

Gimpy stares at me with a humorless expression, seconding my opinion that nothing good can come of taking my health too seriously when I could be attending to his needs. We'll see if he still agrees when Dr. Hollis suggests a round of shots for his fluffy butt.

I leave the Gimp sitting in the shade and head across the parking lot. It's faster to cut through the park behind the station on foot than bike the quarter-mile over to Morales Bail Bonds. Or it *would* be faster, if my safe passage weren't blocked by a pair of angry, ropey, black women.

Amity Cooper and a vaguely familiar, scrawny chick with an Afro wearing gold lamé pants, lean against Cane's squad car. It looks like Amity has just left her brother a note. A square of white paper lies pinned beneath one wiper and an ink pen is clenched tightly in her fist. Considering Amity attacked me with a loaf of crusty bread the last time we had words, I don't want to see what she's capable of armed with a blue Bic. Fernando's warning that the youngest Cooper is out for my blood is way easier to believe when Amity's pen hand rises like a one-fanged serpent preparing to strike. The woman next to her props a hand on her hip and takes a threatening step forward. "That her?"

"Yeah, that's her," Amity growls, the menace in her tone enough to bring back sense memories of the way that crusty bread stabbed the center of my chest.

Right. Running away. Clearly the best call.

I turn back toward the station—even chatting with Dicker is preferable to a run-in with Cane's sister and her henchwoman—but apparently Amity isn't in the mood to let her prey get away so easily.

"Annabelle Lee, get your skinny white ass back here."

"Like you two have room to talk!" I smile as I spin to face them, but continue backing away. Amity stalks across the pavement with Gold Lamé Girl close behind. "Really, Amity. You and your girl need a sandwich. Or maybe some pancakes. Have you two had breakfast yet? Because I was—"

"Shut your mouth." The rumble in Amity's voice reminds me of Cane. She sounds like she smoked a pack of cigarettes last night, and smells even worse. The stink of tar and nicotine lingers on her clothes—

sparkly black pants and a tank top that I'm betting are last night's club wear—making me wince when she shoves into my personal space.

"You want me to hold her?" Gold Lamé Girl asks, slithering up beside me. She smells even worse, but at least her stink gives me a positive ID. She's the woman from the bus, the one who tried to bully me into giving her my beer.

Shit. Maybe if I'd handed it over, she wouldn't be so eager to help kick my ass, or whatever is going down here.

"Come here, girl." One bony hand snatches at my arm, but I twist free.

"Don't touch me," I warn as I stumble away. Amity follows, jabbing her pen into my sternum hard enough to make me wince. My hand whips up, blocking a second stab. This is ridiculous, she can't *physically attack* me every time we run into each other, no matter who her brothers are. "Stop it with the stabbing, Amity. I'm not going to—"

"I thought I told you to shut your mouth," she says, shocking the hell out of me with a full-fledged backhand across the jaw.

Ah! What the hell? What the fracking hell?

My glasses fly from my face. Light gouges at my eyes, and pain blooms in my jaw as I lurch in a half circle, wide-eyed and stupid, too amazed that my boyfriend's sister has actually *struck me* to know what to do with myself. Give me a cracked-out Breeze head and I can fight back with the best of them, but

I wasn't raised to fight with people I've had supper with. People who might one day be my *family* if her brother has his way.

The Jerry Springer–ishness of the interlude is too much for the former junior deb in me to assimilate so quickly, giving Gold Lamé Girl time to grab my elbows and force them behind my back.

"You fucked up this time, girl," Amity says, closing in once more. Her diamond chandelier earrings catch the light and flash, making me wince and rack my brain. Why do those look so familiar? "You fucked up big time. I *know* it was you. You were in the swamp yesterday and you're that faggot's best girlfriend. So tell me where the fuck you put it." She fists her hand in my braid. I'm on my back on the ground at her feet before I can suck in a breath, let alone answer her question. "Tell me!"

It's last night all over again, but this time with a very easily seen and *felt* woman demanding I tell her where some unknown something is hidden. I give myself three guesses what these two are looking for, and the first two don't count.

I remember now where I've seen those earrings before. On the woman in the bayou, the one I tied up, the one working the Breeze operation. This has drug stink all over it. Literally.

The stale, muddy smell of nicotine and the brighter tang of a Breeze high that's been sweated out and dried on the skin linger all around these two. The certainty that Amity is in deep, drug-related trouble hits even before my eyes skim across the marks high on her upper arm. In any other position, I wouldn't be able to see them. But from my place on the ground, I have a killer view of her deodorant-crusted pits, and the swollen injection wounds healing amidst the ingrown hairs.

Amity's been shooting Breeze. Which certainly explains the crazy and the strength with which she so easily lifts me off the ground only to slam me back into the pavement again.

"Tell me, bitch!"

"You better talk up," Gold Lamé Girl seconds, leaning over Amity's shoulder to get a better view of the beating.

I blink and the sky pulses pink and green as my eyes decide whether or not they'll burst from my skull. "I don't know, I don't—"

Amity's fist flies at my face, but I block it, grunting as our bones connect and my forearms bruise. Shoving her away, I try to sit up, but am stomped back onto the ground with one kick of Gold Lamé Girl's boot.

Pain flashes through my skull, humming around to punch at my eyes as Amity gets her hand back in my hair and slams me into the pavement—once, twice, three times. Black and white stars twinkle against the pink and green sky, pulsing and throbbing. I already have a head injury. At this rate, Amity could kill me if I don't get my hair out of her grabby hands.

"Talk up, Lee, I swear to God, I—"

Her words end in a groan as I jackknife my body, sending boot-covered feet surging toward her face. Later, I assume my eyes were playing tricks on me, but at that moment I would swear that my intention connected before my feet. Seconds before my shoes strike her face, Amity arches backwards, chin snapping, feet flying off the ground, as if she's been struck by someone a hell of a lot stronger.

The momentum would have carried her a few feet away—allowing me to regain my footing—if she hadn't maintained her viselike grip on my hair. But she does, and I skid along the pavement behind her, crying out as my jeans ride down and the skin scrapes off my tailbone. Gold Lamé Girl hustles after me with her fist raised.

"Stop it!" I kick in Lamé Girl's general direction, Amity screams something about killing me, and the wind sings a *wah-wah-wah* song that booms through my aching head, promising more pain if I don't get off the damned ground.

I kick my friend from the bus in the gut, then move my fingers to dig into Amity's hands, vowing to cut off all my hair at the first opportunity so there will be nothing for an attacker to hold onto. But before I can claw myself free, a shadow falls on my face and big hands close over mine.

Eighteen

Let her go, Amity! Amity! Let her go!"

Cane. *Thank God*. With Dicker and Abe behind him. Abe already has Gold Lamé Girl's arms behind her back, making me breathe easier even before Cane's shadow blocks out the sky as he pulls Amity away. She gives my scalp one last tug and then she's in the air, tucked under Cane's arm, kicking and thrashing, cursing like a rabid muskrat while Dicker fumbles a pair of handcuffs from his belt.

I bolt into a seated position, and immediately regret it as the world whips in a dizzy circle. Oh crap, I feel woozy, light-headed, and generally like I've been whacked on the head one too many times in the past twenty-four hours.

"Let me loose. Let me loose!" Amity screams. "I didn't do nothin'!"

"It was that bitch," the other woman says. "She threatened me on the bus. She told me she was going to give me her herpes if I didn't give her money."

"Shut up, Monique," Amity says.

"She did! I swear to god!"

"This one's got two priors for public intox and assault." Abe ignores his sister. His lightly wrinkled face remains set in a grim mask. No one observing would guess he's related to one of these women. "I'm going to take her in and book her."

"You can't book me! Book *her*! She told me she's got sores all over her ass," Gold Lamé Girl—whose name is evidently Monique—screams as Abe pulls her away. "Ask those college boys on the bus!"

"I told her they were in my mouth, not my ass," I mumble. Dicker shoots me a vaguely disgusted look, and I vow never to lie about diseases that cause open sores ever again. "And I never threatened her with herpes or anything else, I—"

"She's a liar," Amity says. "She pulled a gun on me! I was defending myself, Cane."

My fingers fly to my gun, which is still safely buttoned in my holster. I didn't even remember I was carrying it. Stupid. Not that I would want to draw down on my could-be future sister-in-law . . . but still, it would have been good for threatening and running away purposes.

"Cuff her, Dicker," Cane says, not buying the gun accusation. "You smell like gator bait, Amity. What the hell were you up to last night?"

"Put me down!" One of Dicker's cuffs snaps around Amity's wrist, and her thrashing becomes a slam dance of crazy. "Let me go, or I swear to God, you'll kill me! You'll kill your own sister! They'll kill me!"

Her voice breaks, and her struggles grow so spastic that Cane nearly drops her. At the last minute, he shifts his grip, slipping one hand between her legs and another around her torso and locking his fists, pinning her like a toddler in the middle of a tantrum. Dicker cuffs her free wrist before scrambling back, as if he fears Amity will take a chunk out of his neck if he stays too close.

"She's on Breeze. Or she's *been* on Breeze." I have to yell to be heard over Amity's now wordless wailing as I sway to my feet. "I saw the injection marks under her arms."

Cane's jaw goes slack and grief flashes across his face. When he speaks, his voice is a raw, painful thing to hear. "Guess that explains the smell."

Breeze heads like to let nicotine build up on their skin. It helps hold the Breeze in longer before they start to sweat out, and smoking cigarettes in endless succession apparently seems like a good idea when you're floating the fairy wind. Cane knows that. He also knows even a few weeks of using Breeze can take years off a life. He realizes the seriousness of what his sister has done; it's plain in every tiny wrinkle around his sad eyes.

"Looks like it's worse than that." Dicker grunts under his breath. "Pin her head back, Cane." After a second of hesitation, Cane tightens his grip, but keeps a sharp eye on Dicker as he points one blunt fingertip at the skin behind Amity's ear. "Call me crazy . . . but . . ." His gaze shifts nervously from me to Cane and back again. "Well . . . that *looks* like a damned fairy bite."

Amity howls, making us all flinch. "That ain't no bite! I ain't got no bite! Fuck you, Dicker. Fuck you!"

Her words morph into more mindless screaming, finally drawing the attention our fight should have attracted five minutes ago. Across the street, the barbershop lingerers—men who spend most of the day inside Sid's Old-Fashioned Cuts soaking up the free air conditioning—have come out to point and stare. Next door, Walter's wide, round face hovers in the window of the hardware store, chubby cheeks working as he traps sunflower shells between his teeth one after another, spying on the festivities from between the rakes and the shovels.

Too bad he didn't think to bring out a shovel and whack Amity and Monique off of me when I was pinned to the ground. I would get my feelings hurt—I consider Walter a friend, whose Eskimo prostitute stories I've listened to enough times at Swallows that he should have my back in a fight—but even Dicker, a man with the authority to make an arrest, was reluctant to engage with Amity until Cane gave the order.

Maybe that's why Amity thinks she can get away with shooting Breeze and attacking people on the street, because everyone in town is too afraid to stand up to the Cooper brothers.

As I move closer, standing on tiptoe to get a look at

what indeed seems to be a scabbed-over fairy bite on Amity's neck, I let my eyes slide up to Cane's face. If he wasn't my lover or my friend, how would I feel about him? Would I still trust him with my life? Or would I wonder if he and his brother didn't have their own agenda in this town, one that included special treatment for friends and family and special punishments for those who mess with those friends and family? Is my relationship with Cane the reason the Junkyard Kings and every other allegedly sketchy or dangerous person in town leaves me alone? Will my life become even more dangerous if I lose that protection, if Cane becomes an enemy rather than a friend?

"Dammit," Cane whispers.

"I'm sorry, man. I'm so sorry." There's real compassion in Dicker's voice. It's a first in my experience, but then everyone knows what a fairy bite means for a family.

"I've got to get her inside, and start making the calls." The misery in Cane's voice makes me want to hug him, but I'm with Dicker—I'm not getting anywhere near Amity's teeth.

Instead, I touch Cane's shoulder. "I'm sorry, too."

Sudden doubts aside, Cane is losing a sister. Amity isn't severely allergic or she'd be dead already, but she'll still be processed and sent to a camp within the next few days. Cane and his family will have to apply for special passes to visit her and only get a few hours, two or three times a year, with a woman they're used to seeing every day.

They'll spend their limited time together separated by a wall of protective glass. They'll never hug Amity again, they'll never spend another Sunday chatting on the porch over endless glasses of sweet tea. And in a few years—maybe five if she's very lucky—they'll bury her before her time.

I've never been a fan, but it makes me so sad. Sad for Amity, and much, much sadder for the man I love.

Cane's brows draw together, and he subtly pulls away from my touch. "Did she or Monique hurt you? Do you want to press charges?"

"No, I'm fine," I lie, ignoring the dull thrumming in my skull. At least the pink and green flashing lights are gone and the wah-wah song has stopped. I'll live. Amity can't say the same.

"You're not fine." He sounds angry, despite the fact that I've given him the answer he wanted. "You need to get to the ER. Dom's right, your eyes are wrecked."

"Okay . . . I will," I say, ignoring the sharpness in his tone. He's just found out his sister will never be coming home again, I can't expect his Sunday manners. "I just need to arrange bail for Fernando and then—"

"Bail was denied. We're holding him." Cane nods to Dicker. "Go get the padded room ready for Amity. Make sure it's clean."

"Wait a second." I hurry to keep up with Cane as he starts across the parking lot. Dicker scurries ahead, chubby thighs churning inside his polyester pants, hustling faster than I've ever seen him move. "What do you mean? How could bail be denied? Fernando has never even had an unpaid parking ticket, I—"

"Perverts who kill kids don't get out of jail, Annabelle," Cane snaps, loud enough to make Amity flinch. Cane winces and tightens his arms in a gesture that's more hug than restraint. When he speaks again, it's in a whisper. "I don't care about his clean driving record, and neither did the judge."

"No, Cane." I shake my head. This can't really be happening. This is insane! "You've got the wrong person. Fernando didn't kill Grace, he would never do something like that."

"I can't talk to you about an ongoing investigation." He circles around me before pausing to throw his parting shot over his shoulder. "And you need to renew your license for that piece. I know it's expired. If I see you carrying it again without a current license, I'll arrest you."

"Jesus, Cane, I—"

"Annabelle! Can I have a few words? Whenever you're finished?" Even from across the street, I can smell Hitch's signature smell. I turn, glad to see him looking healthy and whole in a light blue button-down shirt and a pair of khakis. But really, couldn't he have waited until Cane was inside the station? We haven't discussed my new relationship status, but he has to know that Cane and I aren't "just friends."

Or that we weren't before last night, anyway.

"Sure, just a second," I call before turning back to Cane.

Now there's nothing friendly in Lieutenant Cooper's face. It's almost as if he blames me for Amity's condition, as if I invited some damn fairy to bite her while she was out in the bayou scoring Breeze. That has to be why she was bitten. It might have even happened yesterday, while she was stealing the earrings off the woman who attacked me. My thoughts race, full of suspicions about Amity's connections to the big bad man who attacked me and his big bad drugs that must have gone missing.

Fernando warned me that Amity's place was a hotbed of sketchiness. I should have listened, I should have asked more questions. Maybe then I'd have something to go on to help me clear Fernando's name.

I have to find out more. I have to get Dom to tell me if the footprints in my pictures match the footprints at the Beauchamps'. Or maybe the footprints are still there . . . right outside Grace's window. Maybe I can get Libby to take me on a tour of the grounds this afternoon and get a look at them myself.

"Stay out of this, Annabelle. It's none of your business," Cane says, almost as if he's read my mind. Or maybe he just knows me *that* well. A scary thought, if there ever was one. "I don't want you near a crime scene or inside the station unless you've got legitimate FCC business or you're coming to give Dicker your statement."

"Cane, please. You know Fern, you know he wouldn't—"

"I don't know shit. The past twenty-four hours

have made that pretty clear." The muscle in Cane's jaw leaps and his eyes turn angry with a side of bitter. "I meant what I said about that gun. And keep your hands off FBI weapons, too. Last night was your only free pass."

My jaw drops as he walks away without so much as a goodbye. What was with the parting shot? Was it really a warning about carrying weapons I'm not licensed to carry, or a dig of a more personal nature?

His sister is infected, and he's working a murder case. He has bigger things to worry about than telling his ex-girlfriend to stay away from her ex-boyfriend's "gun."

"Annabelle?" Right. Hitch—and his gun—are waiting for me across the street.

Ugh. Blechk. Blergh.

I take my time gathering my glasses from the ground and slipping them back onto my face, literally dragging my feet as I head Hitch's way. I don't check the street before I cross, either. Getting hit by a car might be a blessing at this point.

"How are you feeling?" Hitch asks when I finally sluff up onto the sidewalk beside him.

"Shouldn't I be asking you that question?"

"You're the one with a head injury and a dozen bite marks." He reaches out, smoothing fingers over the bare skin at my shoulder, inspiring a minor cardiac event. "Jesus, that's amazing. I can barely see them."

I refuse to shiver. The wonder in his voice is for the medical miracle of my mended flesh, nothing more.

The warmth spreading through me as my body celebrates his touch, however, is personal. No matter how wrong that kiss, a part of me wants to do it again. And again. And again, until all the bridges we burned are rebuilt and the distance between our past and present eaten away.

The other part of me wants to run to the station and get Cane alone. Surely, if I talk to him one-on-one, I'll see the same man I saw last night. The one who loves me, who doesn't care about the past as long as he can be my future.

A third part of me just wishes I could see Hitch's eyes. Stupid sunglasses. If I could see his eyes I'd have a clue what sort of "words" we're going to have and my heart might be able to take a break from all the clenching and lurching. A fourth part of me screams that it's time for a drink—damn the early hour and the head injury—Bloody Mary at Swallows! Stat! While a fifth part wants to go home and sleep for a few days.

I am at fifths with myself. It's a . . . fractured feeling.

I clear my throat and Hitch pulls his hand away with a self-conscious flex of his fingers. "Yeah." I glance down at my mostly unmarked skin. Faint, hairline breaks in my pale flesh are the only evidence of the fairy attack. "They did heal fast. I was expecting to get a few scars." I shrug. "Good skin, I guess."

He shakes his head. "Good skin or not, there should be scabbing. You haven't had enough time to—"

"You're right." From a medical standpoint, I know he's right, but in all the excitement, I haven't had time to stress about my battle scars—or lack thereof—and I don't want to stress about them now. "Maybe the bites weren't as deep as they looked."

"No, I saw them." Hitch's know-it-all voice is in full effect as his fingers return to my shoulder, spreading the skin tight, searching for the secrets beneath. "You should absolutely have scabbing, at least some kind of—"

"Sorry to disappoint." I pull away, swallowing hard, trying to ignore how desperately I want him to keep touching me. "Other than acquiring some scabs, what else can I do for you?"

He slips off his sunglasses, tucking them into the front pocket of his shirt, making my breath catch. Damn, he's pretty this morning and looking at me with those eyes. *Those* eyes, the ones I remember, the ones that don't think I'm the lowest form of scum ever to be scraped off the bottom of a cesspool. "I think it's more what *I* can do for *you* that you'll be interested in."

"Oh yeah? And what might that be?"

Hitch squints over my shoulder. "I think your friend is innocent. I questioned him this morning."

Thank God. "Finally. Someone who doesn't have their head up their ass."

"I still want to check out the ground where the body was discovered," Hitch continues, "but I don't think we're going to find any serial killer souvenirs.

My gut is saying Grace's murder isn't connected to the others. But even if it is, I don't think Fernando killed Grace or anyone else."

"I know!" The knot of tension at the base of my neck begins to ease. Fern has someone on his side and Hitch isn't here to talk kisses! Double score for me. "Thank you so much. I can't believe Cane and Abe can't see that charging Fernando with murder is ludicrous."

"It's not ludicrous if you're looking at the evidence."

"What is the evidence, if you don't mind me asking?" I ask, suddenly conscious of the men loitering outside the barbershop a block away. A couple of them are Cooper family friends, and won't hesitate to report anything they see or hear. I take another step away from Hitch and try to look casual. "I don't know what they've got on him, and I know I'm not *supposed* to know, but . . ."

"Walk with me." Hitch gestures down the street. "I'll tell you what I know, but if anyone asks—"

"We never had this conversation," I finish, falling into step beside him.

"Right. Unless I say we did."

"Absolutely. You're the big boss. Whatever you say."

"Right." His lips twitch and for a second I think he's going to smile, but he doesn't. "So, as I understand it, a call came in last night from someone saying Fernando sold them a sizeable quantity of illegal drugs. Breeze, in particular."

Breeze. *Crap.* I'm disappointed. Fern knows better. "Someone like who?"

"I don't know. It was an anonymous call."

"An anonymous call?" That's *strangely* timed. "How anonymous? Was it a man or a woman? If it was a townie, I'm sure someone will be able to recognize the voice on the recording."

"Ah, but that's the bitch of it all." His voice slips into his native drawl, the way it used to when we were alone and there was no need to be anything but ourselves. "The recording was mysteriously erased from the system sometime between last night and this morning. They're blaming the temp on phone duty, but . . ."

"Right. Crap." My concerns about Cane and Abe bump up another notch. All you have to do is mention Breeze to a Baton Rouge judge and you can get a warrant to search anyone, anytime, anywhere. A little lie about a call that never came in is all it would have taken to get the DPD into Fernando's.

"That was my feeling." Hitch turns the corner and heads south toward Railroad Street. "Crap. Shady crap, which is why we're having this conversation. I don't think you're in on the shady crap."

I glance up at him, heart doing a few of those weird squeeze-thump-flutter things it does so well when he's around. It shouldn't feel so good to have this man imply that he trusts me—at least not to be an accessory to crookedness—but it does. "Thanks."

"No problem." He spares me the smile he withheld

before. "So the DPD got their warrant and searched the bed and breakfast and found a mini-fridge with Breeze inside in Fernando's storage room."

"How much Breeze?"

"Not enough to hold him on distribution charges. If it hadn't been for the hair tangled in the refrigerator door, he would have been facing a minor possession charge at the very worst."

"Hair . . . Grace's hair?" It's the only thing that makes sense.

Hitch nods. "Cat hair, and a couple of blond hairs that seem to match a sample from Grace's hairbrush that Libby Beauchamp brought in early this morning."

Poor Libby, no wonder she was sobbing in the bayou.

"We won't know if it's Grace's hair until the results get back from the lab in Baton Rogue, but—"

"But it was enough for the judge to hold Fernando without bail." I finish with a curse. This is bullshit, but I can't see that there's much I can do. At least not right now.

"I seriously doubt the hair alone will be enough to get a conviction," Hitch says, "not unless they find something else."

"Which they won't. Fernando didn't do this. They're not going to find jack."

"I wouldn't be so sure," Hitch says. "Fernando told me someone else put the refrigerator in his storage room. He acted like he had an idea who that "someone" was, but he wouldn't name any names. It seemed like he was afraid to say too much."

"Why would he be afraid while he was in police custody? Unless . . ." Unless he's afraid the police can't keep him safe, or . . .

Or that the police are the ones he needs to be afraid of.

Nineteen

This is bad. "Blergh."

Hitch sighs. "Exactly."

"Cane's sister, Amity . . ." I push away the feeling that I'm betraying Cane with every word I speak.

I have to tell Hitch what I know. He's trusted me with a lot of privileged information about this case. The only way to get Fern out of trouble is to return the favor. I can't let an innocent man, a friend, stay in jail for a murder he didn't commit because I'm afraid I might get my boyfriend, or ex-boyfriend or whatever Cane is to me now, in trouble.

"Amity and a friend of hers attacked me outside the police station this morning."

"Attacked you? Physically?"

I nod. "I was getting my head smashed into the pavement a few minutes before you showed up."

Hitch stops, turning to me with concern in his eyes that I try not to take personally. "Are you okay? Any dizziness? Nausea?"

"No, I'm fine." And I am, mostly. My head doesn't hurt nearly as much as it should, all things considered.

"Annabelle, more head trauma is the last thing—"

"Yeah, I know. I'm fine." I wave away his concern and decide to keep my glasses on so he can't get a good look at my eyes. "But Amity had Breeze injection marks under her arms and what looked like a fairy bite near her face."

"That poor family." Hitch crosses his arms. It doesn't take a genius to figure out he's thinking about his own family, but I know there isn't anything I can say to make that old pain any less painful.

I press on in the name of giving us both something else to think about. "She also kept asking me where 'it' was. I'm thinking 'it' is probably the drugs that were missing from the fridge. The full amount that should have come from a Breeze operation the size of the one in that house." I fill Hitch in on my scout of the Breeze house and environs, about the fridge that was missing, and the fact that I'm guessing the cat hair the police found is from my very own Gimpy. "So maybe Fernando is afraid to name his connection because she's his arresting officer's sister?"

"Could be," Hitch says. "But that shouldn't matter."

My stomach drops. "No, it shouldn't." Not if Cane and Abe are playing fair.

"To be honest, I see an internal affairs investigation in the DPD's future," Hitch says. "I'm going to recommend Stephanie stop sharing information and put in a call to the review board in Baton Rouge. If the DPD planted that evidence, then—"

"No. Cane and Abe wouldn't do that. I know them." I pray my words are true. They might have bent the rules to get into Fern's, but they want to find Grace's killer. Her *real* killer. Sketchy methods in the name of justice, I can believe. Obstruction of justice and framing an innocent man, I cannot. "Someone else must have put it there. Amity, or someone else Fern's afraid of."

"Fern?"

"It's a nickname."

"It fits him." Hitch smiles again, a real smile that makes it hard to breathe.

"It does. Jail, however, I'm sure does not," I say. "But I might have another suspect to throw at the police. The man who attacked me last night was also very interested in where *I* put something he was looking for. I'm guessing he and Amity are both hunting for the drugs that weren't in the fridge."

"But why would they think you have them?"

"I don't know. Maybe because I'm friends with Fernando? Or because I tied that woman up yesterday?"

"Or because you're immune and it would be easy for you to hide a stash where very few people could find it." Hitch bites his lip. "But if Amity and this man are both looking for drugs, then why would either of them plant the empty refrigerator in Fernando's storage room?"

"I . . . I don't know." I shake my head, struggling

to clear out the cobwebs. "Maybe the woman who attacked me yesterday planted it, to throw the other two off her trail? Or maybe there's someone else we don't know about yet. But I definitely think the man in the bayou could have something to do with Grace's murder. The footprints outside her window and the ones I took pictures of this morning could be a match. Dom's looking at them now."

"You've been busy this morning." Hitch turns left on Railroad and heads straight for Swallows. Thank God. He must still have his own caffeine dependency to attend to.

"I wanted to take pictures of the crime scene and the Breeze house before this afternoon. I . . . I thought maybe . . ." I hesitate, wondering how honest I should be with the partner of the woman investigating my performance for the FCC. I trust Hitch to help me clear Fernando, but as far as my own life is concerned . . .

"You thought Stephanie might take it easy on you if you showed initiative?" He grunts. "That could work . . . or not. Were you careful not to contaminate the crime scene?"

"Very careful. I used gloves and the whole bit. I'm not a complete waste, you know."

Hitch reaches for the door to Swallows, but doesn't pull it open. "I know you're not." Tension spikes between us, and the morning air suddenly seems hotter, stickier. "So why did you quit?"

I swallow and stare at his white knuckles. I really

don't want to go over this again. "I'm not going to quit; I'm going to help the FBI any way I can," I say, deliberately misunderstanding him. "Come on, let's get a coffee. My treat." I make a grab for the door, but Hitch doesn't move his hand. Our fingers brush, the world slows, and I swear I can hear his heartbeat speed in response to my touch.

"You know what I mean," he says. "Why did you give up?"

"I didn't give up." I pull my hand away.

"Sure looks like it. Your file was of the saddest things I've read in a while." He leans closer while I hope someone will burst through the door and stop this before it gets any worse. "I know I was an asshole yesterday . . ." Hitch's voice drops, low and intimate, touching things in me I don't want to be touched. "But if any of this is because of us . . . because of the way things ended . . ."

No, he isn't going there. Not here and now, on the street in broad daylight.

"I don't want to talk about this." Screw playing it cool; I just want this conversation to end. Five minutes ago.

"Annabelle, you're throwing your life away."

I manage a disdainful laugh. "Spare me the melodrama, Hitch. I'm fine. I like my life. Things are going great."

"Really? You were brilliant, near the top of our class. You could be saving lives. Instead, you're a borderline alcoholic working a job a trained monkey could do," he says, his words making my jaw drop. A trained *monkey*? "Is that great? Is that what you wanted to be when you grew up?"

"This from the guy who drinks a six-pack every night?"

"I'm not an alcoholic."

"Neither am I, borderline or otherwise, and my job is a job that needs to get done." I'm getting angry. Really angry. "And who the hell are you to pass judgment on my life, anyway?"

"Who am I?" He shakes his head. "I was your *friend*. For years. I cared about you. No matter how things ended, I don't want to see you—"

"Give me a break." My laugh is real this time. "Just how arrogant are you?"

His eyes narrow. "I'm not arrogant, I'm concerned."

"It's been *six years*, Hitch. Six. *Years*. I'm not 'throwing my life away' because I'm still carrying a torch for you, believe me." My tone is so harsh I almost buy my own load of crap. "You think entirely too much of yourself."

"Fine." His jaw clenches and his left eyelid does that twitchy thing it does when he's really angry. "Fuck me for giving a shit."

"No, fuck you for being an asshole."

"Right. Fuck me for being an asshole." His hands lift into the air as he backs away from the door. "But if nothing else, you need to wake up and realize how serious this review is. You could be fired or serve jail time if Stephanie—"

"Screw Stephanie," I say. "Really, why don't you go screw Stephanie and leave me the hell alone." I sound jealous and immature and stupid, but I don't care. I just want him to go away, to take the pity in his beautiful blue eyes and scram before I do something embarrassing. Like cry. Or apologize. Or cuss at him some more.

Or worst of all, give in to the temptation to tell him the truth . . .

What would he say if I confess I can't remember how I ended up in bed with his brother? That the world went fuzzy after those first few drinks?

Last night in the dark, with the fear of losing him so close, maybe I could have said the words. I probably should have said them years ago, on the night he came home with the certainty of my guilt in his eyes. But I didn't. He'd been *so certain* that I'd willingly slept with Anton.

And maybe I did. Maybe I told his brother I liked it rough and we went at it all night like bunnies on roofies, just the way he said. I still can't remember. A few too many drinks coming off a triple shift pulling hurricane victims from the wreckage and I blacked out. I was craving oblivion and Anton had been there with a bottle of Jack and an easy smile.

Maybe, I said yes to that oblivion in all its forms . . . Maybe not . . . Either way, it doesn't matter now. The past is the past and no amount of painful truth can change it.

"I'll go." Hitch's soft voice doesn't fool me. He's

still livid. "But keep your damned phone on. If Stephanie or I call you, I want you to answer on the first ring."

"Yes, sir." The sarcasm is so thick you could cut it with a plastic spoon, proving once again that I am a Mature Adult.

Hitch shakes his head, and smiles an ugly smile. "I should have known this was a dumb idea."

"Yes, you should have. I don't need to be saved. Not by you or anyone else."

"Glad we cleared that up," he says. "Just keep your mouth shut about what we discussed. If I find out you gave anyone on the DPD a heads-up about the pending internal affairs review or compromised either of our investigations, I'll—"

"Don't threaten me. Don't you dare." I swallow, torn between the urge to cry and punch Hitch in the gut. Instead I glare my best, skin-melting glare. "I want to find the man who killed Grace, I want to shut down those Breeze houses, and I want my friend out of jail. I want to help. I've been trying to help all fucking morning."

"Good. Then I'll contact you this afternoon. I'll suit up and we'll go have another look at the Breeze house you found and the other three in the area. It will go faster with two people, and there may be places I can't get to easily in the suit." He looks as thrilled by the idea of spending the afternoon with me as I feel. "We'll leave after your review."

"I can't. I have . . . a meeting."

"Cancel it."

"I can't. I have to give Dicker my statement about last night," I lie, determined to get to the Beauchamps and assure Libby they have the wrong man in custody for her sister's murder. She should be on the lookout, careful and watchful for bad guys prowling around. Not to mention that I still want to get another look at those footprints under Grace's window myself.

"Can't it wait?"

"I've already put it off too long. I don't think he'll be happy if I tell him I can't get around to it until tomorrow." Which is why I'm planning to avoid Dicker or going home to check the messages he's left on my machine until he's off duty and it's too late to call him back.

Hitch sighs. "Then we'll go right after. If we leave by three there should still be enough time to make it through all the houses before dark. Bring your gun and your camera."

"I can't bring the gun." I cast another longing look at the door. Why hasn't *someone* come outside? Probably because half the town is watching me argue with the FBI agent through the glass. Damn sunlight. I can't see anything in the window except a reflection of the street. "My license is expired. I'm not supposed to carry until I get it renewed."

"Then why are you wearing it?"

"I just found out."

"You just found out it was expired?" he asks, his expression achieving new levels of disdain.

"I just found out I'd be *arrested* if I keep carrying it with an expired license."

"Your boyfriend is going to arrest you?" There's something in Hitch's voice, the barest hint of jealousy that makes me feel better about my "screw Stephanie" comment.

"He's not my boyfriend . . . not anymore." Is he? Is it really over? The thought makes my throat tight. "I don't think so, anyway."

"Oh." Hitch looks down, as uncomfortable as I am. "Is that because of . . ."

"There was a camera in the squad car." I do my best not to squirm. "He saw what happened."

"Oh . . ." The word hangs in the air, strangling the life out of both of us.

"It's fine. We'll work it out." I grab for the door. I reached my awkward limit ten minutes ago. "So I'll talk to you la—"

"I can talk to him if you want," Hitch cuts in. "Last night was a mistake, just a response to stress. We both know there's nothing between us anymore."

We do? I loathe this new Hitch as much as I ever loved the old one, but still . . . There was something in that kiss last night, and there's something in the way he's looking at me this morning. Surely this energy between us is more than "nothing?"

"I'm in a relationship; you're in a relationship. We don't even like each other," he says, the confirmation that he can't stand me hurting more than I expect. "It seems like you two are close. It would be a shame for you to lose something good because of one little . . . lapse."

The irony of his statement is clearly lost on him, and it would be pointless and painful to remind him that one "lapse" was all it took to destroy everything we built in three years of loving each other.

"So, your girlfriend understands?"

"My fiancée," Hitch says, twisting the knife another quarter-turn. He never asked me to marry him. We talked about "forever," but he never went down on one knee. Maybe he always considered me a loser on some level, even before what happened with Anton, before I gave him a reason to cut me out of his life. "Stephanie knew before we got here that you and I had a past."

Oh God. It's Stephanie. It really is. He's *engaged* to Stephanie. It makes me physically ill. I'll probably yarf if I order that cappuccino I've been craving all morning.

"She knows life-and-death situations can make people do crazy things."

"Crazy," I echo, trying to laugh and failing.

"Crazy and stupid. Things they don't even want to do." His expression couldn't be more serious if he was talking about shooting Breeze. I am a trashy, shameful habit he can't believe he ever indulged. "Nothing like that will ever happen again. Ever."

It feels like I've been slapped in the face. Worse, even. Amity's wallop hurt, but it didn't make me feel so small and misunderstood, so pathetic and exposed.

Hitch hates himself for loving me and considers what happened last night a moment of insanity that was thankfully forgiven by the woman he really loves. Stephanie. Tall, beautiful, has-her-shit-together, FBI agent Stephanie with the dimples and the soft brown eyes. She's the one he goes home to, laughs with, makes love to.

"I'll see you this afternoon." I pull the door open, but Hitch stops me from opening it all the way.

"I mean it. Assuming he isn't charged with misconduct, if you want me to talk to Cane for you, I—"

"Close the door!" Theresa shouts from inside. "I'm not paying to air-condition the fucking street."

I slam the door, nearly catching Hitch's fingers in the process. "I don't want anything from you. I just want you out of town as fast as possible."

"Then we're on the same page." He steps back with a businesslike nod. "Meet me at the gate near where the body was found at three. We can knock one more thing off the list before we go out to the houses."

"See you at three." I open the door and flee into the cool Swallows air, stalking past the usual stool at the front, needing more distance between me and the table full of men at the door. Judging from the harsh whispers that cease the second I step inside, Patrick and his cronies have seen—and maybe even heard—everything.

The backs of my eyes sting and my fingers itch. I can't remember the last time I felt so embarrassed, so cracked open and leaky. Everything I've tried to become is crumbling all around me. The drama of the past few days has chipped away at my amiable apathy, making me care too much, worry too much, and feel, feel, *feeeeel* more than I ever want to feel again. My muscles ache from all the feeling as much as from my various scuffles.

I slide into a booth at the back and toss my glasses onto the table. I bury my face in my hands and struggle to draw long, smooth breaths. How am I going to make it through this day? How am I going to survive a review conducted by my ex-lover's new fiancée? Let alone an afternoon with a family that just lost a child and an early evening spent hunting for serial killer mementos and crawling through Breeze houses with a man whose biggest mistake in life was giving a shit if I live or die?

The twin *thunk*s of two glasses landing near my elbow make me jump and suck in a breath. I look up to see a glass of water, a gently sweating, thick and spicy Bloody Mary with extra celery, and a grim-faced Theresa.

"Looks like you could use one of these," she says, wiping her hands on her apron. "It's Saturday, right?"

I glance at the frosty glass with the liquid calm inside and think about my giant pupils and my review in less than two hours and the big day ahead and all the reasons I should tell Theresa to take the drink away and bring me a cup of coffee and a stack of pancakes. Instead, I wrap my fingers around the Bloody and pull it close.

"Make it two. And a plate of spicy sausage and toast." Vodka doesn't tell on the breath and the spicy sausage will finish the job of keeping my adult breakfast between me, Theresa, and the darkest corner of Swallows.

"Got it, honey. Out in ten." Theresa bustles away, narrow hips twitching, as I tip the glass back and pour a little peace down my throat.

Fuck Hitch and his judgment and labels and holier-than-thou attitude. I don't have a problem; I have a habit. A habit that holds the fear and sadness at a distance, a habit that keeps me from turning into one of the crazy folks who yell at invisible people on the street corner.

Invisible people. *Shit.*

I down the rest of my drink so fast my brain freezes, temples exploding with cold, agony flowing down into my neck. "Fuck, fuck, fuck," I growl beneath my breath as I dig my fingers into my eyes, hunching my shoulders as I wait for the spell to pass.

The moment is so intense that I nearly miss the soft cry and the scuff of shoes on the tile floor. By the time I open my eyes, all I see is a flash of blue dress and tangled black braids disappearing out the back door. The girl's moving too fast for a one hundred percent positive ID, but I can guess who was watching me wince and curse. There's only one kid who comes looking for me and Marcy on Saturday mornings.

It's Deedee. Percy's daughter, Grace's friend, and

one of the only people who might have seen something that could lead the police to the real killer.

I bolt out of the booth and run, following the sound of dress shoes pounding on the pavement in the alley behind Swallows, ignoring the spinning in my head as the vodka and tomato juice hit my empty stomach and rush straight to my brain and the pain that jabs at my eyes as I realize I've rushed outside without my sunglasses.

None of that matters. Deedee matters.

She stops in the shadows a few feet away, eyes wide and shining, damp trails marking her cheeks with rivers of sadness.

Twenty

Hey." I stop, giving Deedee some space.

She's a cornered animal ready to bolt, and I really don't want her to run away. Everything in me is screaming that those tears aren't just for the friend she's lost. They're for herself, inspired by real and present danger. Deedee is terrified. She saw something, and has information that will lead to Grace's killer, I'm sure of it.

Now I just have to figure out how to make her feel that she can trust me . . . the cussing, crazy woman squinting like a mole ripped from its hole.

"I'm sorry, Deedee. I didn't see you or I wouldn't have said that word. Especially not three times." Or four times? How many times did I drop the f-bomb?

My short-term memory is getting cloudy as the vodka swims through my bloodstream, taking me from zero to intoxicated in a startlingly short amount of time. It's just like last night. The alcohol hits me in a way it normally wouldn't, impairing and aggravating instead of soothing. I have to fight to focus on Deedee, to keep from swaying on my feet.

"I . . . I'm sorry."

"You already said that," Deedee says, leaning back against the brick wall behind her and curling her chin to her chest. Her body language tells me to leave her alone, but her eyes peek at me through the braids that have slipped into her face. All isn't lost, not if I can manage to act like a normal human being for a few more minutes.

I stand up straighter, willing away the clouds.

"Yeah, well it was worth saying twice. Marcy would kill me if she knew I was using swear words in public." I figure reminding her that Marcy and I are tight can only help my case.

"She would not." Some of the tension eases from Deedee's shoulders though she stays glued to the wall. "She knows you swear. You swear all the time."

From the mouths of babes . . . Time to shift gears. "Maybe, but I don't think that's what made you cry. Is it?"

Deedee doesn't say a word, only shrinks back into herself.

"You can talk to me," I say, voice as gentle as I can manage. "I promise. You can tell me what's wrong and I'll do my best to make it right."

More silence, but, finally, she speaks in a whisper so soft I can barely hear her over the hum of the air conditioner kicking on behind us. "You can't. Nobody can." Barely heard or not, the words send a chill through me, lifting the hairs on my arms.

"Is this about Grace?" I ask. "About what happened to her?"

Deedee nods, once, twice, before her face crumples. "I took Grace's necklace." Her words end in a sob and fresh tears roll along the pathways already laid on her cheeks.

"You took her necklace?"

"The one with the unicorn." Deedee holds out her hand, revealing a delicate silver chain with a charm dangling from the end. "I took it. I thought she was sleeping. And I *stole* the necklace right off of her."

I can feel her shame echo along my skin, and it makes my heart melt for the kid. "Oh man, Deedee, come here." I open my arms and, surprisingly, she comes to me, flinging her arms around my waist, pressing her tear-streaked face to my stomach. I hug her tight, amazed at how . . . *okay* it feels to hold this little person while she cries, relieved that this seems to be a child-sized hurt instead of something more sinister. "It's okay. We all do things like that, things that we shouldn't and we feel so bad about later. It's okay."

"I just . . . I just wanted it so bad, and Mama said we couldn't afford one like Grace's 'cause it was from Tiffany's in New York, and Grace said it would look ugly on me anyway, 'cause I could never look like a princess like she did," Deedee sobs. "I thought she was sleeping and wouldn't know it was me. But she wasn't, I shoulda known she wasn't. She wouldn't sleep in the barn."

Relief bleeds back into foreboding as the full meaning of "thought she was sleeping" penetrates. Grace must have been dead when Deedee found her. But why was she in the barn? Her body unattended long enough for Deedee to find her and take the necklace? Why would the man with the big shoes leave the body in the barn only to move it outside the gate at a later date?

He wouldn't. And neither would any other killer from the outside. They wouldn't want to risk being discovered by the family.

"Grace was in the barn when you took the necklace?" I ask, needing to make sure I understand what Deedee is saying. If I do, and if it's true, then the chances that the killer is someone Grace knew, maybe even someone from her own family, are about to skyrocket. "She was in the barn when you thought she was asleep?"

"But she wasn't sleeping." Deedee's arms tighten around me.

"But she was in the barn? It's important." I lean back, trying to get a glimpse of her face, and failing when she tucks her chin tighter to her chest. "You have to tell me if Grace was in the barn when you took the necklace, Deedee, and what time it was if you can remember."

"Please, don't tell my mama," she chokes out. "She'll kill me."

"She won't—"

"I don't want to go to jail!"

"I won't tell your mom, and you're not going to go to jail, sweetie." I cup Deedee's chin in my hand and urge her to look at me. "I promise, you're not going to be in trouble. I just need you to tell me if—"

"What's wrong with your eyes?" Deedee asks, arms loosening.

"Nothing. I got hit on the head and it made my eyes look funny." I fight the urge to grab Deedee's shoulders as she begins to back away. Forcing her to stay isn't going to erase the fear creeping across her face or get her to tell me what happened the night she took Grace's necklace. "You don't have to be scared, just tell me if Grace was in the barn. I won't tell anyone that you took the necklace."

"You look like her." Deedee stumbles back another step, fingers closing around the necklace in her hand. "Like she did after she got the magic."

"Like who?" I ask, struggling to be patient. This is why I don't deal well with children. Because they don't make any freaking sense! Having a linear conversation with an eight-year-old is next door to impossible and down the street from exasperating.

"She was bad after she got the magic. She was really bad," Deedee says, tears welling in her eyes again. "She didn't deserve to get everything all the time. She was bad and—and—I'm glad I took her necklace!" She turns and runs, feet flying, disappearing into the sunshine at the end of the alley.

"Deedee, wait!" I call after her, but I know better than to give chase. I'm in no condition to go running after anyone. I'm so dizzy and . . . drowsy. If I let myself, I could lie down in the shade where Deedee just stood and go straight to sleep.

Pass out, you mean.

I close my eyes and suck in a breath of sour, trash-tainted air. No, I'm not going to pass out, not from one measly drink. I'm going to pull it together, go back inside, have some coffee and second breakfast, and try to make sense of a conversation that's probably equal parts truth and fantasy. Deedee is obviously confused, but I believe that she found Grace in the barn and that Grace was probably dead when she took her necklace. Surely she would have woken up if she were alive.

Though . . . how many times have I watched Marcy pick a child up out of bed and hand him over to his parents without the kid so much as snuffling in his sleep? When kids sleep, they sleep hard. Maybe Grace simply drifted off in the barn, slept through Deedee's theft, and was found by the killer sometime later? Maybe—

A sharp buzzing from my back pocket makes me jump. It takes me several seconds longer than it should to realize the buzz is my set-on-vibrate phone ringing, and several seconds longer to pull the thing from my jeans. By the time I get a look at the screen, the call has already been sent to voice mail.

Good. I wouldn't have answered it, anyway.

It's Jin-Sang. Probably calling to yell at me about

something. Work calls on a Saturday are never good news. I'll just wait and check the message. Later. Maybe much later. No need to pick up and actually talk to—

Before I can finish my thought, the phone buzzes again. This time, however, it's someone I want to talk to. Marcy! She'll be able to help me decipher Deedee's kidspeak. I tap the screen.

"Hey, I'm glad you called," I say. "I need to pick your brain."

A moment of silence and then a long sigh from Marcy on the other end.

"Marcy? Are you okay?" A sick feeling settles in my stomach, the kind that always accompanies the certainty that bad news is on the way. "What happened? Is it Traynell? Is he—"

"Annabelle, I need to talk to you. In person," she says, her voice thick with exhaustion. "Could you come by the house?"

"Um . . . sure." It's only a little after ten. I should have time to get to Marcy and back to the police station by twelve. "I'll be over in a few. Do you want me to bring you anything from Swallows? Some pancakes or a hot chocolate or—"

"Just come on over. I'd like to get this over with."

"Marcy, you're freaking me out. What's wrong? Are you mad at me? Is this because I snuck in and got the cat this morning?"

"This isn't about you, honey, it's about me. I'll see you soon." Then she hangs up. Hangs. Up. Without saying goodbye. For a woman who's built her life on the Lord and good manners, it's an unheard-of breach of etiquette. And it scares me. A lot.

Shoving my phone into my pocket, I hurry back into Swallows and drop a twenty on the table where my breakfast and a second Bloody Mary sit waiting next to my glass of water. I down half the water in one big gulp, but can't seem to take my eyes off that second drink.

A little more alcohol might actually make me *less* sleepy. There's nothing worse than one-beer syndrome for making you want to head straight to bed. If I have more, I might rise above the drowsy and feel sharper, more in control.

Or I might be slurring my words by the time I reach Marcy's house. But then, it doesn't seem like I'll be doing much talking. Marcy has to tell me something, something that obviously has her terribly upset. But what?

Cancer. Breast cancer or ovarian cancer or maybe even lung cancer. She used to smoke. It doesn't matter how many years ago she quit, it doesn't matter that—

My hand goes for the Bloody Mary without my conscious approval, but I don't try to stop it from lifting the glass to my lips. Instead, I open my mouth and pour half the drink down my throat, knowing there's no way I'll make it to Marcy's without a little something. I can't think about Marcy having cancer, about losing the only person I have left.

I finish the drink, grab my sunglasses, and head

for the door, grateful for the soothing lap of vodka against the shores of my brain.

"Hey, do you want this to go?" Theresa yells after me.

"No thanks. I'm good." I wave over my shoulder and hurry out into the sunshine, hoping my words will be a self-fulfilling prophecy.

Assuming Gimpy will be fine lounging in the shade of the police station with my bike a little longer, I start toward Marcy's on foot. Biking would be faster, but I don't want to risk a run-in with Cane or Abe or Dicker or any other DPD employee except Dom, who still has my camera, an item I would do best to retrieve before my meeting with Stephanie.

Stephanie, who is *sleeping* with Hitch. Who is *engaged to be married* to Hitch. Who knows that I had *my tongue* in *Hitch's* mouth and his hand up my shirt less than twenty-four hours ago.

"Who am I kidding?" I mutter as I cut through the Greers' backyard. No matter how much kissing up I do, there's no way Stephanie is going to give me a fair shake. Why couldn't Hitch have waited a day or two to confess his sins? At least until Stephanie filed her report?

"Maybe he wants to see me in jail." I kick at a tree root jutting up from the sidewalk and nearly fall on my face. So far, that second drink isn't helping my coordination, but at least I don't feel like passing out anymore. In fact, my senses are still sharper than usual, sharp enough that I hear a woman calling for Deedee a good minute before the battered blue Chevy Impala rounds the corner.

I slow, debating whether to jump into the bushes outside the Tremains' house for a few seconds too long. Percy, the Beauchamps' housekeeper, spots me and sticks a hand out the window, waving so hard that the fat under her arm ripples like there's something alive under her skin. Looking at the way she fills the driver's seat to overflowing, it's hard to believe she gave birth to a wispy girl like Deedee. Percy's a BIG woman. Tall and broad and on her way to being morbidly obese, so massive she has to pull her arm back inside the car in order to stick her head out.

"Mornin', Miss Lee, I was just wonderin' if you've seen Deedee today? She wasn't supposed to leave the house, but when I went out to call her in for breakfast she'd left the yard." Percy's fear for her daughter is plain. Her chubby cheeks sag and a light sweat covers her forehead. "I know she pesters you and Marcy on the weekends, and I—"

"I saw her a few minutes ago," I say. "Over at Swallows. She's fine."

"Thank God," Percy sighs, her hand fluttering to her heart.

"But she ran off without telling me where she was going. Last I saw her, she was heading south on Hammer toward the park."

"Oh, Lord. That girl. I'm just so glad she wasn't . . . I'm just glad she ran off and nothin' else." Percy sighs again and then again, as if she can't quite catch her breath. But then, worrying that your daughter's become the next victim of a serial killer can't be easy. "I'll look for her over near Railroad, then, and I'll see you later."

"You will?"

Percy brakes. "Aren't you coming over for tea?"

Tea. *Great*. Libby is apparently intent on feeding me like a good Southern hostess, no matter what I have to say about it. "Yeah. I guess so. I'll definitely be by this afternoon."

"Good. Miss Libby was working up a sweat in the kitchen when I left, makin' a double batch of her special muffins." Percy's slight smile fades. "I know it'll be good for her to have a visitor, someone to talk to."

"Yeah, I hope so . . . How are you all holding up?" I ask, feeling obligated to pose the expected question, especially since I'm keeping secrets from Percy about her own daughter. But I promised Deedee I wouldn't tell her mom, and I'm not going to break that promise. Just because she's a kid doesn't mean she doesn't deserve her secrets.

"As well as can be expected with all the police and FBI roaming all over the house." Percy's frown makes her cheeks droop until she resembles a basset hound. "It's hard enough for the family without being talked at like a bunch of criminals. It's plain crazy, especially since they've got that man from the bed-and-breakfast in custody already."

"Riiigght." How did Percy know that? As of twenty

minutes ago, the police hadn't released Fernando's identity to the public. Maybe Barbara Beauchamp shared the news with her maid, but not her daughter?

"But the Beauchamps are good people. With God's help, they'll get through this dark time," Percy says, tears shining in her eyes. "We just need to bury that little girl and put this behind us."

The way she says "that little girl" makes me think Grace wasn't a favorite of Percy's, either. Maybe she agreed with her daughter and thought Grace was bad. But how bad?

"Has the family set a date for the funeral?" I ask, nudging Percy's name onto my list of suspects.

"Not yet. They can't, not until the coroner is done with the body. But hopefully in a few days we'll be able to put that sweet baby to rest." Percy swipes her hand across her forehead, catching a bead of sweat that's nearly dropped into her eye. "I better get. I need to find Deedee and head on back to the house."

"See you soon. Good luck." I wave to Percy as she drives away, her words troubling my gut. She seems *too* eager to move on.

Where is the vindictive rage people close to the victim of a violent crime usually feel? Why isn't she more concerned with making sure Fernando is fried in the biggest, nastiest electric chair in Louisiana for what he's allegedly done? Is it just her good Christian heart that knows an eye for an eye isn't the way to inner peace and riches in the heavenly kingdom or whatever? Or is it something more?

Maybe she doesn't want revenge because she knows who *really* killed Grace and it's not someone she thinks should be punished. Maybe herself? Maybe one of the Beauchamps, whom she considers family after years in their service? Or maybe . . . maybe she suspects her own daughter took her dislike of Grace too far?

Shaking my head, I turn toward Marcy's. I can't believe Deedee would hurt Grace, not when she's so devastated by stealing the other girl's necklace that it's breaking her heart. She doesn't have it in her to kill. But maybe her mother doesn't see her daughter the same way? Maybe Percy only seems suspicious because she's trying to protect her daughter for a crime she didn't commit.

The more I turn what I know over in my mind, the more confused I become. Maybe Marcy will be able to shed some light on the issue, or at least help me understand what Deedee meant by "since Grace got the magic."

Is there some book or movie involving magic that's big with kids right now? Some toy or game the girls would have fought over?

"Marcy?" I call, letting myself in the door to the screened-in porch. Marcy will know. She'll help me sort this out . . . after she tells me whatever bad news she has to get off her chest.

I pause in the foyer, skin crawling with anxiety. It *has* to be bad news. There's no other explanation for why Marcy's house has exploded.

The sitting room's filled with half-packed suitcases and every tidy corner of her immaculate front "visi-tin' place" is piled with photo albums, plastic filing cabinets, and two of Traynell's five toolboxes. Clothes sprawl across the couch and Marcy's collection of ceramic babies is already wrapped in newspaper and tucked away in her biggest Tupperware container. The one with the handle.

For some reason, that handle makes me nervous, but not as nervous as the look on Marcy's face when she appears in the doorway to the kitchen, wearing a dirty pink sweatshirt and a tragic expression.

Twenty-one

I've never seen Marcy look dirty, even after a twelve-hour day wrangling two-year-olds, even fresh from working in her garden. Dirt itself usually knows better than to mess with such an immaculate woman. But now . . . Her faded sweatshirt is covered in dust and greasy black streaks, her hair sticks up like clumps of steel wool, and her steady eyes are filled with fear.

I've never seen Marcy afraid, either. It's even scarier than the dirt.

"What happened? What's wrong?" My mind keeps screaming "cancer," but cancer doesn't explain the suitcases, and the wrapped-up knickknacks.

"Traynell and I are leaving," she says, eyes shimmering. "Today. In an hour, maybe less if we can manage."

"What?" *Leaving?* "Why? What's happening? Are you sick? Is Traynell—"

"No. Traynell and I are fine."

"Okay . . ." She's not sick. Then what the . . . "Is

someone else sick? Or is there a family emergency? Because I *know* you're not going on vacation right now, in the middle of an FBI investigation with a—"

"No, we're not going on vacation, honey. We're going away."

"Away," I repeat dumbly, still fighting to make sense of what's happening.

Marcy's gaze drops to the floor. "I don't plan on being here when that agent comes around with her questions. She called this morning to say she had to postpone until tomorrow. I decided to take that as a sign."

"A sign of what?"

"A sign that I should leave town before I go back to prison."

"Wha . . ." My lips go numb and my tongue forgets how to form the "t" sound. What is she talking about? What's happening here? Have I entered the twilight zone somewhere between Swallows and 32 East Maple Street?

"Sit down, Annabelle." Marcy crosses the room, a hitch in her step I've never seen before, as if the process of packing up her beloved home has literally crippled her. She gestures toward the single clothes-free section of the couch. "I've only got a few minutes, but I wanted to—"

"I don't want to sit down." I back away. "I want to know what the fuck you're talking about."

"Don't curse."

"Then don't be crazy," I say, a burst of hysterical

laughter escaping my buzzing lips. "*This* is crazy. You've never been in jail.

"I killed two people. A long time ago, when I was barely fifteen." The earnestness in her voice makes my head spin. "One of them was planned, one wasn't, but I was convicted on both counts. I spent ten years in a maximum-security prison."

"But Marcy . . . I . . . I—I don't understand." I sound about three years old, but I can't help it. It's like someone told me my mom is a killer. But worse. Finding out Mama Lee had offed someone wouldn't be nearly this shocking. I feel like I've been punched in the stomach and shot into outer space. There's nothing left to stand on, nothing solid or sane in the world, no air left to breathe.

"I had my reasons for what I did. I thought they were good ones . . . at the time." The shuttered look on her face makes it clear she doesn't plan on sharing those reasons.

Not here, not now, not with me, the stupid girl who idolized her and been so certain she knew everything there was to know about Marcy. Wonderful, amazing, loving, lives-to-feed-and-take-care-of-people Marcy. Who's devoted her life to social work and children, who grocery shops for every shut-in in town, who takes in stray cats and loves her husband more with every passing decade.

Who also killed two people. And spent ten years in prison.

The paisley wallpaper pulses, crawling off the

walls, making my stomach clench. Tomato juice and stomach acid rise in my throat, burning toward my mouth. I gulp air and close my eyes, swaying slightly on my feet.

"Annabelle? Annabelle?" Marcy's suddenly at my side, thick arm around my waist, holding me up. "Honey, are you okay?"

"I'm fine."

"You don't look fine. You look sick. You—"

"I'm fine." I pull away.

"Annabelle Lee, you should never have left the hospital last night." She crosses her arms and clucks her tongue, actually having the guts to look disappointed. In me. "You need to take care of yourself. You're supposed to be an adult."

"And you're supposed to be Marcy," I shout, and immediately feel awful for it. The hurt in her eyes crushes things inside me, makes me want to pull her in for an "everything's going to be all right" hug the way she's done for me so many times. But I can't. I'm afraid if I put my arms around her, I'll never let go. "I'm sorry. I just . . . You can't run away. Especially for no reason. No one's going to send you to prison," I say, willing her to realize that what she's doing is crazy. "You have bad things in your past, but you had nothing to do with Grace's death or what happened to any of those other girls."

Marcy doesn't say a word, just swallows and studies her nails. All of them are broken down past the quick. Marcy can't grow her nails past the tips of her fingers, they get too weak after all the hand-washing and dishwashing and endless, compulsive cleaning. She can never get things clean enough. She's the straightest, tidiest, non-rule-breakingest person I've ever known.

So why isn't she saying anything? Why?

"Marcy . . ." My voice cracks. I sound like I'm about to cry. "You can stand there and say nothing as long as you want, but I can't believe you would ever hurt a child. Ever."

Her eyes snap to mine. "Of course I wouldn't. Never."

Despite my big words, a part of me breathes a sigh of relief. "I know! Everyone in town knows! You'll have a hundred character witnesses, or more. The FBI might ask questions about your past, but they're not going to—"

"Annabelle, please, honey. Just leave it alone. I have to go."

"No, I won't leave it alone and you don't have to go anywhere. This is the stupidest thing I've ever heard," I say, voice rising. "The police already have a suspect in custody. He's the *wrong* suspect, but they have evidence they think proves he had something to do with the murder. You're not even on their radar, anymore, I'm positive, and I think I have some idea who—"

"I helped Kennedy's father abduct her. I knew Naomi would let her go. I told him exactly when to come get Kennedy off the playground," Marcy says, shocking me into silence once more. "I know she's not dead. I know she's fine and safe and happy, but if I tell the FBI *how* I know . . ." She presses shaking fingers to her temples. "It's just impossible. I have to go."

"But, Marcy . . . why?"

"Kelly didn't take care of that girl." Marcy lifts her chin. "She didn't deserve her."

"I didn't know things were that bad."

"They were." Marcy shuffles to the couch and half collapses into the only clear space. "Kelly's always *on* something. Pain pills, I think. I don't know for sure, but I know she was word-slurring high almost every afternoon when came to pick Kennedy up. Even when she was pregnant with the little brother." Marcy shakes her head. "That precious girl deserved better, and I knew her daddy would take care of her."

"So you decided to help him *take* her?" I can't keep the shock from my tone.

"She's a monster, Annabelle. She left marks on that girl that won't ever heal." The disgust in her tone leaves no doubt she witnessed the evidence of Kennedy's abuse firsthand. "I did what I had to do."

My breath rushes out. "Marcy, there are legal ways to help victims of abuse. You could have testified and helped Kennedy's dad get custody, maybe even helped the younger brother, too. If Kelly's as bad as you say, then that baby shouldn't—"

"Legally, it would have taken months, maybe years, and Kennedy didn't deserve to suffer anymore."

"And there was no reason she had to," I say, exasperated by Marcy's inability to see how extreme her actions had been. "You could have called Child Protective Services, they would have—"

"And they would have done nothing."

"You don't know that."

"I *do* know. Believe me, I *know*," she says, her voice close enough to a shout to make me flinch. She sighs, her shoulders sagging. "Just . . . let it go, Annabelle. There's no point talkin' on things you don't understand."

"I understand, Marcy. I do, but—"

"No, baby. You don't. And I hope you never do." She smiles at me, the love so clear on her face it makes my chest ache. "You've still got a lot of innocence left in you, Mess."

I shake my head. Innocence? *Me?* Has she had her head in the sand for the past twelve years?

"I know you don't think so," she says. "But I know you. You want to think the best of people. You want to believe in this town and the future and good things for the folks you care about. It's one of the things I've always loved about you."

Loved. Past tense. Because she won't be around to do it anymore. My throat gets tight, tighter, tightest. "Please don't leave, Marcy. Please."

"I have to, baby. But promise me you'll be careful. You need to take better care of yourself," she says. "Or marry Cane and let him take care of you. He loves you, and you two would be so happy. I know you would."

"Fine. Maybe I will," I say, shocked that a part

of me is actually considering it. Maybe I will marry Cane. Maybe I'll say "I do," and let him teach me how to love like a grown-up. "But there's no way I'm getting married to anybody without you. Are you going to at least let me know where you are . . . once you get settled?"

Marcy shakes her head. "No, honey."

No. No, with that sad, sad look in her eyes. "So this is . . . good-bye? Forever?" She doesn't say a word. "You're really doing this, no matter what I say. You're really leaving."

"That's why I wanted to see your face," she says, silent tears slipping down her cheeks. "I wanted to—"

"No. Just . . . no." It becomes impossible to swallow past the ostrich egg in my throat. I want to sink through the floor, crawl into the deepest, darkest cave and hide from the finality in Marcy's expression. But the floor isn't quicksand and there are no caves handy. Even if there were, there's no hole dark or deep enough to smother the misery of knowing I'm losing my best friend.

"I can't do this." I back toward the door, blinking fast, trying to keep the tears stinging at the backs of my eyes from falling. "I can't even believe this is happening. I can't . . ." I turn and fumble for the front door handle.

I hear Marcy sigh, but don't turn back around. "Annabelle, wait. Don't leave like this. Come give me a hug, and let me show you the boxes I want you to have."

A hug? Some boxes? As if one hug can last a lifetime, as if any number of knickknacks came make up for her running away from me and this town and everyone who loves her?

"Goodbye. Don't worry, I won't tell anyone about . . . anything." I throw the words over my shoulder as I lunge through the open door, across the porch, and out the screen door onto the street.

And then I run. And run, until my lungs are sodden from the humid air, until sweat leaks down my face and my shirt is stuck to my skin, until my heart pounds and the alcohol in my bloodstream tugs at my muscles, trying to hold me back. But I break through the wall and fly, feet barely touching the ground, mind lost in the rhythm of my rasping breath, running and running and running as if I'll never stop.

I can't believe I've forgotten how good *physically* running away can feel amidst all the other metaphorical fleeing I've done in my life.

In the end, I can't blame Marcy for bolting. I would probably do the same thing. I'm a runner. And now, I'm all alone.

Somehow I end up close to home, though I can't remember how I got there. I cut through a couple of yards and let myself in the back door with my key, too tired to circle all the way around to the front. My legs are trembling with exhaustion, the muscles in my thighs twitching like Hitch's gimpy eyelid.

"Gimpy. Crap." I'd planned to bring the cat home

and crank up the air before I went back to the station, but now there won't be time. I barely have time to grab a shower and change clothes before I have to meet Stephanie.

Or maybe I'll die first.

At the moment, it doesn't sound like a horrible alternative to being interrogated by my ex-lover's fiancée while my other ex-lover lurks in the building, hating me for getting beat up by his sister and not jumping at the opportunity to settle down and make babies.

"Jesus Christ," I curse as my right knee buckles. I barely catch myself on the kitchen table. I'm in bad shape. Awful shape. I need to start a regular exercise program.

Or end it all with a bullet to the brain.

The raw skin on my arm, where the gun holster chafed as I ran, screams for me to go ahead and do it. End it. The gun's right here, nice and handy. A bullet will stop all the various sources of pain—big and small, my fault and not so much my fault—with one sharp *bang*.

"Coward," I mumble. I might be a mess, but I'm not a coward.

I strip off the holster, careful not to touch the blistered place on my arm, and empty my pockets onto the table. A few crumpled dollar bills, a receipt for cat food from the Quik Stop, and my cell phone. A red box on the touch screen reminds me that I haven't listened to Jin-Sang's message . . .

No, Jin-Sang's *messages*, plural. There are two. Looks like he called again while I was running and I didn't notice.

I drop the phone back to the table, pretending I didn't notice that I didn't notice. I have to get through my review. Then I'll check the damn messages and deal with my damned boss.

I limp across the kitchen and grab a glass, running tap water and chugging it. I'm too thirsty to bother with ice or the filtered water in the fridge. So thirsty. Dying of it. Maybe literally dying, whether I pick up my gun or not.

The wall I broke through smacked down on me a half-mile back, crushing my will to run, making me black out for a few minutes. I'd apparently kept walking—I came back to myself on my feet and closer to home than when I faded out—but I still feel wretched. My head throbs like a giant thumb with a splinter pushed deep, and my tongue lies thick and heavy in my mouth. Even swallowing is a challenge. Water runs down my chin and onto my shirt. I shiver, though the air conditioning unit humming away in the otherwise silent house is in the other room.

I freeze with the glass at my lips, hairs rising on the back of my neck.

The other room . . . my bedroom . . . where I *know* I turned off the air conditioner before I left this morning. But now, it chugs and puffs and rattles.

And I suddenly have the feeling I'm not alone.

Careful not to make more noise than I have

already, I sit the glass in the sink and turn back to the kitchen table. I snag the gun from its holster, but don't arm it . . . yet. I don't want to alert my visitor of my presence. Besides, there's a chance it's Cane in the other room. Maybe he came over to talk after filling out Amity's paperwork, let himself in, and decided to stay for a nap.

Except that I locked both doors this morning, and Cane doesn't have a key. No one does, not even Marcy. Whoever is in my home broke in.

As I creep toward the bedroom, I cast a glance at the front door, grateful for the odd design of the house. From where I stand, I can see that the front door is still locked and all the windows shut tight. My intruder must have come in through the bedroom window. It wouldn't be hard to pull out the air conditioning unit, crawl in, and stick the unit back in place.

Especially if you're a man . . . a big man, so long your feet stretch past the end of the bed and your boots dangle in the air even when you're propped up on a mound of pillows.

Even as I arm the gun and aim it at my visitor's midsection, a part of me can't believe there's a stranger in my house. He seems . . . unreal. Maybe it's the way his threadbare blue jeans cling to his obviously well-muscled legs, or how his white T-shirt pops against his out-in-the-sun-all-day tan. Maybe it's the big smile on his face or the long hair—dark blond locks too feminine to top such a masculine form— tumbling over his shoulders.

More likely it's the sky-blue eyes and overall drop-dead gorgeousness of the criminal that make me pause a second too long. No one expects the bad guy to be so . . . *pretty*. Or lounging on the bed with a tattered paperback copy of *The Bourne Identity*, or smiling like he's been looking forward to being discovered. It's too peculiar for my grief-addled brain. It slows my reflexes, makes my trigger finger sluggish, even when Gorgeous flings his book at the wall, revealing a hypodermic needle the size of my hand, and lunges for me.

Before I can shoot or scream or take a step toward the door, he's on me, knocking the gun from my hand. We fall to the floor in a tangle of arms and legs. The breath rushes from my lungs as he straddles my waist and brings one large hand down on my mouth. His skin is dry and rough against my lips, but smells of soap.

Who knows what kind of blood-borne diseases this guy might have, but I would have taken my chances—and a chunk out of his hand—if his thumb hadn't locked beneath my chin, hooking my jaw, pinning my mouth closed.

Biting is out, so I scream. Muffled or not, Bernadette might hear if she's eavesdropping hard enough. I suck in air through my nose and howl for help until Gorgeous grins and sticks his pinky finger in my right nostril. I can still breathe, but . . . but . . . someone else has *their finger in my nose*.

It's such a weird feeling that I freeze up again, giving the man on top of me the chance to jab his needle into my thigh and hit the plunger. For a second, I can't feel anything except the stab of a big-ass needle fighting its way through jeans and skin. Then, whatever he's injected me with hits my bloodstream, and I scream again.

This time, it's a sound of pure, blinding agony. The toxin catches fire, spreading from my leg to my guts to my heart and blooming with a *whoosh* inside my brain. It's like being burned alive from the inside, blood and bone and organs eaten away as I buck and thrash and struggle to find some way out of the pain. But I can't run from my own body. There's no way out, nothing except a slice of black at the edge of my vision, a place I sense there will be no return from should I choose to slip inside.

Still, I might have gone to it, might have leapt unthinking into the abyss if the man hadn't bent down and whispered in my ear.

"Breathe. Breathe, Annabelle. This isn't going to kill you, you're going to be just fine," he says, the certainty in his words cooling the fire, taking the pain to an almost manageable place. "I'm Tucker. I'm here to help. You need what I just gave you. It's going to make it all better."

My eyes flutter open, straining to focus on the face so close to mine.

He pulls back, staring until his look squirms inside me, stealing more fuel from the flames. "But I need you to promise me something, okay? You can't tell anyone about this. Or me. Don't show the injection mark on your leg. Don't ask your doctor for a second opinion. Just forget this happened until you hear from me again. Do you understand?"

I narrow my eyes and wait for him to pull his hand from my mouth so I can scream for help. But he doesn't, he just stares harder, as if my intentions are written on the backs of my eyes.

"Seriously, Red. If you say a word, your life is over," Tucker says, each syllable firm and deliberate. "It won't be me. It'll be someone you'll never see comin' until it's too late. You listen to me now, and do what I say when I make contact, or chances are you won't live to see your next birthday."

Something in his tone, in his expression, in the way his fingers caress my cheek as he lifts his hand, makes me believe. Crazy or not, I can't tell anyone about this. I *won't* tell. He smiles and springs to his feet, heading for the back door. I try to call out, try to sit up, but I'm frozen on the ground.

Still, I hear him loud and clear when he speaks from the doorway, delivering a final warning only a little less confusing than the first. "And stay away from the Breeze house and that woman. She's going to get what's coming to her, for Grace and all the rest of it."

I swallow, but still can't form words. What does he mean? Does he know who killed Grace?

"But if the Big Man sees you talking to her again, you won't get another warning. You'll just get dead.

He knows she's got his stuff," he says, his face appearing at the edge of my vision as he walks a few steps back into the room. "You're just lucky it was me out scouting today and not him. He doesn't want any more new recruits. Not government types like you, anyway. He would have killed you."

"Getting . . . shot up . . . so much better." I force the words out, though my throat is so raw it feels like I've got the world's worst case of strep.

Tucker laughs. "Girl, you have no idea how much better it can get. Just don't trust anyone you can't see. Except me, of course." Slowly, like the Cheshire cat fading out of Wonderland, Tucker's face disappears, until only his bright eyes and killer smile hang in the air. "See you later, Red."

And then he's gone, stomping through the kitchen and out the back door.

Twenty-two

My thoughts race like dominos tumbling over each other in their haste to get to the big finish.

I'm not losing my mind. There *are* invisible people. One of whom shot me up with a drug he swears will help me—though it doesn't appear to be working so far—and others whom I need to "beware." Including the man from the swamp who now knows I don't have his drugs, but isn't interested in keeping "government types" alive.

The rest of Tucker's gobbledy-gook is hard to comprehend, but that much I heard loud and clear. As well as the warning to keep our meeting and my injection a secret, and the strong encouragement to stay away from "her," the one who will pay for killing Grace, the one Tucker saw me talking with today.

Percy. It *has* to be Percy. Tucker must have seen me by her car and decided to come lie in wait at my house. The more I think about it, the more it makes sense. Percy is one of the family, took care of Grace for years, and had complete access. She could have poisoned the girl with her mother's pills a year ago, just as Benny suspected. She could have kidnapped Grace from her room—or even smothered her in her bed—and then carried her to the barn to await the opportunity to dump her body outside the fence. And if Percy is responsible, and if her daughter saw something that made her suspect her mother, it would totally explain Deedee's odd behavior lately.

Her assertion that her mother will "kill her" takes on a whole new meaning, making me flop uselessly on the floor.

Percy is looking for Deedee now. What will she do to her if she finds out Deedee told me about finding Grace in the barn and stealing her necklace? I don't want to believe Percy would hurt her own kid, but she's a big woman. Big enough to do damage, big enough to leave those footprints in the ground outside Grace's window.

Big enough to carry a refrigerator out of the swamp and lug it over to Fernando's, in an attempt to frame him for the murder and throw suspicion off herself and the family. How she's involved in the Breeze operation, I can't say, but the way Tucker said "stuff" makes me certain it's drug stuff. What other kind of "stuff" is going down around here?

Invisible people. More than one. That's definitely "stuff."

Whatever. My gut assures me the voice of reason

is on crack and that Tucker was talking drugs. Selling Breeze would certainly explain how Percy pays for Deedee's nice clothes, and I don't doubt that she's got the guts to get into the drug business. Most people—even those tempted by the big cash payoff of selling Fairy Wind—would be too afraid of a bite to venture out to a Breeze house. But Percy wouldn't have any trouble getting safely in and out of the bayou. She has use of the iron-sided Beauchamp family van and probably even some sort of suit. The storage unit I spotted in the back of the van certainly looked like an iron suit container.

The only piece that doesn't fit is Amity's attack. If she knows Fernando is in on the operation, she has to know Percy is a player, as well. So why was she so certain that *I* was the one hiding the stash?

"She must have already questioned Percy, and Percy made her believe she didn't have it," I tell the ceiling, wincing only slightly. It hurts less to speak than it did a few minutes ago and my tongue actually feels . . . normal. More normal than when I came in after my run.

I do a swift body scan, relieved to find my aching head is also faring better. There's no more throbbing or pounding, only a faint . . . buzzing. It isn't a sound, but a sensation, a low-voltage stream of electricity that courses through my nervous system, keying me up, focusing my energy, enhancing that "sharp" feeling I had this morning in the bayou. It makes me wonder how my eyes are doing.

If only I could move the rest of my body, I might be able to get to a mirror and find out.

Trying to sit up only results in another fish-flop on the floor, and then another, and another, until the frustration of not being able to control my body is replaced by a deep, pressing fear. What if I'm paralyzed? What if that injection lands me in a wheelchair? Will I still feel it's best to keep my mouth shut about my and Tucker's interlude then?

Hell, no. We're calling 911 as soon as you can move your fingers, one part of me insists, while another part assures me that *keeping quiet is our only choice, we* have *to trust this guy, at least until we know more,* and yet another voice—one that sounds a lot like the Marcy of my teen years—reminds me that *the devil always comes wearing a pretty face.*

"He's not the devil," I whisper. I don't believe in the devil.

But then . . . I didn't believe in invisible people until a few minutes ago.

Tucker really *was* invisible when he walked out my door. He was probably invisible when he broke in, as well. That means no one will have seen him coming or going. There will be no witnesses, and a search for the man would prove futile. He can *vanish at will.* Even if I run straight to Cane and have him put out an APB, I'll be shit out of luck. And I would have broken an inplied promise to Tucker. Despite the easy smile, I have a feeling that's a bad idea.

Still, I need some explanation for why I'm going

to be late to my review with Stephanie. Assuming I make it to the station at all. Right now, it's not looking good. I'm still horizontal, muscles twitching, incapable of even dragging myself over to the phone to call for help.

Shit! I have to get up, I have to throw off this poison and—

"Miss Annabelle?" The door creaks on the hinges. "Miss Annabelle?"

Deedee. What's she doing at my house? At my back door, no less?

"Miss Annabelle, are you . . ." Deedee's words end in a gasp. "Miss Annabelle? Are you okay? Are you dead? Miss Annabelle, are you—"

"I'm okay, Deedee." I cut her off before hysteria can morph into a full-fledged meltdown. "I just . . . fell and hurt my back."

"What did you hurt it on?" Deedee's tear-streaked face appears above me, her eyes puffy. Even her lips look swollen, as if she's had one of those epic crying jags that leave your head feeling like an overstuffed pillow filled with snot.

"I just fell. Wrong. I fell wrong." The lie sounds like a lie.

Deedee wrinkles her nose. "You don't look good."

"I'm okay." I try to shrug, but end up twitching my neck. "I'm going to be fine." I hope.

"Can you get up?" she asks.

Can I? Excellent question. "Maybe. With some help."

I will my hand toward her, funneling all my energy into those few muscles, imagining how my shoulder bone should rotate in the socket. After a twitch or two, I achieve movement. Eureka! Maybe that's all I need to do: focus on one piece at a time. Of course, help wouldn't be a bad thing. I'm over the whole "lying on the ground looking up noses" thing. Poor Deedee's is leaking in a major way. If I don't get out from underneath her, it's only a matter of time before I'm christened by snot droplets.

"Just grab it and pull. Don't be afraid." Tentatively, she takes my hand. "Go ahead, pull hard. You won't— Ah!"

My words end in a scream as Deedee hauls me into a seated position with more strength than I was expecting. My back cracks, my tailbone grinds against the hardwood, and for a second I'm afraid I'll fall back onto the floor. Thankfully, my abdominal muscles engage at the last second, clenching tight, holding me in a hunched-over, trollish version of upright.

I gasp, open-mouthed, for air as my brain seeks to assimilate what just happened. It's like I've suffered nerve damage. I can almost feel the electrical impulses hacking through the tall grass that's grown over usually well-cleared neural pathways.

"Sorry," Deedee says, but she looks more fascinated than sorry. "Does it hurt a lot?"

"Yeah. Kind of. Not too bad."

She crouches next to me, peering at my face. "Your skin is really white."

"I'm a really white person. Part of the whole red-head deal," I say, mind drifting back to Tucker.

No one's called me "Red" for years, not since junior high when my hair morphed from carrot top to auburn. The nickname warms my cockles. A little. Not enough to make up for the fact that the man jabbed a needle in my leg and nearly paralyzed me, but it's nice to feel likable and nickname-worthy.

You are pathetic. And insane.

I'm not pathetic or insane. I'm trying to look on the bright side.

"No, you look . . . sick." Deedee pulls her hands from mine. "But your eyes look better."

"They do?" Well, that's good news. My eyes are better. Now, if I can catch my breath, get my stomach muscles to unclench, and stand up, I'll be doing great.

"Yeah . . . they're not like hers anymore."

"You mean Grace's?" I ask, figuring I might as well try to figure out what Deedee's talking about while I cajole my knees into bending. I'm intrigued by the idea that maybe . . . just maybe . . . this isn't crazy kid stuff. "Were Grace's eyes really big like mine were?"

Deedee nods. "After she got the magic."

"What magic? Like . . . a magic trick kit? Or a book or—"

"Like magic. Real magic." She shoots me a look that hints at how frustrating it can be to communicate with stupid adults.

"Like what kind of real magic? Help me out, I'm not a creative thinker."

Deedee shrugs. "I don't know . . . She could move stuff without touching it and, one time, she made her hands disappear. She had no hands. Like, for a whole day."

A shiver runs down my arms, making me wish I could get up and turn off the air conditioning. Invisible hands. It isn't an invisible person, but it's enough to set my mind racing. Grace had the funny eyes, and then she acquired this "magic" and started to disappear. I certainly had the weird eyes . . . but as for the rest of it . . .

My mind flashes on that moment in bed last night when the clock flew across the room—though I would have sworn I didn't touch it—and today, when Amity's head snapped back before my foot connected. Is there a chance that I've contracted whatever Grace had, this . . . catching magic?

"Was Grace ever bitten?" I ask.

"No." Deedee doesn't ask "bitten by what?" Like anyone born after the mutations, she knows there's only one thing you need to worry about being bitten by. "Grace never even left the house. Or hardly ever. Miss Barbara made her stay home after her eyes started lookin' funny. They'd get better sometimes, but she still had to stay inside."

Hmmm . . . I believe Deedee's telling the truth as she knows it, but there's still a chance Grace was bitten. If her wounds healed as quickly as mine, it would have been easy to miss them. And even if a family member knew she'd been bitten, it wouldn't have been strange for Grace's mother to refuse to bring her to a hospital.

A lot of parents conceal fairy bites in hopes of keeping their children from the camps. If the child isn't severely allergic, the family can manage for a time, but the deception never lasts long. Eventually, the kids grow too mad to function. But maybe Grace didn't. Maybe her wounds healed and she acquired this "magic" instead of a case of the crazies.

And maybe . . . maybe Grace's family wasn't worried about fairy bites because they knew Grace was immune.

My mind flashes on the image of her body, ravaged by animals, yet untouched by the Fey, despite the fact that she was out in the bayou for hours before she was found. Grace *must* have been immune, and that's why the fairy bites affected her the way they did.

That's so dumb I'm not even going to comment.

The Voice of Persistent Doom has a point. If immune people were affected by fairy bites—whether in the form of developing magical powers or amazing vanishing skin or anything besides a sour stomach and a bad case of the runs—I would have heard about it. I've seen dozens of immune people with bite scars, and not one of them can move objects with their mind or disappear. Besides, the government would be all over a development like that faster than a fairy swarm on a warm body. There's something I'm missing.

"So Grace looked funny . . . did she act funny too?" I ask. "Was she the one you were saying was bad?"

Deedee's fingers twist in her lap. "Yeah, but I shouldn't have said that. It ain't right to say bad things about dead people."

"It's okay to say bad things if they're the truth. It's always okay to tell the truth." My hand moves to Deedee's without any major mental gymnastics. Thank God. It looks like once I've made contact with a body part, my brain-to-muscle response time is returning to something close to normal. "What did Grace do that was so bad?"

Deedee darts a look over her shoulder, as if she's worried someone might be listening. With effort, I straighten, shifting to get a better look at the door. It's open, but there's no one there. No one I can see, anyway. The knowledge that Tucker or "the Big Man" could be lurking anywhere, anytime, spying on my every move, is probably going to make me paranoid once I've had a chance to think about it. But for now, I concentrate on Deedee, on reassuring her that anything she says won't leave this room.

"Remember when you asked me not to tell your mom what you did? About stealing the necklace?" I ask.

"Yeah."

"Well, do you know what happened right after I saw you?"

"What?" she whispers, gaze lingering on the empty doorway.

"I ran into your mom." Deedee's head snaps around, eyes wide. I hurry on, fingers wrapping around hers in case she decides to run again. "She was worried, so I told her where she might find you, but I did *not* tell her what we talked about. About the necklace or anything else. And I won't. Ever. I promise."

There's a long pause while Deedee checks me out, apparently trying to decide if I'm playing some kind of grown-up trick.

"Even if the police ask you?" she asks.

"Even if the police ask me."

"Even if God asks you? It's a sin to lie to God."

"I won't be lying if I just don't say anything at all." I leave out the part about not being sure I believe in God, figuring the way into a kid's trust isn't by confessing you have theological doubts. "I won't say anything, to anyone. Whatever you tell me will be our secret."

She swallows, casts one last look over her shoulder, and then leans in close. "Grace used to do bad things. With the magic."

Yeah. I got that much, kid. Get busy with the details already!

I do my best impression of a Patient Adult. "What kind of bad things?"

"She . . . She crushed all the bunnies. Every single one. All the bunnies Miss Libby was raising for the charity Easter sale at the church last spring," Deedee says, her voice a terrified whisper and her eyes still busy, searching the room. I get the very strong impression that she's been warned several hundred thousand times never to tell this story, upon penalty of something severe. "I was going to get to have one, my mama said I could. But Grace crushed them all. Even the babies."

Twenty-three

Y ou mean . . . she killed her sister's rabbits?" I try to keep my voice neutral. Deedee sounds sincere, but this story is *hard* to believe. It seems more likely that a precious pink princess who loved unicorns and playing pretend would be *petting* the bunnies and drawing sparkly pictures of their babies, not *killing* them.

And Marcy was so positive that Grace was a nice, normal girl. Marcy . . . who apparently also thinks it's okay to kill people and help fathers kidnap their daughters.

"Are you sure she did it on purpose?" I ask.

Deedee nods, fresh tears in her eyes. "She used the magic. She took the rocks from around the big fountain and dropped them on their heads. Right on top." Deedee's sobbing softly now and snot leaks down her upper lip. I would get her a tissue—if I could move, or if she hadn't just made the gesture futile by swiping her nose with her arm, leaving a glistening trail from her elbow to her wrist.

"You're sure? You *saw* her do this? You saw her carry the rocks—"

"She didn't carry them. She made them move with the magic," Deedee corrects without a second's hesitation, sticking to her story. "And she told me I *had* to watch or she'd tell her mama that I was the one that killed them." She shudders, as if the idea sickens her. As it should. As it *would* anyone but a psychopath or a future serial killer. "I knew Miss Bee wouldn't believe her 'cause she knew Grace was turnin' bad, but I was afraid to leave. I was afraid she'd crush me with the rocks too."

"Wow." The more she speaks, the more I believe. The story is too horrible to be pretend. Deedee's a weird kid, but weird in the "wants to pet mean cats and climb trees in her nice dresses and wipe snot on her arm and leave it there to dry" kind of way, not the "makes up sick and twisted stories to get attention" kind of way.

What if . . . what if Grace really *had been* disturbed? That wouldn't change the fact that she didn't deserve to be killed, but it would certainly add a few people to the list of suspects. Percy still ranks high, but what if she wasn't acting alone, what if she'd been obeying orders like she has every day for the ten years she's worked for the Beauchamps? What if "Miss Bee" regretted adopting a bad seed and wanted out? There aren't many options in a situation like that.

She could have had Grace committed or sent to a home out of state, but how would that have looked to the rest of the Delta royalty? Bad. It would have looked very bad, and Barbara would have lost all those points she gained for adopting an orphan with a heart condition in the first place and a butt load more.

Having a kid in the funny farm for torturing small animals is a good way to become a social outcast, and Barbara seems to value her place at the top more than she values anything. Certainly more than she values her family's safety, or she would have left the Delta years ago. Maybe even more than her children's lives . . . or at least her *adopted* child's life . . .

I keep seeing her on the steps of the Capitol building, so perfectly put together and in such a terrible rush. What was she doing there? Perhaps it was something completely harmless. Or perhaps she was delivering a payment to a top-secret safety deposit box for her trusty maid, the woman who'd done her dirty work for her once again. There's a bank on the ground floor, one of the few that still rents safety deposit boxes.

But could Barbara Beauchamp do something like that? Pay someone to kill her daughter?

No matter how much a part of me likes the story—always ready to believe the worst of anyone who reminds me of my mother—my gut says Percy was acting on her own, with her own motives. If she honestly believed her daughter's life was in danger from a girl who crushed baby bunnies for fun, she might have decided she had no choice . . . that it was either Deedee or Grace.

"That sounds horrible." I pull one leg in with a

slow draaaggg across the floor, and turn to Deedee. "You must have been really scared and sad."

She sighs. "I always wanted a bunny. Even though mama says all they do is sit around and poop all day."

"So you told your mom about what Grace did to the rabbits?" I ask, jumping on the opening she's provided. "What did she think about that?"

Deedee's eyes search mine, confused. "She thought it was gross and bad," she says, the "no, duh" note in her voice making me feel pretty dumb. So far, I've sucked at questioning Deedee like a child. Might as well treat her like an adult and see how far that gets me.

"Right. Of course she did, I just meant . . . did your mom say what she thought should be done about it? How Grace should be punished for killing those animals and scaring you half to death?"

"Mama said Grace was crazy. She said we just had to pray for her to get better." Deedee rolls her eyes, and mutters under her breath. "But I don't see that prayin' ever works. I prayed forever for a necklace like Grace's, but I never got one until I took it."

"Well . . . I guess the Bible does say God helps those who help themselves . . ." I shift my other leg beneath me and prop up one knee, starting to think seriously about standing up. "But I don't think stealing was what the Bible was talking about. Do you?"

"No, prolly not."

"And take it from a person who once had a *lot* of stuff; it's just stuff. It's not going to solve your problems or make you happy." I sound like an after-school special, but I feel strangely obligated to share one of the few lessons I've learned in my life. Good lessons, anyway. "I mean, look at Grace, she had a lot of stuff and she wasn't happy, was she?"

A light sparks in Deedee's dark eyes, as if I might have said something that makes sense. "No, she wasn't, not even before the magic. Even on her birthday, when she got a car that drove around the yard just like a real car."

"See there. She must have been really sad inside if not even something like that could make her happy." I pause, sensing an important bit of information in Deedee's words. "Can you remember when Grace started feeling so sad?"

"She wasn't just sad, she was mad, too. Sad and mad and she never wanted to play with me anymore. Not since her brother James came back to live at the house."

The brother. The mean, cranky brother who treated Libby like an unstable waste of time. Maybe he'd done the same to his other little sister. Or worse. Maybe this doctor in training isn't a healer, but a hurter. I've certainly met my share of sadistic assholes pretending to be medical professionals. It's part of the reason it was so easy to leave med school when things between me and Hitch went to hell. Scarily enough, I can imagine a couple of the doctors I'd known thinking they could get away with "accidentally" overdosing someone who made their lives difficult.

Even if that someone was a six-year-old girl?

Maybe. Horribly, awfully . . . maybe. *Someone* killed Grace. There's no reason that person couldn't be a doctor. Monsters come in every sex, color, and creed, and hold a wide variety of jobs.

"What do you think about Mr. James, Deedee? Is he nice?"

"I don't know." Deedee picks at the dried snot trail on her arm, making me rethink the wisdom of asking for a hand up. "I don't hardly never see him. He's busy. He's going to be a doctor."

"Did you ever see him with Grace? Was he nice to Grace?"

She shrinks. "Grace said . . . Grace said bad things."

"What kind of bad things?" A sound from the other room makes us jump. It's probably just my cup falling over in the sink. Probably. But I can tell from the frightened look in Deedee's eyes that she doesn't think so.

"I . . . I can't tell. I can't tell anything. I shouldn't of told you." Deedee jumps to her feet, hands fisting her dress, fresh tears in her eyes. "Just don't tell."

"I won't, I told you—"

"And don't go to the house, Miss Annabelle. Don't go to Camellia Grove. Not ever never." Deedee turns and runs, streaking out the back door before I can pick my jaw up off the floor.

Holy. Shit. Maybe the murderer really *is* someone at Camellia Grove.

With a grunt and a groan and several gasping

breaths, I drag myself to the baseboard of the bed and pull myself to my feet. I stand on shaking legs, giving my body a few seconds to adjust before taking one halting step and then another toward the kitchen table.

Despite Deedee's warning, I have to go to the plantation and see if I can find out more about who killed Grace. Fernando's life could depend on it. But first, I have to make sure I have backup. Or at least technological support. I need a hidden wire or a pin-sized video camera concealed in an earring . . . or something. Something the FBI is more likely to possess than the Donaldsonville Police Force. Stephanie probably won't want to give me the time of day, let alone access to the FBI's surveillance equipment, but maybe if I kiss up and apologize for—

"Shit." Stephanie. Our meeting. Even before I look over my shoulder, I know I'm late. Still, I'm surprised by just *how* late.

The clock reads nearly one o'clock. *Shit!* I shuffle faster toward the table, my legs thankfully remembering how to function more swiftly than the rest of me. I'm nearly an *hour* late. My ass is grass, dry, patchy, prison grass. Unless I can prove I was incapacitated, or too busy solving the FBI's murder case to make it to the review.

I pluck my phone from the table, ignoring the red dot announcing I have two unheard messages, and scroll down to Cane's name. He warned me to keep my nose out of police business, but surely he'll help if I tell him my future could depend on it. I have to show up at the Beauchamps wearing a wire and catch Percy or James or someone threatening me to keep my mouth shut, or trying to kill me, or something. Anything to prove Fernando is innocent and I'm an upstanding, crime-fighting facilitator who doesn't belong behind bars.

Cane answers on the third ring, his voice hushed and tight. "Where are you?"

"I'm at home, but I won't be for long, I—"

"You need to get over here, Annabelle. Right now."

"I know I'm late," I say. "But something crazy came up.

"Crazy is right. Don't you understand how serious this is?"

"Yes, I do. But this is serious, too." I will him to hear that I'm not screwing around. "Deedee was just here and—"

"I don't care who was there. *Agent Thomas* is here. She's pissed the hell off, and she just got on a secure line to someone with a 228 area code."

"Keesler?" Oh, shit. Oh dear, oh shit.

"I might be able to get her back into the meeting room if I tell her you're on your way, but it might already be too late."

Too late. As in, "taken into custody, carted off to Keesler, and held for a much less cordial review in front of a military judge and jury" kind of too late. Unless I have a good excuse. Which I do. Several good excuses, actually, but none of which I'm prepared to share. I can't tell Stephanie, or anyone else, about Tucker. And I promised not to share anything Deedee told me in confidence. I'm not going to break that promise. Even to save myself. At least not until I'm sure Deedee is safe.

So what the hell am I going to do? How to fast-talk my way out of trouble and into a wireless mic? I turn the problem over in my mind, tumbling it end over end, but can't see a way, not any way out. I'm screwed. I'm completely screwed.

"Annabelle? Are you there?"

"Yeah, I'm here. I'm . . ." *I'm freaking out. I'm fresh out of stories, too tired to think of a good excuse, and I'm pretty sure I'm going to prison.* "I'm on my way, I'll be there in twenty minutes," I lie, hurrying to the junk drawer where I found my key this morning and searching through the wreckage. I'm sure I saw my old college mini-recorder in there somewhere, the one I used to tape lectures so I could nap during class.

"Good . . . and Annabelle . . ."

"Yeah?" I ask, still digging, cursing my stiff, fumbling fingers.

"If you tell anyone I told you this, I'll deny it," Cane says, his words reminding me uncomfortably of Hitch's. "But Stephanie got a call from her partner a couple of hours ago." Hm. Think of the devil. "After she hung up, she asked Dom to start the paperwork to subpoena Theresa Swallows."

"What?" That's weird. Theresa has nothing to do with any of the investigations. She *can't.* I can't deal with another friend on the wrong side of the law. "Why?"

"I guess your ex watched you order some drinks this morning."

"Wh-what?" Hitch was watching me? Spying on me? Acting like he was walking away and then circling back to get confirmation of my lush-i-tude? I curse myself and Theresa for bringing those damned Bloody Marys. I didn't even ask for the first one!

You could have sent it back. She didn't pour it down your throat.

Ugh. Whatever. This is still ten different types of unfair.

"Agent Rideau wants Theresa on record verifying that there was alcohol in those drinks. She wouldn't tell him when he asked nicely, so he's going to have her testimony subpoenaed."

"What! What the fuck? Why?"

"He thinks it's pertinent evidence for your review. I told Agent Thomas the DPD can't get involved since FCC agents are federal employees." Looks like Cane is still on my side, no matter how mean he was this morning. "But that's only going to buy you a day or two, until one of them finds the time to file the paperwork themselves. In the meantime . . . well, you should probably hire a good lawyer."

"Doesn't he have better things to do than ruin my life?" I wail, unable to deal with the thought that I might really need a *lawyer*. "Like solve a murder? Or close down a drug ring?" I finally locate the tape recorder and go back in for batteries, my hand shaking. What's wrong with Hitch? Why is he *doing* this? And what will Theresa say to the judge? She'll have to tell the truth, and what will happen then? An isolated incident might not be that big a deal, but what if Hitch testifies about that empty can he saw in my purse? Shit! How could he do this to me? Who the hell does he think he is? Who the—

The drawer in front of me slams shut with a sharp crack that makes me cry out in surprise. The phone falls from my hand, clattering to the floor and spinning in a slow circle that mocks the racing of my heart.

Distantly, I hear Cane's voice asking if I'm there, if I'm okay, but I just stand there staring at the drawer, breath coming fast, too disturbed to reach for the phone. I didn't touch the damned drawer. I'm *positive* I didn't, certainly not hard enough to make the wood splinter. I'd moved it some other way, using some other part of me that I've only *barely* begun to believe might exist.

Believe it or not, here it comes . . .

Visions of floating rocks and smashed bunnies dance through my head, making it hard to swallow. What if Grace didn't mean to hurt those animals? What if she'd been angry and bad things had just . . . happened? What if she couldn't control her "magic" as well as Deedee thought?

And what if I'm more fucked than I want to believe?

"Annabelle? Annabelle? Are you there?"

I snatch the phone from the floor. "I'm here. Sorry,

I . . . I dropped the phone. I just can't believe this is happening, and I can't talk about it right now. I just can't. Okay?"

"Okay, it's okay. We don't have to talk about anything," Cane says. "You'll get through this. Just get here as fast as you can. Do you want me to send a squad car to—"

"No. Thanks. I'm fine. I'm already on my way." More lies. But I *will* be on my way soon . . . just not on my way to the police station. "Thanks, Cane. And I'm so sorry about Amity and . . . I really . . . I've been thinking of you . . ."

"Me too," he says, then curses softly. "I almost forgot, I had Dicker drop your cat off at Dr. Hollis's office. It was having a fit outside the station."

"Oh no, is Gimpy okay?"

"I think she'll be fine. Maybe she's getting ready to have kittens or something? Her stomach seemed swollen."

"Um, I don't think so." I snatch my gun and holster from the table and start for the door only to curse myself and turn around. "Gimpy's a boy."

"Oh, well . . ."

I rush back into my room, and throw open my closet, searching for something suitable for afternoon tea. I can't show up at Camellia Grove in sweat-soaked clothes, wearing a gun in my armpit. I need to sneak in under the guise of visiting Libby, then find a way to get some incriminating audio from Percy or James.

Or maybe you'll just get a kick-ass recording of a gunshot if the killer's not in the mood to give an evil genius confession before she/he takes care of business.

"Right," Cane says. I know he's talking about the cat. But still . . . his timing makes my nose wrinkle. My plan is a dumb, shitty plan, but it's the only plan I have. I have to make it work.

"Did Dicker talk to the doctor? Did she say what might be wrong?" I grab a brown halter dress with a tiered skirt from its hanger, throw it on the bed, and go digging for the purse that matches. Silk and bare shoulders are a little dressy for afternoon tea, but it's my only dress with matching accessories. The chocolate purse is big enough to fit my gun, cassette recorder, phone . . . and Bernadette's car keys.

My next-door neighbor owes me for all the entertainment I've provided in the past few years. It's time to pay up with the loan of her canary yellow 1964-and-a-half Mustang convertible. Assuming it actually runs. I've never seen her drive it. It just sits in the shed behind our houses, peeking a shy fender from under its tarp, teasing the world with its gloriousness.

"Dicker didn't stick around. The cat gave him a nasty scratch on his hand," Cane says, not sounding particularly grieved by his coworker's injury. "But I'm sure everything will be fine. I gave Dr. Hollis your number."

"Thanks, Cane." I chuck off my shoes and set to work disposing of my pants with stiff fingers, so distracted my mouth continues to function without the consent of my brain. "Talk soon, love you."

I freeze, pants around my knees, skin breaking out in goose bumps. I said it again. Sober. In daylight. Without any excuse to take the words back at a later date.

"I love you too, baby," he says, the warmth in his voice making my throat tight. "See you soon."

He hangs up without waiting for a response—maybe to urge me to hurry, maybe because he knows what a big deal it is for me to say the l-word. Either way, he's going to be really, *really* mad when I don't show up at the station. If I know Cane, I have maybe fifteen minutes before he comes to hunt me down.

Jolting back into motion, I kick off my jeans, toss my tank top, and wrestle into my dress and sandals in record time. My hair is a hopeless tangle, but it'll only be worse after a convertible ride, so I twist it into a clip and pronounce it "good enough." A quick sweep of powder, some lipstick, and a liberal application of laundry-scented body spray—invented by some genius who believes in wearing dirty clothes as much as I do—and I'm ready to dash.

And dash I do, throwing items in my purse as I go, refusing to think about everything that could go wrong in the next half hour. It's time for something to go right. It *has* to go right . . . or I'm going to be in some very serious, maybe even deadly, trouble.

Twenty-four

Y ou can throw your purse anywhere. My mother's out for the afternoon, so no one's going to care," Libby says, smiling at me across the island in the Camellia Grove kitchen.

It really is big enough to *be* an island. A tribe of hunter-gatherer pygmy people could have flourished there unnoticed by man. The oak fixture is twenty feet wide and eight feet deep, and boasts an intimidating slab of granite that would make the room feel weighed down if it weren't just as enormous. The kitchen is three times the size of my house, with a ceiling that arches forty feet in the air.

I feel like I've wandered into the bowels of a medieval castle. I had no idea the kitchen was so immense. All the other rooms in the plantation—the ones I saw on the walking tour when I was a kid—are small and cozy, with tiny beds for tiny people who weren't raised on a steady diet of multivitamins and bovine growth hormones.

"It's okay, I'll hold on to it. Otherwise I'll lose it." I re-cross my legs, and drum my fingers lightly on the oak table, trying to pretend I'm not crawling out of my skin.

So far I've been here ten minutes and have yet to see any sign of Deedee or Percy. Or James. He's home, if the BMW in the driveway is any indication, but apparently choosing not to come greet the company. Libby met me at the door and led me straight back to the kitchen, where she's *still* baking, though four dozen muffins of various flavors sit cooling on the countertop. It must be her version of stress relief, though one has to wonder what she does with all the goodies. She certainly isn't eating them. She looks even thinner standing up than she did in the van.

"Oh, me too. I can never keep up with a purse." She tucks a wisp of blond hair back into her ponytail and grabs her oven mitts. "I even have a hard time with my car keys. I like the kind that click on your belt loop, but Mother says those are tacky."

"Your mom sounds a lot like my mom."

"Really?" I catch the surprised look on Libby's face before she bends to retrieve her latest batch of muffins. I know I don't fit the Southern belle stereotype, but I *did* take the time to put on my fancy dress . . . *for nothing*.

I've also wasted time, furthered the pissed offed-ness of the FBI, and risked almost certain doom, also for nothing if I don't find some way to make this cozy afternoon take a turn for the worse. I need True Crime Confessions, not Muffin Making Musings.

"So where's your mom?" I ask. "Charity work, or liquid lunch with the ladies with a side of Botox?"

Libby laughs as she rises, clutching a pan overflowing with super-sized muffins. She switches off the oven and joins me at the table, setting the muffins on a cooling tray near the tea steeping in a rose-patterned pot. I have to admit they smell pretty damned good. My stomach grumbles, reminding me I missed second breakfast *and* lunch.

"I don't know," she says. "Mother doesn't tell me where she's going. I think she's afraid I'll try to tag along." She rolls her eyes. "As if I'd willingly submit to such torture. Her friends are horrible." Libby smiles, an easy grin that relaxes me and puts me on edge at the same time.

She's so different than she was out in the swamp. Of course, grief is a weird thing. It comes and goes, and then you find yourself laughing and feeling horrible for it, for being alive when the person you love is dead. Libby doesn't seem to feel particularly horrible, but maybe she's just happy to have some time with a female close to her own age.

"I'd rather stay home." She pours two cups to the brim with smoky amber liquid. "Cream or sugar?"

"Yes, both, please. Lots of sugar."

"So . . . I hate to be rude, but I'm just dying to know who the police have in custody." Libby stirs the tea and then passes my cup over before lifting her own—no cream or sugar—to her lips. "Were you able to find out?"

"I was." I stall, sipping my tea, casting surreptitious glances through the picture window. I keep expecting to see Deedee run down the flower-lined path, but so far, not so good. Where is she?

More importantly, where is her mother?

"But you don't think it's the right person." Libby's cup clatters back into its dish.

"No, I don't. He's a friend of mine. It looks like he might have gotten in trouble with some drug stuff, but I'd bet my life he has nothing to do with the murder."

"I knew it." She sighs. "I knew they wouldn't be able to find the killer that fast."

"I'm sorry. I wish I had better news." I wish I could tell her my suspicions, maybe even ask for her help, but I can't trust Libby.

No matter how nice she seems, she's a Beauchamp, and her loyalty lies with her clan. Percy helped raise her, and there's a chance Barbara or James orchestrated Grace's death or even killed her themselves. I highly doubt that Libby would help put one of her own away, especially her brother. She seems pretty attached to him, despite the bossy older sibling routine.

"It's all right." Libby fetches a pair of tongs from the counter and plucks two muffins from the tray, placing one on each of our plates. She sits, and slathers the top of her muffin with butter before scooting the dish and tiny silver knife toward me. "The muffins are strawberry rhubarb. Sweet cream butter cuts the sourness. Makes them a piece of heaven, if I do say so myself."

"Sounds great." I slather away, watching Libby break her steaming muffin open with her fork from the corner of my eye. I expected her to be more upset, or afraid, or . . . something.

"I have a confession to make," Libby says, keeping her eyes on her muffin. "I knew who they had in custody. They told me this morning when I took a sample of Grace's hair by the station."

My fork hovers between my plate and my mouth. She lied to me, and I had no clue. She's good. Really good.

"I'm sorry, Annabelle," she says, big blue eyes meeting mine. "I just . . . I wanted to talk to someone so badly and you've always seemed so nice."

"Nice?"

She smiles. "You're authentic, and I've known so few authentic people. Even James. He used to be so wonderful, but since he went away to school . . . he's just . . ." Her gaze drifts back to the table and one narrow shoulder lifts in an embarrassed shrug. "Anyway. I wanted to try . . . I wanted to be your friend. I should have just asked you over for tea, but I was afraid you wouldn't come. I figured you'd think I was too boring and pathetic to spend time with." She digs into her muffin with a vengeance, shoving two forkfuls in her mouth and chewing with her eyes glued to her plate.

Aw, man. Now I can't be mad. She isn't boring. She *is* a little pathetic, but not nearly as pathetic as I've felt today. "Hey, it's okay. I'm glad you asked me to come. I . . . I could use a friend too."

"You could?" Libby asks with her mouth still full of muffin. Very unladylike. I like her more already.

"I could. It's been a rough couple of days." Said the asshole to the girl with the murdered sister. *God.* I suck at this girlfriend stuff already. "I mean, not as rough as it's been for you and your family, not at all," I hasten to add, "but there have been some—"

"Rough is rough. I understand, I—"

My phone rings, making us breathe twin sighs of relief. I slide my purse off my arm and crack it enough to get my hand inside, hoping my gun is still covered by the makeup bag I threw in at the last minute. "Sorry, I need to check this. Just in case."

"Sure, no problem." Libby waves her hand a few too many times. She still seems nervous. I'll have to reassure her that we're cool.

After I make sure this is someone I *don't* want to talk to. Between work, the police, ex-boyfriends, and the FBI, I can't imagine anyone I'd pick up for, but it's good to know who's sniffing around. It'll give me an idea how much time I have before someone tracks me down.

I find the phone and pull it out in time to see Dr. Hollis's name on the screen. Wow. A *friendly* professional call. Who woulda thought?

"It's about my cat. One second." I tap the green

button. "Dr. Hollis, hey! Thanks for taking a look at Gimpy, I—"

"Hi, Annabelle, I hate to interrupt."

"You're not interrupting. I'm so glad you called. I've been worried."

"I'm sorry. I should have called to get your consent before the surgery, but there wasn't time," she says, her voice tired. "I felt Gimpy's situation was serious enough that I needed to operate right away. If for some reason you don't feel you can cover the cost, I'll completely—"

"No, no, no," I say, heart beating faster. "Whatever it cost, it's fine. I'll pay it. But what kind of surgery was it?"

"His bowels were impacted. An X-ray showed several foreign objects lodged in his intestines. I was concerned they might burst if the obstructions weren't removed immediately."

"Oh, God. It's because he eats weird stuff all the time." I find myself getting sniffly thinking about how adorable it is that Gimpy's a freak who eats plastic fly lures instead of Meow Mix. Who knew I could fall so hard for a stupid cat in just a few days? "I'm going to have to watch him more closely, I mean . . . assuming . . ."

"He came through just fine," she says. "And I think he'll heal nicely. He's obviously a fighter."

"He is. He's a bastard, but I really like him," I say, earning a laugh from Dr. Hollis. "Thanks for taking care of him."

"No problem. I just wanted to call and fill you in," she says. "I'll wash up the things we pulled from his stomach and save them for you."

"You really don't have to." *Ew.* Souvenirs from my cat's innards pretty much top the list of things I can live without.

"Are you sure? There's a heart-shaped hair tie that looks like something my little girl would miss if our cat ate it, and a really nice turquoise ring."

"Oh . . ." Oh. *Ohhhhh.* "Yes, please save those things. And don't wash them, if that's okay. Just stick them in a plastic bag the way they are."

"Really? Are you—"

"I'm very sure." I'm very sure at least one of those objects is a piece of evidence. It has to be Grace's missing hair tie, the companion to the one tangled in her braid when her body was found. Washing it could remove prints or other physical evidence. I'm not sure if fingerprints or blood or DNA can survive a trip through a cat's digestive tract, but better to play it safe than sorry.

"Okay, will do. You can pick those up anytime, and Gimpy will be ready to go home in a day or two."

"Thanks so much, Dr. Hollis. Talk soon." I end the call and clutch my phone to my chest, more rattled than I'd like to admit.

Gimpy ate Grace's hair tie. That would explain how cat hair and Grace hair ended up on the refrigerator. The cat could have carried it back to the Breeze trailer and rubbed it off onto the fridge. Evidence like that will make it harder for a jury to convict Fernando. Assuming he makes it to trial, which I'm not going to. I'm closing in on the killer. I can feel it in my gut.

"Is your cat going to be okay? Is it something serious?" Libby asks.

"He had to have emergency surgery, but Dr. Hollis said he's going to be fine." I reach for my purse, but my phone rings again before I can dump it inside.

I glance down at the screen. Hitch. Probably wondering where the hell I am. "Must have checked all the bars in town already," I mumble, before turning off my ringer and shoving the phone back into my bag. Let him leave a voice mail.

"The bars? Is that the doctor again?"

"No, just . . . someone I don't want to talk to. Not an emergency." Yet. Once he and his partner find me, however . . . *Shit.* I'm running out of time. "Libby, I need to ask you a favor."

"Sure, but you have to try your muffin while you ask. I'm dying to know if you like it," she says with a nervous swallow, as if my enjoyment of her muffin is the fragile thread connecting her to something resembling good self-esteem. "They're best when they're warm."

"Absolutely. They smell great." I grab my fork and stab a hunk of fluffy, steamy goodness. "I was just wondering if you've seen Percy recently. Like, in the past hour or so?" I slip the bite between my lips, and my taste buds do a happy dance. Libby was dead on—the sweet cream butter tames the slightly sour rhubarb into pure fantasticness. I stab another bite, and then another, cursing myself for waiting twenty-eight years to try rhubarb.

"Good?" she asks, uncertainty lingering in her eyes.

"Very. These are amazing. You should bake muffins professionally." What a dumb thing to say. She doesn't have to do anything professionally. She has a trust fund. But thankfully, Libby doesn't seem to think I'm a dweeb. On the contrary, she seems flattered. Really flattered.

"Thank you so much. I'm so glad you're enjoying it." She draws a shaky breath, pinches at the skin on her empty ring finger, and watches me take another bite. My praise has nearly moved her to tears.

Yikes. She's going to have to toughen up if we're going to make this tea-and-muffin thing a friendly habit. She's just a shade or five too emotional for my taste. She brings out the anxious in me, making me wish my tea was tempered with something more serious than cream and sugar.

"Or Deedee. Have you seen her?" I ask. "Percy or Deedee, either one would be good."

"No, I haven't seen Percy or Deedee today." Libby says. "Did you need to speak with them? I can put out a call over the intercom system. Percy usually has Saturday afternoons and Sundays off, but—"

"No, that's fine . . . I . . ." I finish chewing and set

my fork down, knowing what I'm about to confess isn't something best said with my mouth full.

"What is it? Is something wrong?" Libby asks, leaning forward, wide eyes glued to my face. I must look as stressed as I feel.

"I don't know how to say this, but I . . . I think Percy might have something to do with Grace's death. If I'm wrong, I will apologize to her and you and everyone else a hundred thousand times, but . . ."

I fill her in on my suspicions, leaving out the part about her brother or mother potentially being involved. Still, it isn't easy stuff to say. Even dancing around the subject of Grace's personality quirks and potential issues with Deedee makes me squirm. By the time I finish, my throat feels like it's closing up from exposure to pure Awkward.

"So . . . yeah." I tap a toe beneath the table. "I don't know if the police took a look at Percy's shoes, but it might be worth a gander to see if they match the prints outside Grace's window. And they should probably search the barn if they haven't already." I snatch my tea and take a long, thoughtful drink, watching Libby over the rim of the cup.

"I'm overwhelmed." Libby stares down at her hands. "Percy has been a part of our family for years. And Deedee and Grace were good friends."

"Even after the incident with the rabbits?" More throat closing, so bad I have to swallow hard to get my tea down. Blergh. This is scarier than I thought it would be. How am I going to successfully interrogate

Percy or James when even saying things like this in front of Libby freaks me out?

"Who told you about the rabbits?"

"I can't say. I promised I wouldn't."

Libby nods slowly, graciously accepting that I can't betray a confidence. "All right. Well . . . things were tense between the girls after that. But Grace apologized. She was just . . . having a bad day."

"Killing defenseless animals seems more serious than just a bad day." I keep my voice as gentle as possible.

I remember how hard it was to hear anyone say anything negative about Caroline after her death. Knowing she couldn't defend herself made me ten times the protective sister I was when she was alive. Before our camping trip, I would readily agree with people who called her a stuck-up, spoiled ice princess, even though I knew the snob act was just that— an act. It was our shitty family that made Caroline the way she was.

Libby probably has similar reasons for defending Grace, but at this point I need her to cut the bull and be straight with me. Lies aren't going to help us discover if she has a killer living under her roof.

"Listen." I work my jaw, trying to get my throat to relax. "I know she was your sister, and you were close, but—"

"We weren't that close. Not at the end. But I loved her very much." Her fingers worry the skin where her ring usually sits.

Her ring . . . her *ring*. She's missing a ring. Dr. Hollis found a ring . . . inside a cat who lived in the bayou and ate a dead girl's hair tie . . .

"I'm sure you did." I stare at the white band of flesh and wonder things I don't want to wonder. "Um, I know this is a little off topic, but have you lost a ring?"

She looks up, surprised. "Yes, I did. I lost it while I was potting flowers, but I can't seem to find it."

"Really? What did it look like?"

Her fingers still. "It was turquoise," she says. "My birthstone."

Turquoise. Just like the one Dr. Hollis pulled from Gimpy's stomach. There's a chance Gimpy found his way inside the gate to where Libby was doing her potting and scarfed the ring down along with a few petunias, but my gut knows better. My gut knows Gimpy swallowed that ring because it was dropped outside the gate, probably near Grace and the heart-shaped hair tie that drew his eye. Maybe it slipped off in the rain . . . while Libby was wiping her fingerprints off her sister's dead body.

I swallow—trying to think of some gracious way to excuse myself and make a run for the police station—then swallow again. Or at least I *try* to swallow. But the liquid in my mouth simply sits there for a few seconds before finally trickling down my swollen throat.

It isn't emotion that's choking me up; it's some kind of allergic reaction. My tongue tingles and itches and my throat keeps squeezing tighter and tighter, until my next breath leaks out with a wheeze.

"It was Grace's, too. She was born two days after my birthday. She was so beautiful." The tears in Libby's eyes spill over, leaking down her pale cheeks. "I really did love her. She was everything I ever dreamed my daughter would be."

Oh. *Smack*. Literally, I would *smack* myself in the face for not at least suspecting that Grace was Libby's if I weren't in the middle of choking on my own tongue. Barbara Beauchamp didn't just happen to adopt a girl who eerily resembled her older children; she adopted her own granddaughter, keeping the girl in the family while sparing herself the shame of a pregnant unwed teenage daughter. Libby must have been only fifteen or sixteen, and scared to death.

A part of me feels for her. The rest of me fears her. I have to get out of here. I have to tell Hitch and Cane that there's a damned good chance Libby is the killer.

I set my tea back in its saucer and bring a hand to my throat and then to my lips, trying not to panic when I feel just how inflated my face has become. Shit. *Shit!* If I remember my rare food allergies, some people are as allergic to rhubarb as I am to shellfish. I must have hit the allergy jackpot. It's just my luck that I decide to try a new food capable of sending me into anaphylactic shock only minutes before I figure out my new best friend is a murderer.

I fumble with my purse, but my hands are also

swelling, making it impossible to open the simple latch.

"Annabelle? Are you okay? You look—"

"Call . . . 911 . . ." I gasp, praying she'll understand me.

"Let me help you," Libby says, pulling my purse from my lap.

For a second I consider snatching it back, but think better of it. So Libby's going to see my gun? So what? She's seen it before and I don't have time to waste concealing the fact that I'm concealing a weapon. It's getting harder and harder to breathe. I'm guessing I have fifteen or twenty minutes before my throat closes up completely.

Libby grabs the phone, lifts it high above her head . . . and *smashes* it down onto the table with enough force to shatter the glass. Then she turns back to me with frightened eyes, as if *I'm* the one who just destroyed a choking woman's property. "I'm so sorry. I didn't want to hurt you, Annabelle. I really *did* want to be friends. I promise."

Twenty-five

Oh no. Oh hell, no. I curse myself and my crappy poker face. Libby must have smelled my suspicions and decided against letting me share them.

Her hand shakes as she tosses the broken phone onto the table. "Percy told me she talked to Deedee and that all three of you knew about Grace being in the barn . . ."

Okay. So maybe it wasn't my crappy poker face that tipped her off.

"I didn't think I had any other choice." She sucks in a breath and coughs it back up with a sob. "I remembered what you said about the shrimp. So I ground some up. They were . . . They were in the muffin. I'm *so* sorry."

Holy. Southern-fried. Shit. She did this on purpose. She's trying to kill me with a shrimp muffin. It's positively diabolical, Martha Stewart School of Murder with a side of Extra Craftiness.

I dive for my purse, hoping to get to my gun. If I

can't call for help, I can at least make enough noise to attract attention. Or shoot Libby and take my killer out with me.

Libby and I wrestle for the purse for a few seconds—skinny fingers digging into skinnier fingers and knobby knees bumping under the table—but I'm not fit for a struggle. My wheezing becomes choking, choking becomes gasping, and I slide to the floor in a dizzy fog, all focus devoted to the momentous task of sipping in my next breath.

"I'm sorry. I'm so sorry," Libby repeats, her voice rising into hysterical territory. "I'm so—"

"Libby? What's wrong? I heard you all the way in the—" James breaks off with a swift intake of breath. I can just barely see his shiny black shoes through the clawed feet of the table, but I suppose he can see me just fine. "Oh my God. What happened?"

"She, um . . . she-she," Libby stutters. "She-she-she—"

"She what? Spit it out, Libs." James hurries to my side, gently rolling me onto my back and probing at the swollen skin at my neck. I bulge my eyes and jab a finger at Libby, but my words come out as a sickly groan.

"It's okay. Just relax," he says, mistaking my freak-out for antics of the normal "I'm about to die" variety.

"She ate some shellfish by accident," Libby finally spits out. "She said she's allergic."

"Shellfish. That makes sense." James nods, but keeps his eyes on me, continuing to evaluate his patient. "We're going to get you some help. You might be going into anaphylactic shock, but your airways aren't closed. You're going to be fine as long as we get moving." He turns over his shoulder, directing his next words to Libby. "Get the van keys. We'll take her to the ER. It'll be faster than calling the ambulance."

"But I—"

"But nothing. We've got to move. Let's go." James slips his arms under my knees and shoulders and hoists me into the air. I never expected this guy would be my savior, but I'll take a savior in any form I can get.

"No." Libby punctuates her refusal by raising the gun she must have rummaged from my purse while James and I were playing doctor. She takes aim at her brother's chest, clicking off the safety with the air of a woman who knows her way around a firearm.

"Libby? What are you doing?" James asks, as stunned as any innocent man would be. "Where did you get that gun? We—"

"I can't let you take her to the hospital," Libby says with a ragged sob. Fresh tears spill down her cheeks and her nose starts to run. She swipes at it with the back of one hand, reminding me of Deedee and the trail on her tiny arm. God, where *is* Deedee? If she told Percy what she confided in me, she must have done it recently. Like in the sliver of time it took for me to get dressed and get to Camellia Grove. She must be here . . . somewhere, hopefully someplace far from this kitchen.

"Libby, please, she needs immediate treatment." James starts forward, but Libby—and her gun—step into his path.

"She knows." Libby sniffs. "She knows I put the shrimp in her muffin on purpose."

"You what? You—"

"I had to do it." Her bottom lip trembles. "Deedee saw Grace in the barn before I moved her. I don't know when, but she could have seen me put the rag on her face. She could have seen me moving her. She could have seen anything!"

"Well, if you'd just carried her farther from the gate, then this wouldn't—"

"I couldn't."

"You *wouldn't*, because you're too—"

"She was heavy! And I was crying!" Libby screams, then hiccups, then sobs some more.

"Okay, calm down," James says. "We'll figure this out."

Oh. Shit. *Again.* Brother's in on it too. I would punch him in the face if I weren't working so hard to stay alive. As long as I remain limp and relaxed in James' arms, it's possible to pull in shallow breaths, but it might not be for long. I can feel the swelling getting worse, puffing up my cheeks until I can't close my mouth without catching flesh between my teeth.

"Who else knows?" James asks.

"Deedee told Annabelle and Percy," Libby says. "And I think she told Annabelle about the rabbits and my missing ring. I think that's all, but I can't be sure."

"Where are Percy and Deedee now?" James turns first one way and then the other, uncertain what to do with me now that he's decided I'm a necessary casualty.

"Percy's in the cellar. I hit her over the head with the cast-iron skillet and she fell down the stairs. I couldn't find a pulse. I'm pretty sure she's dead." Libby whimpers, as if horrified by her own words. Holy Moses. This woman is on her way to being a mass murderer.

"And where's Deedee?" James asks, fear in his voice.

"I don't know, but she'll probably be back soon."

Thank God. Deedee's okay. For now.

"I don't think she'll go to the police," Libby says, "but we have to decide what to—"

"Dammit, Libby." James curses as he heads across the kitchen. Libby follows, gun floating to her side. "Why did you do this? These people didn't have to die."

"What was I supposed to do?" She eases in front of him, opening a door and flipping a switch on the wall inside. Seconds later, James hustles down a set of stairs into a musty-smelling place I'm betting is the cellar. Where Percy's body lies at the bottom of the stairs, where *my* body will lie if I don't figure some way out of this mess. "If anyone told the police about Grace's body being in the barn, then they would guess it was someone in the house. We're the only ones who have the keys to the barn. And when they find out Grace isn't my adopted sister, they—"

"They won't find out."

"The FBI agent asked for some of my hair. The man came by this morning after the woman left." Libby stops on the stairs, watching James carry me the rest of the way down.

Hitch. He was here and suspicious of Libby. Maybe he'll come back. I cling to the thread of hope as I suck in another desperate breath. I loathe the damsel in distress role as much as any intimacy-and-relationship-avoiding, self-sufficient, modern woman, but at this point, having someone save my ass is my only chance.

"What?" James stumbles off the last step and edges around a large obstacle. From my position in his arms, I can't see anything but the planks of the ceiling and a single yellowed bulb lighting the darkness, and I'm glad of it. I don't want to see the body of a woman I talked to less than an hour ago, a woman I stupidly thought was a murderer.

"Agent Rideau came by while you were on the way to Baton Rouge," Libby says. "He said he needed a sample of my hair."

"And you just *gave* it to him?"

"I had to. If I refused, it would have looked suspicious." Libby stays on the stairs, watching as James moves a bag of potting soil and puts me down on a table in the center of the room. My blood pressure spikes as I imagine being stabbed in the heart with a garden trowel and buried in the rose garden to fertilize Barbara's award-winning Pink Promises.

He won't stab you. All he has to do is wait for you to suffocate and then throw your body in the swamp. Much less mess.

"God, Libby." James stares down at me with a concerned expression. "Now they're going to find out that Grace wasn't adopted. They'll be able to pull DNA from the hair and—"

"I know that, James. I'm not stupid. That's why we have to leave."

"We can't leave. It'll kill Mama if we leave right after—"

"It's going to kill Mama anyway, when she learns what we did. We can't wait. The police are going to find out."

"They'll find out that Grace was your daughter," he says. "But they didn't have to. Mama got the birth certificate out of the safety deposit box and hid it somewhere no one will ever find it."

Not what I'd thought Barbara was doing in Baton Rouge, but it makes sense. She must have known the investigation would lead to questions about Grace and wanted to make sure there was no paper trail connecting Grace and Libby.

"And I was taking care of the rest of it," James says. "I was making sure someone else was going to be blamed for everything."

"I know what you did." Libby takes another step

into the cellar, but still seems reluctant to join James by my side. "You put the refrigerator we found in the swamp in that man's house, with some of Grace's hair."

So *James* had planted the evidence. I *knew* the drugs and the murder were connected. It's good to know that Fernando is as innocent as I thought. My detective instincts aren't completely off base, just off base enough to get me killed.

It's getting harder to breathe, even when I lie still. The beams above me waver and my head feels light enough to float away and leave the mad, mad world behind.

"How did you know?" James asks.

"I told you, I'm not stupid." Libby's voice is soft, hurt, but tender at the same time. "I know you were trying to help, but that man is a good man. He's innocent."

"Innocent people go to jail all the time," James says, turning his back on me to confront Libby directly. It's the perfect opportunity to make a run for it, but I can't. I'm too dizzy, spinny. "We could have gone to the police and said we remembered seeing a man matching his description hanging around the house. We could have waited until he was convicted and then moved away. We—"

"And how would we pay for that?"

"I'm going to find a way to sell the stuff in the refrigerator," James says, answering the burning question of invisible men and Amity Coopers everywhere. Where are the fucking drugs, you ask? Why, *James* has the fucking drugs, thank you very much. "I've got some connections at the hospital. One of the nurses has a brother who—"

"It won't be enough. We're still going to lose the house. Mama only got that extension from the bank because of what happened to Grace. We're not going to be able—"

"Nothing *happened* to Grace." James voice edges towards a yell. "You *killed* her. If you hadn't killed her, *none* of this would be happening."

"If I hadn't killed her, we could never be together," Libby says, pulling my drifting mind back into my body. James and Libby? Together? Like . . . *together* together? "You know that. You know how she was once she saw us in your bedroom. She was out of her mind. She was going to tell Mama."

"Mama knows." James' shoulders slump. "Don't you think Mama knows by now? Grace . . . she . . . she looked just like me when I was a kid."

Oh. Wow. Yeah, *together* together, all right, and *together* together for a long-ass time if James is Grace's father. *Ew.* So, so . . . wrong. I can tolerate a lot in the name of love, but brother-sister relationships are just . . . *ew.* Not to mention genetically unsound. Grace's heart condition and developmental problems suddenly make a lot more sense.

"She was your niece. There was a good reason for the family resemblance," Libby says. "Mama never suspected anything. She still thinks it was that boy at symphony practice. She never would have known if Grace hadn't—"

"Grace never would have told." James turns back to me, disappointment that I'm still conscious etched on his face. "She didn't even understand what she was seeing. She was only five."

"So why did she kill all my rabbits?" Libby finally gets up the guts to come down the stairs, stepping gingerly over a bulky shadow at the bottom. I still can't see Percy's body in the darkness, but there's no doubt that she's dead. Nothing living could lie so terribly still.

"The rabbits were just . . . She was just seeing what she could get away with. And I think she—"

"She hated me, James." Libby steps to James' side, small hands smoothing up and over his shoulders. "You know she did. Why else did she make all the canning jars fall on me while I was in the pantry?"

"We can't prove she did that," James says, but his heart isn't in his argument. "She wasn't even in the room. She was standing outside."

The magic. He's talking about magic, Grace moving things with her mind the way Deedee said she could. The words spark something within me, a fragile thread of hope.

Can I . . . Maybe . . .

"She did it. You know that. Somehow, she did it." Libby shivers and lays her cheek on James' chest. "I could see it in her eyes, the second she decided to punish me. And when she didn't kill me that way, she put that fairy in my bathroom to see if it would do the job."

"She knew it wouldn't kill you."

"No, she didn't. She didn't know for sure. Mama never told her I was immune, only that *she* was, and that's why it was okay not to tell anyone about the bites."

I was right. Grace was immune. She must have inherited it from her mother, the woman who killed her. *God*. I want to live just to see this waste of a woman rot in jail for the rest of her stupid life. How can she stand here and try to justify slaughtering a little girl, no matter what Grace had done?

"She wasn't going to stop until I was dead," Libby says. "She wasn't right in the head after the bites. You know that."

James sniffs. "I know . . . I just . . . I loved her, Libs. I loved her so much."

"I loved her, too," Libby whispers. "But in the end it was her life or *our* life." Libby's eyes meet mine before she takes James' arm and turns him away, making me wonder which "her" she's talking about.

Maybe me, maybe Percy, maybe Grace, maybe all three. At this point it doesn't matter. We're all going to die for Libby and her secret. My skull is a helium balloon filled to bursting and my neck a thread set to snap in two. The pale blond heads a few feet away blur, and when I try for my next breath only a whisper of air makes it into my aching lungs.

I'm done for, unless . . . unless . . .

I shift my attention to the bulb hanging overhead. It's a small chance, but if I can plunge us all into darkness, maybe I can slip off the table and drag myself upstairs in the confusion. Maybe there's a phone in the kitchen, maybe I can force out a cry for help, maybe I'll live until the ambulance and police arrive.

Or not.

Maybe or not, here I come. I close my eyes and think nasty, rage-filled thoughts.

I was angry when the drawer shoved closed on its own, when I kicked Amity before my foot touched her face. Anger had worked before; it might work again. It might be the key to harnessing my new potential.

Forcing fear to the back of my mind, I reach down deep, gathering all the rage Libby and her twisted family have inspired, pooling my hatred into a big, fiery cauldron. I wait until the heat of it burns inside me before I open my eyes and direct my rage at the bulb, willing it to swing, to shatter, to break.

At first, nothing. Nothing. Lots of frustrating, agonizing *nothing*. But then, finally, the bulb . . . twitches. Once, twice, and the filaments burn brighter.

It's happening. I'm *making* it happen. I really am. The wonder of it cools my anger, and the bulb dims once more.

"That's why you're still here." Libby's voice floats to my ears. I ignore her and refocus, homing in on my anger, imagining the light bursting, glass raining down on Libby and James. "That's why you took the drugs. You want a life together as much as . . ."

"Lights out, that's a good idea," a deep voice whispers, so soft beneath Libby's words I can barely hear him, so close I can feel his breath warming the shell of my ear.

Focus shattered, I jerk my head in the stranger's direction, but thick fingers on my cheek urge my attention back to the light. After a second or two, I let him move me. There isn't anything to see, anyway. It's the man from last night, the invisible boogeyman come to take his vengeance.

Tucker's warning that the Big Man knows who has his "stuff" drifts through my mind. I assumed he was talking about Percy—that she was the "her" I shouldn't be caught hanging around with—but Tucker must have seen me talking to Libby out in the swamp. Somehow, he must know that she killed Grace and helped her brother steal the drugs from the Breeze house.

When you're an invisible person, it's probably easy to get the inside scoop on the dastardly doo going down in a small town like Donaldsonville, but I have a feeling this goes deeper than a pair of decent drug runner types working vengeance for a murdered child into their own agenda. The way Tucker said Grace's name . . . it makes me think he and the man now running a calloused finger along my swollen throat knew the girl personally.

"Lights out, girl. I know Tucker gave you what you

need. Now let's see if you've got what it takes," the man whispers. "If you do, I'll see about saving your ass. If not . . ."

The way his words trail off isn't particularly comforting, but at this point he's my only shot at getting out of here alive. If he wants the lights out, then I'll do my damnedest to make it happen. I just have to make the bulb explode, to plunge the room into darkness and then . . . and then . . .

God only knows "what then." Incestuous relationships, murdered sibling-daughters, and stealing drugs from Breeze houses to finance a flight from the law I can understand. But magic and invisible people are still beyond my comprehension.

But maybe not beyond my reach . . .

Anger is even easier to access the second time around. My face is so swollen my eyes are slitting closed and my tongue fills my mouth to overflowing. I'm pulling air down a pathway smaller than a coffee straw. I'll stop breathing soon; die to protect a child killer. Unless I do something. Now.

The bulb twitches again, harder than before, hard enough to make the light flicker and draw the attention of the Beauchamps. Some part of my mind acknowledges that they've stopped talking, but the rest of me thinks only of the light and the glass and the swing, swing, swing of the chain, the swinging that will bring the glass in contact with the wooden beam above it in just a few—

"Freeze! FBI! Put your hands where I can see

them!" The woman's voice cuts through the air seconds before the glass shatters. The cellar is plunged into darkness, but the woman remains silhouetted in the door at the top of the stairs.

Stephanie. She's come to save the day. Or get herself killed.

If I could form words, I would call out a warning, let her know that Libby has a gun and there's a third man in the basement. But I can't speak, I can only flinch as one gun fires and then another, and listen in horror as Stephanie's body tumbles down the stairs.

Twenty-six

Libby and James scream, but the two cries couldn't be more different. Libby's is a scream of shock and despair, as if she can't believe she's shot an FBI agent and sent another innocent human being to their death. James' is a howl of pain—raw, horrible, skin-peeled-from-your-face-while-you're-still-alive, you'd-rather-be-dead-than-feel-anything-like-that kind of pain. Simply *hearing* that scream is its own breed of torture.

My nerve endings wail along with him, and something primitive in my brain demands I run.

Run! Run fast! Now! Before the monster in the darkness gets you too, before—

James' cry ends in a liquid gurgle, a bone-chilling squish, and the layered *karumph* of a limp body hitting the floor.

Run! Now! Run!

Adrenaline dumps into my bloodstream and rockets through my heart, giving me the strength to shift my weight and roll off the table. I land with a thud—

knocking what breath I have left from my body—and writhe on the ground, feeling the fish out of water metaphor with every fiber of my being. Each second that passes without air is an eternity of hyper-aware agony, accompanied by thousands of thoughts jamming into my head, desperate to be thought before I can't think anymore.

I'm not sure I'll ever breathe again, but after a few seconds, I suck in one tiny breath and then another. Bit by bit, oxygen flows in and carbon dioxide out, just enough to keep my soul in my body. I'm on my stomach now, and gravity is helping ease the pressure in my throat enough to keep me alive.

"James? James?" Libby calls, her voice high and hysterical in the dark.

"James isn't here anymore, sugar." The Big Man's voice oozes from the shadows, seeps out of the earth, seeming to come from everywhere and nowhere at the same time. "James is dead."

"No. No! James!" Libby gasps as she falls to her knees, hands blindly searching the floor where James was standing.

Or at least I imagine that's what she's doing. I imagine it so clearly, that I can almost see the moment she finds what's left of her brother, can almost feel the hot, sticky mess coating her fingers.

"James! James! Ja—" Her keening ends in a gag that sends my adrenaline levels spiking once more, reminding me that I have more important things to do than lie here and listen, waiting for my turn to die.

This time, however, I don't make any sudden moves. I force myself onto my hands and knees and start crawling—slow and steady, quiet as a cockroach sneaking in to steal the sugar—toward the stairs. If I can get to Stephanie, maybe she'll have a phone. Or a gun. Or both. Maybe she'll even be alive and able to help me.

"It's done, Libby," the Big Man says, voice calm and smooth, as if he's chatting over tea, not strangling a woman with his bare hands. "It was done even before you broke your promise and let your brother take my stuff."

"I'm sorry." Libby chokes on the words and gags again. "Please. Help James. You can help him. You can bring him back. I'll give you anything you want."

"You don't have anything I want."

"I know where he put the drugs. I know—"

"I found the Breeze in the barn, fourth stall on the left, stashed in the hidey-hole where we used to put Grace's medicine." The man sighs, his disappointment thick and heavy, weighing down the air until it's even harder to breathe. I sway on my hands and knees, dizzy and shaking, but refuse to let myself lie down. If I go down, I won't be getting up again. "Why did you stop giving Grace her shots, Libby? I thought we had an agreement."

Shots. Like the one Tucker gave me? I store the information away, and inch closer to the stairs, willing myself to be as invisible as the man a few feet away.

"I don't know." Libby sobs, the knowledge that she's run out of bargaining chips clear in the clutching sound. "I don't know."

"You do know. You're a smart girl." His tone demands an answer; even *I* can feel that and I don't have a hand around my neck.

"I . . . I wanted to forget about my mistake. I wanted to finally be happy." Libby whimpers as the Big Man expresses his lack of satisfaction with her answer. "Fine! I wanted her to die! I did. I thought she'd die without the shots."

"But she didn't, did she?"

"No." Soft whisper, so soft I wouldn't have heard it if I weren't listening so hard.

"So you smothered her and put her out for the animals."

"James was going to leave. She made him ashamed." Libby sniffs mightily, covering the shuffle of my hands and knees through the dirt.

I'm close now, close enough that I'll have to ease into the light creeping down the stairwell soon. The straining sun barely illuminates the pile of limbs at the bottom of the stairs—not enough for me to make out where Percy's corpse ends and Stephanie's body begins—but it's brighter than the darkness. The Big Man will be able to see me if he looks this way. I have to be ready to move quickly, have to save my energy and rush from the shadows to Stephanie's side at the best possible moment.

"Once she saw us together. Once she knew . . ."

Libby lets out a shuddering breath that I envy. It's a miracle I'm still conscious considering the minuscule amount of oxygen my heart and brain are currently receiving. "It changed everything. It wasn't the same. He was going to leave forever."

"I saw her that morning, before the police found her." The Big Man sounds unimpressed. So am I. I'd seen Grace, too. I'd carried her tragic little body out of the bayou. "Animals had chewed her face off. Did you see that, Libby? What our Grace looked like after you threw her away?"

Libby sobs again, a cry that turns into a yelp of pain. "Please, please! I'm sorry. I'm so sorry. I thought she was evil! I thought she was possessed!"

"You're a good liar, Libby. I always liked that about you . . . before."

Libby gags and the frantic sound of legs churning against the dirt floor fills the air. "Please! Please!" Her words end in a tangled choke as she begins to suffocate in earnest. It's time. I'm not going to get a better chance.

I scramble into the light, ignoring the numbness in my hands and the lightness in my head, hustling as quickly as I can to Stephanie's side. I half fall over Percy's bulk, but force away the horror of touching a dead woman, and lean over to peer into Stephanie's face.

She's alive. I know it immediately, though her eyes are closed and blood covers her chest. Still, she needs medical attention, the sooner the better. She's losing a lot of blood and who knows what internal injuries she sustained during her fall down the stairs. I have to get help. I have to save her life, my life, maybe even wretched Libby's life. I don't want Libby to die here in the dark; I want her to live to suffer for what she did.

I fumble in Stephanie's suit jacket pocket, fingers questing for a phone even as I strain to see where her gun fell when she tumbled down the stairs. Nothing. *Nothing!* Her pockets are empty and the gun nowhere to be found. What the hell am I going to do? There's no way I can make it up the stairs. I'm too dizzy, too—

"My belt," Stephanie whispers. My eyes fly to her face, relieved to see her conscious. "There's . . . another gun . . . on my belt."

I reach for her waist, find the pistol at the small of her back, and work at the heavy snap holding it in place with my thick fingers. My heart races and the room spins. It gets harder to keep my eyes open with every passing second, but still I pull and tug until finally, *finally*, the snap gives with a pop.

I cringe—certain the Big Man heard the sound—but after a moment it becomes clear he's still busy with Libby. She's weeping hysterically now, babbling about being good or better or best, whatever she thinks it will take to spare her life.

"Tell your brother I said hi. I'm sure he's warming up the hot tub in hell for ya," the Big Man says, not a trace of pity in his tone.

"I called . . . for backup," Stephanie whispers,

the effort it takes for her to form words obvious. "Please . . . don't let him . . . hurt me."

Good grief. Isn't *she* the professional who's supposed to be protecting my sorry ass? Still, who am I to judge? I'd be peeing myself if I wasn't fairly certain the Big Man isn't planning to kill me. He might let me choke to death, but he seems like the type who reserves torture for people who've personally offended.

I pat Stephanie's hand, assuming she can see well enough to know why I won't be whispering any words of assurance, and turn back to the weapon, making sure it's ready to fire.

"The baby . . . I don't . . ." She winces and the softest moan slips from her lips. "Lose . . . the baby."

Oh, God. She's pregnant. With her fiancé's child. Hitch's child. The thought would make me physically ill with complicated ex-boyfriend-related emotions at any other time, but we've got much bigger things to worry about right now.

A juicy crunch echoes through the room. Libby stops crying, stops breathing, stops . . . being. I can feel the moment her soul abandons the playing field, leaving me and Stephanie alone in the dark with the Big Man.

The Big Man who knows exactly where we are.

"Annabelle, I'm not real happy right now, as you can probably guess," he says, footsteps landing heavily on the dirt floor as he crosses the room. "This wasn't supposed to happen. *You* weren't supposed to happen." He sighs, the effort-filled exhalation of large man who's exhausted himself with a double murder. "Grace was going to be the last one. She was such a sweet kid, and so . . . powerful."

I fist the gun and sit up, positioning myself between Stephanie and the Big Man, fighting to stay conscious. Stephanie said she called for backup, but until it arrives it's up to me to protect her and the baby.

The baby. *Hitch's* baby.

Does he know she's pregnant? Or will he find out after we're both dead and the autopsies performed? Will he blame me for taking everything he loves away from him? For ruining his life a second time?

"But Grace's sister didn't keep up her end of the bargain. She stopped giving Gracie her shots, and the kid started to lose her damned mind. Now she's dead. It's time to move on. To adapt. That's the name of the game around here." The air stirs, knees crack, and I know he's squatted down to my level. He's close. Close enough to touch, close enough to be certain I'll hit some part of him if I aim the gun hidden in my lap in his direction. "So I'm going to give you a unique opportunity. I know Tucker slipped you a dose without my permission, and I saw the work you did on that lightbulb."

I flinch as the Big Man's fingers brush my knee only inches below where Tucker pierced my jeans with his needle. Slowly, carefully, I move my other hand to conceal the gun. Has he seen it? Does he know? Should I shoot him now, or wait for him to prove that I have no other choice? If I wait, will I get another chance?

"So, there's no reason a shrimp muffin should be making you look like the goddamned kid from *Mask*. You ever seen that movie? The one with Cher? Damned fine film, and that woman looks *good* on a motorcycle." He laughs, a genuine chuckle, as if he's truly put the horror of the last few minutes behind him. That laugh scares me. A lot. Enough to edge the gun ever so slowly in his direction. "You ever ridden a motorcycle, Annabelle? I think you'd look good on a chopper. Get people to take you more seriously than that bicycle of yours."

The barrel of the gun peeks through my fingers and tilts up, up, toward the sound of his voice, stopping where I guess his torso would be if I could see it. My heart races impossibly faster, until I wonder if it will actually burst from my chest.

"Let me tell you what," the Big Man says, shifting his weight, making me second-guess my aim and my sweat-slick finger ease off the trigger. "If you get your act together, take care of yourself and your friend over there, and prove you're more than one unlucky *pichouette*, then I'll buy you a real bike myself." His knees crack again as he stands. "How's that sound?"

It sounds stupid, *really* stupid. The only good news is that it doesn't seem like he's going to kill us himself. He's going to let us take our chances on whether help will arrive in time.

The stairs creak as he climbs toward the light. I let the gun fall back into my lap. There's no reason to shoot him, not if he isn't posing a direct threat to my or Stephanie's safety. It isn't my job to play judge and jury for what he did to the Beauchamp kids, especially not when I had similar impulses myself. Minus the torture.

"I'll be locking this door from the inside and arming the plantation security system," the Big Man says from the top of the stairs. The door swings shut but for a few inches, ensuring it's too late for me to rethink my decision not to shoot the bastard. "The FBI lady might live long enough for the cavalry to ride in and save the day, but you're about two minutes from pitching over, Annabelle. Better reach down deep and figure this shit out."

The door slams, plunging the cellar into complete darkness, leaving me alone with a dying pregnant woman, three dead bodies, and nothing to hold on to except a gun and the age-old question of whether it's better to die of asphyxiation brought on by anaphylactic shock or a bullet to the brain.

I throw the gun into the dark, knowing it's better to be unarmed than in possession of such a tempting out. I have to keep fighting, have to "reach down deep and shit myself," or whatever it is the crazy man told me to do.

"Who . . . who . . ." Stephanie sucks in a breath that's too gurgly for my liking. "I . . . couldn't . . . I couldn't see . . ."

She couldn't see him, either. So at least I'm not crazy. That's good to know.

Not just good. Vital. He really is invisible. Grace really did make things move with her mind. And so did you. Pull your head out of your ass and do it again. Before it's too late.

The inner voice . . . it might have a point for once in its worthless, self-bashing life. I made that light-bulb move. I shifted matter with my mind. And what is my body if not matter? There's a chance . . . if I focus . . . if I "reach down deep."

I start with my throat, imagining the walls of tissue receding, the swelling fading away until I can pull in a deep, cleansing breath. I visualize so hard it feels like my skull is turning inside out, but nothing happens. Nothing. Nothing, fucking, *nothing*.

And then Stephanie has to go and open her big mouth. "He . . . still . . . loves you. He just won't . . . admit it. It's why . . . I wanted to punish you. For him."

Hurt and rage spike inside me. How dare she? How dare she think she has any right to "punish me"? How dare she talk about Hitch and me and what either of us might feel, as if it's her business? How dare she force me to spend my last few minutes of life listening to her clear her fucking conscience?

The anger washes through my cells, honing my energy to a knifepoint. A few seconds later, the pressure on my throat abates enough for me to pull in a breath, a real breath, one that washes through me from head to toe. My brain celebrates the influx of oxygen by ordering my mouth to tell Stephanie to "shut up."

Except it comes out more like "shuh uh," since my tongue still lies thick and useless in my mouth and my lips are puffed to three times their normal size.

Better than five times.

Yes. Yes, it is. At this rate, I might not be checking out today. If I can just stay angry, I might be—

"I requested this . . . assignment," she says. "I thought if he saw you . . . were a failure . . . I thought . . ."

Anger achieved. I visualize my face smoothing, lips shrinking, eyes opening wide, then move on to my hands. I'll need my fingers in good working condition to slap Stephanie across her stupid face.

Except that I can't slap her. Because I don't go around slapping people who haven't slapped me first, and because she's pregnant. *Pregnant.* She's having Hitch's child and they will be connected forever, no matter what. The thought is so painful it makes me want to scream, summoning a fresh wave of anger and grief, banishing the knots from my stomach and the puff from my cheeks.

"I'm . . . sorry." Stephanie moans again, a mewl of pain that makes me hurt for her in spite of my anger. "It was a mistake."

"Shuh up," I say again, words clearer this time. "You uh hurt. And bleeding."

"But I—"

"Shuh up." I'm pretty sure I'm going to live—at

least until help arrives. It's time to make sure Stephanie isn't going to check out before I can use everything she's told me to blackmail her into writing me a stellar review recommending a full pardon for my mistake out in the swamp.

My hands reach through the darkness, finding the sleeve of her jacket and patting over to the shoulder where I think most of the blood is coming from. The second my fingertips smooth over the entry wound, I know she's in trouble. I'm willing to bet serious cash the bullet's gone into the pleural space surrounding her left lung, causing part of it to collapse. A doctor will need to listen with a stethoscope and maybe order an EKG to be sure, but I just . . . *know* what's happened. I can almost see it, all the sad pink tissue straining to pull in breath despite the screwed state of the air pressure in her chest.

Pneumothorax doesn't have to be deadly, but it's certainly a medical emergency. Depending on the severity of the collapse, she could suffer from hypoxemia—insufficient oxygen in the blood—within a few minutes. And if the oxygen levels get too low . . .

"Tell him . . . I love him." Stephanie sniffs, her voice rich with grief and the knowledge that she might not snap back from this. "Don't tell him . . . I knew . . . about . . . the baby."

Well . . . there's one question answered. Hitch doesn't know. And if I don't do something, he might not know until it's too late for that baby to be anything but one more thing to cry about.

"I'm not going to tell him. You're going to tell him." I place my hand over her chest, send out a quick prayer to that God I'm not sure I believe in, close my eyes, and think. Hard. As hard as I've ever thought.

I think about my mother and father and the way they threw me away, even before Caroline's death. I think about Grace and the adulthood she'll never have, about Hitch's brother and what he did when I still had a hint of "young and trusting" left inside me. I think of poor Deedee without a mother, and James and Libby and their arrogant assurance that they were worth more than the rest of us, and innocent Fernando who could have spent his life behind bars for a crime he didn't commit.

I think and I think and I send all the furies I've summoned into Stephanie's lung, willing it to expand, to recover, to heal.

But even as I do, a part of me can't stop thinking about dead rabbits. About how much easier it would be to use this rage inside me for something else. Something evil.

Twenty-seven

Three and a half weeks later . . .

September is a sweaty, sticky, summer month in the Deep South. Days creep by, the heat a drug that boils your brain and leaves you too spent to do anything not absolutely necessary to life.

But September nights . . . The nights can be downright glorious.

Cane and I linger under the shade tree where a few rare fireflies drift in and out of the gathering darkness. A late summer wind whips down the street, carrying the smell of magnolia, the screams of the neighborhood kids riding their bikes, and the songs of the Junkyard Kings, something bluesy about the women who've done them wrong. As if any of them has touched a woman in the past decade. But the song is nice. More than nice. It's a lovely evening, one that will come damned close to perfect if Cane lets me convince him to stay.

"Come on, you're off duty in ten minutes." I want to flick open the snaps at the top of his uniform shirt, but keep my hands at my sides. We've been out to dinner a few times since that day at Camellia Grove, but physically we're on a "time out" until I decide things that are too big for me to decide right now. "I made a pitcher of mojitos, and Fern's pouring three glasses."

"No. I don't want to interrupt your girl talk."

"You won't. We can girl-talk with you here. And Fern's not mad at you anymore."

Cane grunts as if he doesn't quite believe me. "That's forgiving of him."

"He's a forgiving guy. And he knows you were led astray." I shift closer, nudging his hip with mine. "So stay. Have a drink on the porch." I figure my best course of action is to get Cane drunk enough that he forgets about happily ever after and focuses on happy for now.

So far, he's having none of it.

"I've gotta get to the shuttle," Cane says. "I told Mama I'd head into Baton Rouge and grab a few things she can't get here in town. You need anything while I'm there?"

I shake my head. Screw Baton Rouge. I haven't been there since the FCC—*cough*, Jin-Sang, *the ass*—suspended me for a month.

Despite Stephanie's recommendation that I be reinstated, I'm still on the not-fit-to-scoop-poop list. But whatever. It's probably for the best. The bayou has been wild the past few weeks, with immune teams from Keesler raiding Breeze houses and collecting people from the swamp like crazy. Including Skanky, who I could barely keep from hugging when I saw her alive.

But I didn't hug her. And I didn't confirm any of her nutsy stories about the invisible people *really* running her Breeze operation, either. Cane didn't believe her, of course. No one did. Just like no one would believe me if I was stupid enough to open my mouth about Tucker and the Big Man. Everyone else thinks the Big Man is just a garden-variety bad guy.

The footprints outside Grace's window and the footprints of the man who attacked me were an exact match. I know now that the Big Man was probably watching over Grace, trying to keep her safe from her own family, but there's no way I can tell the police that, either.

Stephanie is the only other person who's *not* seen the Big Man—Fernando dealt solely with Amity for his Breeze, and Amity isn't doing much talking about invisible people or anything else from the camp at Keesler. I'd briefly considered e-mailing Stephanie about it, but decided it was best to let it go. She must have convinced herself there's another explanation. Just like there's another explanation for how her lung reestablished pressure by the time Hitch and the DPD broke into the big house and found us down in the basement. There'd certainly been nothing about invisible people or regenerative powers in her report, though she *did* mention seeing me swollen from an allergic reaction caused by Libby's would-be killer shrimp muffins.

An allergic reaction I don't have anymore. I've had crawfish three times this week alone. It's as yummy as it always smelled.

"Maybe some frozen crawfish tails?" I ask, realizing I'm running low. "If you have room in your cooler."

"I've got room," Cane says, brow furrowing in a way that makes me want to smooth my fingers across his scruffy head. I miss his head. I miss a lot of things about him. "But are you sure it's smart to keep eating those things? What if your allergy comes back?"

"It won't."

"Seems dangerous to me."

"What can I say? I'm wild and untamed."

Cane laughs and threads his fingers through mine. "Tell me about it."

And suddenly we're not talking about crawfish anymore, we're talking about us, but it's . . . okay. There's no anger in his voice, just that same patient, persistent affection. He'll wait. At least for a little longer. Maybe a lot longer. When he leans down to kiss me, pressing those soft, full lips to mine, I can feel how deep his feelings run. Cane's love is a still, quiet pool that I could dive into and maybe never touch bottom.

As my lips move against his and my breath grows faster, I wonder if maybe I should jump, just dive in and trust that I can learn to be all the things he needs me to be.

"Have a good night, Lee-lee," he whispers, and presses one last kiss to my forehead.

"You too," I say, heart tugging in my chest as he slips into his cruiser. "Tell your mom 'hi' for me."

He smiles, his dark eyes sparkling in the fading light. "Will do. See you Sunday."

"Sunday." I wave goodbye until he disappears down the street before turning back to the house. Fern slams out the screen door a second later, confirming that he's been watching me and Cane, waiting for a good moment to interrupt. Still, he knows better than to say anything about Cane's departure.

"You sure you don't have some Cuban in you?" he asks, swirling the icy drinks in his hand as he bounces down the porch steps. He doesn't look too bummed that there'll only be two drinking tonight. Maybe he hasn't forgiven Cane as completely as he insists. "Because these are *amazing*."

Or maybe he's just glad there will more mojitos for us.

He hands me my drink and claims the hammock, leaving me the plastic folding chair. I flop into it just as another strong breeze sweeps through the front yard, making the leaves whisper. It really is a lovely evening, one of many I've had in the past few weeks filled with drawn-out sittin' sessions in the yard with Fernando or Theresa and her sisters or Bernadette, who's finally stopped listening at the window and joined the world.

Since the afternoon I borrowed her car we've been driving in her convertible six or seven times.

I find driving therapeutic and Bernadette unexpectedly charming. She's no Marcy, but I enjoy her stories of Donaldsonville in its prime, of days when the river carried an endless stream of fascinating people to our town. In the time before the dam, and the poverty, and the crime, and the fairies.

Always the fairies.

They come to me almost every night now, filling my dreams with their strange language that—in my crazier moments—I swear I can understand. I do my best to ignore them. For now. I need time. To rest, to recover, to make sense of the impossible things that happened in the darkness beneath Camellia Grove.

"This mojito tastes exactly like what Granny used to slip in my sippy cup." Fern sighs and smacks his lips. "*Exactly*. You're hiding a spic in that family tree of yours, I'd put money on it."

"Nope. No spic. Just Irish and more Irish and a couple of cousin-lovers way back." I take a slow pull on my drink, relishing the perfect mix of lime and cane sugar. It *is* a damned fine mojito, if I do say so myself. I love the way the rum lurks beneath the rest of the drink, secretive and so easily underestimated until it swirls through your head with a sudden one-two punch.

Ahh . . . sweet punch. So nice. So very nice. I'm so glad the only thing I'm good at quitting is quitting itself.

I lasted a day and a half without liquor, until Hitch called from the hospital in New Orleans to assure me that Stephanie and the baby were going to be fine. He sounded so happy. So . . . complete. I decided I just *had* to help him celebrate with a shot or seven of Jack Daniel's and a long cry in the shower. The next day, I bought some beer and other sundry supplies and continued with business as usual.

"You know you can't say that word, right? Only Hispanic people can reclaim that shit. You're going to have to stick with reclaiming 'slut,'" Fern says, but the joke falls flat.

We're still recovering from our brief falling-out after he was released from prison, when I wasn't sure I could forgive him for the lies and the Breeze. In the end, I had no choice. With Marcy gone and Cane and I still on the fence while I decide if I'm ready to Commit, I've been in dire need of companionship.

Besides, I've hardly been a slut *lately*. Aside from a few graphic dreams, I've been a nun. A lonely nun. A nun who's realized the reason she can't promise forever to the second man she ever loved is because she never really fell out of love with the first. Of course, it's far too late to do anything about that. Too late to tell the truths I held back, too late to show Hitch I'm still the girl he thought I was . . . deep down.

"Thinking about him?" Fern asks, humor leaving his tone.

"No," I lie.

"Good, he's not worth it."

We both know which "he" he's talking about, and it isn't the tall, dark, and handsome cop who just drove away. It's the man with the fiancée and the baby due in February, who I'll probably never see again now that Grace's murder is solved and the Breeze houses near Donaldsonville dismantled.

I know I should forget about him, pretend he's dead and buried, but I can't. He comes to me in my dreams, too—sometimes angry, sometimes laughing like we never lost each other. The happy Hitch dreams are the worst. Those are the ones that make me wake up in physical pain, aching all over for what could have been. Sometimes, on those nights, I reach for the phone and dial, needing to talk to Marcy so badly that I forget she's not going to pick up.

Marcy doesn't seem to be coming back, despite the fact that no charges were filed and most people assume she's away caring for a sick relative. That's the story she fed Regina, the woman who took over for her at Blessed Hands. That's also the story I fed Deedee when she ran away from Sweet Haven. She showed up at my place in the middle of the night last week, begging me to call Marcy and ask her if she'd adopt her.

"Sorry, honey, I don't have her number and her . . . aunt is really sick," I said, hating the lie and the fact that I couldn't listen to that voice inside that said maybe I could take care of Deedee . . . maybe just for a little while . . . until Marcy gets back . . .

"Gotta take a piss. You want me to go for you?"

Fern rolls off the hammock with one smooth movement, keeping his empty glass perfectly balanced in one hand.

"No, but get me a refill on your way out." I hand him my cup and squirm my bare feet deeper into the grass. It's nice to have grass. I'm glad I let Bernadette convince me to lay sod.

Now if I can keep it alive, we'll see about other, larger, more delicate things, like a child whose mother's death I feel responsible for, even though it wasn't my fault. Really. At least not entirely.

"More ice?"

"No, just booze," I say.

Fern laughs and disappears into the house. The screen door smacks closed behind him, leaving me alone for the first time since I fetched my mail and the blue envelope with my name on it from my box. I didn't want to open it in front of Cane or Fernando . . . just in case . . . in case it's something more menacing than its innocuous color suggests.

After a quick look over my shoulder, I pull the square from my back pocket and open it, my stomach knotting when I see what's written inside.

9. 12. 2. 3.

That's it. Just four numbers, separated by firm, black dots. It's . . . weird. Ugh. I've had enough weird for one summer.

Good thing it's nearly fall. Another season, another reason, for makin' weird.

"That's whoopee," I say aloud.

"Talking to yourself again?" a familiar voice asks, making my head snap up.

There he is. The man I would have sworn I'd never see again, standing on the sidewalk in front of Bernadette's. He's snuck up on me, footsteps hidden by the sound of children's laughter and the blues.

"I'm good company." I shrug, playing it cool, like Hitch pops up from New Orleans for a visit all the time, like I'm not wishing he'd shown up a few minutes earlier when Cane was here. Of course, it wouldn't have really mattered if he had. Hitch has a fiancée and a life. He wouldn't be jealous that I might be on my way to having the same. The fact that I'm even *thinking* about jealousy is only a sign of my own patheticness.

The thought makes my forehead wrinkle. "What are you doing here?"

He sighs and runs a hand through his hair. No gel this time, just curls throwing a fuzz party all over his head. "That . . . is an excellent question."

"I'm full of them." I stand, shoving the envelope in my back pocket, refusing to acknowledge the quickening of my heart.

He hasn't come here to tell me he's left Stephanie and their unborn baby and rushed back to reclaim our long-dead-and-started-to-rot-and-stink love. There's some other reason, some good reason that he's standing here in a beat-up Barenaked Ladies T-shirt and a torn pair of jeans, looking so much like his old self that it's all I can do not to give him a hug.

"I'm here on business," he finally says, the words sounding like a lie.

"Hmm. Where's your suit?"

"Personal business."

"Oh . . . okay." Oh. God. Could it . . . it can't . . . but what if . . . what if . . .

"Possibly illegal business," he continues with a nervous grin. "That could get me fired. Or put in jail."

"Oh." My foolish hopes crash and burn.

"So I figured . . . since you still had some time before you head back to work . . ." He shuffles closer, onto my new grass, until I can smell his Hitch smell. "I thought maybe you'd want to help."

"With the illegal business that could get you fired or put in jail?"

"And you fired and put in jail, too. Of course."

"Of course," I say, the yucky feeling in my stomach fading. He's here to ask for my help. Doing something illegal. It's way more flattering than it should be. "Are you going to tell me anything more specific?"

"A man I worked with was part of the task force that tracked down the locations of the Breeze houses around Donaldsonville." He runs his hand through his wild hair a second time and swallows. When he speaks again, his voice is hushed. "Two days ago he was murdered."

"Oh my God. I'm so sorry."

"But before he died, he sent me a package." Hitch stares at my new sod, obviously not wanting to talk about his friend's death. They must have been close for him to be so upset. "He found something else while he was out in the bayou, something someone didn't want him talking about."

"What was it?"

"The entrance to a cave," he says. "And several former FBI employees going into the cave with captives and coming out alone. He took some pictures and did some digging beyond his clearance level in the FBI database, and found out two of the people used to work in chemical weapons development."

Wow. "So . . . he hacked into the FBI's computer, and—"

"And fourteen hours later, he was dead."

Oh. Shit. "So you're thinking . . ." I let out a long breath. "If it was someone in the FBI, you're risking a lot more than getting fired, Hitch. If whoever killed your friend finds out you're looking into this, they could decide you need to die, too." And anyone who's helping him would likely share the same fate. Hitch is asking me to risk my life.

He nods, and gives me a look that says he'll understand if I have to tell him no.

"What about Stephanie? Does she—"

"Stephanie knows I have to do this," Hitch says, a bite in his tone that assures me Stephanie is a subject he would prefer remained off-limits. Fine with me. It's easier to pretend she doesn't exist if I never speak her name. "So . . ." He steps closer, nudges my bare foot with the toe of his tennis shoe, an action that sends electricity skittering across my skin. "What do you think?"

What do I think? I think it sounds like possible suicide. But it also sounds noble and important and Agent of Justice-y. And there's a chance I can keep Hitch safe. I saved my life and Stephanie's life, and so far my new "powers" seem to be going strong. I haven't had the chance to inflate any lungs lately, but I've been practicing moving things around the house with my mind. Usually when I'm drunk enough not to be freaked out by seeing the contents of my fruit basket float across the kitchen. I've gotten better; able to manipulate matter without getting angry the way I had to at first.

I haven't had any contact with Tucker or the Big Man and I'm still not sure what's happening to me, but I know I can be useful to Hitch. And then there's the staggering knowledge that *he* thinks I can be useful, too—or he wouldn't be here. That feels pretty damned good considering he branded me a Drunk Waste of Brain a month ago.

Besides, helping Hitch is certainly a better use of my time than sitting around drinking with Fern, worrying about invisible people, and waiting to go back to scooping poop.

"Absolutely. Sounds like fun," I say. "When do we start?"

"You're sure? You understand that—"

"I understand." I meet his tired eyes and nod. "I want to help."

The relief and gratitude in his expression light me up from the inside, and I know in that moment that I would risk my life half a dozen times to see that look on his face again. "Good," he says. "I'll meet you at Swallows at seven tomorrow morning?"

I wrinkle my nose. "Make it nine."

"Eight," he says with a grin.

"Nine," I counter, trying to ignore the vaguely sexual vibe weaving through the air between us.

"Eight-thirty."

"If I'm going to end up in jail or dead, I want a good night's sleep first," I say. "Nine. Take it or leave it."

"Okay. Nine." His grin becomes a dimpled smile that makes my foolish heart want to throw itself into the blue sea of his eyes and drown. "See you tomorrow."

"Tomorrow . . ." I watch him turn to go, resisting the urge to see if his butt still look as fantastic as it once had in that beat-up pair of jeans. "Hitch?"

"Hm?" He turns back, an almost shy glance over his shoulder.

"Thanks for . . ." Thanks for what? For coming back? For smiling at me? For asking me to risk my life for something important? For trusting me? For maybe, just maybe, considering me a friend? "Thanks for . . . thinking of me."

"I think of you all the time."

And then he turns and walks away, strolling slowly from the scene of the crime. It *has* to be a crime to drop a bomb like that into an interpersonal landscape like ours. What did he even *mean* by that?

"Annabelle! Annabelle Lee!"

I turn, startled by the urgency in Fernando's tone, hoping he hasn't seen Hitch. I'm not in the mood for another lecture. "What?"

"Why the hell didn't you tell me you have a bike?"

This was worth screaming my full name? "I've always had a bike."

"Ha ha. You're funny. And insane. How did you get it into the kitchen? I was only in the pisser for five minutes."

What?

"And FYI, the cat looks pissed."

"The cat always looks pissed." Gimpy pulled through surgery just fine and is back to his hissing, weird-stuff-eating, blue-cooler-cuddling ways. He's snuggled up with Old Blue in the kitchen right now, staring at the wallpaper, or the backs of his own eyes, or the fifth dimension, or whatever it is cats see when they stare off into space.

"More pissed than usual," Fern says. "And I can't blame him. There's no room for a Harley in your kitchen."

A what? A . . . Harley . . .

Suddenly, I'm back in the dark at the bottom of the stairs, listening to a promise I don't want the Big Man to keep. *Prove you're more than one unlucky* pichou-ette, *and I'll buy you a real bike myself.*

As far as I'm concerned, the best thing that could

happen to our relationship is for us never to see each other again. I assumed—from the silence the past few weeks—that the Big Man thought the same. But now . . . Surely, he didn't. Surely . . .

"How did you even fit it through the door?" Fernando asks as I rush by him, heading toward the kitchen. "It doesn't look like it's wide enough to—"

"Shit." I freeze in the doorway. There, no more than three feet from Gimpy's bed, filling my tiny kitchen to overflowing, is a big, black and red, shined-until-I-can-see-my-startled-face-in-the-chrome Harley-Davidson motorcycle. With a matching helmet on the seat.

I shuffle forward, touching it with a finger and drawing back as if it's burned me. It's real. It is completely real. And in my kitchen. Where—according to Fernando—it hadn't been a few minutes ago. I spin in a circle, wondering if *he's* close enough to see me, to watch my reaction to his gift.

"What's wrong?" Fernando asks, vaguely amused. "You look like you've seen the ghost of the man who gave you herpes."

"I don't have herpes."

"Amity's friend, Monique, said you did. She's been in Swallows talking some serious smack about your ass. You know who else has been in? *Barbara Beauchamp*, and girl, that woman can tie on the Kendall Jackson Chardonnay like nobody's—"

"I have to go to sleep now, Fern." I turn and shove at Fernando's chest, urging him back toward the front door. If the Big Man is out there, he's probably peeking in the back window, the better to see my shock and dismay. I don't want to risk that he might come in while Fern's here. I don't want to lay the burden of the Big Man's acquaintance—or the danger associated with it—on one of my only remaining friends.

"You're kicking me out?" he asks, appalled. "Because I think it's crazy that you brought your toy into the kitchen?"

"No, because I'm tired. Really tired."

"You're full of shit."

"Yes, that too. I have to take a huge dump before I go to sleep, a really huge—"

"La la la, not listening." Fernando smashes his hands over his ears and lets me push him the rest of the way to the door. The man has serious problems acknowledging that women do number two, which I find strange considering he doesn't even like to sleep with women. What the hell does he care what does or doesn't come out of our anal cavity?

"See you tomorrow," I say, forcing a smile.

"So we're still on for supper?"

"Yep. Your place. You cook, I'll eat." I open the door and shove him onto the porch where he stops and turns back to me.

"You're really kicking me out," he says, befuddled. "What about my drink? Don't I even get a red plastic cup for the road?"

"No. Go. Talk tomorrow, love you, 'bye."

"Okay, 'b—" I shut the door gently in his face and

make a run for the bathroom. I duck inside, slam the door, and wait the interminable twenty seconds I know it will take Fern to stare inside after me and then finally turn to leave. Then I wait a few seconds more, hoping some trick of magic might cause the motorcycle to disappear before I make it back into the kitchen to investigate.

But I should know better. Magic is clearly on the side of the invisibles.

When I creep back into the kitchen, greeted by a low yee-owl from the Gimp, the bike is still exactly where it was before. I stalk around it, staring at all its massive parts, wondering just how in the hell I'm supposed to get it *out* of my house. The key is in the ignition, but Fernando was right, it doesn't look like it will fit through the back door. Then I notice the storage compartment on the back. The *locked* storage compartment, with a row of shiny silver combination lock numbers, the first of which is a perky number 9.

Unexpectedly, it doesn't take me long to connect the dots between my present and the letter in my mailbox. I pull the envelope from my pocket and spin the numbers on the dial until they match the numbers on the card. 9. 12. 2. 3. The storage area pops open with a click and I slowly lift the black-leather lid, cautious until I see the cylinders lying all in a row. It's full of shots. I'm safe.

Or mostly safe. If you call being in possession of a dozen prepped syringes *safe*.

Despite the fact that each one is topped with a red

cap, I still have a hard time reaching my hand inside to grab the scrap of paper on top. I can't help but feel that they're dangerous, maybe even deadly.

You'll need a booster every four weeks. Take the first in three days, and enjoy the ride. Looks like somebody likes you, Red. You'll find the Big Man's a good friend if you know how to keep his secrets. Keep your mouth shut with the police and the FBI and you'll do just fine. If you're good, I'll be in touch soon to teach you a few tricks, Tucker.

Shots. Just like the ones Libby stopped giving Grace. Every four weeks. For how long? And what the hell is in them? Am I poisoning myself if I do, or if I don't? And what's the story with Tucker? Is he friend or foe? And is the Big Man a super-duper bad dude I shouldn't trust, or just your garden-variety drug dealer/vigilante? He killed two people—that I know of—but he also seemed to care about Grace, and I *have* felt much better since I had my first shot.

And now he's given me a Harley. Surely, nothing says "I care" like a shiny motorcycle full of prepped syringes.

Gimpy growls, making me turn to his side of the kitchen in time to catch a flash of movement. I jerk to the left, wishing I had the gun I locked away in the safe beneath my bed.

Thankfully, it turns out to be nothing worth shooting over. Just one of the full glasses Fernando left on the kitchen table floating into the air and out the door, accompanied by deep laughter that makes me shiver.

Tucker. Who knows how long he's been there? For a second, I consider calling out to him, demanding he come back and give me answers. But I have a feeling he's already told me everything he's going to tell. If he wanted me illuminated, he'd be chatting me up, not stealing a mojito and wandering onto my back porch.

So instead of calling after him, I focus on my own drink, willing it up into the air, floating it into my waiting hand, showing him I've already learned a few tricks of my own.

"To magic," I whisper, and lift my glass.

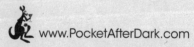